DEADLY DARK DANCE
THE LOST WOMEN SERIES
BOOK THREE

D. D. GILLESPIE

TABLE OF CONTENTS

Acknowledgements	vii
Dedication	ix
Cast of Characters	xi

Prologue - May 1983	1
Chapter 1 - The Devil's Brigade: Saturday-Sunday, May 7-8, 1983	3
Chapter 2 - Willow Whisper and Velvet Dawn: Monday-Saturday, May 9-14	14
Chapter 3 - Nora Gets a Message: Tuesday, May 10	22
Chapter 4 - Spyder Zorman: Tuesday, May 10	26
Chapter 5 - Willow in the Dumps: Saturday, May 14	31
Chapter 6 - Nora's Predicament: Wednesday-Sunday, May 11-15	36
Chapter 7 - Spyder and Slash on the Edge: Monday-Wednesday, May 16-18	43
Chapter 8 - Stephanie Benson: Thursday-Friday, May 19-20	50
Chapter 9 - Nora Gets Ready for a Special Assignment: Friday, May 20	57
Chapter 10 - Internal Biker Politics: Friday, May 20	63
Chapter 11 - Pine Ridge Resort: Saturday, May 21	66
Chapter 12 - Kayaking: Sunday, May 22	71
Chapter 13 - Steph Makes a Move: Sunday May 22	75
Chapter 14 - Nora Faces the Music: Monday, May 23	79
Chapter 15 - Willow Comes Back: Tuesday-Wednesday, May 24-25	82
Chapter 16 - DC Benson Speaks Out: Wednesday, May 25	87
Chapter 17 - Setting Up the Bush Gigs: Thursday, May 26	92
Chapter 18 - The Brandy Arms: 2000 hours, Friday, May 27	95
Chapter 19 - Vigdis Dahlberg: 500 hours, Sunday, May 29	101

Chapter 20 - Nora Gets a Break: 0930 hours, Sunday, May 29	105
Chapter 21 - The Search Begins: Monday-Friday, May 30-June 3	117
Chapter 22 - Nora and Luke at Odds: Friday-Sunday, June 3-5	123
Chapter 23 - Mike Sinclair Weighs In: Friday, June 10	128
Chapter 24 - Nora, Bunnie and Vee: Monday, June 13	133
Chapter 25 - Nora Makes the Break: Tuesday-Friday June 14-18	139
Chapter 26 - New Beginnings: Wednesday-Monday, June 22-27	144
Chapter 27 - Special Ops Training: Monday-Saturday, July 4-9	148
Chapter 28 - Spyder Sees That Willow Is Trouble: Saturday, July 9	155
Chapter 29 - Nora Recruits Vee: Saturday, July 9	161
Chapter 30 - Chloe and her Cosmobile: Monday-Wednesday, July 11-13	167
Chapter 31 - Complications: Thursday July 14	174
Chapter 32 - Progress: Monday, July 25	178
Chapter 33 - Nora Encounters Snags: Monday-Tuesday, July 25-26	185
Chapter 34 - Complaints, Classes and Commercial Real Estate: Tuesday, August 2	189
Chapter 35 - Preparations All Round: Wednesday, August 17	194
Chapter 36 - Chloe Uncovers a Clue: Friday-Friday, August 26-September 16	199
Chapter 37 - Chloe and Slash on the Road: Saturday-Saturday, October 1-15	207
Chapter 38 - Chloe Goes Dancing and Diablo Makes a Move: Saturday, October 15	212
Chapter 39 - Slash Meets Chloe: Saturday, October 15	217
Chapter 40 - Chloe Does Business: Sunday, October 16	221
Chapter 41 - Luke Gets Ready: Sunday, October 16	225
Chapter 42 - Chloe Confirms her Quarry and Tests her Cover: Sunday, October 16	229
Chapter 43 - Diablo Unchained and Luke Meets Chloe: Sunday, October 16	233
Chapter 44 - Vee on Edge and Diablo Out of Control: Sunday, October 16	239

Chapter 45 - Slash in Turmoil and Franz on the Prowl: Sunday, October 16	243
Chapter 46 - Franz Gives Diablo the Slip and Vee Meets Chloe: Sunday, October 16	247
Chapter 47 - Slash Takes Over and Franz Shows his Hand: Sunday, October 16	251
Chapter 48 - Luke Makes a Play, Candy Checks In, Vee Learns a Lesson: Sunday, October 16	257
Chapter 49 - Willow and Diablo in Crisis: Sunday, October 16	262
Chapter 50 - On the Edge: Monday, October 17	266
Chapter 51 - Chloe Uncovered and Willow Overcome: Monday, October 17	271
Chapter 52 - Slash Takes on Diablo and Vee Steps Up: Monday, October 17	275
Chapter 53 - Into the Fray: Monday, October 17	280
Chapter 54 - Willow Whispers: Monday October 16	286
Chapter 55 - Nora Goes for a Swim: 2300 hours Monday October 16	290
Chapter 56 - Karma Time Assault Team in Action: 2330 hours, Sunday, October 17	294
Chapter 57 - Candy, Osprey, Angel and the Hawk: 100 hours Monday October 17	298
Chapter 58 - Debrief, Inquiry and Aftermath: Tuesday-Friday, October 18-21	306
Chapter 1 - East Side Easy	315
Dear Reader	321
Also by Dianne Gillespie	323
Next Series after The Lost Women	325
About the Author	327

Copyright © D. D. Gillespie 2022

All rights reserved. No part of this book may be reproduced or transmitted in any form or by any means, electronic or mechanical, including photocopying, recording or by any information and storage retrieval system, without written permission from the author, except for the inclusion of brief quotations for a review.

This is a work of fiction. Names, characters, historical events are either products of the author's imagination or are used fictionally. Any resemblance to actual persons, living or dead, is entirely coincidental. The author has no control over nor responsibility for third party web sites or their content.

Cover art by Sherry Andrychuk

ISBN: 978-1-7387811-0-2 Print Copy

ISBN: 978-1-7387811-3-3 Electronic Copy

ACKNOWLEDGEMENTS

I would like to thank my faithful Beta readers for their willingness to read and critique when the story was still unfinished: Marion Hunter, Mary Bendsen and Denny Hughes. I thank my daughter, Katrina Roldan, who also provided invaluable insight for the development of the story. I need to acknowledge the wonderfully detailed feedback and helpful suggestions from my editor, Allyson Foster. Without her work, the story would have been much less coherent. Jacqui Nelson has likewise provided very helpful technical support. Lastly, I thank my understanding, loving husband, Stewart Brady, for his patience and forbearance as I struggled to finish this story.

DEDICATION

I wish to dedicate this book to my beloved mother, Dorothy Paus (nee Bailey), whose encouragement and support have been the basis of my emotional well-being for so many years, and whose kindness and wisdom I will miss forever.

CAST OF CHARACTERS' ALIASES AND CODE NAMES

<u>Character name - Code Name - Also Known As</u>

Nora Macpherson - Candy - Chloe LaJoie
Luke Gallager - Osprey
Bonita Burrows - Hazel - Bunnie
Dave Yang - Eagle
Stephanie Benson - Angel - Willow Whisper
Vigdis Dahlberg - Ladonna - Velvet Dawn

Franz Bernhardt - Hawk - Dieter
Slavko Dracul - Wolf - Slash
Milko Zorman - Grizzly - Spyder
Bogdan Lakovic - Lucky - BB
Dimitrios Zorman - Loverboy - Diablo
Devil's Brigade - Karma
RCMP Special Op against the Devils' Brigade - Karma Time

PROLOGUE - MAY 1983

From above, the carpet of spring-green meadow appears like velvet rolled out to border the snow-tipped blue granite of the Coastal mountains that thrust to meet the clouds drifting in the azure skies above. Below, the Bulkley River, raging with spring run-off, cuts a valley that run northwest and southeast for a hundred and sixty miles. After the waters merge in the broad expanse of the Skeena River Valley, below Hazelton and the Kispiox Range, they open in a powerful flow to the North Pacific.

The forty-something helicopter pilot, travelling southeast toward the Telkwa Range, scanned the ribbon of highway between Hazelton and Prince George, taking detours: the NorthCo logging camp northeast of Kitwanga, the Justice Silver mine south of Moose Forks, and the Sedako open pit mine east of Simon Lake. He was a private contractor with a troubled history– a stint as an eight-year-old in the last cohort of the Hitler Youth. His parents, skilled printmakers, had emigrated to Canada when he was in his teens. He had been orphaned in his early twenties and earned his rotor wings in the RCAF as a twenty-five year old.

His ice-blue eyes missed little of the astounding country below as he fingered the scarlet bungy cord that wrapped around the throttle.

It was the same hue as the red lace on the g-string that dangled from a hook glued to the pilot's side of the instrument panel.

Dipping to follow Highway 16, the Yellowhead, he buzzed over a squadron of black-leather jacketed bikers headed northwest. He swooped down, almost skimming the wrinkled sparkle of the Bulkley River surface. The helicopter fishtailed as it swung from one bank to the other, as if stitching the banks together with invisible thread. Outside of Glacier Lake, fly-fishers from beneath ball caps gaped as the helicopter hovered over their section of water, no doubt swearing as the racket disturbed both the elusive steelhead fish and the tranquility of their backcountry idyll.

Just before Prince George, as the sun dipped, the helicopter swerved left and headed northwest in the general direction of Fort Saint Jacob.

CHAPTER 1 - THE DEVIL'S BRIGADE: SATURDAY-SUNDAY, MAY 7-8, 1983

S lavko "Slash" Dracul, second-in-command of the Devil's Brigade, led the bike club on a "recruiting" run along Highway 16. They had just left Prince George and were far from their mother chapter, the most bad-assed, best-equipped, biggest heavy-hitter biker club out of Edmonton, Alberta. Slash signaled a stop just before Brandenhoff, BC. At a roadside rest stop, the club swung their bikes into a semi-circle around him, dismounted, and lit up smokes. They were a group of twenty, fifteen guys and five chicks. All the guys sported devils-on-motorcycles Brigade patches on their denim vests, the one percent insignia prominently displayed. All looked menacing, with scarred faces and tattooed necks and arms. The women, off the bikes, clung to the backs of their rides, their faces smeared with eye make-up, their hair in rats. Several sported tattoos pledging lifelong obedience to 'Grinder' or 'Axel' or 'Tiny'. Nobody smiled.

Slash spoke with deep, guttural authority. "Listen up, scum. When we get to town, stay focused. Brigade's gonna control all o' the rackets on this entire stretch, just like we done in the South along the 97—Williams Lake to Prince George. Strippers, escorts, prostitution, trafficking—we want all o' it." Slash ground his smoke with his worn boot. "This has gotta be done right—not too heavy, but enough so's they know we mean business. We don't want 'em runnin' to the cops."

The motley crew of ragged bruisers erupted in hoarse guffaws. They liked a good fight. Hell, their rep depended on their willingness to take a hit, so Slash needed to echo the call for moderation every time the Brigade got an assignment.

"Listen, you idiots, I don't know what you're laughin' about! I don't remember sayin' nothin' funny here!"

The bikers quieted. Slash was second-in-command. On the road, his word was law. They had spent the last week visiting every nightspot south of Prince George to convince the owners that they needed "protection" from the Brigade for themselves and their dancers. Now they were expanding west, sidestepping most of Prince George where the Renegades, a puppet gang of the Hell's Angels, held sway. The exception was the Hillcrest Hotel on the outskirts of town where the Brigade had established their first PG beachhead.

Perched on the pillion of Slash's Hog was his new ol' lady, Willow, an exquisite, slim brunette with hair down to her ass. The club knew they were avoiding PG because of her, too. Slash had sweet-talked her out of one of the Renegade bars where she was subbing in for exotic dancers who had missed their gigs. His plan was to use her and three others waiting for them in Terrace to work the off-road logging and mining camps for untraceable cash. No one in the club dared challenge Slash's decision to bring Willow along. A few of the others had women riding with them, but these women were "Mammas", sexually available to anyone in the club. Willow was exclusive to Slash.

"Alright, Brigade. Let's roll. Next stop, the Brandy Arms." Slash swung onto his bike and hit the throttle, gunning the engine for effect. Willow leaned in to speak to him. He paused a moment, then shook his head and flipped up the bike stand.

∼

Riding towards their next destination, Slash pondered Willow's dark beauty and fearlessness. He had just refused her plea to dance a gig at the Brandy Arms. Her response to his refusal was "Fuck you. I want out!"

He might have known she'd get antsy. Now, barely two days after he had rescued her from those flea-bitten Renegades, she wanted out. While they were spending those weeks together in Prince George, Slash had set about grooming her to do "contract" gigs for the Brigade, ones where she would be a private dancer, unseen by any but the high-end, paying guest. He thought he had convinced her this kind of work would be good practice for her possible Vegas debut. He didn't really think she's make it to Vegas, but she didn't need to know that.

Just before they had left for the road, he had made clear to her she would be nominal Brigade property, but really his. She had been silent then, but he had sensed a shift in her attitude. She had become less pliant, willful instead of willing. She had refused to sleep with him saying she needed her "beauty sleep". She had refused to be left with the Mammas when the gang stopped on the road for a beer break. The supple beauty that had entranced him now seemed more like the tease of some kind of witchcraft. He felt as if she were keeping him on the hook of her sexuality to play with.

The thought of losing her gripped him in a way that the loss of no other female ever had. *She was just another chippie after all!* No, he had to admit. She was different. She had wormed her way into his affections enough that he dreamed about her, wildly sensual fantasies with her, eager and lusty, worshipping his body, massaging and polishing his skin with her long silky mane of hair. He had *never* dreamt about another broad! He had never before met a woman with such erotic, voluptuous, animal magnetism. That was it. He had fallen for her.

Slash, realizing his attraction to Willow, and knowing the penalty he might pay for it, understood he had to nip her rebellion and "diva" pretensions in the bud. He would cut her cold, leaving her under guard with some gofer he could trust. From Brandenhoff on, she would ride pillion with Bogdan 'Bobby' Lakovic, known as "The Kid".

As a six-foot-four, nineteen-year-old brown belt prospect, the Kid would be up for looking out for Slash's interests, and he could trust him not to cut his grass.

After they finished the recruitment phase of the road trip in Terrace, he would cut back to Edmonton to report to the boss, "Spyder" Zorman, and leave Bobby to take care of the stable of four bush gig dancers. In the meantime, the rest of the Brigade, with Spyder's son, Dimitrios "The Pest" Zorman, as leader, would continue on with a "enforcement" tour, running herd on the mules doing drug deliveries within the Brigade's turf.

That decision made, Slash rode easier. In his gut, he knew independent women, especially beautiful ones, were too much trouble. Better to stick with the Mammas. They never played coy or expected special favours. Once in Brandenhoff at the Brandy Arms, where their presence was tolerated as long as they kept clear of the general public, Slash ignored Willow in favour of snuggling down for the night with raven-haired, buxom Duchess, a Mamma who knew her place.

∾

FOR HER PART, WILLOW WAS INCENSED BY SLASH'S IGNORING HER. When she had been riding along behind him, his broad, muscled back shielding her from the wind and grit of the road, she had decided she needed to confront him about what he had promised her. This didn't feel like she was headed to Vegas anytime soon! What was the point of cutting herself off from family and friends just to be treated like second-class baggage? But he never gave her the opportunity. From Brandenhoff on, she was The Kid's back warmer.

∾

THE NEXT DAY, ONCE THEY WERE SETTLED INTO THEIR TERRACE HOTEL base, Slash called an update meeting–members only–and, for security's sake, crowded the fifteen bulky men into his own hotel room. The place reeked of body odor, fuel oil, cigarette smoke and old leather.

"I got some announcements here. First, I'm leavin' tomorrow to check in with Spyder in Edmonton. He needs an update. Okay? We're lookin' for a helicopter pilot to take four strippers to bush gigs starting this month." Hearing no objections, he continued, "Next, I been thinking about our two youngest club members, the newbies, the Kid, and the Pest–"

Diablo interjected, "I tol' ya, I don't like that handle!"

"It's okay, I fuckin' know that! Ya didn't let me finish! Ya got a new road name now–Diablo! Back off, Pest!" Slash knew how to get the crowd to laugh. "I gotta a job for you. I want you to take all the club except for the The Kid here, and..." he looked around the room and lit on the beefiest bikers in the room, "and... uh... Axel and Gypsy... okay? Leavin' them out, I want you, Diablo, as the Boss's son, to take the rest of the club to do enforcement."

This, the club knew, meant they would visit their latest acquisitions across Highway 16 en masse and make sure there were no backsliders. It was an important job and Diablo knew it. His chest puffed up with new importance.

"Kid, yer new name is BB. These two have names with meaning. BB's–a good name–a kind of ammo. It's little, but BB's not!" The bikers, sizing up BB's six-foot-four three hundred pound frame, erupted in raucous laughter. "And Diablo is a name to fear. Live up to it! Just *not* with the strippers! Okay?" The assembly clapped and cheered.

"Now BB, you and Axel and Gypsy, yer job is maintenance. Yer gonna run herd on the strippers here in Terrace. Right now we have four of our best broads who are contracted outta BawdyWorks from Vancouver doin' regular stripper and body-painting gigs in the hotel bars, and private escort and lap dance gigs in hotel rooms in the area. Soon those four will be doin' the bush gigs. There are others workin' all along the Highway 16 circuit. Diablo and the rest of the Brigade will see to them at the same time they're doin' enforcement. No messin' with any of strippers. Lemme say that again. No messin' with the dancers. Leave 'em alone. Just keep an eye out for 'em and make sure they understand ya mean business.

"Roxie, Fantasia, Bambi and Willow are the four strippers who are gonna do the bush gigs. Lookin' out for them will be your main job, Kid, Axel and Gypsy. I'll get a pilot all lined up to get 'em out and back probably Tuesdays, Thursdays and Fridays or somethin' like that. Ya gotta go with them and make sure there's no problem, right? Some of those miners and loggers get horny! While they're here at the hotel in Terrace or anywhere else, these broads are to be kept close, locked up, escorted to private gigs, and otherwise left alone without interference."

"Hey, Slash, I want that job! Why do I gotta be the on the road?" Diablo Zorman had a reputation as a cocksman. Everyone knew that fact, and why he wasn't babysitting the dancers. Slash didn't want anyone hassling the girls for "favours", in particular, not Willow.

"Remember that last bit I said, asshole? 'Without interference?' Ya *know* why ya don't get that job! And that goes double for the other strippers workin' along the circuit, Those broads ya need to protect. The rest of the club, along with ya, will have this hotel as yer base, but ya will be on the road most of the next two weeks doin' the enforcement. If ya don't like it, and I find out ya ignored me, there'll be consequences. We all know what they'll be." The room erupted in nervous laughter. Slash was infamous for his road-rash 'parties'. Nobody wanted to be the featured "guest". The group started trading stories of past abrasions.

Grinder offered a nugget. "Remember when Slash caught Leftie holdin' out on him? That ten bucks? It cost him his ass rubbed raw from being hauled behind Slash's Hog with his britches off."

"That wasn't so bad." Diablo offered. Remember when Grinder misplaced his colours? He got hauled on his *front* with his gear off. Ouch!! No nooky for him fora looooong time!" The gang erupted in full-throated, belly laughter.

"Hey, listen up, you scum!" Slash waited for the furor to die down. He waited for total silence. "Diablo, meet me here in my room tomorrow mornin' before you ride out...about nine? Yeah? And BB, I want a word here before you go."

Diablo raised his hand and shrugged by way of acknowledgement. Slash caught the disdain written in the young biker's face as he slouched out of the room. He knew he had to nip this disrespect in the bud.

This young punk is bad news for the new territory, like a rotten apple in the barrel. The sooner he earns his patch on the Edmonton turf, the better. Then he's Spyder's problem.

BB stood there looking expectant. Slash took him by the arm and turned him so his back was to the door and no one could guess at their conversation. "Uh...about Willow. She's gonna be someone the cops wanna find, okay? I don't need to fill ya in on all the details, but ya hafta keep her under wraps, until I get back. It don't matter how much she whines, she says locked up away from the other girls and under guard. And no one else needs to know we had this little talk. Ya got it?"

BB nodded, his eyes like saucers. Slash flipped his hand, signifying the end of the interview, and BB exited the room, closing the door softly.

Slash lounged on the bed in his room, troubled by a new sensation. He was wary of any of the Brigade getting to Willow. If he didn't know himself better, he'd say he was jealous!

I've never fallen for any other broad! Why her?

He reflected on the character of the girl. Feisty, but sensual, she ticked all the boxes for him. Whatever she had going for her, he knew he was vulnerable. Willow had gotten to him in ways he didn't know how to resist. That meant he had to keep her at a distance.

∽

JUST BEFORE CLOSING HOUR, DIABLO AND BB, ALONG WITH SEVERAL other Brigadiers, were hanging out in the Terrace Hotel pub throwing back a few beers before crashing. At nineteen and twenty-five respectively, they were the youngest members of the club. BB, especially, was often ID'd because of his baby face, and tonight he had had enough beer to be feeling the effect.

"Hey, Kid!" Diablo didn't like BB and knew calling him by his 'hangaround' handle would get his goat. "So I got the nod to do the enforcement tour instead of you! I don't have to worry now about who's watching my back now that yer demoted to pussy sitter! I'll have real muscle behind me on the road."

BB, his face red and blotchy, rose up and hung his six-foot-four muscular frame over the much shorter Diablo. "Ya sayin' I'm deadweight on the road? That I don't stand behind ya and look tough enough? When we were riding duo on that reconnaissance tour Spyder sent us on in April, I showed the muscle you *ain't* got, chump! Don't forget I got a brown belt. I can wipe the floor with ya!"

In the bar, total silence reigned as the other members of the club watched to see how this dispute would unfold. Diablo scanned the room. This wasn't the first time he had tried to provoke BB. It was a kind of deadly game he liked to play. Diablo glowered at the barman who then left the room looking scared, so that only bikers were left as witnesses.

Diablo, conscious of being the center of attention, worked to solidify his credibility in front of the club. "Yeah, but I was the one to do the hard stuff, convincing those mutts, the strip club managers and owners, that they needed our protection. I was the Brigade's voice; *you* were just back-up muscle."

"We're the same rank in this outfit, Pest. "Just because yer daddy's the Boss don't mean you'll get the nod next. I think Slash's got the jump on ya."

"Yeah, we all know ya hero worship the Slash. I notice he's having trouble keepin' *his* hands off Willow so he's got no call to be dumpin' on *me* for samplin' the goods... and don't call me 'Pest", ya dipshit!"

"You're such a whiner, *Diablo!* That's where ya get that 'Pest' label. What Slash does is not yer problem. He's the boss on the road! And as for ya being the voice, sure, ya did the talking, but without me, ya wouldn't have got them to agree to the dope dealing."

"That's bullshit, BB! We all know the guys up here along this highway are cryin' for nose candy! They're so whacked out from loggin' and minin' they can hardly wait to get into town and score a little blow."

"But the bar owners won't take the biz'ness in their patch unless they have to! Seein' me made them see they had to, or get hurt. And the recruitment tour we just done with Slash proves we done good. That makes us both look good, Diablo, so I don't know what yer bellyaching' about."

"Yeah, whatever... I still get to do enforcement... uh... while you sit on your ass babysittin' these whores."

"It's no wonder ya never score with them, with a mouth like that! Ya kiss yer mother with that mouth?"

"Leave my mother outta this!" But he was chastened. "Whatever..."

BB knew how to take the wind out of Diablo's sails.

∼

THE NEXT MORNING, SLASH MET WITH DIABLO ALONE IN HIS HOTEL room to remind him what he needed to do as enforcement. It was better not to have too many overhearing this conversation in case the police picked up a Brigade member and interrogated them about the leadership's directions. Above all else, Slash needed to remain above the fray and out of jail to oversee the club's various operations.

The boss's son stood before him, slouched in disrespect, his black hair a mass of loose curls, his Hollywood-handsome face marred by a scowl. His was a lean, wiry build that promised quick reactions and slick dexterity rather than endurance or strength.

Sizing up the boy's body language told Slash that Diablo resented him and was doing as he was told because he had no choice. Diablo knew his father, Spyder, would thrash him if he broke discipline. In private, Slash was sure Diablo aspired to the club's leadership, replacing first Slash, and then Spyder. He also knew the boy resented how close Slash was to Spyder. Their expansion west into BC would make room for Diablo to move into Slash's place as second-in-command in Edmonton so Slash could focus on the new turf.

But in Slash's mind, the boy was too immature and impulsive for a leadership role, too eager to scratch his own itches. He didn't always have the welfare of the Brigade top of mind. Giving him this job was more a nod to his ol' man, Spyder, than a vote of confidence in Diablo's leadership potential. Still, the fact was that no other club member had the cred to be a leader. Most of them were just meatheads. Diablo was sly, but not stupid. Maybe this assignment would teach Diablo an important lesson, give him some of the experience to become that leader his father wanted him to be. Now, Slash needed to remind Diablo what his enforcement role involved.

"Diablo, the main thing is ya need to get noticed by the strippers on the regular circuit to remind'em we mean business. We want'em to be antsy enough to beg their agents to get the Devil's Brigade for protection. And we want the owners to see us as real bad asses. They pay up, and we don't fuck with'em. Ya got that? And remember, ya puff up muscles and act tough in front of the strippers. Ya don't screw them! We just want'em respectful and scared, ya get it?"

Diablo nodded, saying nothing.

"And the other thing is... ya gotta lean even more on the owners and managers to buckle under to the club and pay up. We want the money yesterday, right? And one more thing... lay off the nose candy. We need to be in control, not wasted and power-trippin', okay?"

Diablo nodded, his eyes hooded and glittering.

Slash imagined that convincing the owners not to backslide would take some arm-twisting, a job Diablo wouldn't mind at all. Some owners might fight back with some lip but would give in fast enough when Diablo took out his brass knuckles and his knife. Without BB as back-up, Diablo would have to depend on Grinder or Tiny, both meatheads, but effective as muscle threats.

"So, once ya have them cooperating–don't rough'em up too bad– then remind them the deal we brokered last week included a free pass for the drugs. If that business runs smooth, the Brigade will leave the girls alone. But the girls have to see us as bad asses for the plan to work, right?"

"Yeah, whatever. I know already. Ya don't gotta rag on me all the time, Slash. I ain't a dummy!" Slash could hear that Diablo's voice dripped with resentment.

∼

On his way back to Edmonton across Highway 16 to check in with the boss, Milko "Spyder" Zorman, Slash worried about whether BB and Diablo could manage their respective jobs well enough so there would be no screw-ups. He had his doubts.

CHAPTER 2 - WILLOW WHISPER AND VELVET DAWN: MONDAY-SATURDAY, MAY 9-14

Willow, except for when she was doing her private gigs, was under lock and key in a standard hotel room with twin beds, not even able to hang out with the other bush-gig dancers, Roxie, Fantasia, and Bambi. She was none too happy.

Willow liked the fact that BB, when he was not managing the other three dancers, hung out with her and seemed to try to cheer her up. She suspected that, being close to the same age as herself, BB could imagine how she felt being cooped up. She liked when he lounged on the other twin bed and shared pizza or Chinese take-out while they watched her favourite television shows. "Just for Laughs" was a new comedy show that got her smiling. "Coronation Street" somehow became addictive; "Do It for Yourself", a how-to show for women, reduced both of them to gales of laughter. The best show for both was "Fraggle Rock", Muppet mayhem that kept both howling.

But Willow, who could handle just so much incarceration, looked forward to her private gigs. Even though she didn't get to keep the money, at least she was meeting some real people, often getting to travel to other nearby towns. The actual 'dancing' in the hotel rooms almost always ended in a distasteful mauling by the client, but usually with BB's help she managed to pull away before the situation became more serious, not to mention much more expensive for the client. The deal was for a lap dance which the client assumed included actual intercourse. BB relayed the bad news: the cost for providing that 'service' was steep, five times the lap dance price. Few clients were keen to partake at that rate.

Left on her own with a guard outside her door, Willow thought back to how she and Slash had hooked up. He hadn't been wearing his colours when she met him. Now she realized that was deliberate: they had been on Renegade turf. He had come into the strip club where she had just danced her last routine of the night and invited her to sit for a drink. Against the strip club policy, she had agreed.

He had bought her a mixed drink, a Mai Tai, and asked if she was hungry. When she declined any food, he offered her a cigarette, which she accepted. He was well-built and roguishly handsome with his black mustache and goatee. He wore his wavy, dark hair long over his collar. His silver-grey shirt was cut to fit his broad chest, his black jeans slung low on slim hips. His baritone voice was a soothing rumble with the slightest of accents. "So how did a gorgeous, classy young woman like you end up dancing in a Prince George biker's bar? You should be doing Reno or Vegas... at least I think so."

She had looked at him through new eyes then. Here was a man who saw her worth! Someone who recognized she had more potential than just eking out a humdrum existence in this dump of a town! Someone who saw she was a talented dancer, not just a run-of-the-mill stripper you could see in any joint. "Really?" she had said. "Do you really mean I am good enough to play a place like Vegas or Reno?"

"Of course you are! You're something else...What's your name? Uh..." He looked at the billboard advertising the club's current and coming attractions. "Willow?" Each word was enunciated slowly as if considered beforehand.

"Yeah, my stage name is Willow Whisper... but my real name is Stephanie... uh... Benson."

"Oh, I like Willow much better. Yeah, you're supple and graceful as a weeping willow, sweet and willing Willow... I like it." His slate grey eyes glittered in appreciation, and he smiled. It was a charming look when he smiled, quite boyish and unguarded somehow. At least she had thought so then.

"So do you like it here, Willow? I mean, would you like a chance to get away and dance in better places?"

"Would I ever!" The excitement of the possibility had made her heart bounce in her chest. Her breath had come in gasps. She had reached out to touch him and felt the warm bulge of his arm muscle. That touch somehow had been thrilling. "Uh... Mister...what's your name?"

"Oh, you can call me Sly. You know, like Sly and the Family Stone?"

"Anyway, Sly, what do you mean when you ask if I'd like to get away from here?"

"Just what I said, darlin', that you could do better than this place. Do you want me to help?"

"Oh, would you? I mean... I... don't know where to start by myself. Do you know about places like Reno and Vegas, maybe Palm Springs...?"

"Oh sure. There's nothing so special about them, except they're American and bigger than places up here. But don't worry, sweetheart, I got connections!"

"I'd be so grateful if you could help me! I'd do anything to dance in Vegas! Wow!"

Slash hadn't said anything more except, "Sure, I'll help you. You wanna come with me now? We'll find a quieter place to talk and make plans, okay?"

That had been the beginning of a two-week-long dream-come-true, she had thought. Sly had been attentive and chivalrous, opening doors for her and helping her on with her coat, even buying her expensive new outfits. A really generous gentleman! He had paid for fancy meals in fashionable restaurants and taken her to night clubs to listen to blues and jazz combos. They had gone everywhere by taxi during those weeks.

Their nights together had been even more amazing. Willow had not been very experienced sexually, but Sly had been a considerate and skillful lover, revealing to her the mysteries of her body and never leaving her unsatisfied. She reveled in the thrill of her fully awakened libido. He seemed to know all the positions and techniques to arouse her to overwhelming passion, from masturbation to meditation, massage and delayed penetration. She had felt she was the luckiest woman in all of creation to have found such a man to love.

And she did fall in love during that time. She had become unable to imagine her life without him, and for his part, he had seemed besotted as well. In fact, he scarcely had left her side, except for the occasional long distance phone call from their hotel room. She thought she had overheard him refer to Edmonton on the phone, but he never invited her into these private conversations.

The real mystery for her had been the secrecy with which he concealed his naked body. He had always showered alone and emerged fully dressed. When they went to bed, he had made sure the lights were off, and he had insisted on leaving his undershirt on, even when making love. She could see that he had heavily tattooed arms, and that had intrigued her. But she had wondered what lay under the t-shirt covering his chest. However, she was too smitten to question his actions.

Then, after these two magical weeks, it had become clear that the Renegades, the bikers who controlled her old strip club, were tailing them. All of a sudden, Sly had become brusque and urgent in his treatment of her.

"Willow, girl, we have to leave town. If you want to get away from the Renegades, I'll take you with me tonight. Okay?"

She had nodded and asked no questions, so hungry had she been, by that point, to be with him always. Looking back, she might have wondered why they had to leave like thieves in the night, why he had never introduced her to any of his friends, or why he hadn't allowed her to say good-bye to Monica, her roommate, or to her father.

The next day, she was riding pillion behind Sly on his Harley, and she realized that all she had accomplished was to trade the Renegades for the Devil's Brigade. "Sly" was really Slavko "Slash" Dracul, second-in-command of the gang, and he was no longer so charming.

∼

DURING THE TIME IN THE TERRACE HOTEL WITHOUT SLASH, WILLOW was never privy to the club "protection" business nor allowed to mingle with any hotel guests or dancers. She did her private gigs freelance, in hotel rooms rented for the purpose and handed the money over to BB. With everyone else but BB, she was uncommunicative and wary, unhappy to have so little control over her life.

One afternoon, she asked, "BB, why did Slash leave me behind? I did nothing but ask to do a gig." Willow was ironing her hair, a process that took at least an hour, and BB was there to make sure she didn't lose her balance when she lay her hair along the ironing board.

"Uh... I don't know, Willow. He has to get around fast, maybe. You would slow him down. Besides, you can't do your gigs on the road. Think of all the dough you'd miss."

"Big deal, I don't get to keep it, anyway! Shit! I just burnt my fingers!"

"Be careful, you don't wanna burn your hair off! Uh... you get everything you need... you get your meals and room free... Anything you need from the drugstore, we get for you. You have the outfits you need for dancing... some pretty fancy shit, too. That black outfit last night looked real glam." He smiled to reinforce the compliment.

"You liked that, eh? You think I'm sexy, BB?" She regarded him through her hair hanging sleek and flat to the floor.

"Nah, I think you're a scrag! Stupid question!"

"You do not!" She stuck her tongue out at him. "Here, hold this hank of hair so I can comb the back..." BB, ever patient and long-suffering, did as she asked.

"BB, why can't you always be the one to guard me? That Axel, with all those scar and tattoos... ugh... he gives me the creeps! I don't like how he looks at me, like he wants some... I dunno...some *action*, you know? I couldn't stand for him to even *touch* me!"

"Aw, Willow, ya don't need to worry. Those guys can get action, as you call it, from the Mammas anytime, or maybe even Roxie. I think she might do a little biz'ness on the side."

"Oh, that's just gross, BB! Roxie! I didn't know that. You know, you're the only one I ever talk to, the only one who doesn't make me feel like... I dunno... like a piece of meat!" Seeing BB shake his head, she continued. "No I *mean* it! I hate being cooped up here. I have no life! BB, you gotta see that!"

Looking at his watch, BB dived for the door. "Sorry, Willow, I hafta go. Roxie's gotta private gig across town in a half hour." He was gone, closing the door behind him. She knew Axel would be sticking around, guarding the hallway where all four elite bush gig dancers were lodged.

∼

ON THE ROAD, DIABLO WORKED TO GET THE STRIP CLUB OWNERS ON side. The bikers expected the managers to turn a blind eye to the occasional deal being brokered away from the stage in the dark nooks and corners. The regular contract dancers still felt apprehensive, especially Vee "Velvet" Dalhberg, Willow's replacement on the regular circuit. She was a recent recruit to stripping, one whom BawdyWorks, the exotic dancer agency, had just supplied from Vancouver. Blonde and supple as a gymnast, she had never met Willow. The dancers had all heard how Slash had picked her up, and she had disappeared. The bikers would have terrified Vee regardless, as she had never even seen any up close and personal before. Just knowing they might abduct her made her even more petrified.

Diablo found Vee alone one day in the Glacier Lake Hotel lobby reading a Vogue. As soon as he neared her, she stood up and tried to get away. He was greasy, quite repulsive, she thought. His response to her escape effort was to pat the chair seat in a gesture that told her to sit back down and relax. He sat several feet away by the exit door and lit up a smoke. She sat, staring, as if transfixed by the insignia on his clothes.

Seeing her stare, he took off his vest to show her. The back of his leather "cut" or vest sported the Devil's Brigade patch, a crimson, devilish character riding a Harley Hog. He had Devil's Brigade curving across the top and "Edmonton" below. The one percent sign, an MC cloth piece for "motorcycle club", and a "13" completed the collection.

"You want to check out this vest, Velvet, honey?" She shook her head, saying nothing.

"No? You sure?" His laugh was cocky and too loud.

She just continued to stare, her face suddenly ashen and tense.

"You want a cig, Velvet?"

"I.... I don't smoke, thanks."

"Ya gotta have some pleasures... here, you might like it!" He tossed her the package across the room, but it fell short of her lap and landed at her feet.

"No, thanks." Looking at the Export "A" package on the floor, she stooped to pick it up. She noticed that Diablo took that opportunity to check out her young cleavage. Trembling in response, she held the package out. "I gotta go... now... here are your cigarettes." She tossed them into his lap, passing him by as fast as she could. She ended up running almost sideways in order to keep her eyes on his hands and her butt out of his reach.

As she turned her back to pull the door open, he slapped her ass and laughed. "You're too uptight, Velvet! Ya gotta let go..."

Vee vowed she would never again let herself be caught alone with Diablo. Just his presence gave her the heebie-jeebies, making her feel queasy. She knew by instinct that, given half a chance, he would take whatever he wanted. She wondered how the other girls felt.

∽

DIABLO STARED AT VEE'S RETREATING BACK, WONDERING WHY WOMEN had to be so jumpy. He could have any of the Mommas anytime he wanted, but he was tired of sharing. One big plus of being the chief would be he could have his own woman, any one he wanted, and he knew which one he wanted. Willow, the slow-eyed beauty that Slash had tucked away, was perfect. Nubile, hot and athletic, she haunted Diablo's dreams.

Even thinking about her with that stuck-up bastard, Slash, made Diablo burn. Standing up, the cigarette package Vee had tossed back to him fell on the floor. He kicked it across the lobby in anger, then looked up to see the young hotel receptionist watching him, a smirk on his face. Diablo yanked his vest back on and flashed a one finger salute to the kid behind the desk.

I'm surrounded by fuckin' assholes! Everyone either stupid or wet behind the ears!

CHAPTER 3 - NORA GETS A MESSAGE: TUESDAY, MAY 10

Nora woke up surprised and confused. McNab, her grey tabby cat, perched on her chest. He never did that!

"What's up, Mac? Something..." She stopped, smelling the air full of smoke. Was something left cooking on the stove? No, the smoke came from the front of the house, not the kitchen in the back. Her little one bedroom bungalow was compact and comfortable. The space heater in the front room had been keeping it cozy, but she had been keeping it damped down all week putting out the minimum heat. They were enjoying a warm spring for a change. The problem couldn't be the stove.

Her throat was already raw from inhaling the acrid air, her eyes watering, her nose running... *What the hell!* Through the bedroom door, she saw flames licking up the curtains of the living room. This was no overheated stove; her house was on fire!

Where was McNab? She had just seen him, but now he'd disappeared. Where was he? Him and her camera... those were her first thoughts. She groped across the living room to the corner of the kitchen, where a darkroom for her hobby was located. She grabbed the Pentax and the Canon and her purse, and hanging them by their straps over her shoulder, started calling, "Kitty, kitty, kitty...! Oh, where are you, dammit? Kitty, kitty?"

A faint 'meow' emanated from the windowsill above the kitchen sink where the window was ajar an inch or two. The clever cat had found some fresh air! She lifted a tea towel hanging over the cupboard door, and soaking it in water from the tap, dabbed at her eyes. She was having trouble breathing now, too. When she opened her eyes again, McNab was nowhere to be seen.

Has he jumped out the window? No, it is just as it has been... where in hell is he?

Now her heart began to race. The heat of the flames was unbearable. Fire was eating its way through the wall between the living room and kitchen. The hair on her legs below her nightgown was becoming scorched. She had to keep squeezing water into her eyes to see anything. She had to leave, cat or no cat.

The fastest way out was the back door, an entrance tucked into a small enclosed porch that served as a storage space. Here, at the door, Nora found a hissy McNab. She grabbed him by the scruff of his neck, and, wrapping the wet tea towel around his head, stepped out onto the porch. There she found gumboots to wear. As she stood in the backyard in her flannel nightgown gazing in shock as the flames shot from the eaves, she could hear the distant sound of a siren. Someone had called the fire station.

Gruff old Oliver Grissom was volunteer chief this night. He climbed out of the driver's seat of the chief's car with a thermos of black coffee and a blanket to wrap around her. The crew with the firetruck were busy getting the hoses hooked up. It was five in the morning.

"You hear anything before you smelled the smoke?"

"No, my cat woke me up. I didn't even notice it until then." She could feel tears streaming down her face, the result of smoke, shock, pain...

Somehow she knew this was just another in the series of personal attacks she had been suffering ever since Dulac School had been destroyed several years before. At first, the attacks had been small, almost trivial incidents: chalk insults on the walls of her garage, egg splattered on her living room windows, rotten tomatoes in her mail box, cow-dung piled on her front walkway. But then, about a month before, they had upped the ante: slashed tires, and nasty epithets spray-painted on her Ford Mustang–these committed when she had parked the car in town. Now, she was the victim of arson. The thought chilled her to the bone, blanket or no blanket. She was terrified.

The fire crew found the evidence. Whoever had done it had not even bothered to dispose of the gasoline can. The arsonist had tossed it into the ditch across the street.

The fire chief tried to be reassuring. "We'll get the fire out, Constable, don't worry. But the damage will be considerable. Accelerant will do that. You better plan on filing a complaint, but I guess you know how to do that!" Grissom chuckled at his own joke.

"Yeah, I'll get on that." At least, she still had her job. At least there, she could feel competent. She knew the fire was not her fault, but she still felt overcome by a feeling of remorse.

If I had handled my relationship with the Fredericks differently...

In Nora's mind, these attacks were all connected to her close relationship with the local Rocky Creek Band, especially Della Frederick, the impressive matriarchal healer who had become a close friend and confidante. More disheartened with each incident, Nora recalled the hostility she had experienced from the beginning. Several townspeople had not hidden their displeasure.

Brandenhoff was a conservative community, not very sympathetic to the Saik'uz Indigenous band on its doorstep. She had tried to act as liaison in promoting an Indigenous wellness centre on the old Dulac property, but had run into opposition from all the churches in town who felt the land should be sold, and the money returned to St. Joseph's, the local RC parish. Nora half expected to discover that Howard Currie, her boss's father-in-law, or his equally disapproving son, Barry, had been behind the harassment. Even though they were both elders of the local Gospel Church, and apparently respectable citizens, their malice towards her had often been obvious.

Oliver Grissom broke into her thoughts. "The sarge is here, Constable. I thought you should touch base, you know..." Nora turned to see Mike Sinclair, the Brandenhoff Detachment head, arriving in a cruiser.

He jumped out of the car and stood for a moment, taking in the scene. "It looks bad, eh? The house seems to be a total loss, but the garage didn't get touched."

"Yeah," Nora nodded. "It's a furnished rental, so mostly I have lost clothing and personal effects. My car is still okay, and I saved my cameras." When she held them up to show him, she noticed her arm was shaking uncontrollably.

He came over to her side, and after bending his tall frame to study her face, gave her a brief, brotherly hug. "You need a place to stay?" he asked, his sparkling blue eyes clouded with concern. Nora nodded, mute and exhausted. Her teeth had begun chattering.

"Come on, I'll take you home. Patsy said you can use the bed in the basement rec room. You'll just have to put up with the boys in the morning before they go to school..."

"Uh... gee thanks, Mike. That's sweet of you... and Patsy, of course." Mike's school-age sons were noisy, but at least they would be away to school soon so she could sleep. Patsy was another matter. Nora was sure her boss's wife suspected Nora of having designs on Mike. In Patsy's mind, women shouldn't be police officers, and if they were, shouldn't be single. She had never hidden her distrust of Nora, and now the two of them would be stuck under the same roof. Not for long, Nora decided.

CHAPTER 4 - SPYDER ZORMAN: TUESDAY, MAY 10

Slash took his time making the run from Terrace to Edmonton. He had risked a stopover in Prince George–Renegade territory–to check in and collect some drug money, then continued on for brief collections in McBride, Jasper and Hinton. By the time he reached his home base, he was exhausted, with just enough energy to flop in a bed in the clubhouse under The Hog Barn.

Before Slash could sleep off his exhaustion, a gravelly, vocal blast blared at him, "Wake up, ya Pussy!" Milko "Spyder" Zorman, the owner of the best bike shop in Edmonton, The Hog Barn, which specialized in servicing and customizing Harleys, had climbed downstairs to The Hell Pit, the Brigade's clubhouse located below Spyder's living quarters in the back of the shop. "It's noon already! Ya've slept long enough!

Slash knew that Spyder couldn't abide slackers. Just three years before, in 1980, he had arrived from the old country as a forty-six-year-old after escaping the unrest in the Balkans following the death of Tito. He had brought his wife, Elizaveta "Bets", and his son, then twenty-two-year-old Dimitrios, 'Diablo', an apprentice mechanic. Even before their emigration to Canada, the cash to fund the bike shop operation had materialized through connections made in

Europe. That money and Spyder's mechanics papers made immigration easy, the federal government not being too choosy about the financing of new businesses, especially in the under-developed North.

Slash rolled over and gazed through bleary eyes at the Boss. "Yeah, I'm awake. Lemme get a shower, and I'll come up and give ya the scoop." Spyder grunted agreement and trudged back upstairs.

While shaving his two-days' growth of beard off, Slash considered his appearance. Not bad for thirty-five, he decided. His sooty-black, shoulder-length hair framed his slightly pock-marked, dark skin, a moustache and goatee concealing the beginning of a double chin. His slate-grey eyes conveyed a blunt, ruthless practicality. He was six-foot-two, heavy-boned and muscular. He showed a small paunch, just enough to show he could hold his beer. He sported many arm, chest and back tattoos, mostly dark blue and red, biker-themed ink. One shoulder sported an iron cross and the other, DILLIGAF, meaning 'Do I look like I give a fuck?' Slash liked how he looked.

Sitting across from Spyder at his kitchen table, Slash filled him in on the latest excursion. Spyder grunted approval upon hearing about his son, that Slash had given Diablo leadership of the enforcement phase.

"Has he got the cred with the guys, you think?" Spyder, like many fathers, hoped his kid would follow in his footsteps.

"That depends on whether he can keep his hands off the merchandise. You *know* how he likes coke, and how he makes the dancers nervous..."

"He's just a boy, come on... still got the eggshell hangin' from his ass!"

"Yeah, but if he wants to be in charge, he has to keep his nose clean."

"Tell him to get an ol' lady. Someone young and clean, you know? If she don't work out, he can turn her out for tricks..."

"Look, I got better things to do than manage your kid's sex life, Spyder! He'll learn to keep his hands off the goods, or blow it."

"Yeah, whatever..." Spyder never admitted he was wrong. "Okay, what's the take this trip?"

The conversation drifted into the club's financial business. The club did much of its business on the road, but behind and underneath The Hog Barn motorcycle repair shop was the Hell Pit, a sizable cellar with a well-concealed entrance where the club conducted the real money-making business. It was a dimly-lit cavern filled with worn, black, leather seating that smelled of stale smoke and dead beer. The only lighting came from dim lightbulbs attached to the rafters overhead. Here was "church" where the Devil's Brigade held regular meetings.

The real money behind Spyder's bike shop–revenue came from the club members who paid a percentage of anything they made as members of the Brigade, as well as 'rent' to keep their dealings well and truly private. For the last few years, club members had been making the money from shaking down local businesses for "protection", selling drugs in local bars, and running hookers in neighbouring hotels. For whatever reason, the cops looked the other way.

"So you feel good about this expansion idea across Highway 16? We didn't go too far?" Spyder didn't seem too worried. Slash figured he wanted some reassurance that they hadn't started a turf war with anyone–the PG Renegades, for instance. Spyder tended towards anxiety.

"Nah, it's all good. We'll get a pilot for the bush-gig tours. Those should bring in a bundle over the summer. The strippers on the circuit are all covered. I told the guys to make the girls too scared to act up, and, just like I said to Diablo, to keep their mitts off. This week or so, the enforcement crew are out all across Northern BC on Highway 16, reminding the bar owners to cough up."

Spyder gave Slash a thumbs up as he left for the basement clubhouse.

∼

THAT NIGHT, SLASH LAY BEDDED DOWN ON THE CLUBHOUSE COUCH trying to catch some sleep. Through the ceiling, he could easily hear Spyder and Bets involved in a heated discussion upstairs.

"Spyder, you're only forty-nine. Ya can do all the one-armed push-ups and weight-lifting ya like, but it's not doing to help fix that ache yer always complaining about in yer gut!"

"Whaddaya mean, Ol' Lady? I'm as fit today as I was when we hooked up! Mr. Cool, that's me! I ain't Milko anymore, am I?"

"That don't matter Spyder, honey. That's a common Serbian name. You don't need to be ashamed of it."

"Aw, it's a shitty name, Bets! It makes me sound like a pansy! I hate it. I hate the very sound of it! I'm the toughest sonovabitch in the Brigade, and everybody knows it! That's why I'm still Numero Uno! I'm in my prime!"

"Listen, you stupid Bohunk, if ya were so sure you were still good, ya wouldn't be constantly making yer gut ache worse by abusing yer body. Ya wouldn't still be pushing weights and crushing beer cans, or drinking like a fucking fish! I'm getting tired of nursing ya. Ya don't care how much I worry, or how I have to cover for ya."

"Ya can be such a bitch, Elizaveta! Be careful or I'll pop ya one! Ya just got over your last shiner... "

"Cool off, Ol' Man! You're starting to get all red in the face..." Slash heard this detail and held his breath.

The Boss is a powder keg alright. The only thing poppin' might be his ticker!

"Don' worry. I can count on Slash to hold things together for now. He's a selfish motherfucker, but he's solid... uh... loyal, ya know? He'll do good buildin' the new chapter out in BC. And Diablo... uh... he's comin' along. He's just a punk still, but ..." At this point, Spyder's voice dropped and Slash couldn't really hear anything except Spyder's bass rumble and Bets' soft murmur.

So Spyder knows I'm the one to build the new chapter in BC!

"Soon, I can quit the bike shop, leave it to our boy and head south maybe, check out Vegas or San Diego. I'll even take ya with me if ya quit being such a nut-grinder!"

"It's not wrong for me to worry about your health, ya stubborn jerk. Why do ya think ya have that ache, in yer gut eh? What about that yellow tinge in yer eyes? Hell, even yer skin is startin' to turn yellow. Be careful, or you'll look like a Chink!"

"Yeah? Do I look that sick? Nah! Nothin' wrong with me that a coupla days o' rest won't fix. And I need to get Slash back on the road. Not good fer him to see me like this..."

So Spyder wants to keep me at a distance... He must be worried I might push him... and Diablo... out! Would I do that?

The mere possibility, tantalizing as it was, made for an uneasy night.

CHAPTER 5 - WILLOW IN THE DUMPS: SATURDAY, MAY 14

BB waited at the Terrace Hotel for Diablo's "enforcement of protection tour" from Edmonton to Prince Rupert to finish. When Diablo with the rest of the club returned, he mentioned to BB that everything was running like clockwork so there should be enough revenue to go ahead with the expansion.

BB knew that The Brigade was planning to buy a new property in the area to house a new chapter of the club. Staying in hotels all the time when they were on the road was becoming too expensive. Slash had tapped Diablo to check out likely sites to buy, so he had been spending his days cruising the countryside outside of Terrace looking at property. In the evenings, BB noticed, Diablo hung around the bar, hoping, against orders, to catch some action with the strippers.

BB had to be extra careful not to let Diablo interact with Willow who kept agitating for the freedom to go shopping or out for a movie. BB, running short on patience, had continued to refuse, suggesting if she made trouble, he would send Axel to sit with her in the room. BB knew that Willow, upon seeing the grimace on Axel's tattooed face, would quit complaining for a while.

Axel and Gypsy stood guard over the other dancers when BB took Willow to do private dance gigs and escort service work in the bigger towns like Kitimat and Prince Rupert. She was none too pleased to be seeing the same venues over and over again.

"Hey, BB! How long do I do these little one-horse towns? Slash said he would get me Vegas bookings, for God's sake!"

"Give it up, Willow! We're only doing these bookings until we start the bush-gigs. Then you'll be happy to come home to Terrace..."

"Who's doing those with me? I won't be the only dancer, will I?"

"Nah, we got three other girls ready to go as soon as the helicopter pilot says he's got time in his schedule, maybe by the beginning of June."

He, Axel and Gypsy had always kept her safe in guarded hotel rooms, and given her little time with the other off-contract girls. Roxie with her jet-black mane of hair, platinum-blonde Fantasia and honey-haired, tiny Bambi who all lived together in a kitchen suite of the hotel, were also working escort and dancing gigs in the town. These three were pros who knew the score, so the club had little trouble collecting their money and keeping them in line.

～

WILLOW SAT IN FRONT OF HER MIRROR, EXAMINING HER APPEARANCE. Staring back at her was a pale, gaunt face with great dark splotches under lifeless eyes, a face with washed-out skin and a sullen expression. She would have to work some real magic with her make-up to make herself look alluring for her gig tonight!

Why was she even trying? It wasn't as if her guards commented on her looks or health. She thought about her routine since being drafted to the Brigade's private performance and bush gig crew. She was kept apart from the other dancers, probably, she suspected, because she was a favoured dancer, and Slash didn't want her telling the others that she was bound for the big time. Since BB had reminded her that the only option for working her way up to exotic dancing spots in Vegas or Reno was to outshine the others, she had been working on extra private lap-dance gigs several nights a week, usually in Terrace, Lake Else or Prince Rupert. She told herself all this extra effort would impress Slash and motivate him to follow up on his promises.

The actual gigs involved flirting with paunchy middle-aged men, drinking a few beer with the clients and snorting a little coke that Axel provided to keep her focused. When she was finished at three on the morning, she played with a plate of bar food–French fries and a sub, or pizza. She was used to awaking around noon for toast and coffee, spending the afternoon seeing to her toilette, costumes and make-up, exercising to keep her body limber or watching the usual selection of sit-coms and commercial television gameshows. In the afternoon, BB would sometimes share some food with her, but she was often alone.

The windows to her room didn't open, and the only view was the brick wall of the building next door. She got outside for fresh air only when she was transferring from the chase vehicle to the lap-dance venue or vice-versa. She was smoking more than ever, about a pack a day to control her appetite, but even then, if she didn't toe the line and play the game, even the cigarettes were withheld. No one except her clients ever touched her. She had become immune to their overtures, willing her face to wear a sultry expression as if she were some kind of sex doll, and numbing herself to the pawing and probing of enthusiastic, potbellied customers.

Tonight she was in Rupert, where it was raining in buckets, and the heat in the hotel rooms was turned up too high. What she wouldn't give for some unrestricted down-time with fresh air, wholesome food and different company! Her energy was low. BB had told her tonight's gig was important, some guy the Brigade wanted to bring on board. Willow couldn't care less. The lap-dancing had become a mindless routine she could perform in her sleep. But BB had hinted that her performance was important, maybe the key for her to being rewarded with a little more freedom. She sighed and wondered if she was expected to allow this guy to have sex with her. She'd find out from BB. It didn't matter anymore; she didn't care what she had to do. She just felt beaten down by it all, with no way out.

BB felt they had perfected the routine with Willow so well that the little chippie had finally become submissive. She no longer expected to keep the money, or whined about wanting more 'freedom'. She still refused to deal with the other guards, but BB could always get her to cooperate.

On this Saturday night in Rupert, BB went to take her back to her room from an outside gig, and contrary to his usual routine, he led her through the hotel bar. Taking up altogether too much space at the counter was a squad of six RCMP regulars.

They approached Willow first. "Excuse me, Miss. Can I see your ID, please? We're doing a routine check for compliance with off-sale liquour here, and you look too young to be in here."

BB lost sight of Willow when three other big officers surrounded him, demanding his ID as well. He protested in a loud voice, "Hey, I'm legal, what are you buggin' me for?" The province had lowered the drinking age to nineteen at least a decade earlier, but BB had a round baby face and didn't look his age, which was, in fact, nineteen.

"Hey, settle down, sir. If you're legal, there's no need to worry, right?" BB produced his wallet and ID with ill grace. When the cops turned their attention back to Willow, he left the bar, watching the action from the hallway. He was worried about getting hassled for wearing his colours.

But he worried more about Willow, because her ID gave her real name, and BB suspected the cops had been watching out for her. Moreover, at seventeen, she was underage. Too late, he realized he should have made sure she left her wallet in the room. After arresting her, the cops spirited her away before BB could think about intervening, not that he would have been successful.

It turned out that Diablo had witnessed the entire scene from the back of the bar. When BB met him for a beer afterward, Diablo was contemptuous.

"Yer a dipshit, BB! Ya know yer not supposed to bring the girls through the bar! What were ya thinking! Fuck! Is Slash going to be pissed at ya! I told him I should have been the one in charge of Willow! This wouldn't of happened!"

BB had to agree, at least about Slash being pissed. *Such crap luck!* He knew that all of them, Axel, Gypsy and himself, would be answerable to Slash. He had never had any chick watched the way he had been having Willow guarded. What would Slash say or do now?

CHAPTER 6 - NORA'S PREDICAMENT: WEDNESDAY-SUNDAY, MAY 11-15

Nora appreciated the bed at Mike and Patsy Sinclair's place but she knew she wouldn't last there long. There wasn't much privacy as the two younger Sinclair boys, twelve and eleven, were used to spending their off-school hours in front of the rec room television. Also, McNab was unfriendly with the Sinclair's Jack Russell terrier, something Nora was at a loss to manage. The result was the cat spent most of the time outside, yowling.

A quick survey of her burnt-out place had confirmed for Nora that there was little worth saving. It was a furnished rental anyway, and if the police could be seen to have conducted a thorough investigation, the insurance company wouldn't quibble about covering the loss for her landlord. She filled out the required paperwork so the investigation for arson could proceed. Then, two days into her stay at the Sinclairs, the hassle with McNab and the Jack Russell, Bronco, motivated her to look for a room and board situation somewhere in town.

Since her life was already turned upside down, she also considered asking for a transfer to some other detachment, maybe Glacier Lake where Luke Gallagher, her five-year steady, remained stationed. Since his promotion to corporal had come through, he had been making serious overtures to her about something 'more permanent' in their relationship.

On the Friday after the fire, before she left the detachment at the end of shift, she found the energy to make a call to Luke whom she knew to be on office duty in Glacier Lake.

"Hey, Luke! I have news you won't want to hear..."

"Hi, baby doll! What's up?"

As always, she cringed a bit at hearing the sexist endearment, but said nothing. "My house got fire-bombed early yesterday morning. I spent all of yesterday sleeping off the smoke inhalation and trying to save my cat from Sinclair's dog. Sorry I didn't call. I was just too miserable."

"Fire-bombed!" The line crackled with a few well-chosen profanities. "Arson, eh? Poor sweetie. Are you okay? No injuries?"

"No, just smoke inhalation and puffy eyes. I'm off work until tomorrow. I'll be fine by then. I'll use the time to find a room and board, I think."

"Have they got a lead on who did it? Who do you think? How did they do it? How much damage is there?" He heaved a huge sigh and stopped firing questions for a moment. "You have to take this seriously!"

The barrage of questions had come so fast and furious that Nora was overcome at first, not knowing which to answer first. His last statement, though, was almost insulting.

He cares so much, but I feel as if he doesn't trust me to look after myself!

"Uh, Luke, I don't know who, but you know there have been so many nasty incidents over the last few years. Whoever did this wants me gone, one way or the other. The arson squad will investigate of course. The fire crew found a gasoline can tossed into the ditch across the road, so it was a quick flash up with accelerant. Maybe they can get a trace on the gas can, maybe fingerprints. I'll leave that to Mike. I lost clothes mostly, because it was a furnished place, and my insurance will cover those."

"You think you should stay in Brandenhoff? Where *are* you staying anyway? You mentioned Sinclair's dog?"

"I'm at Mike and Patsy Sinclairs, but I'm looking for a room and board. McNab isn't working out there. They've got a dog he doesn't like…"

"Look, Nora, maybe it's time to consider a transfer to someplace else, like…"

Nora cut him off. She knew what he was about to suggest, but she remained unclear in her own mind about her ongoing romance with Luke Gallagher. She *had* been thinking of moving to Glacier Lake, but now, with his comment about taking the arson "seriously", she felt she had to reconsider.

Nora found Luke very attractive, and they worked well as a couple. Even after five years, they had phenomenal sex. He was kind and intelligent, but she was ambivalent because, despite her attraction to him, he was paternalistic and over-protective so that she felt he compromised her options as a Mountie. Maybe it was time to take a break.

"… No, Luke. I can't just walk away. I don't want them to think they've beaten me…" She couldn't give in to bigots like the Curries, Patsy Sinclair's family. Howard Currie, Patsy's father, had never hidden his disrespect for her. As a cop, she knew him to be a source of the tension in town. But could she find evidence to tie him to the acts of vandalism, to the attacks on her property, to the arson? She now knew she had to leave the management of the case to Mike, who, as Howard's son-in-law, would have to recuse himself from the investigation. Likely, Hugh Bland, the second ranking constable at the detachment, would pick up the case.

She realized she'd been mulling over her career options for several months at least. She just couldn't accept ending her friendship with the Frederick family even though they had been implicated, but unproven, as culprits in the unresolved arson at DuLac Residential School. Somehow, her own Indigenous roots, her part Ojibwa mother, and her own pride refused to allow her to bend, to cut off any social connection with the powerful native healer and her family. She regretted not being able to solve the arson case at DuLac a few years before, but now this arson had made clear that her life was in danger. She had no choice but to consider a transfer.

Luke was insistent that she examine her predicament. "What's the point of staying someplace where you feel people might want to beat you? And who would that be? The town? The church? The native band? You can't even point a finger for sure! Nora, I think you need to cut your losses and start over. I'm serious! You know how I feel about you!"

"I know, Luke. I know... I'm not beaten. I just can't talk about this now. I'm too... tired... no proper sleep for a couple of nights... and... I'm just fed up! Let me recoup, and I'll call in a day or so when I'm less stressed, okay?"

～

LIFE AT MIKE'S PLACE WAS AWKWARD ENOUGH, AS NORA HAD NEVER GOT along with Patsy, and she had known from the first that staying there had been an interim solution until she could search for a room and board situation. But the scenario became more complicated when McNab had been added to the mix. McNab had started by behaving as all unhappy cats do, wetting on furniture and pooping in flower pots. Patsy had made clear that she wasn't a "cat person" who would tolerate such a lack of feline manners.

On Thursday, when Nora came home from a day shift, she discovered that Patsy had tossed the cat out in the backyard with Bronco, the Jack Russell. The two had battled in a knock'em out drag'em out fight that left the dog much the worse off. The boys were up in arms at the damage sustained by their pet, and Patsy had launched into hysterics.

"For crying out loud, Nora! (Patsy never swore.) Get rid of that cat! He's a menace! He's not even fixed! Look at the damage done to our Bronco. One torn eye socket, and both ears mauled, neck clawed to the bone... the vet bill is enormous! And the kids... they're heartbroken. They've had Bronco ever since he was a puppy!"

When Nora offered to pay the vet bill, Patsy was mollified, but the central problems remained. Where could she live? What would she do with McNab?

~

She spent a fitful night mulling over the problem and decided she had to move to a hotel until she found a room and board situation, and find another place for McNab. She was sitting in her detachment office the next morning flipping through the yellow pages looking for a kennel when Mike called her into his office.

"Uh... Nora... William Benson, the District Commissioner in Prince George called me... uh... you know who I'm talking about?" Nora's mind was blank.

"Oh, sorry, yes. I know District Commissioner Benson to see him. We haven't met. Uh... sorry, I was thinking about my cat. I'll pay the vet bill, Mike. I know Patsy's upset..."

"Oh, don't worry about that! What kind of self-respecting dog gets himself beat up by a cat, anyway? Don't give it another thought! Will your cat be okay in a kennel for now?" Nora nodded.

"Yeah? Good. Listen, I have a great idea for you... it's a temporary fix, but just might give you the time you need to sort yourself out."

Mike launched into the reason for DC Benson's call. "He has a personal problem. His seventeen-year-old daughter, Stephanie, ran away a few weeks ago and got herself mixed up with the Devil's Brigade biker gang in Prince George. After a quick investigation and quiet undercover work, her father extricated her from the gang while they were in Prince Rupert, and he brought her home to Prince George."

"Lucky girl," Nora murmured. "That bunch don't sound too wholesome..."

"Yeah, *I'll* say! But the problem doesn't stop there. Steph remains vulnerable there in PG as the gang–DC Benson refuses to call it a 'club'–can trace her whereabouts because they know she's a cop's kid."

"Do you mind me asking, Mike, why DC Benson called *you*?"

"Oh, he's an old buddy. We've known each other for years. We both come from the same little town in Alberta. Anyway, he called me as friend to ask if I had an idea for hiding Stephanie away for a few months. Bill needs some limbo time before he could get his daughter into a counselling and rehab program in Vancouver, and he needs to act while he is still legally able to supervise her behaviour as a minor. Stephanie is young and healthy, but still insists on indulging in marijuana and too much alcohol. When she's sober, or straight, she's tractable, but booze and dope combine to bring out the rebel, I guess."

Nora, who realized Mike saw her as homeless and somewhat compromised as a peace officer in Brandenhoff, listened with moderate interest. Mike continued, "I wonder if you would be interested in taking on the custody of this girl, a special assignment, only for a month or two. Because she's so close to legal age, the judge in the juvenile court considered remanding her, but her father was able to make a deal for staying her charges for possession of cocaine and marijuana as long as she cooperates."

Nora's first impulse was to reject the offer. What sane person would want to spend months 'babysitting' a delinquent young woman? It would be a thankless, irksome assignment. "Can't he find a way to keep her secure without involving the Force? I mean… it's a fairly minor charge…"

"Bill thinks she needs to learn a lesson. It's not her first brush with the law, and he's bailed her out a couple of times already."

Nora was still not keen, but when she looked at Mike, his face was so open and friendly, and his blue eyes sparkling with such good humour, that she relented.

"Alright, Mike, as a favour to you, I'll try it, but only two weeks to start, okay? I'll be able to see by then whether the girl and I can work together." She avoided adding that she didn't want to leave McNab in a kennel for any longer.

Nora mulled the proposal over as she walked down the hall toward her office. On second look, the offer of two weeks of extraordinary duty was appealing. The plus-side was that the custodial arrangement would stipulate Pine Ridge Resort, a remote, luxurious lodge, as accommodation. It came complete with a live-in, bonded security staff to protect the whereabouts of the girl, as well as canoes, kayaks, fishing gear, and a stable of horses for trail riding. The venue was one the Force had used in the past for special assignment training. The resort was in a pristine wilderness due north of the city on the upper arm of the Parsnip River. It *could* be a wonderful break!

Adding to the appeal, was the fact that she could be away from town where the arson investigation was going nowhere. She had got to the point of avoiding Constable High Bland, who had inherited the file, because he always regarded her with a hangdog look that said, "Don't blame me! This town is locked up tighter than a drum protecting the Curries." In her heart, she knew nothing would ever be found to prove them to be the culprits.

CHAPTER 7 - SPYDER AND SLASH ON THE EDGE: MONDAY-WEDNESDAY, MAY 16-18

Just before midnight, Slash sat in the Hog Barn clubhouse with three of the Brigade veterans playing stud poker and drinking beer. Ever since overhearing Spyder and Bets' conversation on the previous day, Slash couldn't help brooding about Spyder's health. He knew he had to find out where Spyder's rep stood. If the other bikers in the city were to discover the Devil's Brigade had a lame-duck leader, there would be blood on the streets as they clashed for territory. Slash knew Spyder was even sick enough to prompt brazen action from the Hell's Angels or even Satan's Choice, who were expanding from their base in southern California. They could always smell a vacuum.

Spyder yelled to come in when Slash knocked using their club signal. The boss was lying on the couch watching a rental, Martin Scorsese's "Mean Streets", on his videotape machine. Hands in his pockets, Slash stood by the door until Spyder looked him up and down and nodded for him to sit.

"What's up? Ya got problems ya can't handle?" Spyder's aggressive foray into conversation was predictable. He liked to look for a weakness in others.

"Nah, boss, not really. Ya know I got the chops to..."

"Cut the crap, Slavko, I know ya got some kinda beef, or ya wouldn't be up here so late."

"Uh... I think we gotta get ya out showin' the flag, ya know... yer the president of this mother chapter, and lately, there are lotsa wannabes biting at our heels out on the streets." Slash knew he had to be careful in his wording. Spyder was notorious for his thin skin.

"Shit, Slash! Yer the vice-president! *You* show the fuckin' flag! I don't gotta do that!"

Slash weighed his next words with care knowing that Spyder would react no matter how gently he phrased the criticism. He knew The Boss well enough to be careful of igniting his temper. It was his worst weakness, Slash thought, something that would sink him, in the end, something immature and stupid. He knew where Diablo got his temper.

"Spyder, man, I don't wanna say it, but ya ain't really been out for months and there's talk... like... ya know... hell, the Rebels and the Warlocks are crackin' jokes about ya... even calling ya... ya know... um... Milko."

Spyder exploded off the couch, and leaping across the room, grabbed Slash by the throat. "What did ya call me, motherfucker?" He was tightening Slash's swastika chain necklace, twisting it into a garotte. "Say it again, asshole! I dare ya!"

Slash was pushing on Spyder's arms, trying to break his grip. Meanwhile, his face was turning beet-red and then purple as the chain twisted ever tighter.

Slash soon realized that, although Spyder might be sick, he wasn't yet weak. All that can-crushing was paying off! Slash was about to clutch Spyder's hair when Bets, hearing the ruckus, appeared from a back room.

"Sonovabitch! Leave him alone, Spyder!" Her interference broke the boss's concentration. He loosened his grip, and Slash slid down onto the easy chair beside Spyder's couch. Spyder glared up at Bets from where he had also collapsed on the couch.

Bets stood over Spyder, frowning at Slash. "He hates that name, ya know… Even Dimitrios calls him Spyder, never 'Dad'. Last time he said it was when we got married. Ya shouldda known better."

Spyder turned on Bets. "Shut yer hole, woman. Ya don't open yer yap in front of club members. Nothin'! Ya hear? Not even Slash."

She tightened her ponytail, set her mouth in her phony, beatific smile, and walked away to sit at the dining room table on the other side of the room.

Slash, coughing into his sleeve to minimize attention, nodded. In his own defense, he croaked, "Yeah, I know, how ya hate the name, but ya should know those dipshit newbies are calling ya that… should know they're crowdin' the Brigade on the streets here."

Spyder reared up again. "Who's fuckin' crowdin' us?"

"I told ya, the Rebels and the Warlocks, they're taking over on Whyte Avenue, hanging out at Blues and the High Note."

"Oh yeah? We gotta do somethin', eh?"

"Yeah, but we gotta keep it outa town. The heat are watchin'. The Queen's Cowboys don't come into 'Chuk much, but they will for a turf war with bikers. Anyway, the Edmonton Police Service are lookin' for reasons to ban us."

"What time is it? The bar's still open. Let's go."

Bets, who has been watching the interaction from the sidelines, piped up, "Too late to go anywhere, Spyder… remember ya got a reason to take it easy… remember?" She looked sideways at Slash and then moved towards Spyder. "Just beer… okay, Old Man? Just beer. No hard stuff, eh?"

He backhanded her so hard she collapsed back against the wall, her nose bloody.

"Enough of the pussy-shit… I'm goin' with Slash to Blues. I ain't heard good sax in a long time."

∼

THE SCENE AT THE BLUES CLUB ON WHYTE AVENUE GOT LIVELY around two am when the regular clientele thinned out, and the band got into its dope. The air was thick enough with ganga smoke to chop with a machete. Spyder and Slash leant back against the wall by the exit and mellowed to the sounds of a sax medley–everything from Pink Floyd's "Money" to Gerry Mulligan's "Big City Blues".

Slash waited for a pause between tunes, "So, no sign of Rebels or Warlocks tonight…"

Spyder growled, his face a mask of misery, and took another shot of tequila. "Yeah, whatever… they likely heard we're here and are too pussy to show their ugly mugs… I'll…" Without warning, his head plummeted, and his face hit the tabletop, blood spouting from his mouth and nose.

"Spyder! Man! What the fuck!" Slash, astounded by the volume of blood, jumped up to avoid being soaked and hailed the barman. "Hey, Artie! Gimme some towels over here, will ya? Spyder's gotta nosebleed…"

Spyder, wracked by spasms, continued to vomit. Slash, knowing Spyder wouldn't want to go to Emergency, asked Artie to call a taxi. Spyder spluttered between spasms, "Fucking ulcers! My liver's shot too! Sawbones says it's cirrhosis."

Slash did his best to be sympathetic. "Take it easy man. We'll get ya home to Bets. Maybe the tequila was a mistake, eh?"

Spyder choked out, "Screw that! I can't drink pussy stuff in public! I got a rep in this dump!"

∽

SLASH SHEPHERDED SPYDER HOME AND TOLD BETS THE STORY. SHE called the club's doctor, one who could no longer practice because of getting caught doing abortions. Slash knew it wasn't the first time someone had called Doc Roussopoulos to see Milko "Spyder" Zorman.

The Doc was not known for his bedside manner. As Slash waited listening by the basement door, Spyder got a rare tongue lashing, one he couldn't threaten away. "I told you the last time this happened, Mr. Zorman, that you were courting serious health problems, even deadly ones. I told you then you had to quit drinking alcohol, especially the hard stuff. You have cirrhosis of the liver and stomach ulcers. There's little I can do, really."

Slash knew to leave then. Bad enough to be so sick. Spyder didn't need to lose face in front of his Number Two, as well.

Slash got a couple of club members to bring his and Spyder's Harleys back from in front of the Blues Club. It wouldn't do to leave them there too long and attract the notice of other bike clubs or the cops. Slash felt a lead weight in his gut thinking of how weak Spyder was.

To himself, he pondered how long before the other clubs would know Spyder was living on borrowed time. Word of his collapse at the Blues Club was doubtless already on the rumour mill. Spyder would have to tap Leftie, the club's money man, to show the flag in town until he could get back on his feet. Even that might not do the trick.

Slash knew a new clubhouse based in BC was more critical than ever. Then, if Spyder wanted to retreat to somewhere down south, he could leave the business to Diablo. Once Slash had the BC chapter set up, he would invite the Edmonton club to join him in BC, likely around Terrace. If Diablo wanted to keep the Hog Barn going, he's have to work to keep the Brigade members from leaving. Slash grinned with self-satisfaction. Bikers knew good leadership, and Diablo wasn't it!

～

ON TUESDAY, THE NEXT DAY, BB, AXEL, AND DIABLO ARRIVED BACK IN Edmonton with the bad news about Willow. BB didn't pick up any reaction from Slash to the news of Willow's disappearance. It was as if he couldn't care less, BB thought. Slash's eyes surveying the two youngest gang members were leaden. He took occasional sips of the beer beside him on the clubhouse table.

Slash spoke first to Diablo, motioning him to take a seat while BB was left standing. "What's the scoop on a new clubhouse site? Find anything?"

"Nah, not yet. We want a business outta town that can act as a cover. Not that easy to find. Maybe a ranch, maybe a logging camp... somethin' will turn up." Diablo was enjoying his time in the limelight. "I was wonderin'... if I can place a want ad in the Terrace paper? Ya know, might save time..."

"That's a dumb idea, Pest! What an idiot! Ya should know better! We never advertise our stuff. The less the public know about us the better!" Shaking his head, he flung his arm up to dismiss Diablo who wasted no time in slinking away out the clubhouse door. "Now BB, about that fuckin' Willow..."

BB stood in dread about what Slash was about to say him, so he was surprised to be invited to take a seat. Slash's reaction to the disappearance of Willow verged on unflappable practicality. His voice was low and steady. "We gotta figure out how we lost her. That's an asset those fuckin' cops have stolen from us. I wonder if she would be on her way back to her cop-daddy. Fuck women, especially young, good-looking ones!" Slash took a moment to make a decision. "Anyway, I'll send some gofers... uh...Grinder and Tiny... back to Terrace to nose around to find out what had happened to her."

"Uh... thanks, Slash... can I get some sleep?"

"Yeah, get outta here." BB's dragged his dog-tired carcass across the expanse of the clubhouse to where several dilapidated couches were grouped in a dark corner. He was so exhausted, he collapsed and slept around the clock.

～

BB AWOKE BEFORE MIDNIGHT TO THE SOUND OF SPYDER AND SLASH hammering through the details of expanding the club into British Columbia. Spyder was speaking, his voice hoarse and windy. "I don't like what's happening here in Edmonchuk. Too many run-ins with the other clubs... too much heat altogether. I figure we should set up our main BC headquarters in Prince George... easy road to Van from there... it's nice and central..."

"Spyder, I'm tellin' ya, we gotta skirt PG because the Renegades have got it sewn up. We should concentrate our efforts on Brandenhoff and west of there. There's no biker action, or at least, little that we could see from there to Terrace... just a string of jerkwater towns with lots of young loggers and miners lookin' for a little action on the weekends."

"Do they want what we have to offer, though? Those little towns got a lot of Bible thumpers...might not be many customers..."

"Oh, hell, Spyder, when was the last time ya spent a stretch there? Those guys come to work from all over the country. They got no connections in the towns, nothin' except cash to burn...it'll be a licence to print money!"

"Okay, Slash, I hafta go with what ya say 'cause I ain't goin' to check it out myself, I don't think."

BB couldn't remember a time when Spyder had given in so easily. He noticed a serious change in Spyder from when he had last seen him before the tour, a lessening of vigour, a dullness in his eyes. Yet, neither Slash nor Diablo had mentioned the change.

They're afraid to piss off the Boss by hinting he doesn't look too healthy.

Later that day, BB approached Slash in the clubhouse. "Uh... I wonder if the boss is self-medicating too much, ya know... pushing himself with too much weed or downers..." When he caught the gunmetal glint in Slash's eyes, he stopped dead. "Just wondering..."

Slash turned to face him square on and growled, his words stinging the boy who hero-worshipped him. "I thought the screw-up with Willow would have taught ya something, BB. Mind... yer... own... business... Spyder is okay, just getting over a flu."

CHAPTER 8 - STEPHANIE BENSON: THURSDAY-FRIDAY, MAY 19-20

Nora drove to Prince George to meet Stephanie who was being held in a segregated juvenile lock-up. Nora hadn't done any research in the girl's case file, preferring to form her own impressions first before having them skewed by the therapeutic spin of the intake medical crew. All she knew really was what Mike had told her when he had asked if she was interested in the assignment.

The custodian, a severe-looking older woman in khaki with her grey hair pulled into a no-nonsense bun, showed Nora through several barred doors secured by deadlocks. The clang of each door as it closed behind them echoed down the hallway.

In the visitor's room, pacing like a caged cougar cub, was Stephanie Benson, an intense, slender pixie with enormous amber eyes and a braided mane of ebony hair that fell past her waist. She wore an olive-green prison jumpsuit several sizes too large. Right from the beginning, the girl's fragile dark beauty struck Nora.

Stephanie looked Nora up and down, a derisive scowl marring her beautiful face.

Nora felt her way with great caution, knowing the girl was skittish. "Hi, Steph, I'm Nora Macpherson. How are you?"

The girl regarded her, an antagonistic expression in her eyes.

"How do you think? Cooped up like a fuckin' chicken..." She dropped into an armchair at the large table and slumped, her elbows propped to support her head, her eyes on the ceiling.

Nora, although a bit shocked by the girl's salty language, forged ahead. "Uh... your dad has asked me to check with you to ask if you're interested in going somewhere else, a high-end mountain resort, a kind of retreat, I guess... better than here anyway..." Nora gestured to the sterile beige walls and functional brown, Naugahyde couch and wooden tables and chairs.

"Yeah, whatever..." she said, her twitching leg thumping relentlessly against the underside of the table. "So my father sent you? You a cop?" Nora nodded in response. "I might have known Daddy wouldn't do it himself..."

Nora was taken aback by the girls' blunt honesty.

Not just a pretty face...she's gutsy... not afraid to say what she thinks!

"I think your dad is just a busy man, Steph. And he probably thinks you could use a fresh set of ears..."

"Oh, really?" The tone was sardonic and argumentative.

The force of girl's sustained hostility surprised Nora. She tried to pivot to a focus on her interests. "Can you tell me about yourself a bit, Steph? What you enjoy? What you're good at? Uh... I'm just trying to get to know you, yeah?"

"No." Her eyes locked on Nora with surprising intensity. "My head aches, my body aches. I. Don't. Need. No. Fucking. Cop. Babysitter. Tell my old man that! Tell him to face me himself!"

For all her bravado, Nora saw that Steph was high-strung, so brittle and tense that she seemed ready to explode at any moment. Her eyes were frantic and her movements jittery, the tattoo of her knee on the table bottom becoming ever more insistent, her hands clutching her head as if to crush away some pain.

Hmmm... frenetic movement... headache... muscle ache... aggression... this behaviour is likely withdrawal... It's futile to push for a breakthrough while she's so volatile. I'd better leave her to dry out.

She buzzed for the lock-up doors to be opened and had to wait for the custodian and the automatic system to work. To fill the silence, she attempted another interaction. "Good-bye, Stephanie, I'll see you tomorrow, okay?" Stephanie's only response was to fling herself upright and to start pacing again.

On her way out, Nora let the stolid prison custodian know she would come back the next day. She needed to spend some time on research. Maybe she had made a mistake in thinking she could wing it on her first contact with Stephanie Benson.

∼

Nora spent that Thursday evening pouring over the case file Mike had given her. The file had been assembled from information her father had supplied, reports from the arresting team in Prince Rupert as well as data collected from the psychiatric team at the juvenile lock-up facility in Prince George.

From the father's tersely written report, Nora found out that Stephanie was a December baby, born in 1966, whose mother had died when she was six, and Bill had never remarried. He had sent Steph to an all-girls' school run by the Anglican Church, where she had had little freedom. She was an intelligent girl and skipped a grade so was always hanging out with kids older than herself. On summer holidays at home in her early teens, she had had a couple of brushes with the law, mostly bouts of public drinking underage and minor vandalism in local parks. These had resulted in fines that her father had paid.

So as a December baby, she was surrounded by peers older than herself at school, perhaps always trying to win approval, proving herself...

When she had graduated in June 1982, she was still six months away from her seventeenth birthday. She had refused to continue her schooling, so her dad had allowed her to get a sales job in a women's clothing store and to share an apartment in Prince George with a girlfriend, someone she had known for years at school.

As if he had no idea that arrangement was a recipe for disaster! If she had already had run-ins with the law, you'd think he would have been more circumspect.

For the few months, the father, himself working long hours, had little connection with his daughter beyond helping her make ends meet on her minimal salary. The father thought Stephanie had tried, but was not mature enough to manage her scaled-back lifestyle. Bill Benson had noted that she had started asking for money more often than he was prepared to give her any. There were also notations about police calls to noisy, late night parties in her apartment which Bill had mentioned as embarrassing for him. He wrote that as a result, he and Stephanie had argued, and the upshot was a complete breakdown in communication. Benson had not seen her or given her money since just after the previous Christmas.

So she had been trying to make it on her own for several months, four at least...

The psychiatrist's report from the juvenile lock-up picked up where her father's information left off. Stephanie had admitted that, since that falling-out with her father, she had started spending much of her income on partying, booze and drugs. By Easter, she had found herself so much in debt that almost all her salary was going to pay off money she owed to a friend of Monica, her roommate. This friend was part-owner of some local night-spots, and it had been he who had suggested she should get a second job. The unnamed friend (Stephanie had refused to identify him) had even offered to introduce her to a club that featured exotic dancers. She would be an occasional substitute for girls who missed their gigs through illness or lateness. The friend assured her that she would be doing him a favour, and that the money she made would provide enough income to fill the gap. Before long, she had quit her sales job, given up her apartment, and was part of the troupe, working a regular circuit across Northern BC. The file noted at the end that Stephanie Benson showed a love of risk-taking that was habitual, perhaps a non-verbal plea for attention.

Daddy issues... Despite the appearance of vulnerability, Stephanie seems determined to go her own way, like someone who is fond of taking risks just for the reaction she evokes in those who care about her.

Nora pushed back from the desk feeling numbed by the girl's

story. Nora, who had lost her own mom when she was eleven, knew a little bit about growing up motherless. Her heart went out to this thrill-seeking girl who, she suspected, only wanted her sole remaining parent to pay attention for a change. She wished she could say as much to DC Benson, but somehow she didn't think he would listen to her. She, herself, couldn't be sure her assessment of Stephanie was objective and not a projection of how she had felt when her mother had died. She remembered feeling that the bottom of her world had fallen out, that she was at loose ends without an anchor. Thinking back, she shook her head, dismissing the comparison. Her father hadn't been remote the way Bill Benson seemed to be. He had stepped up and done his best for his only child. And she still had been connected to her Ojibwa grandmother on the reserve outside of Brandon, Manitoba. This girl seemed to have no one but her rather distant father.

∼

BEFORE LEAVING AGAIN FOR THE LOCK-UP IN PRINCE GEORGE THE NEXT day, she stopped in to chat with Mike. As an old friend of the Commissioner, she thought Sarge might have a sense of the sort of person Bill Benson was out of uniform.

"Mike, can I have a word?"

"Hey, Nora! Have you checked in with Stephanie Benson yet? I know her dad is hoping you can bring her around... uh... but by the look on your face, I don't think I have much reason for optimism."

Nora tried to adjust her facial expression from worry to one of wry concern. "That's why I'm here, Mike. I don't think this dad has connected with his daughter for a while. Steph's so angry with him, she doesn't want any part of a plan if he has anything to do with it! She's a gorgeous girl, Mike, and someone who is a very strong-willed, a risk-taker, I would say."

"Stephanie gets that from her dad, I'd say. Bill Benson is where he is in the Force today because he knows what he wants, and he never stops trying to get it. He's one of the most stubborn, gutsy people I've ever known... but a damn good cop."

"Well, I think he should have taken some time off to spend with his daughter. We can force her to go to the resort and drag her out for lots of activities, but I wouldn't place any bets on how successful the effort will be unless we get her full cooperation."

Mike's forehead wrinkled in concentration. "One thing I remember about Stephanie is she was crazy about horses as a little kid. I know this ranch has a stable and some nice mounts. Perhaps that will provide enough inducement to get her thinking it's not such a bad idea..."

∼

When Nora returned to the lock-up that afternoon, Stephanie was waiting in the same room, but her attitude was changed. Seated at the table, she smiled, her body calm and composed. "Yeah, Nora? Is it? I'm sorry about the yesterday. You're right. I don't want to be here. Where do you want us to go?" Her amber eyes were sparkling with goodwill.

Nora stood stock-still in astonishment.

What has happened? How believable is this sudden transformation?

Despite her confusion, she managed a positive response. "Oh, great, Steph! What made you change your mind?"

"Oh, I realized what a dump this place was compared to what you were offering..."

"Yeah, I think this place sounds so cool! It's called Pine Ridge Resort. It's a five-star rated place in a pristine wilderness with all the gear for enjoying the terrain up in the mountains: canoes, kayaks, fishing gear, and a stable of horses, too!"

"Horses, really? Are you kidding? I love horses! Oh, wow! I used to ride a little, you know..."

"Yeah, we can go trail riding and kayaking, rock-climbing, do a little fishing maybe... it'll be fun!"

"When can we go?"

"Well, it sits a little way out of town on the Parsnip River, so we'll need travel time."

Nora remained in shock at Steph's sudden enthusiasm. It seemed such a turnaround from the previous day that she questioned its credibility. Could someone overcome the effects of drug withdrawal so fast? She checked with the supervisory staff at the holding centre to ask what they thought. The woman custodian agreed that Steph had seemed to improve right after Nora had left the previous day. She said she's seen similar reversals before, usually when they'd spent a few days in the lock-up and became bored.

Nora arranged for them to travel to Pine Ridge, leaving early the next day.

CHAPTER 9 - NORA GETS READY FOR A SPECIAL ASSIGNMENT: FRIDAY, MAY 20

That night, Nora spent more hours checking the report filed by the arresting officer in Prince Rupert. There was little information about Stephanie's 'career' as a dancer, only that she had ended up working out of the Hillcrest Hotel, a club recently infiltrated by a biker gang, the Devil's Brigade. According to the other dancers interviewed in Prince Rupert afterwards, the gang leader, a thirty-year-old Serbian immigrant, Slavko 'Slash' Dracul, had 'befriended her' and signed her up to leave the regular strip circuit to work special contracts for the gang. The Brigade was an Edmonton-based club and ran a regular network across BC and Alberta where they supplied security for girls at their stripping gigs, and the Force suspected, ran a prostitution circuit.

Were it not for an unexpected RCMP raid of the Prince Rupert Skylark Hotel for illegal liquour off-sales, on May 8th, the police might not have apprehended Stephanie in time. There had been a BOLF for her issued by the Prince George RCMP, but since she was only seventeen, she was arrested for being underage in a place of alcohol sales. The arresting report also contained a note from Bunnie Burrows, whom Nora knew by reputation. Bunnie worked undercover along the stroll in the Downtown Eastside, but also kept her ear to the ground with the exotic dancers on the circuit around the province. The word she had picked up among the other girls was that Steph would work the Brigade's next set of bush gigs, flying into a series of remote mining and logging camps.

From the file, Nora learned Steph had been in custody for just six days since being picked up in Rupert, and the diagnostic team had assessed her in a police-run, medical lock-up facility. Nora noted that the medical file listed alcohol, marijuana and cocaine as the substances found in Steph's system. It also detailed a set of psychological concerns: insomnia, nightmares, depression and difficulty concentrating. Nora decided the girl needed to be kept busy with dawn-to-dusk outdoor activity. If she became tired enough from healthy exertion outside, Nora bet she should sleep well.

Nora had the Friday afternoon and Saturday to sort out her stuff, pack for two weeks at the resort, and decide what to do with McNab. She had a sudden brain-wave that Luke might help her out by taking the tabby for the two weeks. She reached him by phone at home around supper time.

"Hey Luke, how are you doing?"

"Not much, Hon. How about you? Have you recovered from the smoke inhalation?"

"Oh, yeah. I'm much better, thanks. Uh... the reason I'm calling is that I have a special assignment for a couple of weeks." She briefed him on the short-term custody assignment at Pine Ridge Resort.

"Pretty amazing that a high-ranking dad can muster up such perks for a wayward daughter, don't you think?"

"Yeah, I agree! But it works for me, and I was wondering if you wanted a visit from our feline friend for that time?"

"Oh, you mean McNab? Oh, sorry. I wish I could help you, but to be honest, I'm off first thing Sunday to take a computer training course in Prince George. I'll be away for two weeks myself."

"Okay. Too bad, but that's cool. We are all going to need to know that stuff."

"To tell you the truth, I'm not sure. Computers mean a lot of sitting on your butt. I like to be up and moving around more. But I guess we'll need to do some of that keyboard tapping stuff, too. The less the better is what I say!"

"Okay, Luke. Well, get as much as you can out of it. I'll need to figure it out, too, and it'll be easier if I have a computer-tutor buddy!"

"Will do! Talk soon! Good luck with Benson's daughter!"

∼

NEXT, NORA PICKED UP MCNAB FROM THE CAT KENNEL AND CALLED ON Della Frederick to ask for her help. She held McNab, wrapped in a towel in her arms. She hoped Della would be grateful enough to take McNab because Nora had intervened several years before to help Della's niece, Carla, stay clear of some unhealthy influences at Dulac School.

"Hi Della. I'm in a spot and need to board my cat for a couple of weeks."

"I don't know, Nora. I'm really more of a dog-person..." She peered at McNab nestled in Nora's arms, and Nora saw Della reach out her hand to examine the bite marks on his forehead. "Oh, look at him. Was he in a fight?"

"Yeah, he had a difference of opinion with the Sinclair's terrier."

"Mike and Patsy Sinclair? The RCMP sergeant?"

"Yes, I'm afraid so. The dog got the worst of it though... so you can't take him for a bit? I don't want to leave him in a kennel anymore. He *hates* it there. He can't go anywhere, and he's not eating. I'll pay you..."

Della threw up her hands. "Oh, don't be silly! I don't want your money! Is he an outdoor cat? Is he a mouser? If he can pull his own weight, he can stay. Our kids' dog, a Lab-Shepherd cross, is a tolerant old girl, and won't even lift an eyebrow with... McNab? Is it? Good name for a cop's cat!"

Heaving a great sigh, Nora grinned. "Oh, Della, you're an angel! I was so afraid I would have to take him to the SPCA! Thank you!"

Della smiled and asked, "Would you like some tea? Have you got time? I haven't seen you since your house burned down. I'm so sorry! Any idea how it started?"

"We fairly sure it was set deliberately. There was an empty gas can thrown in the ditch opposite the house."

"Sit down and take a load off. I'll be right back... just put the kettle on..."

From the kitchen, she called back, "You know who might have wanted to do this?" When she came back to the living room, she sat back down on the couch, and struck her head as if to knock the memories loose, "Oh, right... you've had all kinds of nasty stuff this last couple of years... vandalism, dumps of manure... of course there's someone, or maybe a couple of 'someones' who'd like to see the back of you."

"I haven't asked around," Nora explained. "It's such an unpleasant topic that I hate to burden anyone else with it. The detachment has started a file, and someone there will pursue it. I don't know what evidence is possible, maybe fingerprints on the gasoline can handle. It happened in the early hours of the morning so I doubt there was anyone awake amongst my neighbours who could be a witness." She didn't mention Hugh Bland's lack of progress.

"Anyway, enough about me. What happening with your family?" Nora had played an important role a couple of years before in helping to steer Della's niece away from some unhealthy influences at school.

Della knew that Nora's interest in her family was genuine, and was happy to provide an update. "Carla's finished high school and is training to be a practical nurse at New Caledonia College in Prince George."

"Oh, good for her! That's a big step!"

Della nodded, "I have to admit I'm a little leery about Carla being so far from home, but I know there was not much opportunity for young people in Brandenhoff. It's too small, and the white people are not kind to us".

"How's your brother-in-law, Pete?" Carla's dad's drinking problem had been at the bottom of Carla's isolation and of Sally, his wife's, decision to leave him and relocate to Prince George, taking the younger children with her. He had also been implicated in the arson of the DuLac Residential School a couple of years before. Nothing had come of the arson link, and Nora was hoping Pete had stayed sober.

"He's got Sally to move back with the younger kids to the reserve. So things are looking better on that front. I don't think he's had a drink in more than two years."

"That's wonderful news!" She couldn't help but feel happy for this family's success in combatting the drinking problem. They were admirable in their love and support of each other, and for being reliable workers and community participants, but for many in the town, they still carried the stigma of being native. She was sure the lack of progress in the arson investigation as well as her continued friendship with Della underlay much of the hostility she had experienced from some locals. She wished she could help these so-called Christians see past their bigotry.

"Well, I have to make a decision soon about whether to stay or go. My value as a law enforcement officer is pretty limited if I can't get people's trust. I hate to admit defeat, but I need to work where I feel needed."

"Of course you do. Oh Nora! I hate to see you have to leave! You're the kind of cop we need in places like this! But I get it. I do. I bet those Currie creeps are responsible for the fire at your place. I remember one time when Barrie Currie let the air out of one of my tires when we were in church. My kids saw him do it and chased him away before he could get to the other tires. When I approached his father, all Howard would say is that boys do stupid things sometimes. He never said sorry, or even said he would deal with his son or send him to apologize. I was never sure if the 'stupid' remark was about the actual mischief, or his kid getting caught doing it!"

"Yeah, I think they are likely suspects... uh... but proving it? Not so easy..." She reminded herself how open they were in their hostility to her, and despite their standing in the local church and community, clearly, at least the son was capable of the kind of mean, childish attacks she had suffered.

As she drove back to the Sinclairs' place for her last night for a while, Nora thought about her own mother, who, as a Metis, had had to pretend to be white to fit in when she had been a young woman. Nora's championing of the Indigenous had been a natural impulse, coming from her admiration for her mother, but one that had cost her the support of the Brandenhoff's power-brokers. Now she had to decide whether to let it drive her away.

Thoughts about the difficulties of being Indigenous led her to think back to her previous brushes with predatory behaviour along Highway 16. K.C "Casey" Mitchell, whom she had heard about when she investigated the murder of Rosemary Joseph, had been a predatory character, she was sure. Circumstantial evidence had him in the area where many young women had been assaulted, strangled and left for dead. Not all of their bodies had been found, but Mitchell's body had turned up near Prince Rupert in 1977, so *he* couldn't be still responsible for all the recent attacks. She reviewed the list of recent victims: Belinda Williams in 1977, Monica Jack in 1978, Tracey Clifton in 1979, Jean Marie Kovacs in 1981, all within the last ten years. One suspect, Edward Dennis Isaac, was listed as at large, but she didn't think he couldn't be responsible for all the disappearances. In Nora's mind there was no doubt: there was another serial killer on the loose.

CHAPTER 10 - INTERNAL BIKER POLITICS: FRIDAY, MAY 20

As Slash sorted through his saddlebags, he cast around the dim interior of the club's Edmonton clubhouse, the Hell Pit, trying to decide what to do. He was mulling over his latest order from Spyder. For two days after the stomach problem, the boss had stayed in bed. Then he had called for Slash.

"Okay, Slash, I want the boys out on the road across Highway 16 from PG to Rupert. If we're makin' a move to buy property up there, we gotta be on the ground! We don't control the action from way over here in Edmonchuk. We gotta set up another chapter of the Brigade in Terrace."

"Yeah, I know. That's why we're doin' the bush gigs, to make the dough to buy the property. While that's happenin', I need the rest of the club to step up. Boss, we already done three tours across there in the last little while–we done a recon, a recruitment and a reinforcement. Ain't that enough?"

"Nah, we gotta keep the pressure on so that Renegade scum knows we're serious. More follow-up, remind the owners what could happen if they fall behind. We gotta keep our thumb on the mules too, and I don't want the Renegades even knowin' we gotta new chapter comin' until it's off the ground."

The Boss is acting as if his ulcer attack has pushed him into being even more hard-nosed.

"Spyder, I need a break from the road. I been goin' full out for months!" He could hear the fury in his own voice. "Why don't you... " He stopped, realizing he couldn't tell Spyder to do this tour himself.

I wonder whether Spyder is keeping me isolated on purpose, so I don't make a power play to replace him?

"Why don't I *what*, Slash?"

"Nothin'. I know you ain't feelin' the urge to ride just now..."

"That's right. I gotta mind the shop and let Diablo learn the road while he has the chance. Leftie will have to step up here in 'Chuk. He's the treasurer so he can run the Hell Pit for now..."

"Okay, Boss. I'll get organized to go. The Brigade are due to meet up in PG at the Hillcrest this coming weekend. I'll be there to tune'em up." Spyder was still looking at him, his fist raised, as if he expected more back-talk.

"Don't worry, Spyder. I got it covered. I got some stuff to do before I take off."

Slash saw Spyder as a sick man, but he knew himself to be sluggish, too. Losing Willow had taken something out of him. He felt embarrassed and annoyed to realize he had been losing control, fretting about his image in the club, not the sign of a confident leader. He would use this trip to re-establish his mojo.

He had been crashing here between road trips for the last few months, having been away so often he needed nothing more permanent to call home. He was wavering about leaving because he felt listless, and because he didn't know what had happened to Willow. If he did as Spyder insisted, he would be absent for a month getting the new chapter up and running. He'd have little time to worry about Willow, maybe a bonus... she was an itch he shouldn't scratch.

He had mostly abided by the strict club rule of "hands off" with the dancers and he knew, if Willow came back, that he needed her at a safe distance, away on the bush gig tour, working the camps for tax-free cash. She must be so scared and isolated she dare not disappear again. But he couldn't keep tabs on her himself if he did as Zorman demanded and took to the road again. Should he make a play for Spyder's place now?

He needed to eliminate both Spyder and Diablo, something he wasn't sure he wanted to try yet. He would have to have the club on his side. They would have to judge Spyder as a liability, as a leader past his prime, someone likely to make costly mistakes. They also needed to see Slash as the obvious successor. That would happen once he made all the money for the club from the bush gigs. It would be *his* achievement–not Spyder's or Diablo's. It would be *his* money that bought the new club property.

How many would see Diablo, Spyder's son, as the legitimate heir? What would happen when they established a new chapter in Terrace? Who was the logical club member to lead that? Diablo, as a mechanic, should want to inherit the Edmonton Mother Club, The Hog Barn. The Terrace turf, by rights should come to Slash, especially if he fought to establish it. But if Diablo was the one to find the property, he might feel he should take the lead. But Diablo couldn't do both, and Slash was betting he would want to stay with the Hell Pit. Besides, Diablo did not have much of a following within the club. Any slack he got was due to his father's position. For the most part, the Brigade saw the son as an impulsive, insecure punk.

Slash had been toying with the idea of monkeying with Spyder's grub, but after considering the club's hunt for Terrace real estate, he decided that would be a dumb move–to handicap the mother club just as there's a new chapter in the offing. No, he would do this new tour of the Highway 16 territory. If Willow showed up, Diablo and BB would escort her on the helicopter bush gigs, keeping her out of sight of the public and, even better, away from him. That would leave the rest of the club free to ride enforcement when he needed them. Once everything was in place, he would move to control the Terrace chapter. Then he could decide about Willow.

CHAPTER 11 - PINE RIDGE RESORT: SATURDAY, MAY 21

After driving all morning to get to The Pine Ridge resort, Nora and Steph spent an exhausting Saturday afternoon exploring the hiking potential of the resort. They had risen early to make the drive and by noon were on a four-hour hike through the mountain trails behind the resort. They had taken packed lunches and trucked up to above the tree line of Black Rock Mountain, where they could see far below the sapphire blue water of Little Kelsey Lake, set like a gem in the valley. There they rested and opened up the bag of ham and cheese buns, juice, and apples provided by the resort kitchen.

"Look over there!" Nora's sighting of a grizzly bear foraging the side hill for spring greens broke the calm. "Shhhh! Don't move or make a sound!" she whispered.

She knew to be wary of the animal, even though it was several hundred yards distant, because the tempers of hungry spring bears were notorious for their unpredictability. They watched it for a few moments to determine which direction it was heading, and to see whether it was a sow with cubs.

With binoculars, Nora followed the movements of the grizzly, remembering her terrifying encounter with a much bigger one six years before on the Bar-T Ranch south of Moose Forks. She and

Luke had had to shoot it at close range in order to protect Hank Talbot, who had not survived its attack. Nora had no delusions about the danger of the adolescent animal she and Steph were observing.

"Is it a boy or girl?" Steph had taken the binoculars and was watching, fascinated.

"Hard to tell when they're young like this one. An adult male is always bigger than the female, but this young one hasn't reached its full size. If it stops to pee, we can try to see if it does it behind its back legs... that's a female. If it pees to the front of the back legs, that's a male." Steph nodded, handing the binoculars back to Nora who continued to follow the grizzly's movements.

Through the lenses, Nora saw the bear stop and sniff the air as if tasting the breeze to locate its dinner. For a moment, Nora froze, preparing to take defensive action should the bear perceive them close by. She breathed again only when the animal returned to foraging in the lush green growth of the alpine meadow. Steph had been stricken silent by the chance encounter.

When she spoke, she sounded breathless, as if short on air. "Have you had much to do with bears? I've never seen one this close in the wild."

"Yes, once I had to shoot a grizzly that was attacking someone... very scary."

"Oh, that's awful! What happened to the person?"

"He didn't make it, I'm sorry to say."

Steph stared at her intently. "Wow."

Nora sensed some newfound respect from the young girl.

They arrived back at the resort in time to get a quick orientation with the sturdy Rocky Mountain horses the resort used to rent to guests. Dan Woodward, the stable manager, told them the breed was a born mountain climber that had originated in the foothills of the Appalachian Mountains in Eastern Kentucky in the late 1800s. Rocky Mountain horses had been a well-kept secret for years. Reliable and sure-footed on the trail, with an easy gait, the horse was well adapted for mountain riding. Because it could endure rough riding conditions, it had been the ride of choice for many years for mountain mail carriers, doctors, and traveling preachers.

"Hey, Miss, how about you spend some time with Molly, here?" Dan pointed to an eight-year-old chestnut mare. "She likes her coat done with this curry comb, and you can clean her mane a bit, too."

Nora saw that Molly was a sweet-tempered, gentle creature, but Steph expressed no pleasure in connecting with the animal. Her listless efforts to groom the horse betrayed her annoyance with the whole bonding process. She stopped combing her mane after a few strokes and didn't want to bother with the curry comb. Even when feeding Molly treats, Steph showed barely any patience by holding the apple in her open hand, but just dropped it on the stable floor for the horse to find.

"You know the horse will connect with you better the more time you spend with her." Nora wondered how much Steph had actually spent with horses. Maybe she didn't really know what to do?

"Yeah, well I don't feel like it right now."

"Do you want some help? I can show you the basics of grooming a horse..."

"No, I know what to do, I just don't feel like it, I told you!"

"Well how about helping me to feed the horses? Dan said we can give them some straw and oats..."

"Whatever..."

Nora was puzzled by the girl's discontent.

Mike said she was crazy about horses! Maybe kayaking, fishing or rock climbing will be better choices?

They kept Steph busy in the stable until suppertime and decided on a quick ride around the paddock afterwards. Over supper, Nora tried to engage the girl in conversation about her horse experience during her younger years.

Her response was scornful. "Oh, you know Mounties! It's all about the horses, eh? My dad got me taking lessons when I was six, and I thought they were pretty cool. I mean, I was a kid! What kid wouldn't like to ride a horse? But my dad made a big deal out of it... always wanting me to do fancy grooming–you know–braids and ribbons... and spending time on brushing it."

"That's part of the joy of having a horse, the closeness that comes with making it feel loved and comfortable..."

"Yeah, well I wanted to ride real fast with the other kids there, you know, the young cowboys at the ranch where we kept the horse. We galloped all over the place, hung out, ate hotdogs, maybe drank a little beer... They would do the clean-up of the horse later. That's what we paid them for, right?"

"How old were you by this time?"

"Thirteen, maybe? I think."

Nora was no longer sure that the resort horses were a draw for Steph. The 'beer' detail was revealing since it confirmed this girl had been using drugs, at least alcohol, for several years. Perhaps years before, boys and beer had been the real attractions at the ranch? Still, she got the girl to spend an hour in the paddock with Molly. Steph mounted the mare, and Nora tried Boots, a five-year-old black gelding with white feet and forelock.

Molly was at first tractable, but Steph couldn't maintain her balance, and had to dismount and remount many times. She became more and more irritable, and the horse eventually lost patience and shied away. Nora had less trouble with Boots, but he was a stronger, more lively horse, so before long she noticed the muscle strain in her back, legs and arms from trying to maintain control of the animal.

~

THE EXPERIENCE WAS EXHAUSTING FOR STEPH, WHO WAS SO TIRED FROM her day that she collapsed into bed around nine right after her bath. Nora, no less exhausted, pondered whether she could keep up such a schedule, day after day.

On the way to bed, Nora stopped in to ensure Steph was settling in. She found her lying on the bed. "I hope you have a good sleep..."

"Yeah, I wish! I sometimes get nightmares... I hate it!"

"What are your nightmares about, Steph?"

"Oh, just stuff, you know... my mom, my friends..."

"What do you dream about your mom?"

The girl seemed hesitant to confide at first. She stared at the wall at first, and then when she saw Nora was still standing there, Steph heaved a huge sigh. She recalled her dream. "I'm looking for my mom in a store, and I can't find her... and I end up in a room with mirrors on all the walls... and she's walking away in the mirror... but she doesn't turn to look at me when I call..."

"That is scary, especially when you're just a little kid... well, I hope you're so pooped out tonight, that you'll just drop right off. Tomorrow we're going kayaking..."

"Kayaking? I haven't done that in years..."

"Oh, it's not hard. It'll come back to you! Good night."

From Stephanie, there was nothing but a slight sideways nod in Nora's direction as she closed the door. As Nora lay in bed, she cast back over the day. The girl's sudden shifts in mood, nightmares and irritable outbursts were telling. Her sense was that Steph was still experiencing drug withdrawal, maybe even critical symptoms. She decided to connect with a Force psychiatrist on Monday.

CHAPTER 12 - KAYAKING: SUNDAY, MAY 22

The next morning, at seven o'clock, Nora tried coaxing Steph out of bed.

"I'm still tired... besides, I had more bad dreams last night... you know I told you about mirrors? This time, I couldn't get away from the mirrors. It was like I was melting into them... drowning... besides, I feel achy all over... and it's Sunday! I don't work on Sunday."

"You realize you just gave me nothing but a list of excuses? And that the Sunday excuse is completely lame? Come on, Steph. I have arranged for the thrill of a lifetime today. Have you ever raced down a river? On a mountain river run? The kayak goes like a roller coaster... bouncing and jumping all the way... it'll be fun!" Nora was gambling that Steph's love of risk-taking would kick in.

"I don't know..." Steph was snuggling back into her blankets.

Nora challenged her. "You know, the kayak will be far more exciting than the hiking and horseback riding we did yesterday... even more than those gallops on the ranch when you were a kid! There's not much predictability in kayaking."

"Oh, come on, Constable! It's Sunday!"

"At least with a horse there's a rhythm... and..."

"Alright! Alright! You don't give up, do you? I'll get up and go kayaking if you leave me alone. Thanks. Shut the door."

In the end, she was sure Steph agreed to come, if only to shut Nora up.

The truck ride up to the start of the run was scenic, winding through lodgepole pine and cottonwood stands along the banks of the Parsnip River. As they wound their way toward its headwaters, there were outcroppings of early Indian paintbrush, daisies, fireweed and every so often, clumps of wolf's bane, their bright yellow heads dancing along the shoulder of the road.

They left a truck at the bottom of the run so that it was available to carry the kayak back to the resort on their return, and got a ride for themselves and the two-man kayak up to the start of the run with the resort's handyman-chauffeur, Marvin Boychuk. Nora was feeling upbeat as they started off and was glad to see that Steph, for once, had at least a pleasant facial expression.

"That water looks cold," were Steph's first words upon arriving at the top. It was icy. The spring run-off had just begun, fueled by the melting snowfall higher up.

"You'll get used to it," Nora didn't stop to give her any time to object, but started lowering the kayak from the bed of the pickup, gesturing to Steph to take the weight of the front end. Before long, Marvin had helped them sort out the route and situate themselves in the kayak with life vests, sandwiches and thermoses of hot coffee in case they needed warming up. Just before Nora got into the kayak, he made sure Nora had the keys to the truck left below at the point where they would end the kayak run, and Nora showed where she had them stashed in her jeans pocket. Marvin waved goodbye and drove off.

Basic training in kayak management had been part of Nora's detachment experience in the Moose Forks days. She planned on doing the life-vest set-up, paddle drill, and a basic sweep roll practice.

"Steph, we have to do some basic safety training first, okay?"

"Don't we just let the river do the work? Safety training? Like what?"

"For one, you need to learn how to right the kayak if we flip over!"

They spent the next hour doing basic drills in the small back eddy at the top of the run. Steph was not enthusiastic about getting herself all wet by flipping the kayak, but Nora insisted, and the girl seemed to cooperate good-naturedly. After warming up with some thermos coffee, they started the descent.

The river was a beginner run, as it featured only a few areas of mild white water and one gorge. No waterfalls. Still, the descent was not without its perils, as they needed quick reflexes to avoid outcroppings of rocks and low-hanging tree limbs. The trip began around eleven o'clock and Nora calculated they would be at the finish point by one. Because no one expected them back until dinnertime, she decided they had time for a more leisurely pace at the bottom, where the current became gentler.

The ride along the river was both scenic and exhilarating. Nora sensed Steph was enjoying the thrill of the unpredictable up and down and back and forth of the kayak run. At least, there were many whoops and screams as they made their way to the last few miles where the flow became slower.

"Let's pull the kayak in here and have our lunch, okay?" Nora had picked a sheltered cove where a grassy knoll undulated down to the riverbank. The grass was the new green of spring, fresh-smelling like hay and dotted with the first wildflowers, dandelions, and sweet clover. They could hear the buzz of innumerable insects in the grass and trees. Nora hoped it was a perfect day for relaxing and chatting. She was still trying to get a sense of what was bothering Stephanie.

Once on the ground, Steph made a beeline for the bush, "I'm hungry, but I gotta pee." She giggled and looked sideways at Nora, then hurried off into the bush.

Afterwards, munching their lunch, they lolled on the new grass. Nora, pulling out the tender grass shoots to chew, remarked, "I've never been up this way before. It's pretty nice, eh?"

"Yeah, it's nice." Steph had already wolfed down her juice and sandwich and now lay on her back, gazing at the sky, biting into an apple.

"What did you think of the ride so far?"

"It's good. Not as bad as I thought, anyway. Thanks."

Nora prodded for more substance. "Did you find it exciting? Would you want to do it again?"

"Meh! Whatever. It would be more fun with a bunch of people." It wasn't the response Nora had been hoping for... there was no mention of anything close to 'exhilaration' or enough excitement to build dopamine. Steph's threshold for triggering satisfaction was high.

Still, Steph seemed relaxed enough. She had eaten all her lunch, as she had done with all her meals. This slight girl's appetite, which seemed twice her own, had surprised Nora.

"Perhaps your dad could join you up here with one or two of your friends?"

Again that snicker, "Yeah? As if! My dad is more interested in his work than me." Her tone was emphatic. "You know why he really sent me here with you? You're just another babysitter! He's pawned me off again..."

With that, Stephanie excused herself for another call of nature in the undergrowth. Nora lay sunning, pondering what Steph had said, thinking that the girl might not be all that wrong about her dad. It would mean more to the girl to have him spend time with her up here.

CHAPTER 13 - STEPH MAKES A MOVE: SUNDAY MAY 22

When Steph returned, Nora herself took a quick trip into the bush, and when she came back, Steph was already putting her life vest back on to prepare for the rest of the trip downriver. She seemed in a hurry to leave. Once on the river, they made excellent time. The peacefulness of the gentle flow and the fresh spring-green river setting lulled Nora into a contented mindset that lasted almost to the end of the run.

As they came near to the parked truck, there was a large deadfall obstructing their path on the same side of the bank. Nora couldn't prevent the kayak from getting caught up in its branches, so the only solution was for one of them to crawl onto the tree trunk and push the kayak free.

"I'll do it, I should have been able to avoid it," Nora offered. She was already regretting the ease with which she had let the beauty of the place lure her into mindlessness.

"No, let me. Least I can do to... to thank you... uh... for today. I can do it easy!" The lithe, young girl had no difficulty climbing up and extricating the craft from the crooked bough that entrapped it. When the kayak was almost free from the entanglement, Steph took a header into the river on the other side of the tree trunk.

She yelled back, "Sorry, I lost my balance! I might as well just head for shore. It'll be easier."

Nora called back. "Meet me at the shore when I get there. I can't manage the kayak on my own."

But when she at last slogged her way to shore, pulling the kayak behind her, Steph was not available to help. Cursing quietly to herself, Nora slung the kayak onto her shoulders and was trudging up the incline to where they had parked the truck when she saw Stephanie driving away down the hill. Nora clapped her hand to her jeans' pocket in disbelief. Of course, the truck keys were gone! Somehow, they must have fallen out when they were lying on the grass for lunch, and she hadn't noticed. Stephanie, having seen them, picked them up, and from that point on, had started planning a getaway...

After stowing the kayak on the riverbank, Nora began the four-mile walk home along the mountain road. She felt utterly disheartened. She knew Stephanie would not be at the resort when she got there. By that time, the girl would be long gone, to who knows where.

During that hour's brisk walk back to the resort, Nora strategized. She at least needed to get word to Steph's father, and to Mike Sinclair to post a BOLF for the lodge's pickup truck and an APB, an all-points bulletin, for the girl herself. Steph would no doubt not stop on her way down the mountain. Nora wondered where the young woman would go. She was betting she would not bother to stop in Prince George, but would hightail it for a bigger centre, either Edmonton or Vancouver.

Back at the lodge, Nora approached Marvin Boychuk in the garage.

"Marvin, I hate to tell you, but Stephanie Benson has just taken off with that truck you left for us... I'm so sorry... the keys must've dropped out of my pocket..."

Marvin was philosophical. "Won't be the first or last time, Constable. We get all kinds up here..."

"Do you know how much gas it had?"

"Oh, hell, I just filled it up before you come..." So Steph could get a good long way before she had to stop...

"Anyway, do you want me to drive back up and bring back the kayak and paddles... and the life vests...?"

"Nah, you got more important stuff to do. Leave that to me." Marvin waved her away.

Inside the lodge, she contacted her detachment to issue the BOLF and then District Commissioner Benson's office to alert the father about his daughter's escape. Benson was not in, but his receptionist assured Nora that he would get the message as soon as possible and likely contact her at her detachment later that evening. Nora replied she would return to the Spruce Grove Hotel in Brandenhoff, and he could contact her there. Discouraged and cranky, Nora packed up and headed back into town, where she checked into her hotel for the night.

~

WILLOW DROVE DOWN THE MOUNTAIN ON AUTO-PILOT. HER DECISION TO steal the truck and take off had been an impulse born of finding the keys in the grass. She gave no thought to Nora or the fix she had left the cop in.

Stupid cow! She thought I'd be happy to hang out with her! As if!

Now, she had to decide where to go. She checked the gas gauge and saw that the tank was almost full.

Well, that's a stroke of luck! I wonder how much cash I have? I had a few bucks in my bag when they nabbed me. I wonder if it's still there.

She had twenty-five dollars. How far could she get? Where did she *want* to get to? By the time she reached Highway 16, she had a decision to make. Should she head east or west? West would take her across BC back to Prince Rupert where she had been arrested. No. She wouldn't go that way. No way did she want to be back in the custody of Axel. Where would she go if she headed east?

She thought back to her time with Slash. He had been so wonderful at first. And she hadn't wanted to leave. The cops had taken her. He would understand that she wanted to be with him, that she loved him and wanted to be his woman. She ached for him and longed to revisit those two weeks when they had first met. He would welcome her back, she was sure. She would do whatever he asked if only they could be together again. She felt jittery with anticipation. He *had* to want her! Every fiber of her being said so.

But where was he? BB had never said where he had gone, only that he had club business to attend to. But she remembered that Slash had made phone calls to Edmonton… she had also overheard the cops who arrested her mention that the Brigade came from the Edmonton area. Maybe that was the clue she needed. She turned east and drove straight through Prince George along the Yellowhead. Edmonton was several hundred miles away.

Maybe I'll even get some dance gigs in Edmonton to get ready for Vegas!

CHAPTER 14 - NORA FACES THE MUSIC: MONDAY, MAY 23

The morning after Steph's disappearance, Nora awoke to realize that Bill Benson still hadn't tried to contact her.

What kind of father would leave his daughter's fate hanging in the wind like that?

Exhausted from a restless night, she arrived early at the detachment to check the local paper for a place to live. Worrying about her dismal performance with Steph, and the noise from a combined darts and foosball tournament the Spruce Grove was hosting had disturbed her sleep. The racket of the happy competitors had lasted well into the early hours.

Her boss, Mike Sinclair, found her in the squad room pouring over the local newspaper when he arrived at 830 hours. As he hadn't been in over the weekend, he was unaware that Stephanie Benson had taken off. He was astonished to see Nora sitting in the squad room.

"What the hell..."

"Hi Mike, uh... I'm back. Uh... Stephanie Benson got away from me yesterday around 1400 hours, I'd say. She took the resort's truck left for us at the bottom of a kayak run... got the keys when they fell out of my pocket, I guess." Her face collapsed into a rueful grimace.

She watched his face as the words tumbled out. No doubt he was upset to learn that his friend's flighty daughter once again was missing.

"Mike, I take full responsibility... but I will say, with all due respect, that I think this girl needs her father for a few days somewhere relaxing, and wouldn't run away from *him* so fast."

Mike didn't reassure her she had not been careless, or that losing the keys could have happened to anyone under the circumstances. Rather, he said nothing, ignoring her observation about Bill Benson's relationship with his daughter. He stomped out. To herself, Nora thought he was in shock, or angry, or both. She sat in the squad room alone for a few minutes until the intercom called her to Mike's office.

Sinclair was sitting ashen-faced behind his desk. He raised his head, his blue eyes intense, and a muscle under his right eye twitched. "Nora, I needed to take a minute, because... you know... I recommended you for this job to one of my oldest friends, and..."

"I understand, Sergeant. I really screwed up... I should have secured the keys with a carabiner... I was so focused on trying to figure her out, I lost sight of the custodial aspect."

"I get that Steph presents challenging behaviour... I see you would want to try to understand her..." He heaved a great sigh. "So, what do you propose to do?" Mike's voice was light, but she understood the underlying point.

What am I going to do to fix this?

"I requested a BOLF for her and the truck before I left Pine Ridge. Now, I'll think back over my time with Stephanie for any clues about where she might go." She knew she had a slim chance on her own, that she would need the support of the Force to find the wayward girl. Right now, all she could do was pull her weight with the search. Her energy was low, but she needed to find more to offer. Mike regarded her standing at attention before him for several seconds.

"You've had it rough lately, no mistake. All that petty vandalism and then the fire... by the way, Hugh Bland has had that gasoline can sent to forensics and it came back with no sign of fingerprints or identifying marks. He has also canvassed the gas stations in town to find out if any of them remember someone filling up a gas can lately. No dice there, either. The insurance company who covered your place have indicated they're happy with the results of our investigation, It was a small place and not too much to compensate. So what I'm trying to say is that we don't think we can do much more to discover the culprit, not unless more evidence turns up..."

"I... I... understand, Mike. It just makes it hard, you know...to hold my head up in town... and now this screw-up with Stephanie..."

"Don't judge your value by what the public thinks... we all make mistakes." Then he smiled a brief grin and nodded his head in dismissal.

She returned to the squad room and picked up the want-ads again. She found a room and board situation that looked promising. She could pay on a month-at-a-time basis. With no household to maintain, she could focus on her future.

∽

JANE AND PADDY CONNORS, THE LOCAL HARDWARE STORE OWNERS, lived in roomy accommodation behind the store. The youngest of their three sons had just left for a job logging in a camp north of Terrace. Jane confided, "The house seems so empty now that Joey is gone. I'm not used to having the whole place to myself when Paddy is in the store."

Nora felt at home right away. Paddy Connors was a gruff, practical kind of guy who teased her about being a "mounted" policewoman in a one-horse town. It was a classic dad joke. Jane asked what she wanted to eat and went out of her way to accommodate her irregular hours of work. Nora felt welcome like the daughter they had never had. Here, at least, she felt she might recoup her lost energy.

CHAPTER 15 - WILLOW COMES BACK: TUESDAY-WEDNESDAY, MAY 24-25

When Willow appeared in Edmonton at the Hog Barn after being gone for ten days, she looked thin and tired, great dark splotches under her eyes reinforcing a waif look. She pleaded to see Slash as soon as possible. BB reported directly to Slash, "She told me she drove a stolen truck non-stop right here from the BC Interior, from some resort on the Parsnip River."

Slash cast his eyes, totaling mileage. No one was better at estimating highway distance than a trucker or a biker. "That sounds like bullshit. From Edmonton to PG is four-hundred-and-sixty miles, about seven hours. The drive down from the Parsnip in the boonies, took about another three or four hours. If she left Sunday afternoon as she said, she should have been in Edmonchuk by Monday morning at the latest. Today is Tuesday. Where the hell has she been?"

"She just says like I told you already... she got caught in the bust in Prince Rupert at the Skylark Hotel. Says her dad had an APB posted for her, and a squad of regular RCMP doing a liquor-control check recognized her from her photo." BB shifted his feet, avoiding Slash's gaze. "She says she wants to see you."

"Maybe in a couple of days... ask Bets to let her sleep on their couch...You get the truck keys?"

"Yeah... new Dodge Ram... "

"Shame we gotta chop that... but too risky to keep... Get Leftie to see to it." Leftie handled all the club's stolen goods. As BB was leaving, Slash added as an afterthought, "Tell that broad I got no time for her."

~

BEWILDERED BY SLASH'S INDIFFERENCE, WILLOW SPENT THE NEXT twenty-four hours huddled on the Zormans' couch, watching whatever Spyder and Bets chose on TV. Bets ignored her except for pointing at the stove when there was food available. Spyder behaved as though she were invisible.

When Slash called her down to the Hell Pit the next day, he demanded, "Where've you been since you got nabbed in Rupert?" She avoided looking at his stony face across the table from her. He motioned her to a rickety chair that teetered back and forth.

"They sent me straight to Prince George to get checked out. My father made sure I got the full treatment: body search, medical, pregnancy test, cold turkey... You want all the details? It was fuckin' horrible."

"Watch your mouth. We don't want you soundin' like trash."

"I was in custody in a lock-up for six days, and then I got released to this RCMP constable... uh.. Nora... I'm not sure... Mc Something... She took me to this treatment centre-slash-resort on the Parsnip River, and I stayed there from last Saturday to Sunday afternoon. The truck keys fell out of her pocket, and I scooped 'em. Lucky I had twenty-five bucks in my backpack..."

"Where were you from Monday to Tuesday this week? You left BC on Sunday. The trip wouldda been between twelve and fourteen hours if you kept going. When did you get into Edmonton?"

"Yesterday, I drove the truck to a pull-off in Spruce Grove and slept. Woke up hungry. I had no money, 'cause I spent most of it on gas to get here. I had enough for a McDonald's burger and a coke. That's all I ate for over twenty-four hours."

"Yeah, so you went hungry. What else? How'd you find us?"

"I had to work at it. You guys aren't exactly in the phone book!"

"Damn straight! We don't want wannabe bitches findin' us..."

"Slash, I came back to you. It wasn't my plan to be gone in the first place. The cops *took* me!"

"So, you still didn't tell me how you found us... I. Need. To. Know."

"I asked around about where dancers worked and they told me about a bar on Whyte Avenue... I think... and I went there and asked if anyone might tell me where to find the Devil's Brigade. The guy behind the bar phoned someone. I don't know who. Next thing, BB was at the bar."

"Well, I don't want you here. You're a jinx. Stay out of the way until we get you back with the other girls. You shouldda gone back to join them in the first place instead of comin' here."

Willow's stomach dropped.

∽

HER STORY JIBED WITH WHAT BB HAD SAID. THEIR BAR GUY ON WHYTE had contacted him and said there was a Honey looking for the Brigade. Studying her supple willingness, her eyes glued to his, her breath coming in pants, Slash decided she must be wired up for him, exactly where he wanted her. She was still that eager-to-please piece of ass that he had spent an entire two weeks grooming a month before. Then, he had her eating out of his hand. Now, he decided, he needed to get her out of his sight as soon as possible. He got up from his seat and paced the stained wooden floors of the Hell Pit, leaving her seated, chewing her lip.

The loss of her for that a week had shaken Slash more than he wanted to admit. He had sent out Grinder and Tiny to check around Rupert. He drummed up old contacts in the security biz to ask for news at the cop-shop in PG. Nothing. Nobody had seen her. He had felt as if he were spinning his wheels. And that realization of his own helplessness or incompetence was still eating at him. If Willow had not waltzed back in, would he ever have found her? Did he really care if she ever came back, or was it only the lost money that bothered him? No, he had to admit, to himself at least, she had gotten under his skin as no other female ever had. Fuck! He hated her for that.

The cops had grabbed Willow so fast that Slash doubted his own judgment. What kind of idiot lets that happen to his newest acquisition, even if she was a cop's kid? He gave himself a mental shake: any preoccupation with Willow made him focus on something other than the club's business, not a wise choice for a second-in-command. Slash had toyed with the idea of taking her on the road trip Spyder had ordered–he could use a "back warmer"–but there was no way he was ready to lose his focus. He realized he needed to re-establish his cred with the club. Doing that meant getting the bush-gig project up and running. This chick was too distracting.

Willow had been watching him as he mulled over the situation. She appeared compliant and pleasing, ready to pick up where they had left off. "Happy to see me, Slash? I thought after all this time, you would get excited to spend some time with lil' Steph…"

"Yer name is Willow, bitch!" Slash lunged at her, lashing out. "Stop thinking of yourself as anything else! Stick to yer stage name and talk to no one! Or ya won't even need a name!"

"That's not what you said when we met. You said I'd have gigs in Vegas… that we might go together… at least you said I would have regular dancing gigs up front on the circuit!"

"Listen, dummy! That two weeks in PG was a mistake! Ya don't mean nothing to me. Ya were just a pretty piece of ass I could use to add to my bush gig line-up. Vegas? That's a joke! Ya have no hope of ever being Vegas quality! Besides, the cops have a BOLF out for ya, 'Be On the Lookout For'? Ya can't go public anymore. The private hotel room gigs are also out. Bush gigs will start soon. I gotta pilot lined up."

"I don't want to do bush gigs, Slash!"

Slash had reached the limit of his patience. She was a problem he couldn't control unless he pushed her away.

"Oh Slash, I love you! Don't you know?"

"Get real! Love? What's that–somethin' to eat? Grow up, ya stupid bitch! Ya bin livin' in some fairy tale fantasy..."

"I love....."

"Shaddup!" He could not let her say it again. He could not let her see his weakness. Something snapped. He stood before her, his face a mask of thunderous rage and reached across to pull her by her ponytail onto the floor. There, he immobilized her beside the table, his knees on her legs, her arms pinioned above her head with his one hand. Clutching her ponytail as a handle, he banged the side and crown of her head on the floor again and again... roughing her up, without causing a bruise on her face. Any damage make-up would cover.

Slash snarled, almost incoherent with rage. "You'll do as I say–bush gigs in the BC back country. Ya hear, snot-nose? Yer not cop-daddy's little girl anymore! Ya got that? Get ready to work where I say! And while yer at it, cut yer hair short and bleach it!"

When she held her head and moaned in pain, he growled and spat on her. He was no longer the smitten Romeo. All he could think of was the monetary investment she represented, the money spent on grooming her and every other dancer they had recruited for the bush gigs, thousands of dollars, and it and all their hard work going down the tube if she was discovered and their operation outted by her cop daddy. No woman was worth it.

CHAPTER 16 - DC BENSON SPEAKS OUT: WEDNESDAY, MAY 25

Bill Benson called Nora at home later in the day from Vancouver. He said he had been at a top-secret meeting and out of telephone contact since mid-afternoon of the previous Sunday, the date of Steph's disappearance. In fact, unknown to anyone in the Force, since Friday evening, he had locked himself away in a Vancouver hotel with a female companion enjoying a little R & R and a pay-tv broadcast of the Larry Holmes heavyweight championship fight against Tim Witherspoon at the Dunes Hotel in Vegas.

Now he felt guilty and defensive, unsure about how to proceed. "Constable Macpherson... uh... Nora... Bill Benson here. I just got the message about Stephanie."

"Yes, District Commissioner, I'm glad you caught me in. I just got home from work and am on my way out for dinner. I'm also moving into a new place tomorrow, so things are busy."

"Uh, I won't keep you long, I promise. First, Nora, I want to say that I'm not angry with you, because I realize Stephanie is a handful." There was a pause, and he continued, but changed his tone to one more severe. He now sounded more accusatory, harsh. "Did Steph recognize you as the boss, Nora? Like, did she see you as someone in charge?"

"Are you asking if she saw me as an authority figure?"

"Well, of course... dammit! There's got to be some reason why she was able to get away!"

~

Nora had been about to suggest the Steph needed him as an 'authority figure-father', when she heard his temper heating up. This man was not ready to hear he had neglected his daughter.

"District Commissioner, I take full responsibility. Those truck keys slipped out of my pocket. I should have had them secured. All I can do is give my all to find her and get her back. I promise I will do my best."

"Do you have any notion of where Steph would go? Did she talk about any place she liked while you were with her?"

"No, she wasn't very communicative for the short three days we were together." Again she was on the verge of suggesting that Steph needed a parent's attention, but decided she didn't know him or his daughter well enough to venture such a judgment.

All she said was, "She's rebelling, Commissioner. Most girls do at some point, and I suspect she didn't get a chance before because she was in a fairly strict school until the last year or so. I realize it's hard to accept, but I believe she'll see that defying everything doesn't get her anywhere, and then she'll get in touch. She's got to show up somewhere. We've made a notation about her connection to the Devil's Brigade, and I'll patch through an inquiry to the Edmonton City Police where they're headquartered."

There was continued silence on the other end of the line.

"But I believe, for now, you need to let her go." Nora continued. "But we'll keep the file open, of course. You know how we update and review them regularly. That's standard procedure. She's got to show up somewhere."

Benson growled, " I don't like the sound of this, *Constable* Macpherson. My instinct says you're covering for Stephanie for some unfathomable reason only a female would understand."

Nora was aghast.

The man's a sexist as well as short-tempered! No wonder Stephanie is avoiding him.

"Well, thanks for your time, Constable Macpherson," Benson said briskly. "I appreciate your effort and will probably get back to you down the road. Keep Stephanie's case on the back burner... you know... just keep an eye on her file for any developments. We'll ask you to help again when the Force picks up Steph's trail."

"For sure, I'll keep my ear to the ground for any sign of her. I doubt Steph will stick around the area, knowing you and the Force are looking for her. I suspect we'll get word from some other detachment..."

We can only hope...

"Perhaps... but I still want you on the file. You understand? I have a feeling you can help more than others to find my daughter..." A pause ensued. "Right. I'll sign off here."

Nora sat perplexed. Why would he want to continue to involve her when she had failed so spectacularly this time? As it was, she hoped she hadn't earned a black mark on her service record.

∼

When Benson hung up, he placed a phone call to Mike Sinclair. "Mike, about this business with Stephanie..."

"Yes, Bill, I know. It's a pity. Constable Macpherson has done some follow-up..."

"There must be someone keeping tabs on the situation. My daughter can't just disappear into thin air! I want non-stop follow-up! You're my friend, Mike, not just the supervising officer, so I expect one-hundred and fifty percent from you and your detachment. It's like one of our own is missing here..." He felt guilty and helpless, willing to grasp at straws.

Would it have made any difference if I hadn't been AWOL that weekend? Is Steph going to pay the price for my wicked weekend getaway watching that boxing match with Maxine in Vancouver?

"Yes, for certain. We will keep the BOLF open. That's standard procedure. We have a long backlog of unsolved missing persons cases. She'll be at the top of the pile, I assure you."

"Uh... thanks, Mike... uh... so..." Bill hesitated to sign off.

"Is there something else, Bill?"

"I think this Devil's Brigade is behind the uptick in drug trafficking along Highway 16 that recent detachment reports have picked up. If that's the case, then a search for Stephanie will also serve to zero in on that bunch... I also have a hunch about Constable Macpherson. She's a good connection for Steph."

"Maybe so, I don't disagree about the biker connection, though. As far as Constable Macpherson's involvement is concerned, it's a little late now, don't you think?"

"No, I mean she has a feel for how to find her, perhaps?"

"What makes you say that?"

"Just a hunch... uh... is Constable Macpherson close to anyone on the Force?"

"Not sure what you mean..."

"Is she friendly enough with anyone to confide in them? About work stuff?"

"I don't think anyone here in Brandenhoff. She was cordial with all of us, but I wouldn't say she was ever close to anyone here... but I think she has a steady, a corporal at the Glacier Lake Detachment."

"Oh, yeah? What's his name?"

"Why, Bill?"

"Come on, Mike! It's my daughter here! I will use whatever angle I can to find her!"

"Sure, but how will knowing Nora's boyfriend make a difference?"

"He might tell me stuff he wouldn't tell you or her..."

"Like what? What will he know about Steph?"

"Not Steph! About Constable Macpherson... uh... Nora! He might have an inside track on what makes her tick... you know... uh... pillow talk?"

"I doubt he'll have anything to tell you..."

"What's his name?"

When Mike hesitated, Bill sighed, "Never mind, I'll find out from Glacier Lake."

If only I didn't feel that I dropped the ball here. She's my daughter, but I don't know what makes her tick. I guess I feel to blame.

CHAPTER 17 - SETTING UP THE BUSH GIGS: THURSDAY, MAY 26

Slash himself wasn't able to run the bush-gig job because Spyder would have him burning up the highway between PG and Rupert running herd on the mules, making their dope deliveries. He would also check out the real estate Diablo had identified in Terrace, run discipline on club members, and oversee the "maintenance"– making sure regular installments of protection money of the territory got paid.

The Brigade's latest venture required them to hire a helicopter pilot to drop and pick up the dancers from the remote camps that paid for the service. Slash met the pilot prospect, Frank Bernhardt, in the back of the huge basement pub below the Inn of the North in Prince George. He checked his credentials and recognized the training details. As Slavko Dracul, he had been in the Serbian army; he recognized the type who used the service to get a marketable skill that few others had. They were mercenaries... he'd met a few.

"Yeah, man, we're in the market for a helicopter pilot. We have goods to deliver three places: the Justice Silver Mine south of Moose Forks, the Sedako open pit mine east of Simon Lake and the NorthCo Logging show near Kitwanga. Three times a week, once for each location, drop off consignment, pick up four or five hours later."

"Night flying? I'm not interested in any regular night time work."

"No, the customers work in twenty-four-hour shifts, so some are always around at mid-day and in the afternoon."

"What sort of customers?"

"People who enjoy watching women dance…"

"I see… and that's it? Just ferrying these strippers in and out?"

In the next hour, Slash learned that Frank Bernhardt was suitable, but had a couple of problems. First, he was too curious about the biz, asking questions about the competition Renegades bike club and their operation in Prince George. Secondly, he wasn't a biker, but a cager, a regular, four-wheeled type out for a buck, but greedy about it.

Slash didn't like the Kraut. He was also an immigrant, but he was a square head Kraut who'd been in Canada longer and thought that made him better than the Slavs. Slash didn't trust the German, but he needed to use him. The alternative pilot options were all too squeaky-clean, farm boys who had grown up flying crop-dusters, who had little world experience outside of flying school. They wouldn't ignore of the under-the-table action.

With the Kraut, though, Slash felt a real ambivalence. Bernhardt wasn't the type to rat to the cops, but his arrogance was irritating. The grease to ease this friction was money. Slash knew Bernhardt would do just about anything for cash.

The question was, should he send the girls on their own with this guy? His gut said no. Those backcountry boys in the camps would be real rough. He needed to send a guard, someone trustworthy, who would keep his hands off, but be tough enough to protect the goods. He considered his options: only one really, BB. Despite fucking up in Prince Rupert, he had to give him one more chance to prove he was up to managing the girls on the off-road gigs. But he would have to leave the decision to Spyder, whose temperament these days was none too predictable.

Slash thought over what he would say to Spyder. He had no trouble justifying the choice of BB because, although the Kid was just junior, a prospect, and not a patch holder yet, he had a brown belt, and would look after himself without looking or acting threatening. Spyder would want his son to do the job, but Diablo couldn't help but trumpet his pent-up hostility with every thuggish gesture. He would have the miners and loggers at the camps itching for a brawl from the moment he set foot in camp. Slash realized his recommendation of BB as lead on the job would sour Diablo's mood, but he had to take that chance. Also, he recognized he couldn't leave Spyder's son behind in Edmonton to plot behind his back. He needed to keep Diablo as close as possible.

Slash approached Spyder later that Tuesday night. "Boss, I wanna talk about who to send with the strippers in the helicopter. I think BB is a good guy. He's young and big, got a brown belt... Uh... Diablo wants to go, but I'm not sure. You know yourself, Spyder, your boy... he can't leave the broads alone, eh?"

Spyder guffawed, "Neither could I at his age. So what?"

"So I want to send someone else as back-up with BB. Somebody bigger, older."

"Send Axel, and Diablo both as back-up. They can keep each other out of trouble." Axel was huge and ugly, the opposite of chick bait.

"You don't want your boy here, do you? You know, to run the shop?" Slash hoped not, but wanted to give Spyder the chance to say no. On the way out when the end was near, a biker had his pride where death was involved. He liked to be self-contained, with not too many people hanging around watching. But still, Spyder might want his kid around when he checked out.

"Nah, let him go with you. Bets and I can manage this place."

So it was decided.

CHAPTER 18 - THE BRANDY ARMS: 2000 HOURS, FRIDAY, MAY 27

The end of shift on a Friday always left Franz "Frank" Bernhardt feeling antsy. By eight, he found himself tired of his own company even though he had A-class machinery to play with all week long. This week's job had been tiresome–eight short hops every day between Prince George and the Justice Silver Mine south of Moose Forks. The monotonous schedule was not unusual. This week, Franz was twitchy enough that he found the routine unbearable. He needed some diversion, some pleasant distraction to take his mind off the job and the lonely life he led. He was a solitary man, with no family and only business acquaintances–not actual friends. He liked it that way. It was less complicated.

At least he made significant money as a helicopter pilot, so at forty-seven, he owned his own helicopter, a 1972 Bell 205 that could seat twelve on a utility set-up. He free-lanced contracts all across the northern sector of the province. He sometimes made it back to home, a secluded log-cabin property at the northwest corner of Jacob Lake, twenty-five miles from Fort Saint Jacob, a remote area north of Highway 16. But this Friday night, the sun would set at 930 hours and he wouldn't finish in time to get home, so he headed to Brandenhoff, the largest town within range. There should be something entertaining there.

Once landed at the local airstrip, he rented a pickup for the weekend, headed into town, and checked into a motel. He hustled to shower and shave. In the mirror, he examined his appearance: he was a tall, slender, athletic man, with short-cropped, greying light brown hair and intense ice-blue eyes. He knew he was fit with a wiry, rather than muscular, build. *If only....* But he couldn't go there. He was what he was.

After he grabbed a burger, he headed to the bar, where he found what he'd been craving. As he stood at the stage edge, his gaze intent on the young blonde gyrating on stage, he pounded his hand on the table, as if he had untold pent-up anger.

The object of his glacial gaze was unaware of his scrutiny. The supple girl, clad in black and scarlet vinyl, twirled, bent and slid herself scissoring along the pole in the cage set up on the stage. She smiled to herself, her hair a tangled golden cloud that obscured her vision as she spiraled to the recently released tune, "Every Breath You Take", Sting's husky voice reverberating for her, alone.

Franz couldn't take his eyes off Velvet Dawn. She was exactly his type: tall, fair-haired, athletic–the Nordic type. He'd been alone since his parents died years before. Should he make the effort? Try to see her? Take her for a ride in his chopper? The prospect of her, nubile and friendly, sitting up rapt with the beauty of the geography stirred him. After sitting through her first set, he settled in to wait for her next ones.

Sitting next to the stage, he continued to order beer, fantasizing about the young blonde as she gyrated before him. With each beer, his thoughts became darker. What was the point? He recollected all the times he has been so close to feeling something was possible, some connection, some mutual attraction, only to have his advances rejected. The same old anger roiled in his gut, thinking of those others, laughing at him, pointing and hooting, or just dismissing him and leaving him lying in the bed alone. His ice-blue eyes darkened.

Nora was on late night duty for the Friday following her special op with Stephanie. The town of Brandenhoff was hopping with a large contingent of loggers and miners in town for the unusual attraction of exotic dancers at the Brandenhoff Arms Inn, the "Brandy Arms" to the locals.

Nora made a scheduled stop to survey the venue. She stood at the entrance scanning for the hotel manager, Tim Westcott, to let him know she had checked in. When a contingent of intoxicated young loggers surrounded her, she realized she needed to find him fast, or else figure out how to fend off the clutch of interested guys without offending them. The lounge was loud and smoky, the raunchy refrain of "Can't Get No Satisfaction" blaring from the speakers as a bronzed redhead gyrated with seductive skill on stage.

A giant of a young man lurched from his barstool towards her, followed by several of his buddies, eager to check out the unusual sight of a female Force member. Sweeping his arm back toward his seat to offer her a place, the young logger slurred his speech, a dead giveaway to how long he had been perched on his stool. "Hey, Mishus Cop, Honey! Come'n have a drink with ush!"

With as bright a smile as she could muster, Nora shook her head and shouted back that she wasn't staying. She swept her hands down to show off her uniform, emphasizing she was on duty, and that she was there to see someone. The group grumbled good-naturedly and went back to their beers.

It relieved Nora to catch sight of Manager Tim coming to investigate why a crowd had gathered near the exit door. He glanced at Nora, his eyes questioning, but she smiled and gestured that there was no problem. She hooked her finger to ask him for a quiet word, and he came outside with her.

"Hi Mr. Westcott, I'm just wondering about security for the dancers tonight… whether someone will escort them to their rooms and control hotel traffic if they want privacy?"

"Oh, yeah, we have that covered, Constable. Thanks for asking.

We don't expect any trouble. There are four dancers altogether. Three are experienced dancers, but one girl, Velvet Dawn, is new to the business. The more experienced ones look out for newbies, so I'm not worried. Velvet is the next performer, if you want to watch..."

"Sure, I'll stop for a minute..."

I wonder what attracts a girl to this kind of work?

She couldn't imagine why someone would expose herself, be so vulnerable...

Back inside, Nora wandered to the side to stand against a wall to watch Velvet Dawn, whose performance inside the bars of a black ironwork cage was a marvel of nubile athleticism. The girl, in her late teens or early twenties, was a tall, willowy blonde who struck her as more gymnast than stripper. Her graceful routine included back walkovers, splits and handstands, all in rhythm to the pulsing beat of Thelma Houston's "Don't Leave Me This Way". When the girl finished, Nora could see she had worked up a sweat. The athleticism of the routine was undeniable.

For the next tune, "Shake, Shake, Shake, Your Booty", the routine was simplified, a few dance moves with a lot of butt-action. Nora noted that the appreciative audience had festooned the girl's G-string with an array of lengthwise folded tens and twenties. When she caught Tim's eye, Nora saluted and signaled him to follow when she headed for the exit.

"Tim, I'm just wondering what you meant when you said you didn't expect any trouble 'mostly'".

"Uh... I had a phone call earlier today from a Christian women's group who object to the dancers' performance and suggested they might try to interrupt it. They showed up at about nine with picket signs... something about "porn" in their God-fearing community. I got them to leave by saying it was a one-night event, and there were no plans for more in the foreseeable future."

"Is that true? You won't have dancers again? You've built a stage and the cage as a prop...?"

"We use the stage for music acts all the time. The cage... it's a 'go-go' dancer thing... no big deal to make..." he heaved a sigh. "Brandenhoff is small potatoes, Constable. The booking agencies don't bother including us on their circuit as a rule. These protestors, all women, left without fuss, so I didn't bother to report it."

"You know, Tim, you may run your business as you see fit, as long as you breach no 'community standard laws'. Citizens in small communities like this often protest if something flouts common decency."

"You know, I get it. I know what 'decency' is. That biker's gang, the Devil's Brigade was also through town a week ago in force, and the owner of the hotel, Mitch Grady, told me not to worry, but as I see it, bikers are not the kind of people we want deciding to stick around here. Most of us don't consider them 'decent' folks. But they are kept around as security for the dancers. We don't need it here, but I suppose they do in the bigger places." He shuffled his feet and avoided her gaze.

Nora's ears perked up at the mention of the Devil's Brigade, her eyes speculative. In the past, there had been the odd biker in the region, but until this last month, they had never been a serious presence in this town. Were they expanding territory or just cruising on spec? Daily reports had mentioned several sightings on the highway during the last few weeks. She was positive their presence here now had something to do with Stephanie's latest disappearance.

On the walk back to her cruiser, Nora reflected on the performance she had just witnessed at the Brandy Arms. She remembered Steph Benson, and how easily the young girl would make money if she could get some gigs to dance. She would need cash now... Right then, Nora realized she needed to make a point of checking the bars that featured dancers for any word of Steph.

Nora stopped, her key in the ignition. It occurred to her she should interview the dancers for any news. When she got out of the cruiser and looked for Tim, she found him behind the hotel check-in counter.

"Sorry, Tim. I had another thought as I was getting ready to leave. I would like to interview some of your dancers to see if they have seen or heard of a young woman who has been reported missing. She was doing some dance gigs not long ago."

Tim shook his head. "I'd like to oblige, but I've had to promise the girls so many hours off-duty, and they've all reached their workhours limit. You should have asked to see them when you were here between sets."

"How about tomorrow?"

"They'll be off duty and likely unavailable. I can't promise they'd be around."

Disappointed, Nora handed him her card. "Ask them to contact me, please?" Tim's facial expression didn't project much optimistic that they would.

Nora tried to control her irritation. She should have thought ahead and knew it could be a costly oversight. She kicked herself for not planning for interviews when she first read about the Brandy Arms having this one-night stripper show. When was that? Why hadn't she picked up on the possibility then?

She reflected on her recent history: she had just returned from the special op, was looking for a place, and was moving. Lately, her life had been a flurry and a daze. It happened. Once again, she felt like a failure. What would Mike say about her promise to do all she could to find Stephanie if he knew she had blown this obvious opportunity? Would he note it on her file? She got the feeling her career had taken a hit in the last few weeks. She wanted some way to get it back on track.

Nora spent her break that night shift back in the detachment, reviewing the file on Stephanie Benson, searching for any sightings. Neither the BOLF for Stephanie nor the one for Pine Ridge Resort's pickup had yielded any results. As her research into the Devil's Brigade had led her to Edmonton, she updated the BOLF to reflect the news that Stephanie could be on her way there.

On a hunch, she sent a message through the Force's secure system to alert Bonita "Bunnie" Burrows who was an undercover liaison with dancers in the Vancouver strip. She wanted Bunnie to be keeping a lookout for Stephanie Benson on the stripper circuit.

CHAPTER 19 - VIGDIS DAHLBERG: 500 HOURS, SUNDAY, MAY 29

A couple of days later, Nora was seven hours into an extra night shift at around 500 hours when she received an off-radio message to investigate a call from a local taxi driver, a Norm Sandhu. An assault was occurring in Unit 109 at the Starlight Motel. Such third person referrals from taxi drivers were unusual, at least in Brandenhoff. Still, mindful of all the extra action in town because of the exotic dancers, Nora signaled she would check it out.

When she arrived, there was no activity that she could see or hear in any of the units, and no taxicab waiting to provide direction. She returned to the detachment to file her shift report before heading home. At 655 hours, just as she was locking up, the detachment phone lit up again, and Nora trudged back into the office to answer it. The morning office staff would be on at 700 hours, but hadn't yet arrived.

A gruff voice at the other end barked, "Police? Yeah, I gotta a girl here..."

The low pitch of the voice electrified Nora. It was gruff, yet there was an undercurrent of warmth, somehow. "Yes, who is this, please? Your name?" She wondered if there was a connection to the assault phoned in earlier.

"Norm Sandhu. Are you the police?" In the background, Nora could just make out a female speaking nearby. "Yes, Constable Nora Macpherson. Who's the girl?"

"Oh, yeah, the girl…"

"Mr. Sandhu, Norm, let me talk to the girl if she is able…"

"Oh, yeah, I'll ask her…"

Then she heard the hoarse whisper of a woman whose voice was thick as if she had been crying. Nora sensed her own throat constricting in sympathy. "Hello, miss, I'm an RCMP constable. What's your name?" No answer… "Do you need help?" No answer. "Where are you?"

At last, after an eternity, the voice drifted back. "Vigdis. That's my name, Vigdis Dahlberg. I… a guy attacked me tonight. This cabby showed up just in time. I'm so glad. I gotta go back to the hotel where I work so I can pack…"

"Where were you working, Vigdis?" She felt odd saying the name and wondered if the girl used any other. "What work do you do?"

"At the Brandenhoff Arms… you know, dancing…" suddenly, she sounded sleepy, so Nora asked to speak to Norm again.

"Norm, please take her to emergency and I'll meet you there."

∼

FIFTEEN MINUTES LATER, SHE WAS AT BRANDENHOFF MEDICAL CENTER waiting for the doctor on duty to examine Vigdis. She hadn't met the girl, but wondered if she was the young blonde she had seen earlier on stage. She had used her cruiser's radio to contact the detachment to call the Starlight Motel to determine if that individual in Unit 109 was still there. The hotel receptionist checked the roster. The guest in Unit 109 had checked out a couple of hours before. His name was Deiter Bernhardt. Nora made a note to research him in the records.

Nora chatted with Norm, the taxi driver, over instant coffees in the awakening cafeteria.

"It all started as a mistake, you know? At two-thirty, I got a call to pick up a fare at the Starlight Motel. Seeing a light on in only one unit, I pulled up outside it and honked. There was no answer, so I left the cab running and knocked on the door. No reply. I knocked again, and the door was flung open, and a tall guy... really mad... came at me!"

"What did he look like?"

"Six-two maybe, grey crewcut, forty-five or fifty I'd guess... wearing just jeans... real skinny... you could make out his ribs!"

"What else did you see, Norm?"

"There was someone on the bed behind the man, a girl, I thought, and I saw he had her tied to the bed with some bright-coloured cloth. But the door was open for just a few seconds so, in the beginning, I didn't take it in, or even believe what I saw. I guess I was in shock. But when I was driving away, I got to thinking about it, so I turned around. That girl was not lying in a seductive pose. She wasn't there willingly. I know what being willing looks like, and that wasn't it. That girl was terrified.

"So that's when I stopped to phone the police to send someone to check it out. Then, something made me go back there, and I went to pound on the door. It took a long time, but this time, when the door crashed open, the girl, naked except for a blouse undone at the front, threw herself out into my arms. Behind her, I saw a male figure curled up like a newborn baby on the floor... you know... like a fetus."

"So you left him there? Where did you go then?"

"Yes, we got into my cab, and I turned on the heat. I gave her my jacket to cover herself and took her to our taxi stand to phone, but it isn't open until the end of shift for me... uh... seven o'clock, so we just hung out in my cab until Vikram, the daytime radio dispatcher, came in to open up."

"Well, thank you, Norm, for your courage in going back. I'm sure Miss Dahlberg is very grateful, too. Can you come into the detachment later today to file a statement?"

Norm agreed and left. Nora turned back to wait for Vigdis at Emergency, where she found the emergency nurse telling the girl she was ready to go.

"The doctor has examined her and declared her fit to be

discharged. She's just getting into some clothes that we found for her." The ER nurse was writing and didn't look up. The smell of antiseptic in the air was overpowering.

"Please remind the attending physician he needs to file a medical report as soon as possible." Waiting for Vigdis, Nora thought about the medical exam process; there was no formal examination for rape yet available. She knew that a microanalyst from Chicago, a Louis Vitullo, had developed a 'rape kit', equipment for sexual assault analysis, but Brandenhoff was too remote to have any. No doubt, it was not even yet available in Vancouver.

The young woman, Vigdis Dahlberg, was the woman she had seen Friday evening at the Brandy Arms, the performer introduced as Velvet Dawn. No wonder, Nora mused. With that name, I'd be looking for a new one, too!

"Miss Dahlberg... Vigdis... can I give you a lift back to the hotel so you can get some sleep?"

The girl yawned and shook her head. "Call me Vee... uh... I... I don't want to go there. We have to share rooms and my roommate is gross... uh... excuse me... she smokes in the room and wears way too much perfume... Ugh!" The dancer was wearing some flannelette pajamas from the clinic's Lost and Found, so she was decent, but couldn't stop yawning from exhaustion.

By this point, it was almost 900 hours, two hours past her end-of-shift, and as she watched Vee nodding off in the cafeteria chair, Nora realized her own energy was flagging, too.

"Well, you will need to give a statement sometime later today, so we have to find you some place to get some shut-eye. Come on, Vee, let's get to the detachment, and I'll make you a bed in one of the cells."

CHAPTER 20 - NORA GETS A BREAK: 0930 HOURS, SUNDAY, MAY 29

Before heading home, Nora called her sergeant. "Mike, I have bedded an exotic dancer, a Vigdis Dalhberg–she goes by Vee–down in a holding cell to sleep until I can get a statement from her. She's got a blanket and a bottle of water…"

"Okay. What's happened?"

"An assault in a room at the Starlight. A cabby intervened by chance, so she got away without too much damage… attempted strangulation, I would say. I need to get some sleep, and then I'll come back to take her statement."

"That only works if she doesn't object. We aren't charging her. What time is your next shift?"

"2200 hours, but I'll get some sleep and be right back. I am hoping she might know something about Stephanie Benson. There aren't that many exotic dancers doing gigs along Highway 16, so this girl, Vigdis, might help."

On her answering machine at home, she found two messages, one from Luke and the other from Della Frederick.

"Della's voice sounded calm and comforting. "I just want to let you know McNab is fitting in okay. He's earning his keep by catching mice in the house. I've put a bell on him to give the neighbourhood birds a chance. So don't worry about collecting your boy, Nora. He's welcome to stay with us. You can visit him anytime."

Thank goodness for animal lovers! I don't need to worry about McNab at least.

Luke's message was less uplifting. "Hi Doll. I'm still in Prince George at this stupid course... I guess I shouldn't say that, but I am not enjoying it, and I still have a week to go. I can hardly wait to get back to my regular job. Take care of yourself. I'd like to get together soon..."

The message didn't explain why he didn't like the course, but Nora suspected the problem was the expectation that RCMP members could become expert with the new technology, computers especially. Luke was more action-oriented and hated the idea of hours spent sitting at a machine, no matter how useful it might be.

Nora fell into bed and sank deep into dreams of bright dancers, dark bikers, and shady customers, all gyrating in the eerie blue light of countless banks of computers.

∼

Nora awoke to the phone ringing. "Constable Macpherson here."

"Hi, Constable, Hugh Bland here at the detachment... uh... that young dancer, Vigdis... is saying she wants to go, but Mike left a note saying you wanted get a statement from her before she left, so I'm wondering... You think she may know something about Stephanie Benson?"

"Okay, Hugh, what time is it?"

"1300 hours... your shift isn't until 2200..."

"That's fine. I'll be there as soon as I can."

She showered, grabbed some cereal and coffee in a thermos and reached the detachment by 1400 hours.

Vee was still there. Nora caught her anxious glance as soon as she sat down with her in her office.

"I didn't think I'd have to wait so long... I didn't do nothing wrong!"

"Of course you didn't, Vee. We need to hear what happened."

"He was real nice up until....you know..."

Nora nodded in sympathy.

"Did you catch that guy? I would hate to think he might show up at the next gig... Anyway, I gotta bus to catch to our next gig in Terrace and I wanna travel with the other three dancers tomorrow morning, Monday. I got laundry and costume repairs to do, and they won't wait for me because that's the only bus going to Terrace until mid-week. I wanna leave right away."

Nora noticed her neck showed large bluish marks, and her voice was still hoarse. "Vee, can you work with those bruises on your neck?"

"Oh that's nothing. I don't have a gig until next Tuesday... uh... May 31st... two days from now. By then they'll fade, and besides, I can cover them with make-up. Lots of girls have to do that." From what Nora had learned of the exotic dancer life style, she believed Vee. Tolerating physical assault came with the territory.

"You're sure?"

"Oh, yeah. I'm part of a special summer season start-up of shows at the Totem Room at Lake Else, near Terrace. It's worth a lot of money for me, so I really don't want to blow the gig."

Nora turned on her recording machine. "Well, let's get started with your statement. Start by telling a bit about yourself and how you started dancing."

"Uh... okay... My real name is Vigdis Dahlberg, but I go by Vee like I told you."

"And how old are you, Vee?"

"Nineteen last December, born December 14, 1964. I'm from Victoria on the island.

"Vancouver Island?"

"Yeah, of course."

Nora chuckled. "Yes, I guess everybody in BC knows that if someone says 'the island', they mean Vancouver Island."

"Yeah, that's home. Before I got the contract to dance for Bawdy-Works, I never been off the island."

"BawdyWorks... is that an agency in Victoria?"

"No, they're in Vancouver, but the guy in charge... uh... Mr. Cobb, told me they go searching for talent in the dance studios. Uh... he recruited me right from my studio. I been there studying dance for six years."

"What kind of dance did you study?"

"I did contemporary, jazz and ballet mostly. I also did gymnastics at a separate gym."

"So you're very qualified."

"Yeah, he gave me a try-out and then had me sign a contract right away."

"What about your family? Do they know where you are? What kind of work you're doing?"

Vee looked at her lap, examining some frayed spot in the flannelette. "Uh... I told them I had a job teaching dance in the interior of the province. They don't need to know the details..." She looked at Nora then. "You're not gonna call them, are you?"

"No, Vee. You're an adult. But if anything happens, you would want them to help, wouldn't you?"

"Yeah, but I'm okay. Nothing happened...right?"

"We'll decide in a bit what to do... Anyway, how do you like the job? Is it stressful?"

"It's been okay, just tiring. We're on the road a lot. The agency checks out the dance venues and sets up the gigs. This time in Brandenhoff is a one-off. We don't tend to do gigs in such small places. We played here Friday night and had Saturday and today off. We have to catch the bus to Terrace tomorrow early." There was urgency in her voice.

"Yes, I know. This won't take long. How long have you been dancing, Vee?"

"I just started in March this year."

So she's new and worried about keeping her head down, not being troublesome.

"Tell me about the audience that night."

"It was all guys except for one woman, the hotel server, an older woman in her forties, I think. The management, Tim, was good. He kept everyone back from the stage except when they were giving us money, you know..." Vee blushed and kept going with her story.

"What about the guy who attacked you later? Did you see him in the audience?"

"Yeah, he was right up front, watching my every move, but he didn't push to get me to talk to him the way others did. He just stood there pounding his fist in his other hand to the beat of the music. Weird. One of the first things the other dancers said was not to get them talking to you, even if they were cute. They would be just trying to cop a feel... Anyway, the gig went well. At least, I got lots of tips, you know... how they do... but that guy who attacked me later... Dieter, he said his name was... he didn't give me any tip.

"After I left the stage, I went to the dressing room and changed into my street clothes and came back out for a drink at the bar before going back to my room in the hotel. I was avoiding going there because, as I told you, I'm not keen on my roommate. I hope I can switch when we move on to Lake Else. Anyway, I didn't wanna go back right away. I didn't care about whether the other dancers said I shouldn't go for a drink... I'm legal... right? Besides, my biker guard wasn't around for a change, Diablo, he's called... I guess he was buggin' some other dancer for a change..."

Nora nodded, thinking how little social life there was for these girls. Being watched over by bikers probably didn't make for easy social mixing either.

"The guy, Dieter, sat next to me and struck up a conversation. He seemed okay, not coarse in his language, and he didn't try to touch me. The only odd thing was that he had a habit of pounding his right fist into the cup of his left hand... maybe he didn't even know he was doing it. He said he was just lonely and thought I looked like a friendly person who might like to keep him company. We chatted for a while. He said he was a part-time wilderness guide north of Brandenhoff and was just in town for the weekend. He had a rental truck in town and offered me a hundred dollars to come for a ride in his helicopter the next day, Saturday."

"Was there anyone around that you knew while you were talking to him?"

"No, the guards were off somewhere... you know... the bikers. But I said no to the hundred bucks. I said I was busy the next day and couldn't leave the hotel, and I lied... uh... I said I would be on the bus the following day, Sunday. But Dieter, he kept trying, saying then he would give me two hundred dollars and in the end, five hundred, just for the pleasure of my company. He promised me he wouldn't even touch me if I didn't want."

"Is that a lot of money for you, Vee?"

"You bet! Five hundred dollars is a whack of dough! I have to work a full cycle of gigs to clear three hundred for an entire week. I know I shouldn't have, but I said I would meet him outside the hotel the next morning, Saturday."

∽

Vee continued her statement. "The Saturday with Dieter was a surprise. First, we left early so the bikers weren't around. The guy drove me in his truck to a helicopter pad somewhere outside of town. He said the helicopters there were usually used to carry the loggers and miners to places they couldn't get to by road. His helicopter is big. He can carry maybe five or six people, and there's room for stuff in the back. It was empty when we had our ride."

"Tell me about what you saw... how you felt... and how Dieter... uh, Mr. Bernhardt behaved..."

"I was super excited to see the land from the air! We flew along the river that goes west from here..."

"The Nechako?"

"Yeah, I think that was what he called it. We went swooping up and down along the Nechako River and then turned up north towards... McLeod Lake and Mackenzie." She described how the vast wilderness spread out in a captivating, panoramic tapestry of forest green and glittering lakes.

Dieter told her about himself, that he had immigrated from Germany but had been in Canada since his teens. His family had settled in Prince George, where his parents had run a printing business, but they had both died several years before, and he had no other family in the country.

Vee said, "I kind of felt sorry for him when he told me he had no family left. I don't get along with my mom, but I know she's help me if I asked..." She continued recounting her conversation with Dieter to Nora as well as she could remember.

"Dieter told me that, as he was living in Prince George, the wild country drew him right away. He had to get away from the pulp mill stench that was everywhere in the city when the wind was blowing from the East."

"Yeah, it is pretty bad, eh?" Nora nodded. "I've noticed it, too. What else did he tell you?"

"He said that after high school, he had joined the Canadian Air Force and had qualified as a helicopter pilot by the time he was twenty-four. He said his job now was to fly The Top Brass in and out of mining and logging operations across the north."

"Is that all he does, fly VIP's around?"

Maybe we can track this guy through their companies!

"No, he said he added to his income by flying tourists in and out of hunting and fishing camps all across the northern parts of British Columbia and Alberta. He said it was exciting in some ways, to see all that amazing country, but he said he was really lonely."

"How did that make you feel, Vee?"

Does this guy play the 'poor me' card to get the women to comply?

"I had never flown before at all, even in an airplane, so the trip was even more exciting. It was so beautiful up there, like nothing I had ever seen. So I guess I was grateful..."

"That's understandable. But did you feel sorry for him when he said he was lonely?"

"I guess, a little..."

"Okay, what else?"

"We stopped for lunch in Mackenzie and at the end of the day, for a steak supper at a new place in Brandenhoff. Wow! I haven't had steak in I dunno how long!"

Big spender! I wonder if this is his usual MO...

"After supper, when he looked in his wallet, he said he'd used up most of his cash. He said he had to go back to his motel room to get enough to pay me the five hundred. I told him he could bring it back and leave it at the front desk, but he said that was risky, because so much dough might be too much for a night clerk to ignore."

"Did this reason make sense for you, Vee? I mean, did you think it sounded reasonable?"

"Oh, I got it. I've never had five hundred dollars all at once in my hands, either."

"Why did you go with him to his motel? Why not wait for him to bring it back to you at your hotel?"

"We weren't at the hotel when he told me. We were still at the restaurant. Besides, he'd been gentlemanly all day so I thought going with him would be no problem. How could I tell he'd turn mean so fast?... and when we got to the motel..."

"The Starlight Motel..."

"Yeah, I was still thinking he was a nice guy, so I didn't think it was a big deal to go up and get the money in his room... besides, the motel wasn't far from the Brandy Inn. I thought I could just leave and walk back if he didn't wanna drive me." Vee looked up at Nora, her eyes searching for understanding.

"So what did you think were his intentions?"

"To get the money to give me."

This is total naïveté....

"So you never saw him as a threat?"

"No... uh... but when he grabbed my arm when we got inside the room... uh... I couldn't believe how strong he was... like I was in a vice, you know, and he was using only one hand... When I asked about the money, he shook me and told me not to be so stupid...so naïve...

"He said, 'I fed and entertained you all day. Why would I spend even more?' Then he put his other hand over my mouth, so I couldn't make a sound, and he shoved me back on the bed and tied my wrists to the bed frame with coloured scarves and shoved another scarf in my mouth."

"From then on," Vee said, "it was a little blurry."

"When did you arrive at the Starlight Motel?"

"Between 9:30 and 10:00, I think."

So, before the cab driver intervened, Vee was there at the mercy of Bernhardt for at least four hours.

"Vee, as well as you can, tell me what Dieter Bernhardt did to you."

The girl became very silent.

When she started speaking again, she sounded strangled. "My throat is still sore…" Nora could hear her voice breaking from time to time, so that only hushed air sounded.

"I was so… surprised… he didn't try to have sex with me, you know? He just lay on top of me and started massaging my arms and shoulders, like I had pins and needles, and he was trying to wake my nerves up. I felt surprised, at first, because it was kind of relaxing, you know? I mean, when he tied me up, I expected something much worse."

This MO is similar to the MO of the killers of some of the murdered women along Highway 16… no actual intercourse, but stripped and strangled…

"And all this time he had you tied to the bed?" Vee nodded, tears streaming down her face. Nora reached out to pat Vee's shoulder in reassurance. "Go on, tell me what happened next."

"After that, he pressed much harder, using his fingers to rub up and down my arm and shoulder muscles so hard that I cried out because it hurt so much. He did that until I couldn't even move, and then he took my clothes off…"

"Did he untie you then? To take your top off?"

"No, he just undid all the buttons of the blouse… but he did rip my bra enough, so it came off. I thought then he would rape me then, but he just started talking in what I think was German. He getting more and more excited and all I could do was stare at him. I couldn't understand what he was saying... but I got the basic idea... I speak Danish, and German is a bit like it..."

"What was he saying, do you think?"

"He liked that I was almost a German girl... uh... he admired my body... that I was muscular and fit..." She shook as if to rid herself of the memory. "He was so creepy!"

"Go on. What happened next?"

"He was bare-chested, but he still had his jeans on, so in a way that made me feel hopeful... but then, he put his hands to my neck and pressed super hard on my windpipe. I felt he was hard... you know... a bit anyway when he ground his hips into mine. Soon, I could feel my lungs aching as if they were about to explode. It was like time was standing still... All my senses became hyped up... you know... so I could hear everything: his ragged breathing, his wrist bones cracking as his hands worked to put more and more pressure, then... a knock on the door..."

"Then I went blank, floating as if there was no up or down, my body so sore everywhere, my lungs felt as if they would burst like balloons blown up too big..."

"So you blacked out around then?"

Vee nodded. "Then I was conscious again, and Dieter had disappeared. I looked to see where he was and saw he was standing at the motel room door yelling at a dark-skinned, grey-haired man with a very surprised look on his face. But before I could signal to the stranger, Dieter slammed the door shut."

"So that was the cab driver, the first time he came to the motel door?"

That was a lucky break! If he had kept going without interruption, she would have been dead...

"Yeah. After the door shut, then he was on me again, beginning where he left off. But this time he seemed sorta desperate, like he didn't want more interruptions. But he didn't know that I'd loosened one scarf by stretching the fabric enough so the slackness would let my hand slip through. Even while he had his hands on my neck, I was working on the second hand. He was pressing on my neck so hard, my eyes were probably popping out...Then, just when I got my other scarf loose, another knock came at the door."

"What did he do this second time?"

"He just started again, only harder! He was groaning and breathing funny... I was feeling faint and floaty again...I couldn't get no air... but I was so scared I was able... I don't know how... to concentrate enough to get both my hands free and bring my arms down to whack both sides of his head at once."

"Whoa! Really!"

Hot damn! This is one gutsy girl!

"It wasn't a big enough smack to do more than make him kinda stunned, but enough to let me get my knees bent and my feet in place so's I could kick him right where it hurts the most... you know? I got him with a jab to his balls... and then another in the same place." She gulped, as if in wonder at what she had done.

"What happened then?"

"Oh, he yelped and fell off the bed, and ended up in a ball on the floor. He just laid there making strange noises, like he was a little kid. So I crawled off the bed, and when I opened the door, the cabbie was there. I just flew at him, you know? Like he was a saviour!"

"Vee, this is very helpful. You have survived a terrible attack. Thanks for waiting to do this for us." Nora felt excited about the wealth of detail Vee had provided about Dieter Bernhardt.

Maybe this is the perp who'd been attacking along Highway 16! The serial killer!

The interview had lasted until 1600 hours, and Vee was frantic to be gone, but Nora had one last request.

"I think it's important that you press charges against this man, Vee."

Her reaction was immediate and panicky. "Oh, no, I can't. I don't have time to stop and do a bunch of paperwork... I have to get back so's I can get ready to leave. I have to fix my costumes and get my hair done. It's hard to get appointments, you know, with us always on the road. I'm already late... besides, he didn't really do nothing serious to me..."

Nora realized that the Force pressing charges would be a futile exercise if she couldn't convince the victim to cooperate. Even though there was a witness, the cabby, and a positive ID for the accused, the Crown wouldn't be keen unless Vee agreed to press charges. Still, she sensed Vee had connected with her, that the girl was willing to trust, but was stuck in too-tight a schedule. This feeling was reinforced when Vee gave her a brief hug as they said good-bye.

Her regular night shift that Sunday flew by as she contemplated the next crucial steps of her investigation.

CHAPTER 21 - THE SEARCH BEGINS: MONDAY-FRIDAY, MAY 30-JUNE 3

During her shift Monday daytime, Nora reread Vee and Norm Sandhu's statements side by side to check for any discrepancies.

On first impression, she couldn't see any inconsistencies. What troubled her, apart from the obvious intent to murder the girl by strangling her, were the elaborate "foreplay" of meals, a helicopter ride and the atypical non-sexual intercourse nature of the attack.

Was this their serial killer? There had been several young women go missing in the last few years. She would have to research how they had died. None seemed that similar to the MO used on Vigdis Dahlberg.

She searched the Motor Vehicle records for a Dieter Bernhardt. There was nothing, not even a driver's licence application.

She phoned the motel where he had stayed, inquiring what name he had used to register and about the state of the room as he had left it. Anything odd? The desk clerk said he had registered as Dieter Bernhardt. The chambermaid had mentioned nothing, but the desk clerk said he would report back.

He flew a helicopter. Who did he work for? She checked the phonebook for helicopter services and found different companies working out of Prince George: Starburst, McClintock's and Loch Doon. She made a note of the phone numbers.

Within the hour, the Starlight Hotel clerk called back to say the only odd thing about the room was that Bernhardt had disarranged the bedclothes, but hadn't slept between the sheets. Nora imagined Sandhu's appearance had spooked him, and he had bolted soon after.

She had heard back from Bunnie Burrows in Vancouver. She would be happy to keep an eye open for the DC's daughter, but she needed to know her stage name.

Of course! I don't know what name she'll be using on the road. How do I find that out?

Bunnie had also included a cryptic comment. "Why don't you consider Special Ops training so you can look for her yourself?" Nora sent a return message saying she would try to find the name for Bunnie, and that she'd consider her suggestion... She had never considered herself as undercover potential...

Before she knew it, her shift was over and she was writing up her notes in her detachment office. Nora raised her head from the desk and noted the time. 1700 hours. Her exhaustion had resulted from pulling two extra shifts in the last rotation, and her schedule had her going on shift again during the next three days. Afterwards, she would be off for two delicious days. But right now, she was restless. Having stayed up past her tiredness, she was running on nervous energy alone.

After waiting an hour to allow time for him to get home from his day shift, Nora phoned Luke. "Hey there! It's me... is this a good time?"

"Sure Hon, what's up?"

"Well, we haven't touched base since you got back from your computer course. I got your message yesterday, but then work got busy. Did your computer stuff get any more interesting?"

"Not really... a lot of time watching it 'think', or so they called it! I can find my own methods to waste time! The thing is, someone has convinced the brass that computer technology is the way of the future, that we'll all need to use it every day. I don't know… I hope not. Anyway, what got you so busy at work?"

"We had an incident with an exotic dancer getting attacked at the Starlight Motel in town here. It was a weird MO. The sounds the vic made seemed to have aroused the perp, no specific sexual assault as such, but the perp was on the point of strangling her when a cabby interrupted. She was lucky. Anyway, this reminded me of some of the unsolved cases we have along the highway…"

"Yeah, I remember, some were strangled, fully clothed…"

"Oh, she was down to her blouse…he had ripped everything else off, she said…"

"Huh! Interesting! So, any leads on the guy?"

"I have a name and an occupation, and the cabby as witness, but the girl won't press charges."

"That's such a bummer! We can't do anything unless the vic is willing to go that extra step."

"Another strange thing is I can't find any record of his having any kind of license, at least not under the name he used to register at the Starlight…"

Luke's low whistle conveyed his dismay. "Too bad… send me the details anyway, and we can at least watch out for the guy. Uh… no action on that BOLF for Stephanie Benson or the truck either, by the way." She listened to their breathing while there was a pause.

"So, wanna get together this weekend?" The warmth in Luke's rich voice reminded her of why she so enjoyed this relationship.

"Sure, I'll come to you. What will we do… outside?"

I know what we'll be doing inside…

"How about we spend some time hiking the local cross-country ski trails? The alpine meadows will be full of flowers…"

"Sounds good!"

∼

EVEN THOUGH SHE WAS LOOKING FORWARD TO SOME DOWN TIME WITH Luke, in the back of her mind, Nora never stopped thinking about

Steph Benson. On duty, she had to force herself to stay focused on the job at hand. But running across Vee Dahlberg had launched Nora's instinct to explore the possibility of connecting with others who might have a lead on Steph. There must be dancers, bartenders... and bikers in the know.

She thought again about Bunnie's suggestion. She could get the training to go undercover herself. Getting the goods on these people would require some stealth. She knew that people in the netherworld—not quite the underworld, but next door, shady people such as exotic dancers, or strip club owners, were loath to get involved with cops. There were all kinds of operations on the record where members of the Force had tried to infiltrate the clubs where they were sure illicit drugs were being dealt, and where coincidentally exotic dancers were doing gigs, but investigations had come up short.

First, random civilian males inquiring into the industry were suspect so the girls clammed up, and secondly, the dancers were so transient that tracking their movements and protecting them from possible retaliation was difficult. Under those circumstances, it was impossible to convince a dancer to act as an asset. Also, there were relatively few female members on the Force so, with the exception of Bunnie, their usefulness as undercover agents had not yet been explored. Bunnie spent almost all her time in Vancouver. Working up here, Nora reasoned, she could be breaking ground.

Could she do it? Even if she believed she could, would the brass let her? Would the Force fund it? She couldn't do it alone. She would need an "in" somewhere. What about Vee? If she couldn't convince Vee to press charges, could she convince her to be an inside contact? Did Vee have the nerve to cover for her... not tell anyone Nora was a cop?

The idea consumed her spare time during the rest of the week. Could she get a shot at undercover work, posing as someone connected to the exotic dancers' lifestyle? Bartender, barmaid, hotel manager? No, she would also need to be transient to stay in touch with Vee, who would be her wingman... er... woman. What kind of work would she do? Something she could do as a mobile service for the dancers so people wouldn't question her interest in being around them... hair, makeup, costume.... A flash of herself as a hairdresser/cosmetician popped up. Why not? She could do one of those entry-level courses in PG or Van.

The more she thought about the idea, the more Nora became convinced it had potential. Vee had mentioned how difficult it was to find esthetic services on the road, how their schedule was so tight they couldn't always make hair appointments or get their nails done or search for costume replacements.

Also, it would please DC Benson to get some inside help to find his underage daughter as well as get some hard evidence to control a serious drug trafficking problem. And it wouldn't hurt her career either, to have a DC going to bat for her! She felt suddenly energized by the possibilities. She felt sure he'd be open at least to listening to her idea... help her sign up to an esthetician program, get a diploma, about six months' time... during which she could transition from a cop to an ordinary citizen with a mobile hair and nails service! She could come up with a company name and use her vehicle to advertise.

This plan was going to need support at the North District level. She needed a purpose more crucial than merely the apprehension of Steph Benson, important as that objective was. What could that 'something greater' be? Her mind leapt to the image of Vee when she had seen her after the attack. No one had sighted that Bernhardt guy since that night, May 21st... She thought he could be the serial killer who fit the MO of their Highway 16 predator. The problem was that mounting an expensive undercover operation with the sole purpose of looking for one lone killer could be an absurd, fruitless venture. She needed a rationale with a better chance of success.

Then she thought about the Steph's biker gang connection and Vee's comment about the bikers acting as security for the dancers and wondered how much interest there would be at North District level in pursuing criminally organized drug traffickers. There could also be some interest in coordinating with K Division RCMP (Alberta) which might already be tracking the Devil's Brigade. The Alberta Force could be unaware that there might be an expansion into BC and would be interested to keep tabs on what E Division (BC) uncovered. She decided to check that possibility out when she talked to DC Benson.

She thought back to Steph's edgy behaviour and speculated about what drugs she had been using... likely cocaine, weed, maybe the odd opiate. However, the restlessness, nightmares and difficulty concentrating seemed to fit most with a coke habit. She began to develop a plan to present to Benson, one that would cast a wide net for his daughter but would also stand a good chance of catching some of the head gang members. Biker gangs had already been implicated in the procurement and trafficking of cocaine, which had been cropping up across north central BC more frequently during the past couple of years. This idea, she believed, was a better proposal, one that had legs!

Next, she would have to think about why she was the best person for the job. Apart from her awareness of the problem, what advantage could she offer? She had the inkling of a plan...

Before leaving for the weekend, she spent some time perusing the Vancouver phone book and then placed a call for a brochure and an application form to the Bianca McKay Esthetics School in Vancouver, and asked that they fast-track them to her in Brandenhoff. At home, she spent several of her evening hours making a plan to follow up: doing the paperwork to apply for specialist undercover training, consolidating her finances, and finally, contacting Gloria Newsom, her buddy from Depot who lived in the Downtown Eastside of Vancouver, someone she hoped who could help her make the transition.

CHAPTER 22 - NORA AND LUKE AT ODDS: FRIDAY-SUNDAY, JUNE 3-5

Nora spent the next Friday afternoon and Saturday with Luke in Glacier Lake. All of Friday afternoon and evening was a lazy playtime spent catching up in bed. Their sexual play was prolonged and satisfying. Luke was a considerate and skillful lover, and Nora couldn't help matching his passion with her own. At times like these, she couldn't imagine being without him in her life.

On Saturday they delighted in hiking the ski hill trails. The alpine meadows of the area were renowned for their pristine beauty. They stopped in mid-afternoon to lie in a sunny meadow densely dotted with daisies, Indian paintbrush, pea vine and fireweed, the array of white, yellow, coral, purple and rose-pink blooms almost tranquilizing their senses. Overhead, they could hear the high-pitched cries of bald eagles as they soared and swooped, searching for prey.

Nora broached her new career idea in an almost offhand manner, concerned that if she seemed too excited, Luke would disapprove on principle. He was quite conservative, really.

"I'm thinking of submitting a proposal to North District level... an idea I got when I dealt the other week with Vee Dahlberg, you know, the dancer?"

"Yeah? What kind of proposal?" Luke's tone was almost, but not quite, flippant, as if he couldn't believe her capable of dealing directly with North District bureaucracy.

"Uh... I was thinking I could train as an esthetics specialist, you know, a hairdresser, cosmetician... and... then I could... uh... go-undercover-to-infiltrate-the-exotic-dancers-lifestyle-hoping-to-connect-with-Steph Benson." She said the last part in a rush just to get the words out.

"You're joking, right?"

Undaunted, Nora shook her head. "No, I'm not. I think my plan might work..."

"Nora, you're crazy to try something like this, I mean, completely crackers! Do you have any idea how risky something like that would be? How you would be the target of those biker-thugs that provide so-called security for the dancers? They don't play nice, or give second chances!

"I would take the specialist undercover training in Chilliwack so I wouldn't be walking in blind..."

Luke seemed to ignore her interjection and continued with his objections, his voice increasing in volume with each added detail. "Besides, you have no experience with this kind of operation. District would have to be off their nut to set you up to try this! And if you think the District bean-counters would throw money at such a foolish, haywire scheme, well, you are more naïve than I thought. They can't afford the money to keep you safe! They're spending it all on computers!"

Nora refused to have her hopes crushed by Luke's tirade. "I *have* thought it through! What better person to get inside than someone working with the dancers? I think I can get Vee Dahlberg to be an inside contact so I can get access to the dancers, and through them, maybe the bikers who were holding Steph...She was high on a variety of stuff when I was dealing with her. I think they're the dealers...and District is interested in finding who is supplying the cocaine and marijuana along here."

"And I say you're being an idiot to put yourself at such risk, with so little experience!"

"You don't see the possibility..."

"What I see is someone who is already well-known in the area, from Brandenhoff to Glacier Lake, if not beyond, who expects to waltz back in after a few months away with a completely different identity... it's a non-starter!"

"The point is, with my plan, I can change my appearance so much that no one would recognize me, and it would all be a part of the op. I would be legitimate to wear stuff that altered my appearance... I could dye my hair, wear contacts to change eye-colour even..."

Luke's only response was to retch, as if disgusted.

"I would be a mobile service offering these products for sale, so it only makes sense I would model them myself... wigs, false eyelashes, nails, derrieres, and breasts, as well as glitzy stage costumes... Once I am in character, even you won't know it's me."

Luke stared at her in disbelief. "Nora, you are a natural beauty. You wear almost no make-up. I love your hair the way it is..."

She sat up and swept her shoulder-length chestnut hair off her face. The auburn highlights glinted in the sun. Staring at him in wordless fury, she rose and tied her hair up in a no-nonsense twist. His scorn had cut her to the quick. Although she was prepared to alter her appearance and to put herself in lethal danger for a chance at cracking a drug ring, he was adamant that she would be uselessly vulnerable undercover. His disdain and disrespect were palpable. She felt gut-punched.

The trek back down the mountainside was long and silent. Instead of staying over until Sunday, Nora drove off right away with no further effort to resolve their impasse. She cried most of the trip back to Brandenhoff.

~

NORA AWOKE UP EARLY THE NEXT MORNING AFTER A FITFUL SLEEP AND soberly considered her options: should she break it off with Luke and go her own way? She couldn't work at cross purposes with someone who had his heart invested. Knowing she needed to plan her undercover strategy so it was acceptable to HQ, she decided to ignore what Luke thought. As it was she would have to make her proposal attractive enough to justify the four-month wait for her to prepare for it.

The problem of the drug trade across the Highway 16 corridor was serious. That was a given. The question of whether it was being driven by the Devil's Brigade and/or the Renegades was likely not debatable. The existence of a predatory killer working in the area was also at least a serious possibility if not a given. Thanks to Vigdis Dahlberg, they now had a likely identity for that individual. She was betting her approach to an undercover op would be a successful way to target both the drug dealing and the predatory individual who would be attracted to people like exotic dancers.

Nora knew she couldn't depend only on District Commissioner Benson to be the sole backer of her undercover idea because, with his daughter's life on the line, he had too much of a vested interest. Benson's approval would certainly be needed for her acceptance into the Special Ops training, but there were other hurdles she would have to pass. Even though she was sure of Benson's endorsement, Nora knew she needed support from her immediate superior, Mike Sinclair, and the director of the Special Operations Program itself. She would have to have her ducks in a row because whatever she planned must stand up to scrutiny. Luke was right about one thing: she would have to change her own appearance substantially to avoid being recognized in the various communities along Highway 16 where people knew her. It couldn't be merely a dye job either; she would need to change her entire identity: walk, talk, attitude, and looks.

During that first slow night shift after the disastrous meeting with Luke, Nora had much time to think about his scathing rejection of her undercover plan. She felt he was being self-serving in his refusal to acknowledge her right to try the idea. How else was she going to learn if she didn't try? She examined her chances: Nora was sure she would have no trouble fulfilling the demands of the beautician program, but she also had to find out if she satisfied the pre-requisites for an undercover operation. Maybe she hadn't been in the Force long enough? Maybe she didn't have the right personality for such work? Once again, doubts assailed her, and she felt the need to tamp down her expectations.

She had developed and costed out her proposal so that she could run it by Mike Sinclair before she approached Benson with the idea. Mike couldn't be the one to give the final authorization, but he would know where to look for holes in the plan, what steps to take to make it operational and which members needed to give it final approval. Mike was a great 'process' guy.

CHAPTER 23 - MIKE SINCLAIR WEIGHS IN: FRIDAY, JUNE 10

When she sat down with Mike the following Friday after shift, she felt confident she had examined the project from all angles.

"Mike, I think I'm going to apply for Special Ops training so I can focus on the drug trafficking problem up here. I think I'll get leads on Steph Benson and Dieter Bernhardt that way, too."

She could tell Mike was surprised. He hadn't been expecting such a daring initiative. "Um... look, Nora, I understand your frustration about your posting here in Brandenhoff, and I recognize that a change of scene might do you good. But I'm not so sure about undercover work... you're still fairly inexperienced in vice policing, this town not being a hotbed of drug gangs or criminal enterprise... if you get my drift..." The way his mouth buckled suggested some level of suppressed mirth, as if he wasn't ready to give the idea serious consideration.

"But on the other hand," Mike continued, "there is considerable evidence that the drug trade has taken off along this highway. Our little town is an anomaly in not having a very active scene... uh... one of the benefits of an active church community perhaps?" He looked at her sideways to see if she had caught the implication. "In other words, you can't use Brandenhoff as an exemplar community to gauge the peril of your plan."

But Nora's enthusiasm for her Special Ops plan was all-consuming. "My idea is to qualify as an esthetician–hairdresser, cosmetician, fashion consultant, mani-pedicurist–at the same time I am taking Special Ops training in Chilliwack so that I can run a mobile esthetician service through this area, working with the various dancers who do their gigs along Highway 16. The idea is to use that cover to infiltrate the Devils' Brigade drug trafficking operation in this part of the province."

"Is that the only area where you would use this cover?" This was a fair question, since such a service would be a novelty, its possibility of success more likely in the populated south.

"No, I would start in the Southern Mainland to establish credibility, and then work my way up the Fraser Highway, so it won't seem as if I am just targeting the Brigade territory."

"You know you're well-known along this stretch of highway…"

"Oh, I realize that! My cover won't be just a dye job! Part of the reason I thought of the esthetician idea was so that I could alter my appearance without it being suspicious. Also, during the time I was away, people could forget how I used to look."

"It's not just about appearance, Nora…"

"Oh, I'm hoping the Special Ops program will train me in developing an undercover persona… change the way I talk, walk, dress… my body shape… *you* might not even know me!"

Mike's eyebrows rose, his lop-sided smile betraying his amusement. "Maybe… they're a pretty versatile bunch. Who do you see as assets within the business?"

"I know I need an inside asset to help provide cover, someone who would introduce me as a mobile esthetician and back me up if anyone asked questions. I think Vigdis Dahlberg–Vee–would do that. She's new to the exotic dancing business, so not jaded by it, and motivated because of her encounter with the predator. I'll check that first, before any other commitment. But also there's Bunnie Burrows who can help with developing an undercover op. She actually suggested the idea to me."

Mike's jaw dropped. Nora guessed that the initiative of cultivating Vee Dahlberg as an inside asset had surprised him, but hearing that a Force Member had recruited Nora was astonishing.

"That's impressive, Nora. I didn't think you had thought that far ahead. You're sure this dancer, Vee, would cooperate?"

"As I said, I would have to get her commitment first."

"Have you asked Bill Benson if he thinks your idea has merit?"

"No, that's why I'm running it by you first, Mike. If you see any holes in my planning, I'm trusting you to tell me where they are."

"What about cost? This sounds like an expensive proposition..."

"I have checked out a three month program in Vancouver, at the Bianca McKay Centre, an award-winning school established two decades ago, that offers programs where I can start anytime without waiting for the next intake of students. It has basic courses in all the skill areas I would need... for seven-fifty tuition... I've already filled out the application and sent it back by special delivery and asked about starting as soon as possible."

"That's just the beginning..."

"Hey, I know! The actual cost will be the purchase of a vehicle, setting up the mobile business and equipping it with stock. I've costed that out to about eight thousand. My photography will also come in handy, because I can charge for promo shots of the dancers. That will bring in some money..."

"Not enough to cover your expenses, I suspect."

"Oh I realize that... I also have an inheritance from my folks, and I can use some of that for seed money. The Force will fund it, won't they... if it's authorized? Or I can just go ahead and wait for forgiveness instead of permission..." She heaved a great sigh and added, "The thing is I know I need a change, and this Special Op feels right."

"Nora, you shouldn't be so naïve as to think you can dream up an op that you will pursue regardless of whether the Force authorizes it..."

"But if it looks feasible, they'll authorize, won't they?"

"Oh, yeah, they might authorize. But not maybe at the level you might want or expect... Let's just say I wouldn't go spending your inheritance until you get some serious support from District HQ and permission to take the Special Ops program in Chilliwack. Speaking of which, have you checked out whether there's a suitable program coming up?"

"I've read the overview for prospective candidates for the Chilliwack program, and I checked to see whether there's an intake date soon for the Special Ops Program I need. They said beginning of July. Also, I understand there's a shortage of female applicants, so that puts me at an advantage, too. I've checked out applying to the Burnaby detachment for a transfer, and I've phoned Gloria Newsom, a roommate and friend of mine from Depot training days, and asked her to keep her eyes open for a studio apartment near the Robson campus of the esthetics school... and... I *want* to do this Mike... whether *or not* somebody thinks I'm up to it..."

"Now, don't go rogue on us, Nora..." but there was a twinkle in his eye.

"I can do it... but what I want to know is whether you think it might work... you know... do you think it's possible?"

"The more important question is whether *you* think you can do it..."

Suddenly, she felt overwhelmed by the enormity of what she was attempting. Did she have what it would take?

It's either this or quit the Force altogether... and I really don't want to go there... I feel like I'm screwing up, beaten down by all the stuff at DuLac, and the jerks in Brandenhoff, feeling held back by the sexism in the Force...

Mike interrupted her downward spiral into doubt. "The thing is, Nora, I'm... uh... unsure you have the temperament for the gut-wrenching choices undercover work might demand. You know, in that business, they don't pay you for what you do, but for what you might have to do."

Her response was the ultimate defense. Somehow his doubt had hardened her resolve. "I'm tougher than people might think..."

Mike nodded and leant forward. His voice was almost a whisper.

"Maybe, but don't forget, I'm the guy who has seen you break down over animals dying on the highway. In this business you're thinking of infiltrating, you'll see much worse, stuff that will change you forever." He seemed all at once overcome by his recollection of Special Ops horror stories. "Hell, from what I've heard, the training will change you in ways you can't imagine." His arms flew out and up in a 'who knows?' gesture.

Nora was fighting back tears by this point. "Why can't people respect my right to determine the path my career takes? First, Luke, and now you, Mike. They need female operatives. I think I can do the job. I have a possible asset, an informant, Vee Dahlberg, who I am pretty sure will help me. I have a cover story planned–a mobile esthetician service where I will use a disguise with the products I sell–and I have target, Dieter Bernhardt whom we both agree is dangerous while at large, and a young victim, Stephanie Benson who is vulnerable, likely to become one of the many missing and murdered women in this part of the country." She had to stop to catch her breath.

Mike signified an end to the meeting by pounding his fist on the desk as he rose in his chair. "Steph Benson may be missing, but I somehow doubt she'll be cooperative. Okay, Nora, I can see your determination, and I agree that you should be able to have a say on determining your own career path. I'll endorse your application for special training in undercover operations. Budgeting for your cover story will have to wait until you get that training. Walk before running, you know... I'll also apprise Bill Benson of your plan, and I'll ask him if he feels he can expedite your entry into the program, if possible. We also need to work on a story to cover your transfer from here. No one can know you are going for Special Ops."

She resisted the urge to hug him...

CHAPTER 24 - NORA, BUNNIE AND VEE: MONDAY, JUNE 13

Nora, energized by her interview with Mike, phoned Bianca McKay Esthetics to find out the status of her application. They had approved her to begin in July. She asked them to hold her application until she could confirm her ability to move. Next, she phoned the Totem Room of the Lake Else Hotel outside of Terrace to find out if Vee was still there, or if they knew where her next gig would be. She had contemplated calling BawdyWorks, Vee's booking agency, for the information, but had calculated she might need to work with them in her undercover capacity down the road, so she didn't want to compromise that possibility by alerting them to her interest in "Velvet Dawn". The Lake Else receptionist wouldn't confirm anything about the dancers over the phone.

She got Mike's permission to take a day off to travel to Prince George to present her undercover idea to Bill Benson and to check out the dancers' venue at the Hillcrest, where there had been reports of Brigade activity in the last few weeks.

The meeting with Benson went well. Nora got the impression that the DC was relieved to have someone actively trying to find his daughter. "Constable Macpherson, I'm delighted that you're interested in this kind of assignment. It takes a special kind of officer to make the transition to Special Ops. I wish you all the best, and I'll make sure they know in Burnaby that you have my backing." Nora got the impression that his relief was a matter of something off his conscience, and not just a matter of professional expediency.

"I also agree that the drug trafficking problem and the search for a serial predator are an even more important focus which might catch Stephanie up in the search." She left assured of Benson's support when she took her proposal further up the chain of command.

Before she left Prince George HQ, Nora checked out Starburst, McClintock's and Loch Doon helicopter services to see if they could ID Dieter Bernhardt. She made quick phone calls to each office using the physical description both Vee and Norm Sandhu had provided.

"Constable Nora Macpherson of Brandenhoff RCMP detachment here. I'm trying to locate a helicopter pilot called Dieter Bernhardt. Six-two, maybe, grey-brown crewcut, forty-five or fifty... very slim build?"

She had struck out at Starburst and McClintock's and was feeling discouraged when the receptionist at Loch Doon gave her a lead. "Do you mean Franz or Frank instead of Dieter Bernhardt? We have an interim contract with a Friedrich 'Franz' Bernhardt. I never heard him call himself Dieter, though..."

"That could be him. Does he match the description I gave?"

"Maybe... his hair isn't grey though, more like a dirty blond, and he's not over six feet."

"Okay, thanks." It might be dyed hair, and both Norm and Vee were short enough to over-estimate a tall man's height. Nora felt she had made some headway.

∼

On her way out of Prince George, Nora stopped in first at Hillcrest Registration desk to ask if any dancers were there. The hotel lobby was typical of many she had seen in the area: worn scarlet floral carpet with tired-looking, black armchairs and couches. There was a pervasive odor of cigarette smoke and Lysol.

The hotel clerk, a somewhat surly, older man, seemed guarded. "Who's askin'?" He looked her up and down, assessing that her civvies didn't give any clue to her identity or intentions.

Flashing her RCMP ID, she responded, "I'm Constable Macpherson from the Brandenhoff RCMP detachment, just hoping to connect with a young woman who reported an incident to us a while back... the person I'm looking for is Vee Dahlberg... also known as Velvet Dawn..."

"Velvet's not here. I don't know where she is..." His rasping voice echoed in the silent lobby.

Sensing his hostility, Nora backed away with a nod. As she walking towards the hotel entrance, she caught sight of familiar figure: 'Bunnie' Burrows–Corporal Bonita Burrows of the Downtown Vancouver RCMP Detachment. She had already connected with her to keep an eye out for Stephanie. Bunnie would be an invaluable undercover associate. She was a liaison with the dancers, a kind of angel sponsor who had, among other assignments, worked the Robson Street hooker walk, watching and trying to connect with as many of the women as possible.

Bunnie raised a discreet brow, signaling Nora into the hallway off the lobby. Her raven-black hair, sloe-eyed make-up and buxom build called to mind a flamenco dancer Nora had once seen. Just now, she was wearing a form-hugging leotard and a vibrant, multi-coloured, tasseled shawl.

She turned and walked back along the hallway, out of sight of the hotel clerk, who didn't seem to pay them any attention. "Vee was here a few weeks ago, but she'll be working downtown at the Seymour Strip until the end of July, so you can contact her there."

"Why are you here, Bunnie? I thought your usual beat was the Downtown Eastside?"

"Yeah, I'm on the circuit for about a week, filling in for one girl who sprained her ankle. I have an 'in' with BawdyWorks to sub in when they need someone ASAP. They don't ask questions." She winked. "Just keeping my ear to the ground... Hey! I heard about your

BOLF for Dieter Bernhardt. I've asked around here, but nobody remembers running into anyone by that name."

"Could be the wrong first name, according to what I found out today. 'Dieter' may be 'Franz' as in Friedrich or even Frank..." She filled Bunnie in on her chat with Loch Doon Helicopter Service. "We'll have to change the BOLF." Bunnie listened with avid attention, her eyes alert for any interlopers in the hallway. "Speaking of names, did you happen across Stephanie Benson's stage name? It would be a lot easier to track her if I had that."

"No, I'm working on it. I may not be able to find it out until I am down south in Van. But I will keep you in the loop."

"You planning on coming south?"

"Yeah, I'm trying to transfer to Special Ops and the get posted back here."

Bunnie's eyes lit up. "That's great news! I'm glad you're following up on my advice. Definitely keep me In the loop. I can be a resource for you."

Bunnie inspired Nora. On stage in her short bolero jacket and flounced scarlet skirt, she was gorgeous and dynamic, her act based upon a background in ballroom dancing, where she had specialized in Latin varieties: salsa, tango, paso doble, cha-cha, rhumba. Nora certainly didn't want to be a dancer, but she thought she would enjoy a stint of pure feminine indulgence selling costumes and make-up to the ones she had met. She told Bunnie about her esthetician idea, and the dancer whistled in appreciation. "That's awesome, girl, just wicked! Have you applied to Burnaby yet?"

"Just waiting for District to okay my transfer... actually I've been in town to follow up with the DC."

"Well, keep in touch... use the undercover communications system. This gig is a popular spot with the bikers. There's already been chatter about the Brigade moving into this area... Listen, I gotta go. Not a good idea for us to be seen together..."

~

Vee struggled to find the energy to get herself up and dressed. Her routine on the road was wearing her down, the seemingly endless trek across the province a monotonous round of three star hotels and crappy café meals eaten at odd hours. Most time off was spent sleeping and refurbishing and recombining the various bits of dance costume she had brought with her.

The actual work, the dancing, was an outlet where she could drift off into another world on a musical carpet ride, the cage where she danced a secure space–until some idiot invaded it while she was dancing to fondle her legs or butt. Even the joy of dancing was becoming tainted by the leering, foul-mouthed louts who seemed to constitute the bulk of the audience. At least the money was good. The tips she and the other dancers earned nightly–sometimes a hundred bucks each in ten and twenties–were the real bonus. But there were few places to spend the cash. The little towns along the route had little appealing merchandise for a city girl like her.

The security detail of Diablo, Grinder, Gypsy and a new recruit named Tank always lurking in the background was disconcerting. She felt some kind of violence was always in the offing. After her first encounter with Diablo, Vee had avoided being alone with him, but the close quarters of the various cafes and hotel lobbies where they found themselves together inevitably meant she had to tolerate his presence, if not interact with him.

Diablo picked up on her disdain, and used it as a reason to torment her. She couldn't ask him to pick up her dry cleaning or anything from the store for fear that he would tamper with it. He had laced her juice with vodka at least once that she knew of, and her chiffon scarves had come back from the cleaners reeking of tobacco and some other musty smell she couldn't identify.

"Hey, Velvet," he had crooned as he passed the garments to her, "let me into your room tonight and I'll make it worth your while... ya don't need to go out with helicopter pilots when I'm here..."

She had protested, "I don't need anything from you! Leave me alone!" and he had acted hurt, as if he were used to her loving attention.

Even Mona, who was the sleepiest of the dancers, had noticed and asked, "Is Diablo a special guy for you?"

Vee had bristled in response, "*As if!* Why would I have anything to do with that creep!"

"Well, he acts like he's really stuck on you, girl. That's what I notice. He's always askin' where you are and what time your gigs are..."

"Mona, I'm serious! Don't tell him anything. Nothing! You hear me? I don't want him knowing anything about me! Yuck!"

"Okay, okay. Don't throw a hissy fit! A little extra cash always come in handy is all I'm sayin'..."

"Extra cash? From what?"

"You know...." Mona rotated her hips suggestively.

"You don't...! Do you mean... Oh my god!" Vee's naiveté had become a reliable source of ribald humour in the troupe.

CHAPTER 25 - NORA MAKES THE BREAK: TUESDAY-FRIDAY JUNE 14-18

Getting back to Brandenhoff after her encounter with Bunnie, Nora made her next three moves. She confirmed her start date at Bianca McKay, and, since she would have to be posted to a different detachment to attend the training, submitted her formal request for transfer to Burnaby, effective immediately. Last, she applied for the next space in the Special Ops Program at the Pacific Region Training Centre in Chilliwack.

I'll show you, Luke! I'm not all talk, no action... I'm doing this for me... to keep me vital and engaged...

She realized that she would need a vehicle to make the commute from the downtown esthetics campus on Robson to Chilliwack. Despite Mike's advice, she knew financing this career move might mean paying up front and hoping the Force would reimburse later. She knew other programs had got started when determined Force members had forged ahead on their own, hoping for support from the powers-that-be. Most of these efforts had ended in success and had been funded post facto, the few failures being ones where the officers involved had opted to leave the Force or had been compromised by their involvement with the criminals they were targeting. Nora was unwavering in her determination that those would not be her outcomes. Using her own money was a serious risk, but she felt empowered by the fact that she was making an important career decision.

The vehicle, she decided, should be a van that could evolve into her mobile esthetician van, her means of transport. Nora had been saving for five years to buy another vehicle, so she had enough saved up to buy a used one.

Her phone call roused Gloria Newsom, her former buddy from Depot days, who worked mostly nights in the East End. "Hey, girlfriend! Great to hear from you! I've been watching the rental ads for you..."

Nora was happy to hear this cheerful voice. Here was someone who seemed to have chuckles bubbling up unbidden between words. Gloria continued, "You can have your pick of many medium-to-high-rise sub-lets, or take a basement suite in the East End."

"I wonder which place would be the lowest profile for me... medium is a four-story building? Hmmm... nobody in those glorified shoebox structures ever seems to pay attention to their neighbours... in a basement place, I might get a nosy landlady... I'll opt for a sub-let, thanks!"

"Righto, I'll make a first month's payment on a studio for you to hold the place for the first of July, and we can square up later."

"You're the best! I'll be there in a week. Can I camp on your couch for a few nights? Oh, and I need you to place an ad for a van... have the ad say a high-roof van with low mileage–something affordable like a 60s era Ford Transit?"

"Okay, why a van?"

"It's going to be my 'Cosmobile', wheels for my mobile esthetician business. What do you think? Good name for the business?"

"Gotcha! Cosmobile, eh? Like Cosmo Magazine! That's hilarious!"

That night, Nora had trouble sleeping, astonished at how far she had gone down this road. Next, now she had to tell Luke...

When Nora got to the detachment that morning, she put in a call to Luke at home. His voice was sleep-drenched.

"Uh, oh... so sorry, Luke. I forgot you had a late shift last night..."

"Yeah..."

"Uh... we haven't talked since..."

"Yeah?"

"I mean I think we should talk some more..."

"Are you still planning on that transfer?" His voice was no longer sleepy but insistent, somehow aggressive.

"Can I come and see you this afternoon? Are you off?"

"Yeah, I don't have a shift again until Sunday."

"Okay, I'll drive up and maybe we can go for a walk? It's going to be a nice day." She knew their talk would need privacy and that being outdoors in nature would offer both that and some tranquility.

"Yeah, I'll see you."

She wasn't sure when he said that whether or not he had been having misgivings about bothering to meet with her. Somehow his tone had sounded as if he were making some kind of concession.

~

That afternoon, Nora drove up to Glacier Lake to see Luke. She had taken many of the first steps to realize her ambition of becoming a Special Ops member, and now her hope was that she and Luke could at least remain friends. She respected and admired him; she wanted his good opinion, for him to be proud of her.

At first, she felt optimistic. They had gone for a walk around Glacier Lake proper, a scenic expanse of crystal blue water at the foot of near-by James Bay Mountain. Luke has been warm in his welcome at first, but when they began chatting about the beauty of the area and the potential for building a log home on the lake, she had become wary.

"It's an amazing location, Luke. Do you think now is the time to decide?"

"Yeah, I thought I should wait..." He peered at her closely, his eyebrow lifted in a query.

"I don't want to hold you back, Luke. If this is what you want, you should go ahead with it."

"But I can't see building a life here by myself, Nora. I have come to see it as a place for *us*, not just me! But now you seem to be making moves to leave and do something so dangerous and foolish..."

"But it's an important idea that someone can take on, and I want to be that someone! I've thought it through and developed a plan to hide my identity and to maximize my chances of breaking into the exotic dancers network. I've already sent in applications and got the blessing of DC Benton *and* Mike Sinclair."

"You are so naïve, Nora, it makes me heartsick. You could so easily get killed!"

"I think you just don't like the idea because it would take me away from here, so we wouldn't see each other so much. You are interested in me only as a girlfriend and a bedmate!"

"That's not true... I love you... I want much more..."

"But your wanting gets in the way of what I want... maybe I have ambitions too... you just don't see them the way I do!"

"Well, if that's really what you want, then have your fill! Just don't expect me to be waiting, hat in hand, for you to come back!"

"I don't expect *anything* from you, Luke! This. Is. Over. I had hoped to be able to part as friends, but I guess that was impossible. I have been very drawn to you, Luke, and I guess I loved you too, but you're asking too much. I have no choice but to say goodbye and really mean it."

This last bit had been beyond gut-wrenching. Driving back to Brandenhoff with tears streaming down her cheeks, Nora again examined her feelings for Luke. She had felt very attracted to him, seeing him as a potential life-mate, but knew she couldn't accept his expectation that she remain as a regular constable in the Force. She couldn't see herself pecking her way to corporal and then maybe sergeant, if she were fortunate, or not staying in at all, as the demands of marriage, and likely motherhood, interfered with career plans. She supposed he saw her as a life-mate too; two years before, after dating for three years, they had once broached marriage, and decided it was too soon. Now she was answering with her feet.

She didn't know if she would ever find another such love. She thought that, if Luke was serious, he would wait regardless of what he had just said. If he didn't, it wasn't meant to be. She felt regret, because she knew she had hurt him, but in her practical way, she hoped he would mend and down the road, accept her decision and continue to be friends, if nothing else. Still, there was an aching hollow within her heart. She had loved Luke. But was she still "in love"?

CHAPTER 26 - NEW BEGINNINGS: WEDNESDAY-MONDAY, JUNE 22-27

Nora puffed, lugging her bags up the three flights of stairs to Gloria's flat on East Pender in the heart of Vancouver's Chinatown. It had been a hectic, non-stop two weeks of finishing up her files at Brandenhoff Detachment, packing up her few possessions– the remains after her house-fire– saying goodbye to the locals who had befriended her, and breaking up with Luke.

Now at Gloria Newsom's door, she was about to begin a new adventure. When the apartment door opened, she experienced shock at the change in her old roomie, whom she hadn't seen in several years. Glo had been a full-figured woman with a thick mane of chestnut hair the last time Nora had seen her. Now standing in the doorway was a slender, waif-like creature with a pixie cut and a tattooed sleeve.

"Hey, Glo! How's it going? I hardly recognize you!"

Glo chuckled, a raspy cough interrupting as she beckoned Nora in. "I've been getting over an awful cold..." She caught Nora's look of alarm. "Don't worry, I'm okay... on the mend now. Come on. Let's get you settled. You can put your bags in that corner and use the couch. It folds down into a bed."

Later, over tea in her cozy suite jampacked with wicker furniture and Asian art, she elaborated, "I'm working at Main Street Station—a secondment to the Vancouver Police Department—as a liaison with Community Outreach. They're trying something different to stay in touch with the street people. The higher-ups have started moving some of their mildly disabled patients out of Riverview—you know the old Essendale—and there's just no place for most of them to go. They're ending up on the streets here. So I run a kind of store-front detachment office, doing all I can to redirect them to group homes, therapy centres... they're mostly institutionalized, right? They haven't fended for themselves in years... it's heart-breaking..."

"The change in my weight and the short haircut are all about being too busy to eat or fuss with my looks. I have eighteen-hour days sometimes... Anyway, that's my story. I keep super busy, and I'm still enjoying life." Glo broke out into her trademark chuckle.

Nora's reaction was philosophical. "I wonder how I'll look when this is all done..."

"By the sounds of what you've told me, you'll have some great clothes and a totally new look! Not that you aren't gorgeous as you are, but who couldn't use a little makeover, eh? Imagine getting the Force to subsidize you! Oh, hey! Speaking of the Force, what's happening with your course?"

"I'll head over to Burnaby tomorrow. Find out then..."

"You'll do great, girlfriend! Don't get me wrong. From what I've heard, it's not a cake-walk. It'll be exhausting and demanding, but you have the stuff to do it."

"Thanks, Glo. I wish the man in my life had felt the same..."

"Well, I found you a sub-let in a four-story building near the park on Keefer Street, close to here, actually. It's a residential area with street parking for your van."

"How's the entrance? Can everyone see the residents coming and going?"

"I don't think so. There are some shrubs around the entrance, so it's not noticeable. The rental agency said the turnover is high, so you shouldn't have to worry about nosey neighbours. You can move in July first."

∼

She couldn't start her new program until she had connected with her new detachment head and enrolled in the Special Ops three-month introductory course at the Pacific Region Training Centre in Chilliwack. The detachment visit to Burnaby at this point was a mere formality. She wouldn't be taking up any actual position there, as she would spend her time in Chilliwack on course. Her deployment afterwards was also unlikely to be in Vancouver as she aimed to focus her search up north along Highway 16. She had to be on someone's payroll, so she made the long trip out to the new suburban, provincial headquarters of the Force where she spent a full day filling out paperwork.

Next, she enrolled in her program at the Pacific Region Training Centre in Chilliwack. Gus MacGillvery, the Program Manager, did the initial interview and introduced her to Inspector Dave Yang, the Project Management Head for Undercover Ops.

Dave was a twenty-year veteran of the Force, ten of it undercover, and five at the Institute. He was a small man, and likely had had to stretch to meet the RCMP height requirements of five-feet-eight-inches. But he had the build of the proverbial brick shithouse. Solid muscle across chest and back and along all four limbs bulged through his uniform. He spoke in slow, careful phrases and checked her concentration with frequent, deliberate eye contact. His voice was a clear baritone with only the slightest trace of an Asian accent. He didn't smile, but made liberal use of his hands to emphasize his meaning. Yang, as the overseer for placement in the field, had the final decision about her suitability and readiness for undercover duty. Nora could sense the man's strength and authority.

"This is a tough program, Nora. We don't tolerate screw-ups. There are lots of rules and routines you must learn to execute flawlessly. Your success will depend on discipline and dedication... mostly discipline. You understand?"

"Yes, Inspector."

"Call me Dave, Nora. Rank doesn't merit a lot of attention in undercover work."

She waited for him to elaborate, his gaze penetrating hers as he seemed to weigh his next words.

"We don't have enough women recruits in the Special Operations Program. We value those we get, but we also don't make it easy for them because we can't afford to. I don't want to hear of any distractions that might interfere with your focus in training... So this is my way of saying that you need to put your past behind you. It has no place here."

"But Inspector... uh... Dave, I don't feel I have a past that will get in the way..."

"Let's hope not."

"Uh... Inspec...uh... Dave, can I ask? I want to develop an undercover character who can work with the dancers and travel to where they are... do you think...."

"Right now, all you should be thinking about is the preparatory program we offer here. There will be time enough for your idea of how to implement those skills once you've proven you can *execute* those elementary undercover skills flawlessly. Understood?"

Nora nodded without a word. Dave Yang rose from his desk to let her know the interview was over.

CHAPTER 27 - SPECIAL OPS TRAINING: MONDAY-SATURDAY, JULY 4-9

Her first week of Special Ops classes began on the evening of the first Monday in July. There were endless new protocols to learn. The program laid the curriculum out in a binder that had to stay at the school. Nora had to keep everything she learned in memory. No one could know what work she was doing there. If anyone asked where she was going when she was on her way to the Institute, she was to give an alternative address with a voice recorder-linked phone number so she could collect messages covertly. The same system would advise her of any information coming from the Institute. She would also travel to the Institute covertly by picking up a ride in a ghost car leaving from the alternate address. She would take classes every other week at night to enable her to take her esthetics training in the daytime. There could be no deviation from the established routine. Violation of the rules would mean immediate ejection from the program. At first, Nora was shell-shocked by the stringency of the process, but she recognized the need for such security. Her life and the lives of her contacts would be on the line.

THE SMELL OF THE *DOJO* WAS A FAMILIAR AROMA OF INCENSE, WOOD polish and foam rubber. Nora, remembering her *jiujitsu* etiquette, bowed on entering and bowed again to acknowledge the judo instructor, the *Sensei*, who waited for her and the other nine classmates of her cohort. The thick white cotton of her Judo jacket and pants felt stiff and unwieldy.

Paul Nixon, one of her cohort peers, stage-whispered to her from the back row nearest the entrance, "*Seiza Ni-Rei*, Nora..."

"Right, *Seiza Ni-Rei*–the kneeling bow..." She knelt, first on her left knee, then on her right, and bowed forward, remembering to keep her back and shoulders aligned.

In the front row, Callum Knox, the most qualified judoka of their cohort, intoned, "*Sensei Ni-Rei...*"

It's the call to honour the instructor...another bow in the Seiza position... I am starting to remember this stuff... next is Otaigi Ni-Rei, the bow to honour each other and our supporters...

The *Sensei*, none other than Dave Yang, began the drill.

"We begin with breathing... relax... breathe in... hold....breathe out...relax...breathe in..."

Nora allowed herself to become absorbed in the routine, feeling her lungs fill and then empty, her mind empty of other thoughts... her conscious focus on just the present... the exercise before her. The jujitsu and aikido were defensive skill-sets that would useful be when she was on her own in the field needing to subdue an aggressor. Relearning the drill was crucial.

The class continued rotating through the flexing for the bridge and the 'shrimp', the essential movements for grappling and sparring.

Oooh, I am going to be stiff tonight! I haven't done these exercises since Depot!

∾

IN THE AFTERNOON CAME REFRESHER CLASSES IN *KARATE* TO DEVELOP the strength of her hands. This was a more offensive skill-set, one which taught her how to use her body as a weapon, if necessary. Later, she would do a refresher in taekwondo for the kicking of the feet.

Before tackling any upgrade lesson in traditional *Shotokan karate*, Dave Yang made sure the new cohort practised the basic stances (*Tachikata*), punches (*Tsuki*), and blocks (*Uke*). "The kicks (*Geri*) we'll do later. They're the hardest to master," Yang told them.

Nora and her classmates spent the first half hour repeating the three most-used of the fifteen stances in *Shotokan karate*. Being able to assume the correct stance for a particular purpose and transition seamlessly into others in order to block, punch or kick needed to be instinctive. She couldn't expect to think about what stance she needed next for a specific routine. Her body needed to know.

"You need more weight on the back foot for the *Kokutsu Dachi*, Nora." Yang bent to adjust her back leg, pushing her rear shoulder down so the desired effect was achieved. His voice was clipped and clear, the monotone of instruction had a hypnotic quality that demanded focus.

"Next, class, transition to *Kiba Dachi*, side stance... good... remember the feet and knees must be parallel but pointing a bit inward... next... the front stance, the *Zenkutsu Dachi*. Remember, the back foot must be turned out thirty to forty-five degrees. Good. Now repeat... Kokutsu Dachi... Kiba Dachi... Zenkutsu Dachi... AGAIN..."

After the first half hour, Yang moved on to punches. He reminded them how to fold their fingers into their palm and to reinforce the index and second fingers by folding the thumb over top. "All punches in karate used the two knuckles of the index and second finger," Yang inspected everyone's extended hand to confirm correct form.

"Then, the punch or *tsuki* takes the shortest distance between two points...no right or left hooks with the *Choku-Zuki*, the straight punch! You can deliver it from the *Kiba Dachi*. With *Oi-Zuki*, the front lunge punch, same straight line for the arm, but this time your stance is *Zenkutsu Dachi*. Deviating from the straight trajectory costs you power." He demonstrated the two punches, transitioning from one stance to the next, then led the class is a half hour drill of repeated punches and changes of stance.

"We'll finish off with *Uke*, the blocks. Learning to block effectively is likely to be your most valuable *karate* move. You will use it to avoid a hit and maybe injury…"

Nora finished her session that night in a state of total exhaustion.

Jujitsu for the first three hours, then karate for another three! And we haven't even started taekwondo!

∼

"Ready for tradecraft, Nora?" Paul Nixon had been appointed her partner for the class where she would perfect her understanding of undercover technique.

"Yeah, I'm looking forward to it. You?"

Paul grinned. He was a tall, gangly fellow with a shock of carroty hair who looked more likely to be a farmer than a field officer. "It's where we get to playact and be sneaky. How much fun is that?"

Their first exercise was 'the drop', the art of making an inobtrusive transfer of an object in plain sight. In this case, they had to deliver a manila envelope in a busy bus depot. Nora sat reading a newspaper while Paul sauntered by. After looking at her watch, Nora set the newspaper on the seat, rummaged in her purse and then, acting as if she had forgotten something, hurried away leaving the paper behind. Paul sat next to the seat she had left and picked up the discarded newspaper.

"How did that go?" Nora asked Perry Udall, their tradecraft instructor.

"Your enactment was okay, but you looked Paul in the eye as you left. You have to remember to avoid any kind of contact."

Damn! This is hard. You have to act oblivious but really be hyperconscious…

"Thanks, Perry. I'll try that exercise again tomorrow."

"No, you won't. We have other ones to practice. You won't get back to this one until it shows up unexpectedly in a scenario we give you.

You won't get many pre-set trial transfer ops. The next time you'll just have to know to do it right."

Ouch! So that's what this was...'a pre-set trial transfer op'...next time I get no forewarning...they DO play hardball here!

"Now, we're moving on to the art of camouflage. There's a trunk of clothing in the prep room over there. You and Paul decide on outfits and go to Five Corners in the heart of downtown Chilliwack where Yale Road and Young Road intersect with Wellington Avenue. We'll tell you when."

"When do we do this? Now?" Paul was keen on dress-up.

"No. I said we'd *tell* you! Probably on Friday, *when* the time comes," Perry looked pointedly at Paul who gulped.

"How are we connected to each other?" Paul asked.

"I leave that up to you. Use your imagination. Now, I have other cadets to brief."

He left to work with the next set of pairs in the class.

∼

IN THE AFTERNOON, THEY HAD PRACTICE IN MAINTAINING A PERSONA FOR specified periods of time. Whereas the camouflage exercise was designed to hone their skill in melting into the backdrop, and staying anonymous while still effecting a successful maneuver, persona maintenance was an exercise in sustaining a false identity over time. The extent of subtlety and personal identity erosion that was necessary to maintain a covert status was staggering. Nora felt as if her body and face had frozen after standing immobile and impassive for hours on end. This exercise made the kids' play of staring contests seem silly.

"How long have you been in the biz...er...Trudy?" Perry had approached her to test her self-control of a teen prostitute façade.

"Long enough to make you for a cop, big guy! Get lost! I ain't doin' anythin' you can nab me for! I ain't 'aggressively pressing no solicitation', you pig!" She smirked and popped a pink gum bubble in his face.

Feels good to give him some lip for a change!

Udall seemed taken aback, and left her alone for a while. She unpacked another package of bubble gum to refresh her wad and chewed it open-mouth to reinforce her juvenile image.

At least they don't make me take up cigarettes again! It took me years to chuck that habit!

Udall came back twice more to check her appearance and expression for noticeable flaws in the 'hooker' character she had assumed for that afternoon's exercise. He seemed satisfied as he walked off attending to the checklist on his clipboard.

At the end of the session, when the 'all clear' had been sounded, she connected with Paul to decide on their plan for the camouflage exercise. After phoning to check at the Municipal Works office, they decided to become city workers planting a new flowerbed at the Five Corners. They would be able to be dirty-faced in city fatigues with their hair covered by bandanas and baseball caps. Face down in the flowerbeds, their identities should be safe for the requisite thirty minutes.

Udall came to see them early Friday morning, "For your camouflage practice, be there at noon on Saturday, tomorrow. I shouldn't be able to identify either of you for at least thirty minutes. That's a busy time in this town, so you have the benefit of a crowd to cover you. While there, your job is to uncover the drop left for you."

In an ever-shifting cycle of dramatic role-playing, she was a drug addict, a housewife, a teen prostitute, a bank teller, a municipal gardener. The work was exhilarating, yet exhausting. Some days, to shake off the conditioning, she had to stop herself at the end of a session and deliberate on her real identity, to reassemble and integrate the parts of her old self that had been submerged all day. At these times she needed to be alone, something not always possible at the training center. She discovered taking hour-long showers in the center's spa area was the solution. No one bothered her there as few women were in the program, and the hot water was unlimited.

BAM! BAM! BAM-BAM! The deafening din of small arms training was bearable only with ear protection. Nora wished there were some way she could just as easily block the pungent odour of gunpowder. The build-up of the fireworks smell was giving her a headache. Then, there was the strain of holding the Smith and Wesson sidearm itself. Although it weighed only thirty ounces and was just seven-and-a-half inches long, her wrist burned with an agonizing ache that even the support of her other hand could not diminish.

Aaron McAllister, her firearms instructor, came up from behind in her stall at the firing range. He tapped her on her shoulder to signal he wanted a word. "Don't rely on that extra support from your other hand, Nora."

She regarded him, her eyebrows raised in a question. She wasn't sure she had heard him right.

"Your left hand for support..." He pointed at her hold on the Smith and Wesson. "You won't be able to count on it in the field. That right wrist has to get stronger. I suggest wrist supports for now, but also start doing a regular work out with small, lightweight dumbbells. That should pay off in a couple of weeks."

Nora felt a small internal clench of her gut. She feared her capacity for more adversity was limited.

One more flippin' exercise to add to the routine! How much more? Can I do this? What happens when we star training with the C7, the new issue assault rifle? Those suckers weigh eight and a half pounds fully loaded compared to this Smith and Wesson- it's not even two pounds! My arms are gonna fall off!

CHAPTER 28 - SPYDER SEES THAT WILLOW IS TROUBLE: SATURDAY, JULY 9

Willow missed her hair. She had been growing it ever since she could remember and had only ever had it trimmed to clean up the split ends. Now, because Slash had demanded it, she had cut it to a short pixie and bleached it white blonde.

Whereas before while dancing, she had been used to using her luxurious cascade of mahogany tresses like a curtain to seduce the audience, now she adjusted her routine to minimize her sense of being naked and exposed. Her dance routine became one of hide-and-seek, where she dressed in masks and wigs as well as the usual array of pasties and g-string to conceal her true appearance until the very end, when she shed the wig and mask to reveal a pale, elfin face with huge, heavily made-up eyes and a pert little mouth. She had the look of a gamine, a rebellious, playful waif. It played well to the raucous crowds of young men confined to camp for weeks on end who saw in her a lost girl they could rescue, or a stray they could take home.

Week in and week out, Roxie, Fantasia, Bambi and herself were shuttled to cold water, wood-heated cabins to dress and wait for their separate gigs in cavernous cafeterias set up with the dining tables as dance runways, the taped music blaring from tinny speakers set high in the naked rafters. The places all smelled the same–beer, sweat, and cigarette smoke with a whiff of Maryjane once in a while.

And the clientele never varied either. "Comere, sweetheart! Let me see what's behind that mask... ya got such little bubbies! Like a kitten, ya are...here I got somethin' for ya..."

"Leave 'er alone, ya meathead. Don't you see she's more interested in someone younger, classier?"

"Like hell she is... Here, Willow, let me feel that silky skin..." He grabbed her leg and yanked at her g-string, his hands groping like great hairy paws.

She let them touch her, though both BB and Axel said she shouldn't. She enjoyed the idea of defying the bikers–until Axel intervened. Then, thrusting the miner's hand away, she turned tail and pranced for the other side of the room.

She had lost so much already: her innocence, her freedom, her love, her future...She despaired of ever seeing Vegas or Reno. She certainly never saw Slash. What could the bikers do, anyway, if she defied them? She stopped short, realizing what they *could* do–remove her access to dope, her one escape from this nightmarish reality.

Coke got her up and going in the morning. The buzz of a line or two every four hours kept her tuned up all day. Then a couple of beers and a few reefers put her to sleep when she had to stay over in camp for another gig the next day. The habit became so ingrained that, within a couple of weeks, she was hard-pressed to remember a day when she hadn't been semi-stoned...

∼

"S*pyder, ya gotta do what the doc said and lay off the booze!*" Bets had taken Spyder's bottle of twelve-year-old Whistle Pig Rye and was heading for the kitchen.

"Give it back, bitch! If I wanna drink, I'll fuckin' well drink, doctor be damned!" He lunged to pursue her and recover his rye, but he lost steam halfway up from the couch. His eyes blurred and he clutched his belly, then slumped back. "Gimme my bottle, Bets...com'on..."

Bets stopped on her way through the kitchen door and glanced back... Spyder was looking a little queer... "Spyder! What's up? Are you okay?" She rushed over just in time to catch him before he collapsed sideways into the chrome pedestal ashtray beside his easy chair.

"Hey, Old Man! Wake up! You feeling sick? Talk to me, Spyder!" She shook him gently, but could not rouse him.

She was on her way to phone Doc Roussopoulos to come over to check on Spyder when he rose up and bellowed, "Bets, you bitch, don't call the sawbones...I'm fine! Gimme my bottle, or I swear I'll deck you!" He continued, crowing like a cockerel, "Don't test me... I still got it and you know it!" He flexed his biceps and did a demo of his right hook as if to prove his claim.

"You're an old fool! Be damned if I'll try to help you anymore!"

"Gimme my bottle!"

"She threw it, narrowly missing his crown. It crashed against the wall behind his chair and broke, spewing up and over where he sat, drenching his head in twelve-year-old rye.

"There! Drink that!" Bets grabbed her purse and stormed out of the apartment behind the Hog Barn. She was due to be minding the cash register in the shop that afternoon, but in her fury, duty to Spyder was the last thing on her mind. Leftie would have to do overtime.

∼

Constable Stan Kozinski of the Edmonton Police parked his motorcycle outside The Hog Barn and wandered through the open door of the shop. In the back of the shop behind the cash was a middle-aged woman with a ponytail and a bruised cheek, her head down perusing some papers scattered across the counter. When he cleared his throat, she looked up in some alarm and gathered the papers together in a loose pile. He doffed his helmet with its eye shield so she could see his face more clearly. He was aware that the sight of a cop in full riding gear could be intimidating.

"Yes, can help you? Is there some problem?" Her voice was shaky.

"Hello, Ma'am, I'm Stan Kozinski with the Edmonton City Police. Are you the owner of this shop?"

"No, I'm the wife of the owner..."

"And his name is...?"

"Uh... Milko Zorman, but he don't like to use that name...he likes to be called Spyder..."

"Okay... uh... and your name, Mrs. Zorman?"

"Elizavetta.... What's this about?"

"Can I talk to Mr. Zorman... uh... Spyder?"

"Can I tell him what for? He's not very well... that's why I'm here instead of him... uh... so it needs to be important, ya know?"

"Well, Mrs. Zorman, I am tracing the whereabouts of a young girl named Stephanie Benson. We have been asked by the RCMP in Prince George to follow up on a report that she headed to Alberta. We have reason to believe that she came to Edmonton, and that she asked to contact the Devil's Brigade Motorcycle Club. That's the last sighting we have, from... uh..." he consulted his notebook, "The High Note on Whyte Avenue..."

"Uh... I see... uh... just a minute, I'll see if Spyder can get up..."

∽

"Spyder, Ol' Man, wake up! There's a cop here asking about a girl..."

Spyder opened one eye and glared at Bets, his face set in a grimace. "What kinda cop? What girl? What he say?"

"Edmonton Cop... 'Stephanie' he said her name was....Stephanie Benson I think... just that he heard at The High Note that she was asking for the Brigade."

"Those fuckin' idiots! They're not suppost to yap to the heat! That all he said?"

"Yeah, pretty much...he wants to see you..."

"I knew we shouldda got rid of that bitch when she showed up here..."

SPYDER, DRESSED ONLY IN A WHITE SINGLET AND PAJAMA BOTTOMS, hobbled over to the door leading to the shop and peeked through to size up the Edmonton cop. "Huh! He's a motorcycle cop, eh? I see his bike outside the front door. Interesting… I'll put some clothes on…"

When he emerged from the back, the cop was examining a rack of bike accessories. Spyder, in jeans and a black t-shirt, came to the back of the counter and thumped his fist to announce his presence.

Kozinski peered over his shoulder and then turned, his helmet balanced on his hip just above his sidearm, his gloves clutched in his hand. He grinned and nodded, "I apologize for disturbing you, Mr. Zorman, but we are concerned about the whereabouts of a young girl… uh… just seventeen… her name is Stephanie Benson, she's been missing since…uh…the last week of May…"

"What's that got to do with me?" Spyder growled. "Does she ride a Harley?"

"I don't think so… no… uh… she stopped in at The High Note on Whyte Avenue, and someone there directed her here to the Hog Barn, saying she could get in touch with the Devil's Brigade Motorcycle Club here."

"Well, I got no idea where she is. She mighta bin here, ya know. Some of our guys attract young ones, but our rules are no broads in the clubhouse, so she wouldna stayed long, ya know?"

"So you have a clubhouse here?"

"Yeah, so what?"

"Oh, I don't know. We just like to stay in touch with organized bike clubs… you know… stay in the loop."

"Well, the clubhouse is off limits to everybody except the Brigade… even Bets, the Ol' Lady don't go there…"

"What would I see if I did go there?"

Spyder cast him a penetrating look. "Nothin' much… bunch of tables and chairs, ashtrays, some couches, a fridge or two to keep the beer cold… ya know… a club for guys."

Kozinski slapped his gloves in his other hand. "Okay, Spyder, I hear you. Let's hope I don't need to get a search warrant."

"What for! I got nothin' to hide! Don't ya go making threats!"

"Or what?"

"Or... nothin'... I just don't think ya have any reason to get a search warrant..."

"Okay, I'll record that you might have seen Stephanie Benson, but can't be sure. Would that be accurate?"

"Yeah, sure..." Spyder watched Kozinki exit the shop and mount his bike.

I better get word to Slash... that little chippie is trouble...

CHAPTER 29 - NORA RECRUITS VEE: SATURDAY, JULY 9

After her first week at the Special Ops course, Nora's next stop in getting her transition to undercover underway was to connect with Vee at the Seymour Strip Club. She knew she should have taken this step before she had started her programs in Chilliwack and Vancouver, but time had got away on her. She could only hope Vee would be receptive. She phoned and left a message to contact her at Glo's number. Vee called back a few hours later, curious about why Nora was calling. Nora set a time to meet her for coffee at a Starbuck's, the latest hot trending brand from Seattle.

On her way to the meeting, Nora reflected on the efforts of M.A.D.D. and similar groups in Canada, which were having a noticeable effect on the transformation of social venues in the city. Trendy young people were populating the coffee shops much the way they saw on television that European youth did, and the mild, though wet, climate of Vancouver made workable the use of outdoor patios outdoors year-round, something not possible anyplace else, except for Victoria, the provincial capital across Georgia Strait.

Even knowing that Starbuck's was a popular location, Nora was astounded by how hopping busy the place was at ten in the morning.

She saw Vee huddled in a corner spot, hunched over reading a fashion magazine.

Nora reviewed her purpose for the meeting. The point was to do a preliminary screen to see if Vee would work as an inside contact, the fail-safe person she could count on to raise the alarm for her if anything went wrong. She had to trust Vee, and that meant she had to find out if Vee was beholden to anyone else. She had met her soon after Vee first started to dance, and the blonde beauty had already had a frightening encounter with their suspect, Franz Bernhardt.

The problem was Nora hadn't seen Vee for over a month, and almost anything could have happened in that length of time. Standing at the door of the Starbuck's Coffee Shop on East Hasting, she started by assessing Vee's appearance as she sat absorbed by the magazine. Nora was astonished to see the dancer dressed in her best imitation of Madonna: a very short shocking-pink jersey mini-skirt, black fishnet stockings, a lacy, black, off-the-shoulder see-through top bejeweled with glittery crystals, a large pearl-encrusted crucifix necklace, and matching pink fingerless gloves. Vee had topped the look off with a mass of her back-combed-tousled white blonde hair held in place by a huge black velvet bow and headband.

The young dancer looked up and waved, and Nora smiled a greeting, showing with a sweep of her hand that she was impressed by Vee's outfit.

Vee glowed with appreciation. "I'm so happy to be spending some time in Vancouver where I can find cool duds to wear. There's not much gnarly stuff I can find on the road...mostly just jeans and t-shirts."

"Oh that reminds me, Vee, I want to run an idea past you...What do you think of the possibility of setting up a mobile service to provide esthetics and costuming services to the dancers? Can you see this idea as a business that would attract the attention of the dancers? Would they have the money to spend?"

Vee looked blank. "I'm not sure what you're askin', Nora. What kind of business...?"

"Oh, I have this idea that I could do a mobile beauty parlour kind of business. I can do hair treatments... you know... cuts, dye jobs, extensions, stylings... and cosmetics service to offer all the usual toners, moisturizers, and lip and eye makeup, including false eyelashes. Aren't those things hard to find on the road?"

"Yeah...sort of..."

Nora sensed Vee's hesitancy and added, "I can even carry a line of showgirl stage costumes suitable for exotic dancers, quick to remove without damage. They've got this new stuff called Velcro that rips off really quick." She look a great breath to finish off the spiel. "Also, I can also provide breast and posterior enhancers for your off-duty outfits, you know, something to enhance your curves."

"Yeah... Wow...I... " Vee seemed speechless.

"I've even thought of a cute name for my business–Cosmobile! What do you think?"

Vee smiled for a moment at hearing the name, but her eyes were still troubled. "Aren't you going to be a cop anymore?" Her mouth gaped in disbelief.

Nora leant in closer to speak to Vee so others couldn't overhear.

"Vee, my plan is to use this business partly to see if we can find that guy who attacked you in Brandenhoff. We think he's done it before to other girls. In fact, we think he has killed others just as we are sure he would have killed you, if that taxi driver hadn't shown up the way he did."

"How is using this business going to help?" Vee's eyes showed her confusion. She was such an innocent. She'd never imagined that women cops would go undercover.

"I will be a businesswoman following the gigs of the dancers across the North, providing them products they need. I will dress differently so people I have met before can't recognize me. I haven't decided on the particulars yet, but I will let you know what my new identity is as soon as I get it worked out."

Vee's eyes widened in comprehension. "You're doing that for us? I never thought..."

Nora raised her hand to shush her. "I will pay you to be an agent helping us. It's a matter of life and death, Vee. You can't let on you know that I'm a cop. I will be someone you have met here in Van who has given you great deals on make-up and... clothing." She gestured to the outfit Vee is wearing. "I can stock these kinds of items as well as stage wear. Do you think my business will interest other dancers? I have to make it look like the real deal–a successful business venture. I'll look different and have another name. You will be the only one who knows. All I need you to do is introduce me to your dancer friends as someone you know and trust. You can help us get that Bernhardt creep into jail where he belongs."

Here was the crucial moment. Was Vee gutsy enough to become a paid agent? Nora continued, "Maybe a couple of hundred to start..."

"Geez, Nora. This is rad! I mean, I can use the dough too, of course, but... I was scared of that guy... I thought I was gonna die! Do you really think you can find him?"

"Only if you keep your cool, girl. I can't stress enough about how you have to behave like you've never known me as a cop. I'll be a trendy mobile hairdresser from uh... Winnipeg, moved to Van to learn my trade and set up business. My parents are dead, and I'm using my inheritance to get started. As far as you know, I know nothing about who attacked you... Have you told any of the other girls about it?"

"Yeah, of course! I didn't want them to do like I done... I told the girls doing that gig with me... uh... Chrissie, Mona and Tiffany. Why?"

"Then they likely told others... we'll have to make that a part of the story package. I have heard it from elsewhere, some other dancer... that's how I know. Also, I need to be sure you're clean. You know what I mean?"

Vee looked indignant. "I have a shower and wash my hair every day! What a thing to say!"

Nora chuckled to herself. "I mean you aren't drinking too much or using any drugs, are you?"

"I smoke cigarettes... sometimes... I just started cause I get bored sometimes. Do they count? I drink beer sometimes, too, but I don't like the taste. What kind of drugs?"

"We worry about the illegal kind... heroin, cocaine, meth... "

"Oh, no! No way do I do that stuff! That's needles, right? I hate needles even when I'm supposed to get them..."

"Okay. I will need you to see my control officer. Her codename is Hazel. The point of this short meeting with Hazel is so she can recognize you if anything happens. She will set you up with a phone number to leave messages for me in case you see the guy who attacked you. This will go into effect when you go back up to the Highway 16 tour which is when?"

"I am in Glacier Lake, Terrace and Prince Rupert starting in mid-October."

" Okay. So the codenames will need to be memorized by then. Bernhardt's codename is Hawk, and you'll need to know a few others, but either Hazel or I will organize that for you. I'll set up a time and place for a couple of weeks from now. How long will you be at the Seymour?"

"Until the end of July. After that I'm in the interior–Kamloops and Kelowna until September."

"When are you available for me or Hazel to contact you?"

"Anytime between noon and five is good."

As Nora rose to leave, she whispered in Vee's ear, "Remember, not a word to anyone about this deal, okay? I start my esthetics course this next week, so I won't have any spare time."

The girl nodded and acknowledged with a timid smile.

"Oh, yeah," Nora remembers her other reason for connecting with Vee. "Have you heard any word of Steph Benson, a young dancer like yourself, new to the biz?"

Vee looked blank. "No, I don't remember that name... but she wouldn't use her proper name, you know. Do you know her stage name?"

Of course! The blasted stage name again.

"No, I don't know... I'll find a photo..." She would ask Bill Benson for a recent photo of Steph, and then, hoping that the dancers' agency would have a photo display she could examine once she had established her own new identity, she imagined she could identify

Steph with her stage name. No time to lose. She needed to get started on her own transformation, so she would be ready to prep Vee before the dancer left town at the end of the month.

Nora came away feeling quite confident of Vee's commitment. On the one hand, the dancer was young and inexperienced, but on the other, she hadn't had long to be tainted by hanging out with dodgy characters. Their conversation made Nora believe no unsavory connections had already compromised her.

So she had a control officer, Bunnie Burrows, codename Hazel, an inside asset, Vee, a target, Franz Bernhardt, and a set-up, the Cosmobile, for her op. Next she needed a persona for herself, a set of codenames for the principal players, a communications system, and equipment to ensure her own safety.

She would send messages that Vee must memorize and if she wrote them down, burn. Those messages would refer to codenames only, herself as Candy and Vee, as Ladonna.

CHAPTER 30 - CHLOE AND HER COSMOBILE: MONDAY-WEDNESDAY, JULY 11-13

Nora began developing her undercover persona, Chloe Brigitte LaJoie, a tall, flaxen-haired, green-eyed, bronzed fashionista with an eye-popping wardrobe of the latest-fad stage-wear, wigs, and spike heels. Chloe walked with a seductive swing, wore her fingernails like scarlet talons, and kept her hair long with a fringe that appeared to obscure her gaze. She was a tramped-up version of Claudia Schiffer. Next she had to *sound* like a Southerner.

NORA OPENED THE DOOR OF THE LANGUAGE LAB AND PEEKED IN. THE space held a couple of round tables with chair and a dozen or so cubicles with tape decks and headsets.

A petite blonde woman in a sweater set and plaid kilt approached. "Nora Macpherson? Nice to meet you. We don't have many women in this program so I suspected it was you... I'm Suzanne McLeod, your dialectology instructor. How's it going?"

"Uh... fine thanks. Dialectology?" Nora was surprised that training in this skill set was available. "Are you a serving member, Suzanne?"

"Oh no, I've been seconded from UBC. They call me in when we have special dialect training required. So Dave Yang contacted me to ask if I could help you develop a Southern dialect. Do you want a Deep South drawl or the more northern Tennessee-based twang?"

"Uh... I haven't really thought about it... my persona is from New Orleans... uh... so Deep South, I guess."

"Oh lovely. And what is your undercover name?"

"Chloe Brigitte LaJoie."

"Now you must learn to say it as someone from New Orleans would say it." She said the name aloud herself a few times, as if examining its phonetic structure. "The drawl of the Deep South, tends to drop the "R" sound and it sounds softer to the ear as syllables are drawn out. So they would say 'Klo-way Bigitte LaJwah', and with a name like that, you've got a Cajun background. We must introduce you to Dixieland and Zydeco!"

"Zydeco? What's that? I know Dixieland...New Orleans jazz, right?"

"Now you must learn to say it as someone from New Orleans would say it." 'NawLeans'. Both your name and the city name have dropped the 'r' sound. And Zydeco? That's music inspired by the French Acadians–Cajun settlers to Louisiana in the 1700's–who combined it with Caribbean music and the blues. It's very animated, uses accordion, washboard, fiddle and guitar. Now say your name and city of origin for me..."

"I'm Klo-way Bigitte LaJwah from... uh... NawLeans."

"Happy to meet you. When you come here, you become her. Once in the door you are Klo-way. Your identity as Nora stops at the door unless we both agree to Time Out."

"Hmmm... Immersion training."

"Exa-actly, so Aah will speak to y'all in DI-ah-lect from na-ow on...And y'all use your ears to hear the pattern listen for dropped 'r's, elongated vowels and submerged 'i's, like 'Aah' instead of 'I'. Now let's jest talk about anything. The DI-alect will surround ya'll. We have some audiotapes for hearin' the sound. Ya'll kin start there listening to *Gaw-on with the Wind* read to ya'll by Tennessee Williams."

Nora was stunned by the immediacy of the transition they expected. She became Chloe LaJoie twice a week for four hours at a time starting that July day. Over the next few weeks, she learned to say 'PO-leece' and 'CE-ment'. Most important of all, she learned how to slow everything down so there was an extra count between each syllable. Almost as if everyone were talking underwater.

∽

ONCE NORA BEGAN AT THE BIANCA MCKAY SCHOOL OF ESTHETICS, the days flew by in a dizzying whirlwind of classes. Nora enjoyed being in downtown Vancouver at the school. Hairdressing, personal grooming and cosmetics courses were a break from the more stressful Special Ops training.

In the hair salons of the school, she learned the latest techniques in dyeing, streaking, crimping, and braiding hair. The new styles of the 1980's were off the charts in volume and texture. Teasing and perming ensured super-sized profiles; accessories like bows and barrettes were holdovers from a previous era that still found favour.

In the nail salon, she learned the trendy new French manicure as well as the traditional claw and kitten styles. In cosmetology, she learned how to change her appearance to enhance her features, and by extension, how to degrade her appearance to detract attention. Of course, this last objective was not something Bianca McKay taught, but it was knowledge Nora tucked away for when she might need to lie low.

Her fellow students at Bianca McKay were a mixed bag of high school graduates and older housewives looking for re-entry into the work market. There were a few men as well, but Nora didn't get to hang out with them. Mostly she partnered with three others, Molly, a young woman with multi-coloured hair and freckles, Catherine, a motherly, somewhat pious type, and Margot, a recently divorced thirty-year-old from Montreal who had moved to a make a fresh start.

One day, working to convert Molly's hair from its red and blue to an ash blonde, they happened upon the topic of dancers and their lifestyle.

Margot had known an exotic dancer in Quebec. "Yeah, Colette, she made a good living, you know? She said the gigs were easy, and the tips from the customers could be several hundred bucks a week! She worked three weeks and got the fourth off. I almost thought about it myself... but I'm too old now..." She shrugged with Gallic flamboyance.

Catherine, her brow furrowed as she worked the bleaching solution into Molly's hair, shook her head in distaste. "I pray to God I never have to worry about my girls thinking about doing that. What a horror! Having all those creeps looking at you that way!" She looked Margot in the eye, "How could you even consider..." Seeing Margot's face turn red, she stopped. "Uh...each to her own, I guess."

Nora couldn't miss the opportunity to ask Margot about what she knew of the lifestyle. "Margot, did your friend ever talk about whether she felt unsafe when she was out on the road? You know, whether there were problems with customers hassling her?"

"Oh, yeah. That was normal, eh? The girls were told to avoid talking to them when they were off duty. Not much social life for them... between and after gigs they stay in the dressing room or their hotel room. Back home in Quebec now, security is Hell's Angels. Nobody messes with the H.A. Even Colette stays clear of them."

"So that's usual in Quebec, having bikers work security for exotic dancers?"

"Yeah, I think so." Margot didn't seem perturbed. Catherine concentrated on brushing the peroxide into Molly's hair, her mouth set in a semi-scowl.

"Hey, ladies! What do you think if I shave my head and do a mohawk?" Molly's question instantly derailed the biker discussion. The other three laughed in shock. Molly glanced up grinning, "Just kidding!" They all burst out laughing.

Celine Starr, their colour treatments instructor, wandered by to see the source of the hilarity. "What's up, ladies?"

"Nothing much," Catherine volunteered. "Molly here wants a mohawk... not!"

"Well, that's for another class, right? We don't do cuts today..."

The four students glanced around, feeling chastised. Once Celine moved on, they all suppressed giggles trying to avoid being the source of any further disturbance in the class.

∼

LATER BACK IN CHILLIWACK, NORA HAD A CHANCE TO ASK DAVE YANG, "Are biker clubs a regular feature in exotic dancers' lives across Canada?"

"Oh yeah, they always seem to infiltrate the vice crimes: drug and human trafficking, prostitution, gambling, pornography distribution, illegal liquor sales. Exotic dancing lies on the verge, you know, on the fringes of prostitution. It's easier to get a girl to cross the line if she's already involved with taking her clothes off for money. From there, some think it's a quick hop to lap dancing and escort service–the euphemisms for prostitution."

"So my targeting their drug operation could uncover a lot of other actionable crimes?"

"Definitely."

"And any girl I recruit will need to know these risks..."

"Absolutely. You need to check your cover story for viability too. Will your idea stand up to scrutiny by people like that? Don't forget biker gangs are businesses at their heart. Don't underestimate those guys; they can find their way around a balance sheet or financial statement with no trouble at all."

Nora decided she couldn't wait to do a proper business plan.

∼

SHE PHONED VEE AT HER LATEST GIG AND ASKED HER TO CONNECT HER with some older dancers to try out her spiel because Nora needed to know how much business she could rely on from the dancers on the circuit. She asked Vee to get them on the phone for her.

"Hey, do you have your new look yet? I'm really curious…"

"No, Vee, but I'm working on it… I'll let you know soon."

"Okay, I'll talk to a few of the dancers at my club to see if they're interested. I don't know why they wouldn't be, because the prices you mention sound okay… I mean not super expensive. That stuff is ridiculous in the stores…"

∼

The next day, Nora had a chance to chat with Sapphire and Isis on the phone. It was her first chance to try out her new Southern Belle "Chloe" persona.

"Hi Sapphire… Ah'm Chloe LaJoie, a pal of Vee's who is startin' a biz'ness offerin' many of the things y'all could use for your gigs–cosmetics, wardrobe, wigs… Ah have some stunnin' new spike heels, too."

"Oh, wow… that sounds awesome… where's your shop? It's hard to find this stuff here. I usually have to send away for my costumes and pay shipping too. Then I have to wait 'til I'm back in Vancouver to pick the stuff up."

"Bless your heart! There's no shop and no shipping. Ah'm fixin' to offer esthetics services on the road… so y'all can get what's needed when y'all need it. Services like facials, manicures, pedicures, hair-do's… Ah even have a little studio set-up to take promo shots for y'all to post in the lobbies of your hotels… would this interest y'all?"

"Won't that be expensive? We don't clear that much per gig, you know… not after we pay for agency fees and bus tickets…"

"That's what Aah'm checking out, Sapphire, Sugah. How much of your income do y'all spend on costume and personal esthetics now?"

"I dunno… probably about half of what I clear?"

"So what is that if'n ya'll don't mind may askin'?"

"I clear about five hundred dollars a week… so I guess I spend two hundred to two-fifty on make-up, stockings, replacement of pasties and g-strings..."

"Well, Ah think y'all will spend a whole lot less with mah service, especially if y'all talk it up with the other girls. The more biz'ness Ah have, the cheaper Ah can sell, right? And it'll be much more convenient! So are y'all interested? Want to place an order soon?"

"Yeah, I am right out of... I gotta check... Hey and I wanna see the stuff before I pay... you know..."

"Okay, Sapphire, y'all go and check what y'all need and tell Vee. Aah'll get some samples for her to show y'all. Will that work? Now, let me have a chat with Isis, Sugah."

Within a week, Nora took enough orders to satisfy the bean-counters at Special Ops HQ that her business proposal was viable. She knew it needed to sound solid, so she could make a go of it. No flimsy accounting. The enthusiasm of the dancers she talked to assured that the project would seem legitimate.

She made a budget from some hypothetical money from HQ. The estimate of expense ran into the thousands. She had bought the car herself, so it wasn't part of the equation. But she would need maintenance money for the car, and merchandise to sell. After several days of exhaustive research in the worksite library, Nora estimated the operation would set Special Ops back at least ten thousand, more when she factored in travel expenses: fuel, car maintenance, lodging, food... Chloe would need financial support from the Special Ops people to the tune of at least fifteen thousand dollars over six months, if the operation lasted that long.

She calculated that she should submit an Operation Proposal outlining the basics of 'Chloe and her Cosmobile' as soon as possible. She wanted to get on the road in October when her Special Ops training was finished, before the north country roads became too difficult to navigate in winter storms. She had had her share of blizzard conditions and didn't relish white-knuckling through any more. By November, if she hadn't caught any fish, she would move south again to troll around the Southern Mainland.

CHAPTER 31 - COMPLICATIONS: THURSDAY JULY 14

S lash was back in Edmonton at the Hell Pit sleeping off another fifteen-hour straight run from Terrace. The trip had been his choice. Spyder wasn't expecting him. Slash had decided to approach Spyder about taking over the BC operation. He had made the effort to get it off the ground; he knew the turf. In his mind, there was no logical reason that Spyder should object. But Spyder was a visceral guy, and not always logical, so Slash knew he had to be careful. He got up and made enough noise so he would be heard upstairs. No point in freaking the old man out with wondering whether he was hearing things. He made the usual noises of someone starting his day: water running, toilet flushing, throat clearing...

Slash heard the footsteps on the wooden stairs as he was coming out of the shower. "Who the fuck's here?" There was no mistaking the hoarse, smoke-damaged voice tone of the club's chief.

"Just me, Spyder. I got in late and didn't wanna bother ya." In fact, Slash couldn't have faced Spyder the night before. He was too tired to think straight. The last couple of months had pushed him to the brink. The worry about the new venture with the bush gigs, coupled with his anxiety about Diablo and the Kraut had meant he hadn't slept easy in weeks.

"Watcha doin' here?" Spyder, as usual, could be counted on to cut to the chase without any conversational niceties.

"Well, the operation in BC is goin' good, and I thought I'd check in to keep you in the loop." These were both half-truths, but Spyder wouldn't know that. The bush-gigs were going to plan with the club making a big cut, but Slash couldn't stop worrying about the Kraut being a liability. Non-bikers were always suspect. As for keeping Spyder in the loop, Slash just wanted himself on the ground floor for the expansion plan. He had become determined to keep Diablo out of the picture.

"So what do I need to know? Bets! Gimme some bicarb of soda. My gut's achin' something awful... uh...where were we...yeah. What do I need to know? Is Diablo zeroing in on a property for us?"

"No, not yet. We need a business that's not on a main road, you know. Something a bit isolated, but still legit. Terrace is a small place so the fuzz will be sniffin' around sooner than they did here."

"Shit yeah...we don't need no cops nosin' around even before we get set up. We better get our front guy to do the buyin' when the time comes. I think the Doc owes us some time... he can do that... uh... speakin of cops nosin' around..."

Slash was on guard right way. Their Edmonton operation had never had much interest from the cops. "Yeah? What about the cops?"

"We had a motorcycle cop here a couple of weeks ago lookin' fer yer little back warmer."

Slash felt his mind go blank. "What?"

"Yeah, they said they were lookin' fer a Stephanie Benson... isn't that the piece ya called Willow? The cop said The High Note had sent him here..."

"The High Note sent the cops here? That's bullshit! We better pay them a visit and teach them some manners..."

"Yeah, but what about the little broad you brung here?"

"Spyder, I never told her to come here and never brung her neither!"

"Well, she's trouble! And you better deal with it! Ya gotta get rid of her! Who is she anyway? What's so special about her?"

175

"Lemme think about it, okay? I got other stuff on my mind right now..."

I can't tell him who she is...a cop's daughter! Spyder would have me rat packed!

The thought of a beating by the whole gang left him stunned for a moment, until Spyder's next comment made him pay attention.

"Like what? I thought ya said everythin' was goin' good out west..."

"Like who's goin' to sign the papers fer the new business and club-house... who's goin' to be the chief, ya know?" Slash's bluntness amazed even himself.

"Ya haven't even found the property yet, so what's the fuckin' hurry? Ya tryin' to cut my grass, Slash? I got news for ya..."

"I wanna know what yer plans are, Spyder. I gotta right to know..."

"Well, maybe ya gotta clean up yer own problems first... ya know? I gotta right not to worry about cops comin' here!"

"Yeah, maybe... if that's how ya see it..."

"Course that's how I fuckin' see it! Ya wanna be chief, ya gotta build yer own firewall!"

Slash left for the Hell Pit in a foul mood.

Fuck that bitch! She's a cop's kid! I shouldda known she'd be trouble. Maybe it's time for me to make the move...

∽

FRANZ WAS AT HIS RETREAT ON JACOB LAKE. THE WEATHER WAS FINALLY warming, and the lake glittered with sun dancing on the waves. He lounged on the deck of his rustic log cabin overlooking the lake, a cold beer keeping him company. The clearing with his helicopter pad lay behind. He had just finished the dock but hadn't bought a boat yet. So far, he hadn't had enough leisure time to contemplate the pleasures of boating or even fishing. But he vowed that day was coming... if only he could solve the dilemma of how to enjoy it alone...

He thought about the last girl, the beautiful, tall, blonde dancer whirling in her cage. She was the sort of female he'd been looking for, but he had to be sure whoever he settled on would stay. Here, there was no place to go, and no way to get out even if there were a place to go. If he could bring a girl here, she would have to stay until... there he stopped dreaming... she wouldn't want to stay with him once she saw... once she knew he couldn't do... she would just laugh too... there was no point. But he could still bring a woman here, play with her, try it on with her... God! Somewhere, there had to be a woman for him!

He shivered. The late sun was not enough to keep him warm outside. He wandered into the cabin to find something to eat and discovered a bagful of chewy, barbecued moose strips. Inside, it wasn't cozy as most cabins would be, instead almost spartan. The furniture was rough-hewn spruce, handmade without adornment or concessions to comfort like cushions. He stored his supplies on open shelving. To the right was the bed, a thin, double mattress on a cord-strung frame, a down sleeping bag lying open on its surface. A cast-iron Quebec heater with a kettle on top stood cold in the middle of the room with its supply of cordwood and kindling on the floor beside it. To the left, next to a washbasin sunk into a small counter, was a pump that brought water from the lake. A cast iron frying pan hung from a nail above the sink. In the back wall was a door that led to an outhouse, and further back, the helicopter pad clearing.

There were a few items of clothing hanging from hooks by the bed, but otherwise, little sign of creature comforts–no connection to the outside except for a CB radio sitting on the counter. Franz thought about how a girl would look here, lying on the bed, cooking at the stove, chopping firewood... he liked the idea. Then he shook his head, as if to clear the cobwebs. No fucking way. No woman would ever live out here willingly.

He decided that he would have to find a woman to bring here whether or not she wanted to cooperate. He couldn't wait much longer.

CHAPTER 32 - PROGRESS: MONDAY, JULY 25

In Chilliwack, Nora was a bright spark in the night-time Special Ops training sessions. Yang appreciated her intelligence and physical strength. She had absorbed the often-technical content of the course like a sponge. Still, Yang worried about whether she could maintain detachment from "the public", the civilian population. And she had a fiery temperament she had to learn to harness, and there was still the issue of the viability of her undercover identity. Nora was hoping that with time, they would ease up on their objections.

Yang had set the program up so that trainees could begin planning their own special ops once the instructors had signed them off on a varied set of skills. The first of them was "appraise and search", the nuts and bolts of most psychological police practice: how to size someone up, and how to make the case for the suspect's arrest. Next, many search details involved tactical take-downs–Nora had to hold her own in a knock'em out brawl without serious injury. To get ready, she had been swimming laps and pumping iron ever since June. Regular martial arts training had honed her reflexes and bolstered her strength. The posture of her tall, slim body was relaxed, but her grey-green eyes were alert. She was becoming fit for combat.

Her mastery of technical equipment was ongoing. The new

gadgets of the mid-eighties were the Polaroid cameras and Walkmans - portable audio to be used for relaying instructions and surveillance detail. The public would often see her enjoying her "music". She also had a small secret camera hidden in a large, gaudy pendant she always wore for sentimental reasons, because she would say it was the last gift her parents gave her. Last, the program equipped her with a custom-made, stainless steel, five-inch blade that was concealed in the sole of her high-button, wedge-heel, fashion black boots. A flick of her thumb made it a ready, lethal weapon.

By the end of three intensive months, she was slated to have learned much else: the use of new weaponry; negotiating traps, discovery and arrest; recruiting informants and maintaining police contacts; transitioning character, working in code, and last but not least, familiarizing herself with a wealth of new electronic equipment: computer records, secret cameras, sound recorders, body cams, and surveillance wiretaps.

Each night Nora returned to her sub-let exhausted. Her days Monday to Friday each week were taken up with esthetics training from nine to five. During alternate weeks, she worked on her Chilliwack coursework daytimes on Saturday and Sunday, and from six pm until two am during the week. Her schedule was so tight she had little time for anything else.

∽

"BILL BENSON HERE, CORPORAL GALLAGHER. UH... WE HAVEN'T MET, but we've been at the same meetings at HQ here in Prince George..." Benson's voice was taut and matter-of-fact.

"Yes, District Commissioner. I recognize your voice. How can I help you?" Luke was cautious and curious. What did Benson want with him? He knew about the daughter, Steph, through conversations with Nora, but Luke knew he couldn't allow Benson to know that. He waited for clarity, trying to imagine the District Commissioner's motive for singling him out.

"One of my reasons for calling is to follow up with you on the

BOLF for Friedrich, Franz or Frank Bernhardt... uh... I think the initial BOLF named him Dieter Bernhardt? I notice Nora Macpherson has updated with a note that his name is likely Friedrich Bernhardt and not Deiter Bernhardt? I have been wondering what progress has occurred... partly because my daughter has gone missing in this area, and if this Bernhardt is as dangerous as the file suggests, I want to know what's being done to locate him. I'm looking at the file update sent this week, and you have made the most recent notation ...uh... about a complaint at Justice Silver Mine south of Moose Forks... something about an altercation between Mr. Bernhardt and a foreman at the mine?"

"Yes, DC, the foreman... uh... Kyle Parsons, made what he thought was a humorous comment about an article of female clothing hanging in the helicopter's cockpit on the dash. Mr. Bernhardt took great exception to the comment, and Mr. Parsons defended himself against what sounds like a fairly serious assault. Unfortunately, he didn't want to press charges... something about reliable helicopter pilots being hard to find..."

"Too bad... we need these people to step up... Oh well, can't be helped. But keep your eyes and ears open for this Bernhardt guy. I think he's trouble." Benson cleared his throat, as if to suggest further comment.

"Uh... another reason I am talking to you is that I endorsed Constable Macpherson for Special Ops training a while back, and I am concerned that she has a reliable Force member providing back-up once she is ready for the field. I would like you to be that back-up."

Luke was uncomfortable. He swallowed deep and ventured a response. "Well, on the first point, about the BOLF for Bernhardt, as you know, DC, a BOLF is a pretty open-ended thing. I believe Constable Macpherson made some initial inquiries and found out that there is a Friedrich Bernhardt who's a helicopter pilot with the Loch Doon Service in Prince George. But the ID is not conclusive... some discrepancy with physical description, I believe, which she mentioned when we last talked about this case." Luke tried not to think about that last time he had seen Nora.

"Well, Corporal, as I'm sure you understand, I want to know everything is being done to locate Stephanie. I think wherever she is may be connected to the movements of the Devil's Brigade. So I want to stay on top of their movements. Now I know that Constable Macpherson has moved detachments. I thought Steph had clicked with her... had connected enough, you know..."

Luke was dumbfounded. He couldn't imagine Nora keeping such a personal sense of connection from the father.

Sensing the father's distress at not hearing any word from his daughter, Luke asked, "Do you mind giving me a brief recap of Stephanie's history and what you've heard about her since her disappearance in May?"

"There aren't any witnesses to the girl's first involvement, but there were reports of the Edmonton outfit, the Devil's Brigade, around Prince George at the time. She went missing for the first time in Prince George in early May. Since she disappeared the second time, she hasn't been seen anywhere along the circuit. I've had District-level eyes on the Brigade for several weeks with no results. She seems to have gone to ground. After the second disappearance, when she ran off with the Pine Ridge truck in late May, we haven't even had a sighting of the stolen truck. That, in itself, is unusual. Often thieves abandon stolen vehicles; the license plate is stripped off and the keys missing. I remember that from my days as a regular patrol cop. But the licence plate hasn't turned up on any other vehicle either.

Luke sensed that Bill Benson had been a good street cop in his younger days. "Given that we know Stephanie is connected to a motorcycle gang, we can assume that the truck has ended up in a 'chop-shop' that will dismantle it and sell the parts," Luke suggested.

At the other end of the line, Benson harrumphed. "Yeah, I don't care about the truck, except it's evidence to track Steph. Don't tell Pine Ridge that." He chortled, "I'll make good that loss, don't worry. Uh... ahem...!" He cleared his throat. "I'm following up on this BOLF for Bernhardt because I have a hunch he's connected. This assault he's alleged to have done happened just after Steph ran from Pine Ridge. He's an independent contractor who owns his own chopper, so all we have is his helicopter flight records, the ones he keeps for insurance or maintenance purposes."

Benson was silent for a moment. On the long-distance line, a faint crackle took up space in the quietness. Luke leapt into the silence. "There must be some way to trace him through those records."

"If you're sure he's the guy who attacked the dancer, we can trace him through MOT."

Luke's eyebrows raised in conjecture and his face lit up. "We can get a records search through Transport Canada, eh? They have annual paper records on file? And you can network our access to that info? Then we can check to see where this guy's been flying... uh... we didn't do this already because we had the wrong name... and it's easier at the District level..."

On the other end of the line, Benson coughed, and Luke got the distinct impression the commissioner was teary-eyed. Luke could hear his labored breathing.

"Yeah, the thing is, District Commissioner, it was an isolated attack against this young dancer... Vigdis Dahlberg... who wasn't available for long, and didn't seem too eager to file charges, so the case was left on ice–just the BOLF out there hanging around like a dirty smell. Members have had other priorities; at least, that's how it looks to me. In any case, I'll update the BOLF to include the info that Bernhardt's likely working for Loch Doon Helicopters. That way, anyone who checks the file will be able to follow up." There was still no reaction from Benson.

"Uh... Commissioner..."

Benson's voice steadied. "I've checked the record. There's been a thorough investigation of the pub in PG where Stephanie went missing the first time, and of the one in Prince Rupert, where local RCMP apprehended her while they were doing a check on off-sales irregularities... almost on a fluke... The pub in Rupert reported seeing bike gang members during the time that Steph was there, but they seemed to keep a low profile. The management didn't have any particulars about the name of the gang. Anyway, I'm willing to bet it was this Devil's Brigade." He said the name as if he had a rotten taste in his mouth. "In any case, I'm willing to bet there's a connection between Bernhardt and the Devil's Brigade…"

"DC Benson, as I've said before, we need to keep looking. What you've just suggested could very well be true. My nose tells me there's more to this than just your daughter missing."

"I'm glad to hear you say that, Corporal. It makes my decision to involve you as back-up that much more fitting. You sound as if you have some skin in the game…"

"Yes, DC. Absolutely…. finding this perp is important…"

"Right then. I'll sign off, Corporal."

"Do you want to order some action or anything?"

"Yeah, just an idea, mind… I'll get in touch with Special Ops Program in Chilliwack on an informal basis and see how Constable Macpherson's doing. She asked me for a recent photo of Steph to track her when she goes undercover. Maybe she's made some progress. What I want is for you to inquire as well… as her back-up in the field, you should stay in touch wherever possible."

"Undercover Ops Program Training won't talk to me…." He didn't want to add that Nora might not either.

"Tell them Prince George HQ asked for an update. Tell them you've been appointed Constable Macpherson's back-up in the field once she comes up to North Division. Use my name, but only if you have to."

"Righto. Will do, District Commissioner… and… we'll find her. I'm sure we will."

~

LATER THAT DAY, LUKE MADE AN OFFICIAL PHONE CALL TO INSPECTOR Dave Yang of Pacific Region Training Centre in Chilliwack, inquiring about Trainee Constable Nora Macpherson on behalf of North District E Section, AKA Prince George HQ.

"Yes, Inspector, I have been tasked with getting an update on a trainee you have right now, Constable Nora Macpherson."

"Your regimental ID, please?"

"Her regimental number?"

"No, yours first, please."

"Uh... 543LK."

"Your reason for contacting this member?"

"I am following up at the request of PG HQ. I have also been designated as her back-up in the field."

"Yes, but what do you expect to learn? This member is in a top-secret program. No breaches of confidentiality are possible."

"We believe she can help us in our inquiry into a BOLF for a Friedrich Bernhardt. I also want to apprise Constable Macpherson of my appointment as her back-up in North Division."

"Her regimental number?"

"706HS."

"I'll check to see if we can relay you any information."

CHAPTER 33 - NORA ENCOUNTERS SNAGS: MONDAY-TUESDAY, JULY 25-26

Corporal Gallagher's call intrigued Yang. The Force conducted follow-up in a much more formal and faceless fashion. Letters about recruits, identified only by their regimental numbers, were scrutinized and assessed. Few recruits saw anyone or contacted anyone in person during their training period except for the designated Chilliwack staff. This inquiry from PG HQ needed to be an emergency before it would matter.

The next day, Dave Yang sought Nora out. "You seem to be managing the work load well, Nora. This course is exhausting, especially when trainees are carrying on with other course work as well, as you are. The reason I am checking in today is that I've had an inquiry from DC Benson in Prince George who recommended you for this program. He wanted to know how you were progressing and whether you would be in the field on schedule."

Nora tilted her head in speculation. She hadn't expected Benson to be keeping tabs on her, but in hindsight, she realized it only made sense and, in a way, she felt flattered. Given the high profile given this particular file and the initiatives already in place, such as the BOLFs and the APBs, he might see her as his best bet to find Steph. To Dave she asked, "And will I be, do you think?"

Dave's brief nod was somewhat reassuring. "Yeah, I can see you operational by October for the limited op you are planning. You should be putting together the provisional budget and arranging all the backstory cover you think you'll need."

Nora looked up in surprise. "You see me ready by October? That's great news, Dave. Thanks!"

"Yeah... uh... two other things. Corporal Luke Gallagher has also called me to inquire whether you can help with a BOLF you issued for a Friedrich Bernhardt."

Nora blushed, lowering her head to avoid Dave's gaze. "I... I didn't think he would do that... sorry..."

"I don't know, Nora. It seems legit. He was asking on behalf of Prince George HQ... Why is that a problem? Do you know the corporal?"

"We... uh... were in a relationship, but I ended it before I came down here..." She gulped, willing herself not to lose self-control.

"Remember what I said about distractions, Nora..." He caught her eye to emphasize his point.

"Yes, Inspector."

"Dave, Nora. Anyway, I gave no information to Constable Gallagher, who was merely relaying a formal request for assistance with this Friedrich Bernhardt. However, he did relay one other piece of information. DC Benson has appointed him back-up for you in North Division once you are out in the field."

Nora felt embarrassed and irritated. What was Luke doing, trailing her? Being appointed back-up for her? She would need to get *that* changed before she went undercover for real. Moreover, she would be clear when she communicated with Luke that their relationship was over whether or not he accepted the fact.

No doubt he asked to be back-up to keep tabs on me! Well, we'll see about that!

Nora assured Dave, "I'll write him at his detachment and give him my PO Box address so he can write with questions he has about Bernhardt. However, everything he needs to know is in the file. I don't have any additional info."

This feels like a fishing expedition... any excuse to contact me...

That evening, she wrote a formal communication to Corporal Luke Gallagher in care of the Glacier Lake Detachment, telling him the file number of the case relating to Friedrich Bernhardt. She reminded him that the number was all he needed to follow up.

He should have been able to find it himself!

She did not bother to give him her PO Box address.

If he really wants it he can go through Benson!

She also asked that he request someone other than himself be assigned as her back-up. The tone of her communique could leave no doubt her message was professional and impersonal. She could not afford the luxury of venting the anger she felt about Luke's interference.

∼

CHLOE DROVE A NEON-PINK 68 FORD TRANSIT WITH "COSMOBILE" painted in fancy gold paint script. She offered an array of goods and services: cosmetics, wardrobe, bouffant "big hair" wigs, fly-away stage costumes, sequined satin bras, pasties and G-strings, and to pull it all together, a portrait service to create promotional shots for the dancers to display in their hotel venues and if possible, for BawdyWorks to put in their catalogue and display in its lobby.

She made an appointment to run her proposal by Dave Yang for his approval. His reaction was much less positive than she had hoped. "I thought we had gone over this issue before, Nora. What makes you think a person like this could infiltrate the dancers, much less the bikers' command structure on the Northern circuit? Isn't the style up there more rough and tumble? A woman like this would definitely look out of place. And what evidence do you have that the dancers could afford the services you would offer?"

Nora was speechless. Dave's reservations were understandable. How could she justify her persona as Chloe? She had to put that question on the back burner for now. However, in practical terms, she *had* done the legwork to establish a market for her services.

"Dave, here are the orders I took in just one afternoon in early July. These women *are* interested in what I have to offer. In fact, most of them complained about having trouble accessing these products on the road."

Dave regarded her, his eyes opaque. "I can't okay this plan yet, Nora. Your look needs toning down. But I will authorize preliminary funding for the Cosmobile inventory but you have to concentrate on finetuning your undercover identity. Also what do you know about your target? Have you done any recent research on the Brigade to know what you're up against?"

Nora realized he had a point.

CHAPTER 34 - COMPLAINTS, CLASSES AND COMMERCIAL REAL ESTATE: TUESDAY, AUGUST 2

Bambi and Willow were hanging out in the cookhouse lounge of the Justice Silver Mine camp, lying on the couches waiting for their rides out. They, and the other two girls who were still dressing, had danced their gigs earlier in the day. They were not often able to hang out alone. Usually they were kept in their rooms in camp until the chopper was ready to go. But today was different because the work camp staff were short on workers after the long weekend, and the rooms the girls usually used were being cleaned early.

"Did Slash mention anything to you about getting us some new costumes, Willow? I showed BB my collection of stage wear the other day and asked for some new stuff. He said I need to take it up with Slash. Then, I was talkin' to Roxie, and she said Slash told her he might get us some new gear if we were good... what *that* means, I've no idea!" Bambi's bronzed skin was blotched in annoyance.

"Listen, I wouldn't put much trust in Slash comin' through with any promises. My experience is he talks a good line 'til he's gotcha where he wants, then he forgets, or worse, becomes a complete jerk!" Willow recognized that even thinking about Slash still filled her stomach with butterflies. How could he be so callous?

"Well, that's a biker for ya. Nobody ever said they were boy scouts!"

Fantasia and Roxie wandered out from the washrooms. "Hey, Roxie, any word about new outfits for us?" Once Bambi got a hold of a beef, she was all terrier.

Roxie, her jet-black hair tied up in a top-knot, regarded Bambi with a blank stare. She shrugged. "I dunno."

"We can hardly be elite string dancers for the fancy guys in town with our pasties and g-strings in tatters. What do they expect? We're goin' to replace our own stuff? They don't let us off the leash long enough!"

Bambi's voice had been gaining volume so Willow moved to shush her. "Hey, keep it down, Bambi. You want the meatheads coming over and pawing us as an excuse to shut us up? Diablo ain't here on this run, but Axel will shut you up!"

"Oh, you're such a princess, Willow!" Roxie chortled. "Always complainin' about somethin'!"

Bambi rose off the couch to confront Roxie. "So you don't know about Slash getting' us new costumes?"

"No, I don't. Like. I. Said." She sat down on an easy chair and opened up a *National Enquirer* and began to scan the front page. The headline insisted Elizabeth Taylor was hot on some Latino boyfriend...

"But you told me the other day..."

"I said he mentioned 'MAYBE', nothin' fer sure."

"Like I said," Willow interjected. "He talks a good line, but he doesn't come through." She caught Bambi's eye as if to reinforce her point.

"Well, I can't see waitin' much longer. If Slash wants to keep us on side, he better pony up with some new stage wear. I don't like looking like a ragamuffin." Bambi collapsed on the couch as if to punctuate her spineless rag doll state.

∼

IN THE LANGUAGE LAB AT CHILLIWACK, CHLOE WAS HARD AT WORK. "Aah would lak to make a proposal... uh... to bah ya'all a new faar ray-ed TEE-bird." Chloe was immersed in her dialect practice, repeating the phrases and sentences played for her in the taped lessons. "Aah would lak to do that be-fo-wah I bah myself a new yellah dray-ess."

"Foh dinner, we had grayn pays 'n chitlins cuz Mamma said so! Mamma mebbe never had no scole, but she shure knows how to cook and to play the GUI-tar!

"Mah truck had a flat taar. Ya'll are so swate to help fix it! Come own, Aah'll bah ya'll a drink."

"One, two, thray, fo-ah, Aa'm gonna hit the do-ah."

"Why Chloe, Aah declare, ya'll are comin' along lak a house on faar! Now remember, ya'll gotta be able to talk lak this until the cows come home! It don't matter whether ya'll are slap worn out. Remember to smile lots, and ya'll be fine and dandy. Jest keep REviewing those phrases and expressions, Aah give ya'll." Suzanne McLeod, Nora's dialectology instructor, was nothing if not encouraging and up-beat.

Chloe grinned her best. "Yesiree. Aah reckon Aah was goin' to hell in a handbasket with mah op until Aah started yer class, Ma'am."

"Oh, heaven to Betsy, ya'll never was that des-per-ate! Ya'll got gumption, girl!"

"Aah'm fixin' to make this work, Ma'am."

"Aah'm shore ya'll kin do it, Klo-way!"

∽

"I THINK I FOUND SOME PROPERTY FOR US, SPYDER!" DIABLO'S VOICE always rose an octave when he was excited. Spyder thought it made him sound like a girl.

"Yeah? Whatcha got? How much?" In the background, Bets clattered some dishes in the sink. "Shaddup that racket, bitch! Can't ya see I'm on the phone? You ain't with the bush gig, Diablo? I thought you was runnin' security for them?

"Nah, I sat this run out to get the scoop on this place fer us. It's an abandoned loggin' camp on a dirt road about twenty miles offa the highway on the road to Rupert. The site's still got power and the out buildin's are in good shape. All the sawmill equipment is gone, but there's a sawdust and slash burner, a five hundred... uh... and fifty gallon fuel tank, a main building fer a clubhouse and a coupla bunkhouses roughed out with built-in bunkbeds. What's missing is woodstoves in the... uh... bunkhouses for heating and stuff to make a kitchen. They want fifty thou fer it as is."

"Runnin' water? Has it got shitters?"

"Yeah, there's a well so's ya can pump inta the clubhouse buildin' and there's outhouses fer both the clubhouse and the bunkhouses."

"And there's power, ya say?"

"Yeah, the place is wired for 'lectricity."

"Why are they sellin' it?"

"The loggin' permit ran out. The site is bare except fer a few trees aroun' the buildin's.

"Humph..." Spyder cleared his throat. "So we could be sittin' ducks if the cops wanta get cute... ya know... no place to hide."

"But if we say we're buildin' a tree farm... ya know... fer Chris'mus trees 'n stuff, they'll leave us alone, mebbe."

"I dunno, Diablo... need to think about this... where do we get the baby trees...you know...the ...uh...seedlins? To make it look legit? Do you wanna do that kinda work? Grow the seeds, plant'em... now maybe if'n it was weed, that be diffrent..."

"Well, mebbe we can do that, too! The climate is a bit wet though...need greenhouses 'n grow lamps, I think..."

"Nah, a grow-op so close to town would be a magnet fer the heat. I think ya need ta keep lookin', Diablo. This place sounds too complicated. Here, hold on yer ma wants ta say somethin'."

"Dimitrios?"

"Yeah, Ma?"

"I think ya should come 'n see yer dad soon...uh..." Before she could say more, Spyder grabbed the phone.

"Never mind her, Diablo. She don't know what she's talkin' about..."

In the background, Bets raised her voice but got only one syllable out before being cut off, "Spy–"

"Okay, I'll keep lookin'."

"Yeah, get an ol' farm mebbe? We can always say we're a commune...ha!"

CHAPTER 35 - PREPARATIONS ALL ROUND: WEDNESDAY, AUGUST 17

After Dave Yang's heads up about researching the Brigade, Nora got busy digging into the recent chatter along Highway 16. Bunnie was helpful.

"The leadership in the Devil's Brigade is Serbian, arrived from what's left of Yugoslavia. We have had our share of trouble from that area. They come over, many of them trigger-happy ex-militia and infiltrate the vice scene wherever they land. We've had a number of them up on protection racket and procuring charges in the city this last year or two. They're nasty customers, so be careful.

"We have also been hearing about them from the Edmonton PD who want them for all kinds of vice charges. Their chief is a Milko 'Spyder' Zorman and the word is he's not too healthy, so that usually means instability in the ranks and between the clubs.

"Not much has been seen of the other top Brigadiers lately. Word is they are looking for a new site for a clubhouse, probably in Northern BC. We think they're up to something big, but nothing clear yet. Their second-in-command is a thirty-five-year-old ex-militia type–Slavko 'Slash' Dracul, a pretty nasty customer with no convictions, but a thick file with the Edmonton PD."

"Do we know if the Brigade is using helicopters to do their business in the north?" Nora's instincts said there had to be a connection.

"Luke Gallagher has posted that he's doing some cross-checking with MOT to see if he can connect the Brigade to Bernhardt's jaunts, but nothing definite there either."

Of course...him again...

～

OVER THE INTERVENING MONTHS, CHLOE HAD ALSO CONTACTED A variety of strip clubs to create her backstory. She introduced herself and queried their interest in a mobile specialty esthetician service. Her calls to Calgary, Edmonton, Seattle, San Francisco, Las Vegas, Reno, and Palm Springs had been promising. All had said they would keep her in mind. That was, in reality, all she wanted. She had followed up all the phone calls with bright, glossy, promotional flyers with photos of her best-selling lines of products. The flyer included a self-portrait of Chloe with her 'Cosmobile' as a backdrop. A China Town Post Office Box provided contact. If BawdyWorks checked out her story, the places she had sent the flyers should have enough recollection of her to confirm her existence. That was all she needed to back up her cover.

In fact, Chloe's mobile salon was not just a cover. It evoked every young fashionista's dream of making an indelible impression. The magazine rack featured an impressive array of bright, glossy stagewear catalogues, (virtually art books themselves and certainly rarer), and she had plastered the walls of the interior with posters of famous photographic models: from Madonna, Tina Turner, Cyndi Lauper and Debby Harry to Joan Collins and Princess Di. These images gave the specific looks that potential clients would desire. They could say, "Make me look like Brooke Shields!" or "I want a Debby Harry look." Now, having finished her Bianca McKay coursework, Nora as Chloe more or less had the skills and product to deliver on those requests.

One afternoon in mid-August, Chloe phoned BawdyWorks and chatted with Tommy Cobb, the manager. Her aim was to use Bawdy-

Works as the starting point of her search for Stephanie Benson. And to confirm her suspicion that Tommy Cobb was supplying high-end dancers for illegal, under-the-table activity, an idea Yang had relayed to her from Bill Benson when he had sent her a grad photo of Stephanie.

Nora assumed the soft Southern drawl she has been practicing for her new persona.

"Howdy Mistah Cobb. Ah'm Klo-way LaJwah. Aah do believe Aah sent y'all a BRO-shure advertizin' mah new MO-bile esthetics biz'ness?"

On the other end, she could hear a sharp intake of breath and a clearing of his throat. "Uh, yes, Ma'am, I think I remember seeing that in the mail."

"Aah reckon we could do each other a big favour by working together. Aah'm sure yer dancers would be tickled pink with some things Aah have to show them."

"Oh, yeah? What do you have they can't find in the stores here? I mean, we have a wonderful selection of retailers here in Vancouver, you know."

"Oh, Sugah, heavens to Betsy! Aah can get mah service to them on the road! No matter how slap worn out those girls are, they have to truck around to find their costume pieces when they're in the city and supposed to be restin', and then, they can be sure-as-all-get-out that the stuff won't last for the whole tour. Somethin' is always givin' out–spike heels, HO-siery, pasties, garters, I don't know what all–Aah can keep them supplied, when there's no place to replenish their little bits... y'all know what Aah mean?"

"Well... uh.... Miss LaJoie? Yes... ahem... I can tell you have a feel for the business. I think it would delight the dancers to have access to your products while they're on the road. I'd be very interested to meet you in person, myself. You sound like a very exciting lady..."

Nora felt her antennae rise. Tommy Cobb sounded genial but vaguely oily, as if he were assessing her boundaries and defenses. But he'd sounded intrigued by her proposition, for sure. She filled him in on her business plan, and how she had made connections in other major centers in the States and Alberta.

"Well, Miss LaJoie, you come in to the office to let me know when you have the business up and running. I'd like to see the kinds of things you'll have in stock. Then I'll do what I can to connect you with some clients. How's that sound?"

"Fine and dandy, Sugah! Mah biz'ness ain't worth a lick without clients! Aah should be able to get back to y'all later this month. All righty? So long for now, Mistah Cobb!"

Afterwards, Nora felt the urge to have a good hot bath.

∽

IN A KAMLOOPS HOTEL, VEE WAS KEEPING BUSY STUDYING HER NOTES from Hazel. Her roommate, Chrissie, was in the hotel bath for an extended soak so Vee knew she had some time to memorize the list of codenames she had kept hidden in the bottom of her stocking bag. She recited the list in a whisper.

"The Devil's Brigade is called Karma; Nora is... uh... Chloe LaJoie, code name–Candy; Nora's control is Hazel; the creep...uh... Bernhardt is codename–Hawk; I'm Ladonna, Slash is Wolf; BB is Lucky; Diablo is Loverboy; Stephanie, whatever-her- stage-name-is- is Angel; .Tommy Cobb is Slug, HA! I guess Nora....uh... Chloe doesn't like *him*! I don't know who these others are, but I probably need to memorize them anyway... Corporal Luke Gallagher is Osprey, Inspector Dave Yang is Eagle and Milko Zorman is Grizzly... hmmm... I think Diablo's last name is Zorman... I wonder if they're related?"

Vee sat memorizing for a half hour until Chrissie made noises to get out of the tub. By that point Vee was able to recollect the list by heart. She felt somewhat confused about why she needed to know so many, but still had faith that Chloe knew what she was doing.

Vee knew she would be rotating back into Vancouver for September and October, so if she had any worries, she could contact Nora/Chloe then.

~

LUKE TACKED THE WALLET-SIZED GRAD PHOTO OF STEPHANIE BENSON on his bulletin board. Bill had sent it to him with the idea that she might still be recognizable if she should turn up in Glacier Lake. On Benson's direction, he had already sent a request to the Ministry of Transport to allow him access to the maintenance and flight records for Franz Bernhardt's helicopter. He was waiting to hear from them. He hoped those records would reveal clues about Bernhardt's trips across the region. Then he could look for a pattern and track him. The guy was a good pilot, so he didn't put a foot wrong as far as the operation of his aircraft was concerned, but the payload and passenger logs might reveal some illegal activity.

In the meantime, he mused about the terse communication he had received from Nora about his request for follow-up on Bernhardt's BOLF and his appointment as her back-up for Karma Time. This was the code name they had chosen for their operation to apprehend Bernhardt and curtail Brigade drug trafficking along Highway 16. He hadn't bothered to reply as the tone of Nora's memo was so stark, that Luke sensed her anger at his involvement in the op.

Is it worth the effort to let her know I was appointed to this position, that I didn't seek it out? She's so angry I doubt she'd listen even if I could get a message through. Should I ask Benson to make that clear to her? Nah, probably not. The less he suspects that she and I are at odds, the better. I don't want him blaming 'bad chemistry' if anything goes wrong!

CHAPTER 36 - CHLOE UNCOVERS A CLUE: FRIDAY-FRIDAY, AUGUST 26-SEPTEMBER 16

Once Nora had some idea of financial support from Special Ops Budget Office, she invested a chunk of her inheritance from her parents. She had ordered a variety of products COD from connections she had made at Bianca McKay's. The stuff had been trickling in to her personal mailing address for weeks. Her small studio apartment was packed to the ceiling with boxes of specialty garments, wigs, cosmetics and salon supplies.

If anyone asked where she had found the money to fund her business, she would say her folks had died in Winnipeg after moving up with her from Louisiana a few years before. Nora smiled wistfully. It was true, in fact. Her dad had died without warning and left her thirty thousand the year before. She had a tidy sum to play with, but would have to be careful with her money.

She had set herself up with all the merchandise and promo photos she could display. She had transformed her van into a traveling salon with mirrored hairstyling station, sink and hairdryer, a sofa daybed, and a hotplate. She had a hook-up for water to fill both a reserve tank and a twenty-five gallon hot water tank. There was even a porta-potty in a tiny enclosure for emergencies. A padlocked wardrobe trailer was attached behind, stuffed with costumes and wigs. She kept the cosmetic supply and photographic equipment locked inside a cupboard in the van. Overall, it was a carefully detailed project crafted at minimum cost by tradesmen contracted to the training center.

Most important of all, her identity as Chloe LaJoie had been presented at the final planning and authorization meeting with Dave Yang, Gus McGilvery, and Bunnie Burrows, Chloe's control. There had been no haggling over budget. But then, she had done for them an impromptu demo of her 'Chloe' persona, accent, body language, and business spiel.

Although everyone appreciated the work that had gone into the cover, there had still been serious reservations. Bunnie challenged her with the difficulty of maintaining her cover twenty-four-seven, saying that one careless or fatigue-driven slip-up could prove fatal with the likes of a biker gang. Dave Yang's assessment was that the cover still needed work: she would be too obvious; she needed to tone it down, make the clothes less provocative and paint the van a more neutral colour. She remembered the feel of her stomach sinking upon meeting Dave's steady gaze.

She had protested that she was resilient, that she would know when to go to ground and take a break. She didn't want to start planning all over again, to throw out all the prep work she had done. She would make the Cosmobile idea work as it was. She threw herself into even more back story work, spending the next several weeks on a telephone campaign to promote her services to strip clubs across the Western states and provinces.

∽

IN MID-SEPTEMBER, CHLOE PLACED A FOLLOW-UP PHONE CALL TO Tommy Cobb at BawdyWorks to schedule a meeting with him to demo her line of products. She chose her wardrobe and hairstyle with care. She must impress without overwhelming the guy. They had never met, but her instincts said he had an acute case of avarice. His company was new, and he was greedy for profit. She just had to make the offer worth his while financially. She would offer a percentage of the take on her wigs and cosmetic lines. That should be attractive right before Halloween.

Nora dressed with care for her 10:00 am meeting with the exotic dancers' agent. Her low-cut, black body suit, fishnet stockings and black patent spike heels, accessorized with a crop-top, chartreuse jacket, a flounced, sequined mini and a low-slung silver belt would attract attention. Her honey-blonde mane, pulled back with a black net hairband, was topped by an elaborate ebony orchid arrangement.

The air-conditioned lobby of BawdyWorks, scented with some coconut tropical blend that reminded Nora of suntan lotion, featured life-sized posters of legendary exotic dancers: Gypsy Rose Lee, Candy Barr, Sally Rand, Blaze Starr, Fanne Foxe, and Josephine Baker. She noted that there were no photos of the agency's own performers, another service she could offer to provide.

When the paper-white, glossy, black-haired receptionist ushered her in to the manager's office, Nora met a rotund little man with round John Lennon glasses, a curly head of reddish hair and a bright ginger beard. This was Tommy Cobb.

"I am so happy finally to meet you, Chloe."

"And Aah'm delighted to meet y'all, too, Mistah Cobb."

His handshake was moist, his voice warm and intimate as he gestured her towards a sofa and took the seat next to her. "Just Tommy, and can I call you Chloe?"

She nodded and beamed a smile.

"Can I get you a drink, a pop... coffee... tea?"

"Why, yes, please. A diet pop would be nice and dandy..." The circumstances felt cloying as he tilted his head and peered at her, reaching behind to rearrange the cushions at her back. She stiffened her spine to avoid contact, and he backed off, rising to get some cokes from the small hotel refrigerator near the entrance door. She sized up his short, bulky build as he lumbered across the room. He hadn't seen the inside of a gym in a while, and should cut back on the pop.

She shot a dazzling smile at him as he crossed the room towards her, and was amazed to see him blush in response. "So Mistah Cobb... uh... Tommy, Aah have some great little ideas for yer dancers... y'all have seen my bro-chure?"

"Yes, well, I have, but I would like to see more than just a leaflet..."

"Bless your heart! Aah'm fixin' to show y'all right now!" She opened her large black-leather shoulder bag. "Aah have a few samples here for y'all to see... Aah think the quality will delight y'all..." She had been careful to bring only the most delicate and carefully crafted pieces to show him.

The collection impressed Tommy. The lacy silk lingerie in a rainbow of colours lay arrayed on the couch between them. He handled a few gingerly, as if afraid to damage them. "Can I get a few outfits of these to use for when I get some promo shots to send to the hotels?"

"Are these your regular line-up of dancers, the ones who go on tour? These could also be on display in the lobby showcase. That would make a real bang-up display for yer biz'ness! And guess what? Y'all will be surprised to hear that Aah'm also a photographer. Lookee here. These are shots Aah took of one dancer Aah know... do y'all know Bunnie Burrows?"

"Oh yeah! She does some make-up gigs when we have gaps in the schedule. You know her, eh?"

"Y'all like that photo? We can organize a package deal to save y'all some money on shots just like this one. And of course, I can offer you a percentage–let's say ten percent–of any biz'ness you send my way if y'all also purchased some wigs and make-up?"

"Really... this is excellent, Chloe. I should make sure I mention you to my dancers... uh... I guess you wouldn't mind a little free promo? You know, you scratch my back and..." He made a move to sidle across the couch again, but Nora raised her hands in a 'hold back' gesture and scrambled to gather up the wardrobe pieces that lay on the couch between them.

I'm so glad I chose to meet him in his office instead of in my Cosmobile! That instinct was right on!

"Hold yer horses, Mr. Cobb. Let's keep this professional, shall we? Which ones do y'all want to order?"

"Uh... okay... I'll take one of each of the black, silver and red ones. How much?"

"I'll send y'all an invoice with that percentage discount we mentioned. Are ya'll also gonna purchase some wigs and make-up?" She took her time to place all the items back in her bag.

"Uh... yes. I'll have to get back to you on that. I'm not sure what to get until I talk to some girls."

"Okay, ya'll do that. Now, before Aah go, let me get a look-see at the dancers' gigs so Aah can organize a photo shoot schedule."

He rummaged around in his desk drawers and came back with a dog-eared notebook. She spent a few minutes making notes of the names of dancers who were currently in Vancouver. Looking over the spreadsheet of bookings for the dancers, she noticed two things: one, that Vee's name didn't appear anywhere, and two, that three names were labeled with 'Brigade Contract'–Roxie Buxom, Fantasia Revere and Bambi Dearborn.

"Tommy, Aah have met a dancer who says she is a member of yer agency, Velvet Dawn? Just where is she listed? Aah don't see her name on the regular circuit, here. I understood she would be in Vancouver from September until mid-October?

"Uh... yes, she was supposed to but they needed her on the northern circuit. I guess that didn't get updated in my schedule." He seemed flustered, his cheeks more ruddy than her first impression.

"Do you sometimes list your dancers by their legal names, not their stage names?"

Tommy scratched his ginger-coloured beard. "No, we never use anything but stage names. I'm not too sure about where to find Velvet... her rotation's not settled yet, because she's just started on the northern run in the province, and the weather wreaks havoc with their schedule."

"At this time of year?" Nora could understand such an excuse in the winter, but it was still September, and she sensed Tommy was being evasive, though she wasn't sure why.

"You know, Mr. Cobb, mah reason for wanting to know is that Aah'm just trying to make a go of mah biz'ness by taking photos and selling hot fashion. Don't all the dancers need costumes and make-up? Especially if they're dealing with really high-end customers, you know like the B-list girls? Aah'd like to offer mah services to as many girls as possible. This is a competitive business, and they all deserve a shot at achieving the best look available. So, the girls not listed here should have a chance, too." She didn't know Steph Benson's professional name, so she was unsure whether she was listed in the schedule Cobb had shown her.

Tommy lowered his head and regarded her over his shiny, round glasses. "Those girls–the B-list–aren't around until later in November. They take a break in town before they head out again after the holiday season... after Christmas and New Year's, you know... big money for them working in town over those days. The thing is... those girls go to Vegas and Reno to spend their money. They get sponsored to work down there by private agencies. But I'll ask if any of them wanna see what you got... best I can do. Call me back around Halloween."

"Do ya'll have a list of who they are? Just so Aah can keep a record of who Aah've contacted? Are they 'Brigade Contract' dancers, maybe?"

I'll bet those girls 'sponsors' in Vegas and Reno wear 1% badges and leathers and ride Harleys! I'll bet they have very high end clients, too!

Abruptly, Cobb's attitude shifted one-eighty. Where he had been cordial he was now unfriendly, even hostile. His eyes shot daggers, and he puffed up in size.

Well, mention of the Brigade Contracts has rattled him for sure.

"No... uh... that don't mean nothing... just a little shorthand note for me to... uh... keep track of things... and as for the B-list dancers, I don't know who might want to get in touch... and I won't know until later in the month..."

"So are the B-list dancers ones with security from a biker group called Brigade?"

Now, Tommy Cobb seemed to be blowing up like a puffer fish, his face all red and blotchy. Chloe saw the warning signs of a temper about to explode. Tommy was feeling that something had pushed him too far. She couldn't afford to have him asking around about her. He could blow her cover, so she made a mental note to find out the identities of the second-string dancers some other way.

"Uh... sorry, Mr. Cobb, I was just thinkin' about a fun idea fer a photo shoot... y'all imagine girls posed on big Harleys with sexy bikers behind?"

Tommy Cobb shook his head.

"No? Okay, then Aah'll just leave it there for now." Chloe found her way to the door.

∽

As she drove back to her flat, Nora pondered Tommy's reaction to her pressuring him to provide a list of the B-list dancers. Something felt "off", as if he had been told to keep those details secret. And there was no doubt in her mind now, that BawdyWorks was abetting the Brigade in providing dancers for illegal gigs.

As soon as she reached a secure line, she relayed her findings to Dave Yang and asked that they be conveyed to Bunnie Burrows as well. She asked for a follow-up meeting with both of them as soon as one could be scheduled.

This info ought to put to rest any reservations they have about the approach I'm taking. If Tommy Cobb is implicated in the Brigade's illicit gigs, then there is another place to look for Stephanie, and the role of Bernhardt as a helicopter delivery service is clear... The best way for me to infiltrate this set-up is to be a part of the action.

Chloe spent the rest of the morning phoning around to the local strip clubs, asking for their line-up of dancers and their show dates. She inquired about which ones had signed contracts with BawdyWorks and crosschecked her list of potential photo shoots. Vee's stage name still was showing up in the September and October calendars, along with Dolly Barton and Lola Mystique. Could either of these dancers be Steph? To decide, she had to see them and compare their appearance to the photo Bill Benson had sent her. She had a mental image of Steph from when they had been at Pine Ridge Resort, but having the photo helped.

That afternoon, when she drove around to the clubs where Dolly Barton and Lola Mystique were working, she crossed them off as possibilities. When she asked Dolly what had happened to Vee, that she was listed on the schedule but was not in Vancouver, the dancer was offhand. "Those schedules are a joke! They're getting changed all the time. She's working some other tour, I guess."

How was she going to find Steph? Was she likely to be dancing in Vancouver clubs over the holidays? Or would she, as Cobb said, head to the States? No doubt the bikers could get her a fake passport. Nora decided to send word to Canada and U.S. Customs with a photo to watch for her.

CHAPTER 37 - CHLOE AND SLASH ON THE ROAD: SATURDAY-SATURDAY, OCTOBER 1-15

Nora was convinced that her cover would hold up and that her back story was clean. Having confirmed the role BawdyWorks was playing and the almost certain involvement of Franz Bernhardt with the Devil's Brigade, she looked forward to her next meeting with Dave Yang and Bunnie.

She approached the opportunity with determination. "Have you heard about the follow-up I have done with strip clubs across Western Canada and the U.S. to support my back-story? Did you get my message after I met with Tommy Cobb, about the dancers labelled as 'Brigade Contract'? Doesn't that corroborate my theory about using the dancers to connect with the bikers?"

"You know, Nora," Yang said, "We have to test your resolve. We didn't say the approach was unworkable, only that it involved risks–ones we were unsure you had planned for. We appreciate the extra effort you've made to reinforce your Chloe identity, but you need to understand that we still have reservations. What you do impacts not only you, but any other operative in the future as well. If your op is compromised by poor planning, we are far less likely to get future ones approved." There was a long pause as if Yang's intent was to let that reality sink in. Then, Yang asked a question she could answer.

"With that said, what security have you got in place to protect yourself if things go south?"

"I've worked with the techies to arrange a phone messaging system to use as contact for the 'Cosmobile' business and taped a generic reply to be used when callers dial me up. It advises everyone to remain in touch through my post office box at the China Town Postal Branch on Main Street. Bunnie, will you collect my mail, and I'll phone once every two days at 6:00 pm to your home number to pick up any messages?"

Bunnie nodded. "That is a routine method to communicate with operatives in the field. We can also send you updates on cassette tapes where you'll be updated in the field on developments we have found through our resources."

Yang added, "We have confirmed Corporal Luke Gallagher as your back-up. He is well positioned in Glacier Lake to respond to any development that puts you at risk."

Nora gritted her teeth, but said nothing, merely nodding assent.

Yang continued, "We understand you have weaponry that is suitable for your assignment. Remember its use is contingent on the same protocols as a uniformed officer would have to accept."

"I understand, Dave."

"Good luck. Stay in touch." Bonnie smiled her encouragement and the meeting was over.

Afterwards, Nora heaved a sigh of relief. There had been no insistence that she alter her undercover persona. In her mind, that meant she had the go-ahead to become Chloe LaJoie.

～

THEN BY OCTOBER 5TH, SHE WAS ON THE ROAD, THE 'COSMOBILE' FULLY stocked and operational. The mini-salon proved its worth with each stop that she made at strip clubs around the Southern Mainland and along the Fraser Highway. The dancers, hungry for new gear, had ogled the colorful array of stage-wear, wigs and make-up, signed up for facials and make-overs, and spent lavish amounts on whole new outfits and promotional shots. She was saving them time and money by delivering products and services on the road. The business model was a success!

Chloe herself was unrecognizable as Constable Nora Macpherson. Her figure was much more voluptuous thanks to padded breasts and buttocks. Instead of her chestnut hair with red highlights, she had become an ash-blonde with jade-green eyes. She had cropped her hair short and wore "big-hair" wigs in a variety of styles that she secured with special esthetician sticky tape. It was a pain to remove so she minimized her changes of hair-do.

The transition has been expensive, especially the contact lenses, but, with her habitual four-inch wedge heels and neon-bright, figure-hugging, low-cut pantsuits and palazzo pant outfits, she appeared much taller and more well-endowed than the slim, athletic RCMP constable. One accessory always on hand was a head-set and Walkman for listening to her tunes. In fact, it played tapes from her back-up contact crew in Chilliwack who kept her acquainted with the latest movements of both the BawdyWorks dancers and the Devil's Brigade. Every day, Chloe (Codename Candy) checked in with her contact, Bunnie Burrows, (Codename Hazel) for the latest news and the location of the nearest drop box where Control had left her any new info tapes about her operation.

Her story was that her parents, who had moved to Winnipeg when she was a teenager, have now died in a car crash and left her an inheritance sufficient to finance the Cosmobile business. When pressed, she was reluctant to revisit the past, as losing her parents had been so traumatic, and she was trying so hard to make a new start. Her customers, who ranged in age from their early twenties to the late forties, all had one thing in common: they were alienated from family and felt the loss, whether or not they would admit the fact. They took to Chloe as one of their own. She was careful not to push her real agenda in her first encounters with the dancers. She just played the friendly, caring big or little sister role and listened as they shared their stories.

By October, 12th, Chloe was heading north to Prince George, where she planned to stop for the weekend, a couple of days to reorder stock and get some downtime. Her plan was to hole up in a decent hotel and pamper herself. She wanted a swim and a sauna. Going public as Nora Macpherson in a swimsuit was a non-starter—too much likelihood of someone from the region recognizing her. No, she would have to maintain her Chloe character to take a dip. The fake boobs and butt would have to remain concealed in a high-cut, full-figured, one-piece swimsuit instead of the bikini she would prefer. Also, the foam inserts would absorb water and take some time to dry out. Fortunately, she had a couple of extra sets. If anyone dared to ask about her modest swimsuit, she would just say her parents had raised her to be discreet. That should dampen their curiosity.

When she pulled into the Inn of the North, she noticed a Harley parked up close to the main entrance, but thought little of it. She hadn't yet heard anything about the Brigade encroaching on downtown Prince George. The Renegades were the local biker gang and the Inn of the North was out of their league.

～

SLASH WAS LIVID. AFTER AN ENTIRE SEASON OF BABYSITTING DIABLO Zorman, taking him on the maintenance runs crisscrossing the northern parts of BC and Alberta, Slash had had enough. Diablo's testiness had won him few allies within the Brigade, so Slash doubted he could manage the Brigade on his own. However, Spyder had contacted Slash to let him know he needed his Number Two back in the Hell Pit. Spyder had said nothing of his illness, but Slash knew to head home in case the old man checked out altogether. But that meant leaving Diablo the Pest in charge of everything on the road, including the helicopter runs. Slash felt very uneasy, as if a slow fuse had been lit, and time was dragging as he waited for the bomb to explode. He had checked into the Inn of the North, taken a quick dip in the pool, and was now in the downstairs pub nursing a beer, pondering the progress of the latest operation along Highway 16.

All summer, "BB" Lakovic had worked to escort the girls, Willow,

Roxie, Fantasia and Bambi on their runs into the various mining and logging camps that dotted the BC northern wilderness. Slash had kept Diablo on the road, so there had been no chance for him to interfere with the dancers, but it hadn't been easy. Now, there would be only "BB" to keep them safe, and Slash feared the worst.

It was bad enough, according to BB, that the helicopter pilot, the Franz the Kraut, was ogling the women whenever he transported them. What were the odds that Diablo, with Franz's help, would out-muscle BB? Slash pictured the Kraut, his icy-blue eyes focused on Willow's slender shape, and clenched his fists. The helicopter pilot had said nothing about the dancers, but Slash felt the itch to punch him out, just in case. Slash had decided he would fake leaving the Brigade in Diablo's charge, and then come back to check in to see how Diablo has managed his responsibility.

This Saturday, Slash was taking one last day and night in Prince George before heading back west to check on Diablo's "management style". Spyder would understand that he couldn't leave to check in on boss until he was sure he could trust Diablo. Wanting some downtime, Slash had wandered into the Inn's steak house for dinner and then to the back of the lounge to listen to a blues combo. The pulse of the Police song, "Every Breath you Take" was playing on the hotel speakers during the band's break. Slash had ditched his leathers with the Brigade patches to dress in casual black denim jeans and a long-sleeved, grey, button-down cotton shirt to cover his heavily tattooed arms. He felt odd being out of 'uniform', but he was on his own and didn't want to attract attention.

From his seat against the wall, Slash surveyed the clientele: the usual array of business people stopping over for the weekend between stops to Terrace or Quesnel. They were all either solitary drinkers or chatty in small groups sharing pitchers of beer. The blues trio, Tree Notes, came back and warmed up with UB-40's "Red, Red Wine" followed by BB King's "Broken Heart". The instrumental versions sounded tepid compared to the originals, but at least the music was fresh. Slash leant back and ordered a tequila.

CHAPTER 38 - CHLOE GOES DANCING AND DIABLO MAKES A MOVE: SATURDAY, OCTOBER 15

Chloe, not wanting to spend too much of her leisure time getting made up, dressed and wigged for her Chloe persona, had spent most of the last three days relaxing in her hotel room. It was down time she desperately needed. She had seen only the spa attendants, who were so wrapped up in their gossip that they paid her little attention while they ministered to her in the private massage rooms, and the room service delivery guy who had cute dimples but was likely still in his teens.

The time spent in the hotel swimming pool had been divine. Swathed in her outsized swimsuit, she had luxuriated in the warm water, floating and dipping into the depths. There were few other hotel guests about, so she let her mind wander. She thought about her dad and how he would laugh to see her appearance as Chloe. He had always encouraged her to test her limits, to take critical, but well-considered risks. She felt grateful to have had such backing. Now, her life without him seemed a little ungrounded, as if she were somehow weightless. Her reflection darkened when her thoughts turned to Luke and her upcoming operation. No matter how she tried to relax, she always ended up mulling over her chances of success in finding Steph and nabbing the drug-trafficking ring.

Toweling off afterwards, she noticed a well-built, dark-haired swimmer at the opposite end of the pool. She hadn't noticed him come in and now could make out little except that his back was heavily tattooed. From this distance, she was unable to discern any detail, but she was struck by how much skin those dark tattoos covered.

Once back in her room, she collapsed in relaxation, and knew she was horny. She hadn't had sex since splitting with Luke in June. Watching music videos on the hotel TV hadn't helped, especially the black and white, stripped down "Every Breath You Take" by The Police. Sting seemed to be stalking the ex. Her thoughts turned to Luke.

Why was he bothering to keep tabs on her? Did she care? She decided she did, but not enough to change what she was doing. Nora wondered how long before he recognized her in her latest incarnation? She wanted to show him she could do the job well enough to survive and catch the perp.

Her imagination wandered to picturing Luke when she had last seen him. Much Music chose that moment to air "All Night Long" by Lionel Richie. Nora, free of Chloe for the moment, flashed to a vision of herself in Luke's arms, pulsating with need... she wanted him like that for sure... she just didn't want him to judge her. Was compromising her ambition the price she had to pay for a permanent, mutually satisfying relationship?

She gnashed her teeth in frustration. Why couldn't she get her mind *off* the man? Why was it so hard to be a strong, independent woman? She was so tired of the hotel room TV. She wandered over to the sliding doors that led out onto the balcony. Opening them, she could hear the bluesy music coming from the lounge six stories below.

She decided it was time to make some fresh memories...

∽

Chloe decked herself out as Madonna, ready to dance. On top, she wore a black mesh tank top with a black satin bustier underneath. The black leotard covering the bottom half of her figure was calf length. Her belt encased her waist in a wide brassy affair of chain links and glitter. Her blonde hair was a frenzy of turquoise and cream feathers and shiny pearl beads with a black velvet headband and bow holding the look together. Large gold hoops hung from her ears. A dynamo of pent-up, physical energy, she knew she must get a workout somehow. The dance floor would be a perfect release. As she walked into the lounge, she noticed a well-built, dark-haired man back against the wall who seemed to follow her with his eyes as she crossed to take a seat at the bar.

Is that the swimmer? The one with tattoos? Hmmm.

~

"Bambi, you gotta be ready for the ride out on time tonight... I tol' ya last night not to keep us waitin'... twelve o'clock sharp!" The dancers were all in the cafeteria of the Justice Silver Mine Camp. BB's patience was wearing thin. Diablo, per Slash's direction, was hanging at the back, keeping a low profile with the dancers.

Fantasia slammed her coffee cup down. "Why do you have to be such a jerk, BB?" The other girls sat transfixed, watching to see how this confrontation would pan out. Then little Bambi, winking at the other dancers, made a show of pouring herself another cup of java.

"I said... get ready..." BB moved to grab Bambi by the arms. Out of nowhere, Roxie, Fantasia and Willow moved to latch onto BB's shoulders.

Even though he was a brown belt judoka, BB knew the dancers didn't see him as threatening, but as quiet, stubborn and rock-hard strong, a protector. Now, as they weighed him down, he feared they saw him as soft. Without a word, he set out to fight them all off. Instinct kicked in. What he wanted was a hold strong enough to kill a girl's mobility for a few minutes, enough to make the others back off, if not scare them off. It didn't help that he was wrestling with Bambi, the acknowledged arm-wrestling champ. She was small but powerful.

∼

From his position in the rear of the empty cafeteria, Diablo was grinning at the spectacle. BB was getting the shit kicked out of him by a female, or more properly, a group of females! He knew he should be breaking it up, protecting BB, but Diablo was eager to see how this little flare-up would turn out. It had all the potential to work in his favour, especially if BB got beaten. Diablo thought of BB as a little more than a twerp who had wormed his way into a privileged position in the club as Slash's pet, even though he was just a kid, not a patch holder. It was high time for BB to take a fall, and then he, Diablo, would come into his own.

∼

Bambi, who BB knew had been used to fighting since she had been a kid in Nanoose, twisted to confront BB. She reached her long, scarlet nails into his eyes and swiped, blinding him in his own blood. He moved through a red canyon to contain her and soon had her throat locked in his vice-grip. Bambi was pounding on his head, shrieking at him to let go, when Roxie and Willow jumped on each of his shoulders to bring him crashing down to the floor. Bambi rolled out from under BB just in time to avoid his two-hundred-and-thirty-pound bulk from squashing her. Fantasia stood back, immobilized with shock.

BB was pinned down, blinded by blood and pain. He wondered why Diablo hadn't come to help him. He thought he must be out having a smoke...

∼

All this time, Diablo was watching near the door of the cafeteria, grinning ear to ear. BB would be out of commission and he, Diablo, would get to take over. He had been waiting for this chance. Now Bambi had given it to him.

CHAPTER 39 - SLASH MEETS CHLOE: SATURDAY, OCTOBER 15

Slash noticed Chloe as soon as she walked into the lounge. The dish swiveled her gaze from side to side, her thick, black eyelashes aflutter. She looked to see where she should sit and opted for a stool at the bar. She perched upright, her long shapely limbs in fishnet stockings wrapped around the stool legs and her riot of blonde curls glowing in the light from the pot lamp overhead. Thrusting her shoulders backwards to lean against the ladder back of the seat accentuated her curvaceous bust and butt. Her silhouette rivalled Dolly Parton's.

"A glass of merlot, pretty please, Sugah." The black velvet bow of the headband quivered as she spoke, her husky whisper barely audible for the bartender. He leant in to place his ear close to the lipstick-pink mouth. The metallic fabric of her top glittered in the dark, drawing attention to the silver rivets of the bustier underneath. In the background, the strains of Annie Lennox and the Eurythmics' "Sweet Dreams" pulsated from the massive speakers on a small stage.

Chloe's "big city glam" look rivalled that of a couple of other young females in the room, but Slash's instincts sensed that something beyond looks set this broad apart from the local ones. She had a presence that invited deeper examination. He had dressed down in civvies with no patch showing, and he was unarmed. He could be a logger in town for the weekend. He moved to the bar.

They both sat there, nodding to the music until the song finished. When Elton John's "I Guess That's Why They Call It the Blues" started up, Slash made his move. "Can I buy you some more wine, Miss?"

∼

HEARING HIS PENETRATING, GUTTURAL BARITONE, CHLOE TURNED TO face him, in a glance taking in his muscular frame and dark good looks. She smiled, recognizing the man from the swimming pool. "Uh... that's very nice of y'all, Sugah, bless your heart, but no thanks. Aah reckon Aah'm not staying too long."

"You know there's a band? They're just on a break. Please. Stay to hear the band. They're just a trio, but not bad..."

Chloe lowered her gaze and made a more careful examination of his body. She couldn't see any bulge betraying a gun in a holster under his arm. Of course, he could have a knife stuck in his boot... there was something about him that made her uneasy, but he was sexy... maybe just a dance or two... something upbeat. He would be good for a slow number, too...

What was she dreaming? She couldn't get up close and personal with this guy... he'd smell something fishy as soon as he discovered her foam rubber fake boobs and butt. He would be leery of her whole set-up and could blow her cover. Her urge to dance had disappeared, but she could do business–maybe he had a girl who'd appreciate some lingerie... or at least, he could appreciate his girl in the lingerie...

"Hey, aren't y'all precious! Aah could dig some soothin' music... Aah'll stay just for a bit 'cause Aah'm worn slap out. And... fixin' to start early in the mornin'."

"Oh, yeah? What's up? What's a beauty like you doing in Prince George?"

"Oh, Aah'm on business. Aah need to be over yonder in Terrace by Monday."

"Uh…" Slash emitted a speculative grunt. "Where are you from and what kind of business do you have?"

"Oh, y'all can tell Aah'm not from around here? Aah come from Nawleans, Mississippi, y'all know, the Mah-di Grah City? But Aah live in Canada now… in the costume supply business, Sugah. Aah have an appointment to do some fittin's just outside of Terrace on Monday."

Chloe caught Slash's raised eyebrows. "Why do y'all seem surprised?"

"The towns along Highway 16 didn't strike me as too heavy into theatrics or Mardi Gras…uh… What sort of costumes, if you don't mind me asking?" He said 'asking' like 'axing'.

"Mah customers are dancers, uh… what did y'all say your name was?"

"Oh… uh… Sla… uh… Steve… Miss. And yours?"

"Chloe… Chloe LaJoie… Mistah… uh…?

"Just Steve is good. My last name is Drake now, but it used to be Dracul, you know, like Dracula? But you can see why I don't use it any more… kind of weird name, yeah?"

Chloe laughs, a breathy little chuckle halfway between a giggle and a snuffle. "Sho 'nuff, Aah can see why…"

That's a Balkan name…this is the Devil's Brigade's Number Two! He looks pretty clean cut, but…if he's the guy from the pool…under that shirt there's a whole gallery of tats.

In the background, Donna Summer was belting out "Works Hard for the Money".

∼

SLASH WAS CURIOUS ABOUT THIS WOMAN. "So… are you here selling theatre costumes?"

Chloe chuckled, "Why no, sir! Y'all barking up the wrong tree! Not thee-A-tah! I sell costume pieces to exotic dancers… y'know, wigs, false eyelashes, feathers, capes, fancy hah-heeled shoes, pasties… all the bits they need to do their gigs. Aah also do make-up, hair, photo-shoots... Aah'm a full-service operation!" This last statement seemed so incongruous, given her appearance and the setting, that they both laughed out loud.

A round of drinks, a beer and another merlot arrived unannounced, and Slash paid. Chloe shrugged, "Thanks, Steve, Sugah. Aah shouldn't, but just this one, okay?" She fluttered her ultra-long eyelashes.

"How about if we do some business? Does that make it alright?"

"Sho 'nuff... of course, darlin'! What kind of business? Y'all want to pick up something for yer girl? Something a little bit naughty, maybe?" She shook her entire body in mock horror. The bow on her headband quivered, the silver rivets of her bustier twinkling.

Slash erupted in a full roar of laughter. "Yeah, Chloe, that's right. I gotta girl needs some new gear. You know, I gotta couple! In fact, I got four dancers who could use some new stage wear."

That's one way of getting' the strippers' loyalty, maybe. I can feel a power struggle coming between me and Diablo. The question is how to make the deal without tipping this chick off that the girls are doing 'under-the-counter' gigs, and without Diablo finding out.

"Why don't we meet for breakfast here in the hotel restaurant... say at 8:00 am, and afterwards, can I take a look? Do you have your stuff close by?"

"Oh, that'll be fine and dandy, Sugah! Y'all gotta see my Cosmo-bile! It's got it all!"

"Done. Now relax and enjoy your wine. Here comes the band."

CHAPTER 40 - CHLOE DOES BUSINESS: SUNDAY, OCTOBER 16

That night, before crawling into bed, Nora contacted Bunnie, her control in Chilliwack, (Codename Hazel).

"Candy here, Hazel. I have a date to have breakfast tomorrow morning with someone here in PG. I think this guy is someone we might know. His name is Steve Drake, but he used to be Steve Dracul. I heard him slip when he was telling me that. What he was about to say started with S... L... A... What do you think? He's a big guy, dark complexioned, good-looking. Has a slight accent, maybe eastern European...?"

Hazel's voice came back sounding hollow, as if she were holding her breath. "That sounds like a big fish you've caught there, Candy. Likely, it's our boy, Slash, Number Two of the Brigade. Don't lose track of him! I'll check into 'Steve Drake' for you. Call me back before you leave town. How long from now will that be?"

"It's six and a half hours to Terrace. I need to leave for Terrace by ten tomorrow morning."

"Be at your phone by nine-thirty."

Nora steeled herself before meeting 'Steve' for breakfast. This guy made the hairs on the back of her neck stand on end. In some ways, she liked the sensation, the adrenaline rush. He was a dangerous man, someone with a serious track record.

At 800 hours, he was waiting in the restaurant, all six-foot-two of him. He looked even more attractive in daylight, dammit! His plain black leather jacket was zipped up so she could not see the insignia on the denim vest underneath. Her research into the Devil's Brigade niggled in her memory, and the hairs at the nape where she has pinned up her morning 'do' were even more on alert. The tats she had seen in the pool would fit with that ID too.

"Hi, Gorgeous!" Steve's smile was dazzling, accentuated even more by the dark hair of a well-trimmed goatee and 'stache. He was eating a toasted bacon, egg and tomato sandwich, the juices dribbling between his fingers. "I've ordered a coffee for you..."

"That's all Aah have most of the time, not a fan of breakfast..." She was never hungry in the morning anyway...

So, he hadn't waited breakfast for her... not exactly Continental manners!

"Okay, I'm almost done. Do you want to get your coffee to go?" He wiped his fingers on a paper napkin and gulped from his mug.

"That sounds like a plan... Aah do need to make tracks' no later than ten."

Ten minutes later, they were across the parking lot at her vehicle, and her layout, in particular her selection of stage wear for the dancers, impressed Steve. Sitting at the little table she used for manicures, he looked incongruous, but there was nothing awkward about how he checked out the merchandise. He selected four different matching outfits and paid cash, then took her business card and tucked it into his wallet. Turning to her, he leveled a penetrating gaze, surveying her face and body as she stood next to the lingerie clad mannikin, sipping her takeout coffee.

"Chloe, I'd like to buy more. If I buy enough, can we make a deal? I've got four dancers who need what you have to offer, but they work unusual gigs. You won't find them in the hotels along the highway, but I can arrange for you to meet them."

"That all depends, Steve. Y'all manage dancers, do y'all? Why didn't y'all say so last night?"

"I ... uh... didn't realize..." For once, he was at a loss for words.

"What kind of deal are y'all asking for? And how much volume in sales can Aah count on? A group of four dancers doesn't sound like too many...y'all want them to get the complete service? Hair, make-up, photos? Aah can do it all, y'know..."

"We'll see. I can only bring one at a time to meet you. What kind of time to give them a couple of new outfits, fix their hair and do... what do you call it...? Uh... the make-up stuff where you make them look like a million bucks?"

"A facial?"

"Yeah, that's it! How long? And how much for the complete package?"

"Uh... Aah guess about an afternoon, let's say five or six hours... as for how much...? Two outfits, a haircut and stylin' with extensions perhaps, a manicure, pedicure and facial..." Because of her excitement at hooking her Slavic fish, she had to make herself slow down to maintain her breathy, Southern drawl. "For each girl, let's say three hundred? That's an amazin' deal for y'all! The usual price is five hundred. At three hundred each, that would be twelve hundred... Are y'all in?"

"Okay. I'll find you in Terrace and bring the first girl. No need to look for me. Your vehicle sticks out like a hooker in the Holy Land."

"Heavens to Betsy! Aah hope it shows a little more class than that!" She took a hands-on-hips stance and beamed her best coquettish smile. Then she laughed her deep, throaty chuckle and shimmied a little to toss her blonde hair, so it fell a bit out of its confine of pins and headband.

"So, darlin'!" She checked the Madonna "Like a Virgin" wall clock, emitted a soft grunt and pointed to the van's door. "Aah reckon Aah need to get going. Aah haven't even checked out yet."

"Sure thing, gorgeous... until Terrace, then..." His hands caressed her shoulders and moved down toward her breasts. Chloe twisted away just in time before he could make intimate contact. There was no telling how experienced those hands might be!

Do falsies, even good ones, feel like the real thing? I better not take the risk of finding out...

"Hold yer horses, darlin'! Let's keep it PRO-fessional, okay?" Chloe felt a little shaken. She could sense the heat of her flushed face, not a good sign. Someone making a pass like that should not embarrass Chloe.

"Uh... I don't mean nothin' by it..." Slash raised his arms in surrender. He was blocking the exit.

"Just fine and dandy... lemme get goin' now..." She moved to edge around him, taking in a whiff of Ralph Lauren's "Polo". He took the hint, opening and holding the van's rear door for her.

Once outside on the parking lot pavement, she turned to face him. "Aah'll keep an eye out for y'all in Terrace, Sugah..."

"Hey, I'm really sorry if I..."

"It don't matter a hill of beans! Now, Aah gotta git! Aah haven't even checked out yet. Have a good 'un'!"

∽

SLASH ENJOYED THE BOUNCE OF HER HIGH-HEELED CURVES AS SHE sashayed away towards the hotel entrance. What a body!

CHAPTER 41 - LUKE GETS READY: SUNDAY, OCTOBER 16

Luke Gallagher had a hunch Franz was moonlighting by ferrying girls out to the camps that dotted the back country. He had checked the Ministry of Transport record of logs for Bernhardt's helicopter and had discovered a regular pattern of trips in and out of the camps attached to the Sedako mine near Simon Lake, the NorthCo Logging show near Moose Forks and the Justice Silver Mine out of Kitwanga.

He had called the main offices of these companies to find out if there had been any authorized helicopter rentals on the dates he had flagged in Bernhardt's logs. They might have been necessary flights for transporting assay agents or new staff in. The records clerk in the Justice Silver Mine office had detailed only one out of seven of the flights as company-authorized. However, she hastened to add that Bernhardt had charged for only that one flight. Two of the ten trips into NorthCo had been for company business. A similar story had emerged from his inquiry at Sedako, where problems with on-site prostitution had arisen a few years before, around the time that vandals had demolished DuLac School. Now, the perps had an even more sophisticated operation. They were hiring a helicopter pilot to transport women into the camps, no doubt for off-market dancing gigs and prostitution.

The question was, what could the Force do about this illicit activity? After Bill Benson had contacted Luke about the BOLF for the Pine Ridge Resort pickup in July, he had stayed in touch, keeping Luke in the loop about Nora's progress on her course in Chilliwack. Designating him as back-up for Nora had legitimized his involvement. Luke had not acted on Nora's request that he remove himself as her back-up. Somehow he couldn't. If she made that request to Benson, he would have to accept her preference.

Thinking back to Bernhardt, Luke realized it had helped that Benson could cut the red tape to allow access to the federal data from the Ministry of Transport. Getting info about this guy, Bernhardt, had been one of Nora's last requests before she had split for the south, and before she had broken up with him. Nora had been sure the helicopter pilot was responsible for an assault on a dancer in Brandenhoff. Luke had mentioned him to Benson in discussions about the cases Nora had been working on around the time that Stephanie Benson went missing for the second time. Luke knew that the DC's daughter's disappearance had played a role in Nora's decision to go undercover, that, and Bernhardt's alleged attack on the dancer. How he wished he could have intervened more successfully in that string of events!

"Call for you, Corporal Gallagher. District Commissioner Benson on Line Two."

Luke stirred from his contemplation. What news from Benson?

"Corporal, I just wanted to let you know Constable Macpherson is travelling undercover now, and has reached Prince George." He filled in the important details of Nora's new cover identity. "She's blonde now with... uh... augmented... ahem...(he cleared his throat) uh.... very curvy dimensions. She'll be wearing an eye-catching outfit and speaking with a pronounced Southern drawl. You can't miss her!"

Luke held his breath, speechless upon hearing the particulars of Nora's undercover plan. "Uh... DC, what colour and make is the van, please?"

"It's a 68 Ford Transit, pink with metallic gold lettering... says "Cosmobile."

"Cosmobile?" Luke was puzzled.

"Yes, Corporal, as in *Cosmo Magazine*? You know? It's a fashion mag for young women... offers all kinds of tips on..."

"Okay, I get it. She's really done it, eh?" He whistled softly.

"It's a provocative, highly singular look she's developed. Personally, I worry she'll attract attention. Not exactly what we're used to with undercover work... but Chief Inspector Yang in Chilliwack has authorized the op and believes she has a good chance of infiltrating the dancers controlled by the Brigade. He's filled me in on some of the particulars of her... uh... look and... uh... accessories Are you available for back-up immediately?"

"Affirmative, District Commissioner. I am available."

"Did you get the photo of Steph that I sent, Corporal?" Benson had sent a graduation photo of Stephanie to post on the detachment 'Missing Persons' bulletin board. Luke detached it from the bulletin board and fingered it now, wondering if he should take the chance to pass it along to Nora. She already knew what Stephanie looked like, but would she want a photo to show anyone else? Showing it could be a risky move. Revealing her interest in a runaway targeted by the Devil's Brigade could put a bull's eye on her back.

"Yes. We have the photo, but we'll keep it on the bulletin board here. May I suggest also forwarding another copy to Canadian Border Patrol and Customs? I saw somewhere in the file that the dancers head down to Vegas in the winter. We might catch her at the U.S. border."

"Good idea. I'll do that. Now, Nora... uh Constable Macpherson, is currently on her way across Highway 16 to Terrace. She will have to pass through Glacier Lake. Keep an eye out for her, Corporal."

Luke pondered his options. He had a verbal description of the Cosmobile and could spend the afternoon in the cruiser between Glacier Lake and Brandenhoff, watching for it. He was dying to see Nora, if only to tell her he was available for back-up. It would look like business, but it was also personal. He couldn't let go. The question was whether he would jeopardize her op by contacting her, or would she even admit she knew him.

Just as Luke was preparing to leave in his cruiser, he got a phone call from Benson's secretary to tell him that Nora had made contact with Slavko Dracul, number two in the Devil's Brigade. She had met him in a hotel in Prince George, and she had been observed having a drink with him both the night before and this morning. She was on her way to Terrace, having left at 10:15. That should put her in Glacier Lake about four hours later, between 14:00 and 14:30. Knowing that ETA, Luke could wait until she came through town...

He paused to contain his reaction on hearing that Nora had been seen with the Brigade's number two both last night and this morning... she wouldn't be so foolish as to... would she? He felt a sickly spasm in his gut. How far would Nora go to infiltrate that gang? He visualized having that greasy biker, Dracul, in handcuffs, his Harley Davidson wheels in lock-up, his cocky bluster (they were all cocky!) flattened, his phony bravado vaporized... Luke was motivated.

He made a quick call to Chilliwack and then hit the road in the cruiser.

CHAPTER 42 - CHLOE CONFIRMS HER QUARRY AND TESTS HER COVER: SUNDAY, OCTOBER 16

Slash observed as Chloe in her fancy-pants van drove out of the hotel parking lot. She was quite the package, he decided, but he wasn't sure it was a package he wanted to unwrap. A woman like that would mess up his plans with the Brigade. Somehow, he knew she wouldn't be cool with his being a biker drug dealer, nor would she fit in with the Mommas. She looked more like the Mercedes-convertible-and-champagne-on-ice type.

Maybe he should just pass altogether? No, he could do business with her, get the girls some new gear and maybe cement their loyalty by doing them a few girly-type favours. Because he already had the two grand in personal cash for the makeovers, so he wouldn't need to take it out of Brigade coffers. But he still needed to be sure Chloe was legit. No harm in following her across Highway 16 to ensure she was who she said she was.

He was on his way about ten minutes behind her, not worried about having lost sight of her because there was only one route west. On his Harley, he'd have no problem catching up. The trick was to lag behind far enough, so she wasn't able to ID him.

Because Slash didn't tail Chloe close behind, he missed the stop

Chloe made at a drop box in a hotel lobby on the outskirts of town. There, she dropped off an envelope and picked up a small package.

∼

Before starting on the highway, she put on her earphones and inserted into her Walkman the latest tape from her contact crew in Chilliwack. Hazel had arranged for it to be rushed north overnight to the local airport on a Canadian Forces' special flight. Before long, she had the update on the activity of the Devil's Brigade: 'Steve' was Slavko "Slash" Dracul, (Codename Wolf). The escorts for the Bawdy-Works dancers, who were being kept busy doing bush gigs, were Bogdan "BB" Lakovic (Codename Lucky) and Dimitrios "Diablo" Zorman, (Codename Loverboy) the son of the leader of the Brigade. She had a list of the trips the helicopter pilot, Franz Bernhardt (Codename Hawk), had made already, but she had no way of knowing his upcoming itinerary.

The taped information provided Nora with the details about steady traffic among the various worker camps, but there was no regular pattern to apply to make predictions. The four dancers and the two escorts had regular quarters in the Skylark Hotel in downtown Terrace. There, according to observers paid for their scrutiny, the dancers kept to themselves, eating in their rooms, and spending long hours away with the bikers who had a van to transport them to the landing pad at the airstrip where Bernhardt parked the helicopter in between trips. Chloe mused about those dancers. These must be the ones Steve... er... Slavko was planning to treat to makeovers.

Where would she meet them? Slavko had said he would bring the girl to her, so she wouldn't get to see the dancer alone in the hotel. It would be best if she stayed put once she settled on a spot, likely the hotel parking lot. She wondered how she would manage when and if she met Steph Benson. Would her disguise fool the girl? Everything depended on this 'Chloe' identity being solid. The question was how she was to get the girl into custody without blowing her cover and screwing up her drug-bust operation? She'd have to ponder that puzzle for a bit.

Chloe had an appointment to see Vee that afternoon to test out her cover. She wondered how the young dancer was managing the rigours of the road. She was such an innocent that Nora worried she would become overwhelmed by the slog of the travel routine and the raunchy character of the clientele. Her latest dispatch from Bonnie (Hazel) has indicated that Vee hadn't had a sighting of Bernhardt (Hawk) and that the Brigade hadn't been a presence in Lake Else, perhaps because it was off the beaten track. Whatever the case, Vee was her best bet to get wind of Stephanie Benson. She remembered that she still hadn't found out Steph's stage name. Maybe some of Vee's dance mates would know. She felt she was at last zeroing in on the DC's daughter.

Driving through Brandenhoff, Chloe had the urge to test her undercover appearance on people who knew her. Resolving to be careful, she decided against the busy gas station in town and instead stopped at Millie's Mile Easymart in Simon Lake, where Mildred Turnbull had added a gas pump since Nora first encountered her. This woman would remember Constable Macpherson from the time she had dealt with the RCMP several years before, when she had accused some Indigenous kids of shoplifting from her store.

Nora filled up and entered the Easymart. The store-owner had not mellowed in the intervening six years. The scrawny woman in her late fifties with unkempt, straggly, gray hair wore a threadbare smock of a nondescript flowered pattern over baggy blue jeans and a greasy-looking turtleneck. Mildred cast a jaundiced eye over Chloe's figure as she entered the store to pay for her gas. Nora remembered Mildred Turnbull had complained about how the closing of DuLac Residential School had affected her business.

My god! Millie hasn't changed her clothes since the last time I dealt with her! I wonder if the new gas pump is helping her to make a go of it?

"You ain't from around here, eh?" Millie's gravelly voice from years of chain-smoking boomed across the store as Chloe stood at the entrance, adjusting her eyesight to the dim interior.

"Why, no, Sugah... Aah'm just passing through." She was careful to maintain her drawl. "Thank god y'all have a gas pump. Aah was fixin' to get some back yonder in the last town 'cause Aah reckoned the gas tank was just about plumb out. But before two shakes of a bunny's tail, the town was behind me. Thank goodness y'all is here..."

Millie's expression was a cross between 'deer caught in the headlights' and someone who has just been gassed. "Yeah... uh... I got it a while back..." She craned her scrawny neck to see outside to where Chloe had parked the Cosmobile by the pump. "That a travellin' show? You some kinda act?"

"Oh, y'all mean mah little old van?" She pronounced it 'va-an.' "It's a MO-bile beauty service, Ma'am, y'all heard of esthetician service? Hairdo's, make-up, manicures..."

"Harrumph!.... uh... excuse me..." Millie's cough was a cross between an expletive and a nasal explosion. "Manicures? You think I got much time for that kinda stuff? This place keeps me so busy I don't know if my backside is punched, bored or pecked out by crows! All's I doin' is puttin' in time waitin' for the gover'ment drip feed for my droolin' years..."

"Well, bless your heart! What a thing to say! Heaven to Betsy, you need some TLC!"

"No, I don't! All I need is thirty bucks for gasoline, Toots!"

"Well, Ma'am, no need to get riled! Here's your money... but honestly, y'all can catch more flies with honey than with vinegar, Sugah, and y'all should really think about moisturizin'..."

"Harrumph!" Millie's hostility was palpable.

Climbing into her van, Nora smiled in satisfaction. At least, her undercover disguise was intact! Mildred Turnbull had shown no sign of recognition.

CHAPTER 43 - DIABLO UNCHAINED AND LUKE MEETS CHLOE: SUNDAY, OCTOBER 16

Around noon, Diablo Zorman checked in on BB, who had spent the night in great discomfort on the twin bed in the hotel room he shared with Axel, whom Diablo had conned into doing his collections in Hazelton. Getting Axel out of the picture was part of Diablo's grand scheme so he could have free rein. Now he had BB where he wanted him. He didn't know who he hated more, BB or Slash. He despised Slash because he had this stuck-up attitude, this puffed-up ego that said, "I'm the winner and you're a loser!" BB was just a snot-nosed suck-up to Slash who didn't deserve the cred the rest of the club gave him. Now he regarded his brown-belt adversary with disdain.

BB, still dead to the world on some downers Diablo had given him the night before to kill the pain, had wrapped an old black and white bandana over his eyes, but many of the small white dots of the pattern had soaked up blood. The night before, Axel had hauled BB out to the helicopter at the camp and helped Diablo get him up to the hotel room, but no-one had done any first aid. Looking at the blood-soaked bandana, Diablo grunted. BB stirred.

"Who's there? Can I git some water?"

"Yeah, it's Diablo. Yer eyes still bleedin'?" He handed him a thermos of cold coffee.

"No, just crusted shut. I need somethin' different from this thing..." He pulled the bandana off.

Diablo recoiled from the sight. BB's eyes were both swollen shut, the gouges from the fingernails having left bloody cuts above and below the eye socket. BB was lucky his eyeballs were undamaged.

"Yeah, I'll get ya some gauze and stuff for that." Some disinfectant ointment was a small price to pay for having a free hand with the dancers until they had to make the next hop to NorthCo Logging north of Kitwanga on Tuesday. He headed down the hall and knocked on Willow and Bambi's door.

After no answer, he knocked again. He heard a muffled noise from inside. "Hey, girls! You awake?" No answer. "BB is in a bad way... you girls did a quite the number on him last night!"

From inside, there was a yell. "So what? I ain't sorry! He was hurting my arm. It's all bruised now!"

"Uh... Bambi, is Willow there?" Diablo has been hankering after Slash's broad ever since he first set eyes on her.

"Yeah, but she's busy..."

"Doing what?"

"What's it to you? She's having a bath."

"Ask her if she wants me to wash her back..."

From inside, the woman exploded in laughter. "AS IF!"

"Open up, you stupid bitch! I oughta thrash you for what you did to BB last night!"

There was a noise of something metallic being knocked to the floor, a burst of profanity, and the door was yanked open. Bambi confronted him, bleary-eyed with mascara and eyeshadow streaking down her cheeks. "What in hell you doin', Diablo? You know Willow isn't interested in you!"

"Let her tell me that herself, wagon-burner bitch!"

"Who you calling 'a wagon-burner bitch', you fucking Bohunk, lowlife bastard!"

Diablo has a short fuse. Bambi's slur had hit home. "*Jebiga!*" His

Serbian soul said to 'Fuck it!' He shouldered his way past her into the room and, gripping Bambi by the shoulders, threw the girl onto the closest bed. "Stay there! What I do is none of your fucking business!"

He turned to the bathroom, where he heard the water from the tub gurgling down the drain. Entering in silence, he locked the door from the inside. A shriek burst from Willow, and then silence. Next, Bambi heard the occasional muffled squeal and rush of breath from Willow and then, a few moments later, a rhythmic, masculine grunting.

∼

BAMBI LISTENED, STARING VACANT-EYED AT THE CONTENTS OF THE ashtray knocked onto the carpet in her haste to deal with Diablo. Willow was being raped. There was nothing she could do to stop it. Trying to interfere would cause her to get the same, no doubt. She was now regretful they had incapacitated BB. He was a muscle head, but at least he wasn't a pig!

When Diablo emerged from the bathroom, Bambi was up and dressed in her usual black turtle neck and tights, sitting with arms and legs crossed on the one easy chair in the room. He looked her over and laughed. "Brighten up, Sweet Cheeks! Your face could use a wash..." Bambi swiped at her smeared eye make-up and glared until he left the room.

Willow limped out several minutes later, wrapped in a towel, her face red from crying and the pressure Diablo had applied to keep her from screaming. She looked forlorn and short of breath as she collapsed on the bed.

"You should clean yourself again... uh... inside, you know?" Bambi was being practical. Nothing ruined a dancer's options like an unwanted pregnancy.

"Yeah, I know," Willow whispered. "Wait 'til I tell Slash..."

∼

Luke Gallagher intercepted the Cosmobile at a turnoff just north of Glacier Lake. The thoroughness of Nora's preparation for this undercover assignment impressed him. The vehicle looked legit, but if he hadn't known it was Nora behind the wheel, he wouldn't have guessed. Still, he needed to let her know he was available as her back-up.

She rolled down the window. "Howdy?"

"Your vehicle registration and driver's license, please."

"Why, Officer, Sir, is there a problem? Was Aah goin' too fast? Or are mah signals broken down?" She fumbled to find her ID in her large Louis Vuitton carry-on bag. She passed the ID out the window to him. "Aah don't know what all might be wrong. Jest had this VEE-hicle checked when Aah knew Aah was fixin' to hit the road."

∼

Luke examined her licence. "Well... uh, Miss LaJoie?" Nora nodded to confirm her identity.

"Would you get out of your vehicle, please?"

"Heavens to Betsy! What have Aah done?"

She watched Luke struggling to control his laughter.

What was so funny? Godammit! Of all the cops who could have stopped me, it had to be Luke!

"Well, Miss, I must confess to some curiosity here. I've never seen a van rigged out like this one... are you on holiday, camping or...?

Somehow maintaining her poise, Nora exited her driver's seat. "Bless your heart! No! This is a business vehicle, Officer, Sir. I'm a MO-bile esthetics service on my way to an appointment over yonder in Terrace. Do you want to see inside?" She leaned back and pointed to the interior of the van.

∼

Luke stared in amazement at the newly expanded dimensions of Nora Macpherson. 'Chloe LaJoie's' bustline was considerably bigger than Nora's, as was her butt. He shook his head in disbelief, and forced himself to look only in her eyes, which weren't the right colour either...

"No, I believe you. Do you have a business licence to show me? You don't seem to be from here. I want to be sure you have complied with our regulations, Miss... uh... LaJoie..."

"Why no, Officer, Aah'm not from around these parts... jest moved here... that is, to Vancouver, to be my home base for this biz'ness. Aah have a biz'ness licence for... uh... Vancouver and Burnaby and New Westminster..." She fumbled in her big bag to locate the paperwork.

"And you are planning on doing business in Terrace, you say? Do you have a business licence for Terrace, Miss?"

"Oh, rats! Really? Isn't there one for the whole province? Do Aah have to get a new licence for every itty-bitty town Aah come to?"

"I'll have to check to see what covers a mobile service, Miss. You're not planning on setting up shop here, in Glacier Lake, are you?"

"Why no... y'all stopped me, or Aah wouldn't be sittin' here at all."

"What kind of business do you do, Miss... uh... LaJoie? What would you provide for a customer?"

"Why, Aah do manicures, pedicures, facials, hair-dos, wigs, hair and eyelash extensions, stage-costuming..." Luke was trying hard to pay attention. "... lingerie, high heels..." She seemed to have come to the end of her list when her eyes lit up, and she added, "Oh, and photography! Aah have a camera to take promotion shots."

"Well, Miss, I think you are going to need several different business licences to operate all those services... it could be quite expensive. You need to contact the Board of Trade in Terrace as soon as you get there to get your applications processed. Did you say photography? Might I recommend you consider informal portraits of young people, perhaps like this one." Luke showed her a small wallet-sized photo he had stored in his button-down shirt pocket. It was a picture of a somewhat younger Stephanie Benson.

For a full thirty seconds, Nora stood speechless!

What is his point?

"This young lady's father thought someone like you might run across her, and perhaps contact me?"

"Someone like me?" Abruptly, the Southern accent had disappeared. "If and when I find Stephanie, I will follow protocol, Corporal." With that, Chloe turned, opened the van door, and slid back into the driver's seat.

Rats! He shocked me into blowing my cover!

Luke moved over to the still-open window of the driver's side. "Candy," he said the name in a whisper, as if someone might hear. "I am your back-up as arranged by Hazel and Eagle. I am in place because I have been following this op from the beginning, and I know the territory where it will probably play out. I have a message for you about Karma Time. You are not to travel into the bush with the Karma, especially not with Hawk. This comes straight from Eagle. I spoke to him this morning."

Chloe listened with rapt attention. So Benson and Yang had filled Luke in on the operation, code names and all! They had decided she couldn't go anywhere into the bush with the Brigade or Franz Bernhardt. "Well then, Officer, if y'all goin' to cramp my style like that, y'all need to help me get them business licences pretty quick!"

"I'll notify the Terrace Detachment that you'll be coming in..."

"Don't Aah apply through the Chamber of Commerce like in other towns?"

"Of course, but a courtesy call to the RCMP Detachment is usual in these parts. We like to say hello to new businesses..."

"My, my! Y'all do have your little rules to abide by..."

Luke nodded, smiling and conferring a casual salute as she drove away.

CHAPTER 44 - VEE ON EDGE AND DIABLO OUT OF CONTROL: SUNDAY, OCTOBER 16

Outside of Terrace, Vee was trying to enjoy a Sunday morning sleep in as she did after most late Saturday nights working her dance gig in the Lake Else Pub. The problem today was that Vee knew Nora... uh... Chloe was due into town in the afternoon and she couldn't sleep. Vee was rehearsing her sales spiel for the other dancers, Chrissie, Mona, and Tiffany. Across the room, her roommate, Mona, was dead to the world, so Vee was trying to be extra quiet by mouthing the words to herself.

"Uh... Chloe LaJoie, esthetician and stage wear specialist, hairdresser, photographer, born in... not too sure... uh... Southern States... came from Winnipeg... parents dead... starting up a business using her inheritance money... She has a fab collection of burlesque costumes–stilettos, bras, tear-aways, g-strings, pasties, garter belts and stockings, body stockings, teddies, leather and vinyl options, wigs, extensions, false eyelashes..."

Vee recalled the meeting she had had last summer in Vancouver with Hazel, who had drilled Vee on the details of Chloe's background, business set-up, and Vee's own history with her. She had to show she could remember all the codenames for the police and gang members, too. Hazel had reminded Vee how important the Cosmobile Operation was for the dancers. The extra three hundred bills a month was welcome, too.

She recited the code names to herself, "I'm Ladonna, Chloe is Candy, her Cosmobile van is Vogue, Steph Benson... wherever she is, is Angel, Tommy Cobb is Slug, that creep who attacked me is Hawk... uh... Slash is Wolf, BB is Lucky... uh... Diablo is Loverboy... hah! That fits!" She saw little of the Brigade, but what she had seen had made her hyper-sensitive about anyone who lurked on the dancers, and that behaviour characterized Diablo's attitude to a tee. She knew she must always use the codenames when she communicated with Chloe... uh, Candy... about the secret operation.

Vee knew that what they were doing was dangerous. The Brigade was not technically any part of the BawdyWorks contract. Tommy Cobb, himself, had made the dancers' arrangements by phone with the management in each hotel where the dancers stayed and performed. Still, Tommy was a long way off in Vancouver, and the Brigade was the unofficial security detail for the dancers. One of the gang, either hulking "Tiny" or hatchet-faced "Grinder", always seems to be around, and the hotel security seemed to defer to them. Vee shivered. It wasn't what they had promised her when she signed on. She wondered how much Tommy knew about the bikers... Thinking about them, Vee couldn't help but harken back to the time Bernhardt had assaulted her. Mightn't they do the same thing?

Across the room, Mona stirred. Vee had said nothing much about the Cosmobile yet, but she knew Mona would be a great customer for Chloe. Just yesterday, Mona had been complaining about her shoes, how the heels were unstable. Also, she would want to try some wigs and stage wear, especially the g-strings and pasties. That stuff was unavailable outside of the city. Vee was positive Mona would buy a ton of stuff from the Cosmobile.

∼

IN DOWNTOWN TERRACE, BB'S HOTEL ROOM PHONE AWAKENED DIABLO, who had crashed on Axel's bed. On the other bed, BB moaned in discomfort, his eyes still stinging from Bambi's assault the night before.

"Yeah?" Diablo's telephone manners were rudimentary. He listened for a minute, then grunted agreement. "Uh-huh. I'll keep my eyes peeled."

He listened again, the voice on the other end rumbled on for another minute, and Diablo said, "Yeah, I said. I'll watch out... No, he's okay, still sleeping... Axel? Ah, he's around. I'm just hanging out with BB. Listen, I gotta go. I just woke up."

BB, who had been listening, asked, "Who was that?" Diablo looked at him, a sardonic grin creeping into place.

"Oh, nothing to worry about, Baby BB. I got it!" BB didn't need to know that there was a suspicious cop-snitch on the way. With the Kid and Axel out of the way, Diablo had the reins of the operation... for now. Slash was on his way, but Diablo planned to be long gone when he got to Terrace. "I gotta get the girls to NorthCo for Tuesday. I think I'll take'em a little early. Capiche?"

BB sat up, alert to this change of plans. "What for? That's not what we said... no change in schedule until Slash says so! You gotta wait a day or so, and I'll come with you like we said..."

Diablo turned on him with a vicious poke to the throat. "Well, I got the 'say-so' now. You stay here. Matter of fact, I'm just gonna take Willow. I'll let the other girls baby-sit you!"

"No fuckin' way!" BB thrashed about in anger. He swiped the gauze from his eyes and glared his best bleary-eyed, bloody stare at Diablo. "You got no right to spend any time alone with her, or any of the dancers. Slash will have your balls!"

"Yeah? Do I look scared? Or can you even see me... you pussy! Letting yourself get beat-up by some dizzy strippers! You stay here and worry about your own balls. That Bambi is coming for them next!"

"You cocksucker! I don't need baby-sitting... I can see good enough to fix your clock!" He rose to his full six-foot-four-inches and lunged at Diablo, who easily sidestepped the hit. BB's eye injury had affected his depth perception. He landed in a heap by the door. Diablo, hooting in derision, stepped over him on his way out of the room. BB yelled through the door, "Hey Diablo! Where's Axel?"

There was no answer.

Next, Diablo was down the hall pounding on the dancers' door, yelling, "Willow, get your stuff! We're headin' out!"

∼

BB LAY ON THE FLOOR IN AGONY UNTIL HE HEARD THE HOTEL ROOM phone ring. He crawled on hands and knees to grab the receiver. "Hullo?"

On the other end, Slash asked for Diablo. BB, his voice still hoarse from Diablo's hit, croaked out, "Diablo's not here, boss. He's out of control... messin' around with Willow... says he's takin' her early... just her... to NorthCo."

An explosion of anger on the other end of the line caused BB to hold the receiver away from his ear, but he could still hear Slash's tirade. "That motherfuckin' piece of shit! What's he doin' goin' anywhere near Willow? BB, above all, I tol' you to keep her away from Diablo! Do I gotta do it all myself?"

"I know, Slash, but I'm hurt, see? Diablo says he's in charge 'cause I can't see so good... long story, I'll tell you later. But you gotta get here fast! Axel isn't around. I don't know where he is..."

BB nodded as he listened to what Slash had to say. "Yeah, I get it. There's maybe a problem with a cop so we gotta get the girls away early anyway... I'll contact the Kraut and tell him you say not to fly Diablo and Willow ahead of time, but to get ready to go this afternoon."

Another quick response from Slash, and BB signed off, "Yeah."

CHAPTER 45 - SLASH IN TURMOIL AND FRANZ ON THE PROWL: SUNDAY, OCTOBER 16

Slash sat on the side of the highway near the Glacier Lake gas station, his gut twisted in knots. The follow-up phone call to Diablo and BB had been to alert them to keep the off-circuit girls out of sight for the Sunday and Monday night until he got there. He had planned to spend some time checking up on this Chloe dame. But having found out from BB that Diablo had made a move on Willow, Slash found himself caught in a squeeze between knowing what Diablo might do and wondering what was up with Chloe. His order to BB to get the girls out of town early had been a knee-jerk reaction to seeing that Chloe woman's long chat with that cop. Just as much, though, he had reacted on a protective impulse for Willow he was reluctant to admit he felt.

Starting up his motor, he gunned it for the satisfaction of venting his anger. As he swung out westward onto the highway, he reconsidered what he had seen when Chloe was talking to the Queen's Cowboy. Maybe the chick was clean... the cop might have stopped her just because her rig was so weird. Yeah, Slash realized he had to hope she was what she appeared to be, because right now he had bigger problems. Fuckin' Diablo!

Slash hoped BB got through to the Kraut in time. That was the only way he could be sure Willow stayed safe, if being anywhere near Diablo could be 'safe'. As it was, he had to make tracks to get to Terrace before it was too dark for the helicopter to fly to Kitwanga. Slash revved up his Super Glide II Harley Davidson, careening around the loops of Highway 16 at dangerous speeds. When he caught up to the Cosmobile a few miles past Martinville, he overtook and passed without bothering to signal recognition.

~

CHLOE COULDN'T HELP BUT NOTICE SLASH WHEN HE BARRELED BY. She wondered what had got under his skin enough to catapult him along the highway at such dangerous speeds. She flashed back to being stopped by Luke and wondered if Slash had noticed or become suspicious.

Chloe had butterflies thinking about what kind of reception Slash would give her when they met up in Terrace. She decided she should make a tactical move and mention being stopped before he could ask about it. What would she tell him? Luke's inquiry about business licences afforded an obvious excuse. In fact, maybe Steve knew about licensing a mobile business if he had dancers who moved from place to place. Or did he even worry about such bureaucratic details? She thought he would play by the rules at least for the regular circuit dancers. If she played up the business licence idea well enough, he shouldn't think much was amiss. She had to pray that was the case, anyway.

Nora allowed herself to drift to thinking about Luke again. Her first instinct was to resent his involvement. She wondered if he had been tracking the Brigade as they travelled the highway. That would make sense. He might have a clear idea of where they might go. Did he have an RCMP helicopter available? Now, that would be a game changer! She might almost forgive his interference for access to that kind of rig.

Thinking about Luke reminded her of how opposed he was to her going undercover. Or had that changed? She didn't recall any disapproval in his behaviour dealing with her, but then most of their conversation had been between Chloe and a supposedly unknown RCMP constable. Only at the end, had Luke called her "Candy" and mentioned the codenames for her superiors, so she was sure he knew her identity and the details of her operation. Nora felt her stomach churn and her breath catch; she was still not free of her involvement with Luke. Damn him.

∼

BB WASTED NO TIME TRYING TO CONTACT THE KRAUT, FRANZ Bernhardt, to arrange for an earlier flight to Kitwanga. After trying his hotel room and getting no answer, BB tried the office of the local heliport where the receptionist called Bernhardt to the phone.

"I'm busy doing some maintenance this afternoon… won't be ready to fly until tomorrow… Monday afternoon at the earliest. What's the hurry, anyway?"

"You gotta understand, Slash is the one asking for the change, not me. He's got his reasons, don't worry. Your job is to fly us where we want, not ask questions!"

Franz retorted, "Well, if I don't feel ready to fly, I don't. My job is to fly safe. The chopper needs work, and I can't keep putting it off."

BB, puzzled by Franz's adamant refusal to cooperate, phoned the Restawhile Motel, a local two-star, to arrange rooms for the remaining three dancers and himself. He could barely see the phone book, so had to ask the desk to make the calls for him. He kept replaying the conversation with the Kraut in his head. As far as BB could recall, the pilot had never before delayed a departure or refused a change of schedule. Why had he been so set on delaying their flight this time?

∼

WHAT BB DIDN'T KNOW WAS THAT DIABLO HAD ALREADY MADE A DEAL with Franz to fly Diablo and Willow for the night into Franz's lakeside retreat at Jacob Lake, northwest of Fort Saint Jacob. He was rushing to get in the air while he still had enough daylight to make the trip. He needed at minimum two hours; it was already past noon and the sun would set at six-thirty. There was no time to waste. Diablo and Willow were on their way to the heliport on Diablo's bike.

Franz was excited to think about spending uninterrupted time with the dancer. He visualized her naked, helpless and pleading, her hands and feet bound to his bed. What about Diablo? Franz frowned. He would have to sideline him somehow, but he didn't dare finish him off and have the Brigade on his ass forever.

Franz had been so booked with his helicopter pilot job he hadn't had a night off since... he tried to remember the last time. He grimaced, recalling the fouled-up episode in Brandenhoff the previous spring. What a mess! He had almost got caught when that stupid Paki taxi-driver ratted on him. Afterwards, he had made a promise to himself never to use rented accommodations. From then on, he promised himself that he would always find a fail-safe spot to play with his captive... to enjoy the submission, to feel the ultimate power over another living thing...

Now soon he would play again... this deadly dark dance with another twisted, wicked woman whose greatest pleasure was to tease and entice, but never commit to giving out what she offered. He didn't care for the actual copulation, reasoning these kinds of women were too dirty for that kind of coming together. No, he just wanted the sexual release that, for him, came only with the ultimate conquest, the crushing of his victim.

Franz caught himself daydreaming, getting hard just thinking about the girl... Willow? He thought that was her name. It didn't matter. Any of them would do.

CHAPTER 46 - FRANZ GIVES DIABLO THE SLIP AND VEE MEETS CHLOE: SUNDAY, OCTOBER 16

Diablo arrived at the helicopter pad with Willow just after noon. As Bernhardt had told him, he was in the hangar, up to his elbows in maintenance—nothing too big. Now he realized the Kraut had been reorganizing the seat configuration of the helicopter. He had all but two out on the deck of the hangar and was busy wrenching in one passenger seat next to the pilot's seat.

"What's up? How long before we can get outta here?" Diablo pointed at the two seats in the helicopter cabin, his eyebrows raised in suspicion. "Why you doin' this now? Why are the other seats out here?" Diablo had ridden in this machine several times and knew it carried up to eight people, the rest of the space left for baggage and supplies.

Franz scanned Diablo's face and winked. He smiled at Willow standing behind Diablo, looking apprehensive and disheveled, windblown from the motorcycle ride. "Relax, big guy. I got this. We'll be off in no time. You can help me by calling in at the office and picking up the flight log." He pointed around the corner to the outside wall of the hangar stall. "You remember the place I showed you the can last time we flew?" Diablo nodded curtly. Franz continued, "I left the log on the reception desk by mistake. By the time you get back, I'll have the other seat installed, okay?" His face was impassive, neither deference nor hostility evident.

Diablo flipped his chin in defiance. "What the fuck! What do I look like, a messenger boy?" Diablo's sense of self-importance was fragile. He was about to refuse when Willow collapsed against the side of the helicopter, blowing out air like a deflating balloon. She was tired of male egos bumping up against each other.

"Hey Big Guy, let's do something. Either help Franz get us in the air, or else take me back to the hotel. I am tired of this BS." She regarded him from underneath her long lashes, her hot-pink lipsticked mouth curved in a derisive smile.

Diablo interpreted the smile as Willow's eagerness to get some alone time with him. He threw the Kraut a blistering scowl, then patted the dancer's ass. "Yeah, Sweet Cheeks, I'll be right back."

∼

VEE WAS SPENDING THE EARLY AFTERNOON IN THE LAKE ELSE HOTEL Coffeeshop waiting for Chloe. She hadn't seen her since the previous July and wasn't sure she would recognize her, but she knew her van, the Cosmobile, would be unmistakable. Hazel had given her the rundown on that. She wondered about what was going on. Getting the extra cash had been helpful, but Vee didn't understand how what she had been doing–memorizing codenames and watching for her mysterious attacker–would produce any result. She knew if she caught sight of Hawk, she had to phone the number Hazel gave her where Candy could get messages. But how fast could she get that message, and how would sending a message help, if Hawk took her, anyway? Vee had constant butterflies just thinking about catching sight of the helicopter pilot again. She knew she would recognize him right away. But would he remember her? And what would he do if he did?

This was the dancers' day off, so the other three were still lazing in their rooms or checking out the hot springs next to the property. Vee was about to try the same when she saw the Cosmobile pull into the hotel parking lot. She did a massive double-take when Chloe emerged from the vehicle.

This couldn't be the cop she had met in Brandenhoff! She looked nothing like her! Remembering Hazel's reminder about being cautious, Vee collected herself in time to avoid making a spectacle of her surprise at the new arrival. She settled back down into her seat and stared at her coffee cup instead of out the window.

Chloe came breezing in, the scent of Estee Lauder's 'Beautiful' emanating in her wake. "Howdy, Sugah! Y'all must be Velvet! Aah'd recognize y'all anywhere from yer photograph!" She said the word as if 'graph' were two syllables. "You are gorgeous, just like Hazel said! Y'all know why Aah'm here?"

Vee, abashed by the fulsome compliment from this stunning woman, blushed deep pink. "I... I guess you are Chloe LaJoie, and you got dancer stuff to sell?"

"Why, sho-nuff, Sugah. That's me! Have y'all been waiting here long? Are there some other girlfriends who want to peek, too? Aah can show y'all everything Aah got, but have to get a little-bitty business licence before takin' yer money. But first, somethin' to wet mah whistle." Vee looked around to see that everyone in the café was staring at Chloe. The server, who has been in the kitchen, hustled over to ask if she wanted a menu.

"No, child. Just a Pepsi Cola, please... or do y'all have Cherry-Coke, or Dr. Peppah?" The waitress gaped at her with complete unfamiliarity, as if she were an apparition from another planet. "Land sakes! Just a soda, a Coke, then." The waitress nodded with a bounce and scurried off.

"So Velvet... is it alright if Aah call y'all that?" Vee nodded, almost like a bobblehead doll. "How many girls are there to see what Aah have?"

"Uh, just four here, Chrissie, Mona and Tiffany... uh... and me. They're still sleeping or maybe in the spa... Oh, hey! Do you want to go for a soak? I was thinking of doing that..."

"No, Sugah, Aah'm allergic to the stuff they put in the water. But that's okay. Y'all go, and Aah'll get checked in." Nora wondered if Vee remembered she was padded to the hilt–boobs and butt, not to mention false eyelashes, nails and wig. She took hours every morning to put it all together. "Y'all stayin' here for a spell, Velvet?"

"You mean here? In the café?" Her bewilderment was clear.

"Why no, silly! Aah meant at this hotel! Just tryin' to decide how long to book for. "Cause Aah'll go where y'all do for a bit. Okay?"

Chloe lowered her voice. "Have y'all seen Hawk or Loverboy around?"

Vee looked away as if to check to see who was listening. "Hawk? No... and I don't want to, either! But Bambi called the other day... uh... she works with some other girls doing some private stuff, and she said Loverboy was with them, like a guard or something.... uh... she couldn't talk much because the bikers are always watching them. She pretended she was ordering pizza to call me..."

Nora's ears perked up... could these be Tommy Cobb's B-string dancers, the ones that Franz Bernhardt had been flying around to camps?

"So Bambi didn't mention someone who might be Hawk? Someone who flies them to work?"

Vee shook her head, her voice still hushed, ".... Uh... she couldn't talk at all..."

"Do y'all know if they'll be able to look at the stuff in the Cosmobile?"

"Beats me! We hardly ever hear from them or find out what they're doing. It's good money. I know that, if you don't mind being pushed around by a bunch of greasy bikers..."

So, Nora reflected, I'll need to get past the muscle to see if Steph is one of them. "Have y'all met any of these dancers up close and personal, Vee, in person, Aah mean?"

"I just know Bambi because she was at BawdyWorks when I signed on... uh... she's real nice, comes from the island. She's native... and real fit! She can beat the guys at arm wrestling!"

"Aah wondah if she wants a whole work-up? Aah'd like to ask her about her roommates..."

CHAPTER 47 - SLASH TAKES OVER AND FRANZ SHOWS HIS HAND: SUNDAY, OCTOBER 16

Slash rolled into Terrace and connected with BB at the Restawhile Motel, where BB had moved the three remaining B-string dancers using the Brigade's chase vehicle. The new location was a no frills, two-star accommodation, with showers and no bathtubs, and no in-house restaurant. The dancers hadn't stopped grumbling since they had arrived.

Axel was now there as well, back from Rupert and providing temporary back-up in case the dancers got antsy about their move. Slash sized up BB's injuries, cleaned his eyes and applied some butterfly bandages. He was relieved to see that BB's eyes themselves were undamaged. He would be able to see well enough to work, at least. He wasn't yet sure what to do with Bambi who had caused the injury. She would at least lose pay, he decided. Then, Slash took over managing the work camp gigs, telling BB to arrange for another rental helicopter because they would still have to get Roxie, Fantasia and Bambi to NorthCo for Tuesday evening.

The hotel contract would be short a dancer until they got a replacement, so Slash put in a call to Tommy Cobb at BawdyWorks, only to find that he couldn't get another dancer up to Terrace until the end of the week. He decided he would take Vee to join the bush-gig dancers, and Mona, Chrissie and Tiffany would have to do extra sets at Lake Else to cover until the new girl arrived.

With the basic club housework done, Slash then turned his attention to the much more serious problem: Diablo had taken off with Brigade property, with Slash's personal backwarmer, Willow. The more serious question was whether they could trust him to bring her back, or whether by taking her, he had thrown down the gauntlet, defying Slash's authority for the leadership of the club. Had Diablo, knowing something about his father's health, been keeping it from Slash? Was this action just the opening move in a power play?

∽

ACROSS TOWN AT LAKE ELSE, CHLOE WAS IN THE MIDDLE OF HER DEMO with Vee when Slash zoomed into the hotel parking lot on his bike. They heard the roar of the bike from within the Cosmobile and looked at each other in expectation. Chloe mused out loud, "Is Slash here to buy a beauty "package" for one of his girls? Will he help get me a business licence?"

Vee's face was a study in tension. The bikers for her were just a source of anxiety, their deafening, polluting machines no less than their bruising, disagreeable personalities. Their dubious value as security was much overblown. In Vee's opinion, they attracted heat rather than dispelled it.

Slash knocked on the Cosmobile door and climbed in without waiting. "Hey, doll!" he directed this endearment to Chloe. Then to Vee, he signalled his thumb over his shoulder towards the door. "Get your stuff ready to go. Tiny will be over with the chase van to pick you up. You gotta take over for Willow."

Chloe interjected. "That's okay, Sugah. Aah'm in Room 315 if y'all want to chat some more about your order…" She peered straight into Vee's eyes when she gave the room number, and Vee felt she wanted Vee to remember it, that it might be important.

But Vee's mind was still focused on Slash's last words, "Willow?

Why? Where is she? I thought..." Vee was so choked she forgot the dancers were never to question the Brigade, especially Slash.

"Did I ask you to think, Velvet? Just get your skinny ass outta here, NOW!" With that, he gave her a vicious yank on her arm and sent her sprawling towards the door of the van.

∼

CHLOE'S REACTION WAS TO INTERVENE ON VEE'S BEHALF BY LUNGING TO protect her from falling out the half-open door. She remained silent, however, aware that feminine vocal protests were especially irksome. Her movement angered Slash regardless. He raised his arm to backhand her, but stopped when he realized she had assumed the classic heiko-dachi, the "ready" stance of karate.

Slash's face registered surprise. "That was quite the move, Chloe, just a lucky fluke?" Chloe relaxed and smiled her best dazzler. "Vee and me, we weren't expecting y'all so soon, Steve. I was surprised. At first, Aah didn't realize it was y'all, to tell the truth. Aah've never really looked at yer... uh... outfit before." Slash was dressed in his full colours, in black leather pants with the denim vest now over the black leather jacket.

"Land sakes, Aah do love leather! How do those pants feel? Are they soft? Can Aah touch?" She moved her hand to caress his leg and laid her head against his chest, pushing the denim vest aside to caress the soft cowhide. She could feel a rectangular shape in an inside pocket–a book of phone numbers, maybe?

Without warning, Slash grabbed her arms and jerked her away at arms' length. "Just what do you think you're doing?" For several tension-charged seconds, Slash regarded her with stony-eyed callousness.

"Why nothin' Sugah... Aah'm jest happy to see y'all. Aah just got into town myself." Her face lit up as she recalled her encounter with Luke and her decision to tell "Steve" before he asked. "Aah gotta tell y'all! Aah got stopped by a cop somewhere back there... some little jerkwater place..." She monitored his face for any change of expression.

Slash's blank glower remained impenetrable.

"Yeah, he didn't want much, just to check me out 'cause he'd never seen nothin' like mah Cosmobile, y'all know? Uh... anyway, Aah wasn't expectin' y'all... reckoned y'all had business to see to first?"

"What did you tell him?" Slash's voice grated out the question.

"Why... uh... the cop? Uh... the same as Aah told y'all, Sugah! What business Aah was in... Esthetician, photos, stage wear... y'all know what I said... Aah got nothin' to hide!" She flung her arms out to her sides as if to emphasize her transparency. Her enormous breasts jiggled with the movement. "BUT... uh... he said Aah need business licences. Y'all know anythin' about that, Steve? Sure enough, Aah don't..." She fluttered her eyelash extensions.

"Yeah, whatever..."

∼

WALKING BACK TO THE HOTEL LOBBY, SLASH CONSIDERED WHAT HAD just happened. The bitch was just as fuckin' ditzy as he thought. Or was she? He flashed back to how long she had chatted with the Mountie, and her knowing how to make that karate move. Just to check, he decided to call Tommy Cobb at BawdyWorks.

"Hey, Tommy, Slash Dracul here."

"Yeah, Slash, what can I do for you? I'm sorry I can't get a replacement dancer to you any sooner..."

"That's not why I'm callin', Tommy. I know it's not the usual thing for me to call, cause we got no official connection with Bawdyworks, but I gotta woman up here sellin' costumes and make-up services to the girls. I wanna know if she's legit..."

"Oh, yeah? What's her name?"

"Uh...Chloe...uh...LaJoie? Yeah that's it. Chloe LaJoie... blonde... big tits and ass...comes from the southern States..."

"Oh yeah, of course. Quite the broad! I met her here in town... I got some brochures from her in the mail. Her products are top quality... heard she has sent the same stuff to other stripper places, too."

"Yeah, yeah..." Enough of that for now. She sounded legit. Now, he had more important fish to fry. Where the hell had Diablo taken Willow?

∼

BERNHARDT WAS GRINNING AS HE SWUNG HIS CRAFT ALOFT, WHILE Willow cowered in the only passenger seat of the helicopter. It had been a piece of strudel to leave Biker Diablo behind and fly off with the girl. All he had needed to do was to flip her in and close the door, which was already in the locking position. Her screams became muted inside the cabin, and besides, Diablo had been too far away to hear...

The sky was overcast with leaden layers of cloud threatening rain or perhaps sleet. There was a brisk wind blowing from the northwest. Bernhardt knew he needed to make tracks before the weather worsened.

"You better strap yourself in. Wouldn't want you flying loose if we hit an air pocket..." He glanced over at Willow, whose face was a sickly, pasty white. Her eyes fixated on the dashboard dials in the cockpit, some of which were fluctuating in jittery cycles.

He followed her gaze and chuckled. "Relax. This thing can fly in all kinds of weather. This here is nothing. Sit back and enjoy the trip. You've been in this rig before, so you have fuck-all reason to be uptight."

She sounded small and somehow strangled. "I... I haven't ever ridden all alone before though... and I don't get why you left Diablo behind." Her voice strengthened as she realized the consequences of angering the Devil's Brigade. "He's going to be pissed, you know. I wouldn't want any of them pissed at me!"

"Listen, Chickee, never mind them. Where we're going, they won't be following..." With that, he banked the helicopter and sped up upwards, skimming in an expert arc across the top of Lean-to Mountain. Once over the peak, he set the auto-pilot with a heading due east.

She caught sight of the scarlet g-string suspended from the hook on the dash. Her eyes widened and she shuddered. "Where are we going?" Willow quavered. "I don't want..." Tears welled up, drowning her words.

"I don't care what you want. And you don't need to know where we're going." The clipped statement was brutal in its iciness. She saw arguing with such arrogance was futile. She slumped against the window of the door and feigned sleep, her face awash with weeping.

Franz Bernhardt surveyed the horizon, noting a solid cloud cover to the northwest and a dark plume of what might be smoke to the northeast. Nothing to get in his way, he decided.

∾

As Willow listened to that cold, nasal voice, her insides felt like lead. Being raped by Diablo had been nasty, short and brutal, but at least the biker had seemed alive and somewhat normal. This guy was like a zombie, flat and grey. Being fucked by him would be horrifying, like doing it with a machine almost. Shutting her eyes, she felt herself shutting down, the drone of the chopper drowning out the man's voice, her tears and snot cutting off all smell and taste, except for the metallic smack of fear at the back of her throat.

CHAPTER 48 - LUKE MAKES A PLAY, CANDY CHECKS IN, VEE LEARNS A LESSON: SUNDAY, OCTOBER 16

Corporal Luke Gallagher was on the phone to PG headquarters. A couple of critical sources had communicated with Benson. Karma Time, the codename for the op against the Devil's Brigade, was entering a dangerous phase. Word from the Terrace Airport Helicopter Watch had reported Hawk had lifted off with a young, unidentified female on board, leaving a furious Loverboy behind. Also, Wolf had arrived in Terrace and contacted Candy, who had checked in to report that Wolf had taken Ladonna to replace a dancer who might be Angel. Wolf didn't appear to realize that Hawk was taking this dancer in the helicopter to an unknown destination. Wolf couldn't yet realize that transport for the remaining bush-gig dancers would be unavailable.

Luke sat at his desk, tapping his pencil in thought. Where was Bernhardt going? Who was the female he had taken with him? Was she going of her own free will? What was Slavko doing with Vee? What kind of danger did these developments mean for Nora? Did she know Bernhardt had taken a dancer with him? How could the Force respond?

The scenario opened up a possibility Luke had never counted on.

The Devil's Brigade was vulnerable, open to the need to trust outside the club. Now he would see if his planning would pay off.

~

After Slash left, Chloe used the hotel lobby payphone to call her control Hazel and let everyone know that Wolf was in play, taking their asset, Ladonna, on a bush gig. Chloe wondered if she could tag along. Hazel didn't give a straight answer, instead questioning Chloe about Ladonna and her toughness. Coming to Vee's defence, Chloe reminded Hazel that their pursuit of Hawk began with Ladonna, that without her, they wouldn't have had any idea who might be the perp of several vicious murders along the highway.

"That doesn't mean she has what it takes to handle the rigours of a bush-gig circuit or the probability of a bust if the Force swoops," Hazel reasoned. "Ladonna was his first victim to survive an assault. From my understanding, that happened more because of the intuition of that taxi-driver, than because of Ladonna's instincts for survival."

Nora's stomach dropped. Bonnie might be right. She may have over-estimated Vee's ability to cope. For a moment or two, she wondered again whether she had taken too much on and would pay for her naïveté with the loss of someone else's innocent young life. But she also knew she had come too far now to just quit. She heaved a sigh. "I don't agree, Hazel. She freed herself from the bonds he had her tied up with, and disabled him long enough to get away. Admittedly, she was lucky to have Sandhu there, but I think she showed some grit in that situation. Besides, if I went too, at least we might have a witness to the illegal activity in the bush camps, and I could keep my eye out for our person of interest."

"Ladonna's vulnerable now with Wolf; we don't want you in the same position… Word is, Hawk has gone AWOL, Candy. Our airport contact patched through a message just a couple of minutes ago. Hawk has taken off with an unidentified female in his chopper, leaving Loverboy behind. It wasn't likely he would do that and then show up to ferry the others to their gigs at the camps. I think we've seen him make the move we've been expecting."

"And he's one of the reasons I'm here in the first place. I need to get him in my sights. Willow, whoever she is, is with him... and now needs to be replaced." Her mind was turning over, calculating. "Odds are that Willow, the dancer who went with Hawk, is Angel, our girl, the DC's daughter. I haven't been able to do a visual ID, but Ladonna thinks Willow's description matches the grad photo I showed her back in Vancouver."

"Yeah, that's possible," Hazel admitted. "All the more reason to do this next stage carefully... last thing we want to do is put the DC's kid into more jeopardy."

"But I could..."

"Candy, just gimme some time to check into what's being done, alright? I know you want to be in on the action, but your cover story has to hold. How would Chloe look, in *her* get-up–high heels, bouffant wig and fake nails–traipsing around some logging camp? Nobody would give two cents for your chances."

Chloe's whole body seemed to deflate as if she were letting the air out of pneumatic breasts and butt cheeks. "Hazel, I don't have to stay being Chloe. I could..."

"I said, be patient. Wait to hear from me. I'll call tomorrow–Monday–around noon."

Yeah, right! Time enough for Luke Gallagher to grab the bust with no input from her. She couldn't forget that Luke said he was her back-up... the sneaky beggar! Would he do *anything* to show her up, to undermine her success in undercover, including horning in on her perp just as she was about to collar him? Nora's vision turned black with resentment. Then she remembered why she had always liked Luke... he was a decent guy who tried to do his job with integrity.

No, I don't know for sure that's what he's thinking. Maybe he's been assigned as my back-up and had no say...

"Candy?" Hazel's voice crackled over the phone.

"Yeah... I know, stand down..."

"I'll be back in touch tomorrow. Be close to the payphone around noon."

∼

WHILE STOPPING AT HER LAKE ELSE HOTEL ROOM TO COLLECT HER gear, Vee protested she wanted to say goodbye to Mona, Tiffany and Chrissie, but Slash said there was no time and whisked her off on his bike to the Restawhile. There, the other bush-gig dancers were being kept secluded with Axel who ushered Vee into a room to share with Fantasia. The quick turnaround bewildered Vee and when they were alone, with eyebrows raised, she turned to Fantasia, who shrugged in reaction.

"Willow got cozy with Diablo, and he took her to spend some alone time, I guess."

"Willow wanted to go?"

"I somehow doubt it, but that was a dumb move, you know, goin' off with one of these guys. If she really didn't want to go, she should have put up more of a stink. You know they share their women, right? But Slash had his mitts on Willow. He ain't goin' to be happy about Diablo takin' her somewhere."

"Where'd they go?"

"Who knows! Likely holed up someplace where she can't get away until he's finished with her. Anyway, none of my business, and you'd be wise not to make it any of yours either."

"I don't want to work off-circuit... can't they get someone else... BawdyWorks, maybe? I don't want to be hauled all over the place by a helicopter..." Thoughts of the Brandenhoff attack by a helicopter pilot loomed like a specter. Could it be the same guy? What would he do when he recognized her?

"Don't be a wuss! We get extra pay, and I heard Slash say he's buying us some new outfits... could be worse."

"Where's he getting the new outfits?"

"I don't know... some connection he made somewhere..."

Vee knew where, but wondered if Fantasia had any idea about the Cosmobile.

"Did he say when we were going to get this new stuff?" Maybe she wouldn't lose touch with Candy after all!

"No idea. Listen. Don't ask so many questions! You're better off being stupid, or at least looking stupid, in this business. Besides, Slash isn't the most reliable... you know? I wouldn't count on any new outfit until I have it on my hot little backside!"

CHAPTER 49 - WILLOW AND DIABLO IN CRISIS: SUNDAY, OCTOBER 16

Three and a half hours after taking off from Terrace, Franz was swinging north toward his cabin on the far west corner of Jacob Lake. The girl hadn't made a move the entire flight. She seemed almost in a catatonic state, wedged in, her shoulders and head hunched against the door.

"Hey, Willow! Is that your name? You might as well look around. The scenery is hard to beat, and chances are you'll never see it again..." He waved his arm as if to emphasize the astounding beauty of the lake and surrounding hills spread out before them. The velvety forest green of the evergreen trees clothing the mountain sides contrasted with the spectacular azure of the elongated lake stretched along the valley.

"What's that supposed to mean?–'never see it again'? How do you know what I might see or not see?" Then she stopped, frozen, as if weighing his words again. Her voice was suddenly tear-sodden. "What do you mean, eh?" Then, as if energized by terror, she shrieked, "What are you going to do with me?" She lunged at him across the cabin but forgot the shoulder and lap seat-belt constraining her.

"Hey, settle down, you dummy! Remember, I'm piloting this rig.

You don't want me to mess with the controls, do you?" With that, he executed a full three-sixty flip, causing Willow to shriek even more. Her head bobbled with its shocking white fringe of bleached hair, and for a moment, suspended in her seat belt harness, she looked as if she were about to barf. She looked at him with a terrified plea, and he righted the helicopter. "There, does that tell you what kind of problem you might cause?"

A quick examination of her face convinced him he had terrified her into submission. Her skin was pasty-white and blotchy, her mouth gaping like that of a fish on a line, gulping and licking her parched lips as if he had sucked all her vital juices out of her. Her eyes were bulging and red-rimmed; all trace of makeup had vanished with her tears. She stared horrified at him as if at last perceiving his intent. She then began to shudder nonstop, gibbering and hacking as if demented.

He lost his temper. "Shut your hole, you stupid cow! Shut the fuck up while I land this thing, or I will open your door and dump you in the lake! And don't think I won't!"

~

"Is... is... that wha... what you did... be... before? I don't care. I can swim..." She could barely contain her terror to form the words. She clicked the mechanism to take off her seat belt harness, at the same time jimmying the handle of the door as if to let herself out, but soon she realized he had locked it.

"Look what I have here..."

Her eyes swiveled to see him raise a pistol, a Walther P38, and train it on her head as he maneuvered the controls with his left hand. "See? It won't take much to finish this altogether. Now sit still, do up your belt, and shut-up, or I will shut you up!" He moved the pistol to two fingers of his right hand as he took the controls to land the helicopter on a purpose-built pad behind a log cabin.

Willow, shocked into silence, leant against the door again, blinking back her tears.

∼

DIABLO WAS RAGING. HE WAS FLYING DOWN A BIG SLAB OF HIGHWAY, speeding at a breakneck velocity back to Terrace to meet up with Slash and BB. He couldn't fathom how that Kraut had put one over on him. He, Diablo, would be the laughingstock of the Brigade, even a pariah! What could he say to Slash? Or to his father? That he lost the chick to the Kraut who had duped him into being a gofer? A patsy! Sucker! Sap! F–U–C–K!!

The club had to help him out, he calculated, or they would risk losing a dancer, not an option considering how much of an investment she had been in costumes, food, lodgings... the thousands of dollars spent on any one dancer was one huge problem, but an even worse snag would be to tell Slash that the Kraut had snatched his main-squeeze! Yeah, Slash would figure how to get her back, or Diablo's ass would be grass and the club's number two the lawnmower! He would be up shit's creek no matter what, he reflected. How could he explain why he had been alone at the airport with Willow in the first place? Maybe he should just cut out? Go back to Edmonton and plead with the old man for a reprieve?

No, he couldn't do that. Not only would the old man tell him to man up and send him back to face Slash, but old Spyder would also take a piece of his hide for trying to weasel out of a just punishment. He was screwed, no matter what he did. What would Slash do? What would the Brigade want to do? What would Spyder do? Would it help that he was Spyder's son? Was that likely?

This array of questions kept cycling through Diablo's mind as he raced ever faster along the Stewart-Cassiar Highway back to Terrace. Where it crossed Highway 16 on the outskirts of town, Diablo picked up some heat.

Diablo seethed in near hysteria. "Fuck! What else is going to go wrong?"

The RCMP motorcycle set his siren and signaled him over.

Diablo slowed and pulled over, staying astride his motorcycle as the cop approached.

When the cop strode abreast of him, he gave the prescribed surly response to any attention from the heat. He left his aviator sunglasses down and flipped his chin. "Uh... yeah, whaddaya want?"

"Licence and insurance, please."

"What for?"

"I clocked you at 120 kilometers along this stretch. That's forty over the posted limit."

"BS! I ain't got that kind of juice in this rig!"

"My radar says you do. Now, are you going to dismount your motorcycle, or shall I call in someone to take you into the detachment and your bike to the impound yard?"

"Whatever..."

"Right." The patrolman radioed the detachment, and Diablo sat fuming in an even blacker funk.

CHAPTER 50 - ON THE EDGE: MONDAY, OCTOBER 17

Corporal Luke Gallagher trained his eye on the latest updates for the Karma Time Operation, calculating how much time he had left to play with before there was a serious risk of losing either a civilian or an operative. Not much. Time was running out.

His hunch to do a records search through Transport Canada had paid off in identifying the most frequently logged destinations for Franz Bernhardt's helicopter. Luke had checked with the offices of the mines and camps that Transport Canada had identified as the destinations where Bernhardt had been flying all season. He picked up the phone and dialed the number for NorthCo Lumber. He hoped they'd be able to tell him something of Bernhardt's movements.

"Good morning, NorthCo Lumber. Where may I direct your call?"

"Good morning. Corporal Gallagher of Glacier Lake RCMP Detachment here. I'm calling to inquire about a contractor you have working for you. Can you tell me please, is Frank Bernhardt's helicopter scheduled to fly for you today?"

"Let me check, please." After a brief pause, she was back on the line. "Uh... seems he was scheduled for a pickup but he's a no-show. We are wondering if the bush fire spotted north of Jacob Lake might have interfered with flying. The wind was coming from that direction."

Luke phoned around to discover that none of the other camps had seen Bernhardt either.

So where would he go when he's not working? His logs showed only the coordinates for some place northwest of Fort Saint Jacob on Jacob Lake. There was no place name associated with the coordinates. Luke bet this spot was where they would find Bernhardt and whatever female hostage he had taken with him. However, there was no road to access the location, and a motorboat would give too much warning...

There was a bush fire in the area. How would that affect possible movement by air transport? A quick conversation with the local meteorologist told him there was rain on the way for the region that should dampen the fire before it became any kind of threat to Jacob Lake. Still, there was no guarantee. Luke decided he had to act.

Luke organized the logistics of his plan. His first call was to District Commissioner Benson, then to Chilliwack. His third call was to a helicopter rental service. Finally, he alerted his back-up crew, Constables Purvis and Wosniak.

∼

CHLOE WOKE EARLY TO PLAN HER NEXT MOVES. FIRST, SHE BUSIED herself with the need for business licences, knowing she could connect with the local detachment through the Terrace Chamber of Commerce.

Setting up her licences was cumbersome and time-consuming, so that by the time she finished, it was almost noon, and she had to hustle to catch the call at the payphone in the lobby of the Lake Else Hotel. She rushed in from parking the Cosmobile in the hotel parking lot, failing to notice Slash sitting behind a newspaper in the lobby.

On the line, Hazel had valuable information for Chloe, the coordinates for Hawk's getaway cabin on Jacob Lake, which Chloe had to memorize on the spot. Hazel reinforced her caution that if Chloe saw Hawk, she was to keep him in her sights, but was not to go anywhere in a helicopter even if she saw that Ladonna appeared to be on edge about travelling. Hazel finished by assuring Candy that Osprey was aware of the situation and planning to deal with it. He was the source of the coordinates.

Chloe hung up, troubled. Was Luke about to take credit for this op?

'Planning to deal with it', my eye!

"You were in some hurry to catch that call, doll!" Slash loomed up behind her, startling her into horrified silence. Had she said anything on the phone call to give herself away? Hazel had done almost all the talking... maybe she herself had said 'okay' or 'yeah', but that was it, she thought...

"Why, Steve... uh... Aah had to catch a supplier. Aah got some gorgeous new bodices comin' in soon..." She made a mental note to order some to cover her story. "... and he needed to double- check on sizes."

"Why didn't you take the call in your room? There'd be more privacy there... nobody like me to overhear..." He moved in closer, as if to challenge her expectation of personal space. "Or maybe you enjoy having me knowin' what's going on with you?"

"Land sakes, Steve! Of course, y'all can know what's happening. Aah use the lobby phone because that way Aah don't hafta go all the way to mah room from the van to get the call. Aah jest put in mah applications for business licences like that cop on the road said Aah needed to... and Aah'm runnin' a tad late."

He looked at her sideways, as if examining her explanation for holes. "And what's up with the licences?"

"Aah should hear pretty quick... the cops have to okay mah applications... uh... just a courtesy, ya know? Mebbe a small town thang? So Aah need to stop by the copshop tomorrow."

"Oh, yeah? The cops got their noses into everything, don't they?"

∼

Somewhere in Slash's mind, there were warning signals going off. The Chamber of Commerce applications needed courtesy back-up from the Queen's Cowboys? Something seemed fishy here...

"Did they say why they have to 'okay' you? Is that the usual routine?"

"Dagnabit, Steve! It's jest a PO-lite connection fer a new bizness! Don't pitch a fit, now! Aah'm jest doin' what Aah have to, here!"

"Aw, Chloe, I just wanna get our business fixed 'cause I got other stuff to do. I was waitin' here to make a date for my first girl. Can I bring Roxie to see you this afternoon?"

"Why sho-nuff, Sugah! I'll be in mah van as soon as I drop mah bag off."

∽

Slash had a lot on his plate. As he rode his bike to pick up Roxie at the Restawhile, he wrestled with his problems: Diablo was nowhere to be found and had taken Willow God-knew-where. Their helicopter pilot was not answering his radio calls, and they had the extra expense of a replacement helicopter. To top it all off, there was something fishy about that ditsy chick, Chloe. What to do? Slash decided he had to check Chloe out.

When he stopped by to pick up Roxie, BB told him he had secured a helicopter for the following day. It hadn't been as difficult as he expected. There had been a cancellation because of some bush fire so they could make their trip to NorthCo, no problem.

He tucked Roxie onto the P-Pad and hustled back to Lake Else. While Chloe was doing her thing, he would check out her hotel room. There had to be something...

∽

At the Terrace RCMP Detachment, Diablo was in custody, and none too cooperative. He knew speeding was just a traffic violation, so he just clammed up and refused to answer questions. Waiting for his one phone call–to Edmonton, he decided–he tried to frame his predicament to put himself in the best light. The old man would be livid about the coupon–a speeding ticket–but he'd pay up because he'd done it for others in the club. He wouldn't mention Willow being missing, as he couldn't trust the cops not to be listening in. Besides, the Kraut would have to bring her back when he's finished with her... maybe a little worse for wear, but nothing she wasn't used to... Yeah, he'd just ask ol' Spyder to wire some money to pay the fine...

The phone call to Spyder did not go as Diablo has hoped. The old man answered the phone, ornery as a wild boar.

"Yeah, who is it?"

"Uh... Diablo... uh... Spyder." He never called him 'Dad'.

"Whaddaya want?"

"Uh... can you send some money to Terrace to pay a fine?"

"What for! What the hell have you done NOW?"

"Just speedin', nothin' serious..."

"Speedin'"? You stupid git! Not even wheelies or jumpin' the meridian? You got a coupon for speedin'? The only thing worse would be getting' stopped for not wearin' your brain-bucket!"

Diablo gulped, "Uh... Spyder..."

"Fuck! I got no time for this! Call Slash for the dough!"

Diablo pleaded with his father, "I got only one call, and this is it. I won't get another..."

For several moments, there was a dead silence on the line. "Alright, you stupid jerk. I'll call Slash for you. Even a piece of shit like you we can't leave in jail... unhealthy place for a biker..."

CHAPTER 51 - CHLOE UNCOVERED AND WILLOW OVERCOME: MONDAY, OCTOBER 17

After dropping Roxie at the Cosmobile, Slash wandered into the hotel and found his way to Chloe's room. He'd made a note of the room number on her hotel key and, using a credit card to slide past the bolt, had no trouble gaining entry.

Inside, he did a quick search of her clothes hanging up. No piece, or any other weapon. She took her chances, not carrying something to protect herself, he mused. The clothing in the closet was new and sparkly, some of it still sporting the price tags. The bed was a jumble of women's underwear, and there were two wig stands on the mirrored dresser displaying long tresses of blonde hair-do's. Scattered about the floor was a variety of open-toed and closed in spike heels. He had to walk carefully not to trip himself up on them. A quick examination of the bras and panties revealed the extensive padding.

"That sneaky bitch! That's not all her!" He laughed to himself, reflecting on his own stupidity. Of course, she would say she was just advertising her products. No wonder she'd been playing so coy about getting felt up! He was about to leave when he decided to search the bedside drawer. There he saw her Walkman under the hotel take-out menu.

What kind of music does she like? Probably nothing like what she says...

He opened the case to check that there was a cassette inside and chortled to see it was a Liberace label. "You gotta be kidding me! Who would listen to this pansy shit?"

He sauntered down to the lobby and, having a while to kill while Chloe worked with Roxie, he checked in with Spyder. Maybe he knew where his kid was. As the operator connected him, he pondered Chloe's music taste. No doubt about it. This chick was weird!

"Yeah? Who is it?" Spyder sounded cantankerous.

"Slash... just checkin' in."

"You know about Diablo? The stupid git got himself stopped for speedin', of all things!"

Slash laughed out loud, astonished to hear the Pest had been picked up for one of the stupidest of rooky beefs. The Boss continued, "Yeah, he needs cash to pay the ticket.... And to get the bike out of lock-up...Okay?"

"I'll see to that, Spyder." What a pain in the ass! Slash's first reaction was relief that Diablo had got caught by the cops. Then he realized that Spyder had made no mention of Willow. What had happened to her when Diablo got stopped? He would have to find out.

On the way to the copshop, Slash flashed back to the Liberace tape in Chloe's Walkman. The choice of music was bugging him. He made a mental note to check it out when the opportunity arose. No point in getting hung up on nit-picking shit when he had bigger problems to sort out. Before anything else, he had to unravel what was up with Diablo, the piece of shit!

~

FRANZ NOTED THE BUILD-UP OF SMOKE TO THE NORTH OF HIS CABIN ON Jacob Lake. He decided it was far enough away and small enough not to interfere with his plans for the rest of the day. The girl was still crouched against the door when he landed the chopper on the concrete block pad carved out of the bush behind his cabin. Once the rotors stopped, he exited the pilot door and, thrusting the passenger side open, uncoupled the seatbelt harness and yanked the girl out. She collapsed onto the gravel, her limbs rigid with fear. Franz, exasperated, picked her up and threw her over his shoulder to haul her into his cabin.

There, he grappled with Willow to truss her hand and foot with rough hemp rope before tossing her on the sleeping bag on the double bed. Without warning, she began to scream, a high-pitched keening that penetrated to his breaking point. He shouted at her to be quiet, that no one would hear her out here, so she might as well save her voice. He realized he had never had the luxury of such privacy before, had never had a girl in his own place to do with as he pleased...

∽

WILLOW SEEMED ALL AT ONCE TO UNDERSTAND THE DESPERATENESS OF her situation and started to thrash and shriek like a person possessed. Her movements were frenetic enough to loosen the bonds he had applied. The realization that she could break free for a moment glowed as a frantic hope in her eyes.

In a convulsive reaction, he backhanded her twice, left and right, the assault causing red splotches to bloom on both cheeks. All the while he was yelling over and over, "Shut up, bitch! Lie still! Shut up, or I will shut you up! I won't listen to your caterwauling like a cow! SHUT THE FUCK UP!"

Willow, terrified, could not control her paroxysms of horror and continued to screech. Franz found an old red kerchief and stuffed it into her mouth, securing it with another piece of cloth ripped from a tea towel by the sink. She lapsed into rhythmic groaning and whimpering, rocking on the bed until, exhausted, she settled into inertia.

∽

Having muffled her sound, Bernhardt built a fire in the Quebec heater, and set the kettle on to boil. A quick glance out the back window reassured him that the bush fire was not advancing; in fact, the accumulating clouds seemed to suggest rain, and he felt reassured that there would be no interruptions to his agenda.

CHAPTER 52 - SLASH TAKES ON DIABLO AND VEE STEPS UP: MONDAY, OCTOBER 17

By the time Slash arrived in Terrace from Lake Else, he had compiled a long list of worries to put to Diablo. Why had he taken Willow? Where had they gone? Why wasn't she still with him when he was stopped by the cop? Where was she now?

Slash hated dealing with cops. He didn't even want to go into the detachment, but knew he had no choice if he wanted to get Diablo sprung loose. He stopped at a gas station to take off his colours and stash them in his saddlebag. No point in riling the Horsemen with pointless baiting. His black leathers would pigeon-hole him as a heavy as it was.

In the cop-shop, he approached the glassed-in front desk and stood quietly while the civilian woman on the phone finished her conversation.

"Uh... I'm Slavko Dracul, here to see... Dimitrios Zorman..." the seldom-used name falling hesitantly from his lips.

"Yes, Mr... uh... Dracul? Just wait here. I'll page the duty officer."

After about ten minutes, a fair-haired young constable emerged from a back office. "Constable Hermann, Mr. Dracul. How can I help you?"

"Uh... I'd like to speak to Dimitrios Zorman."

"You'd like to speak to him?" He consulted the roster on the counter in front of him. "I see he has a fine for speeding, and his motorcycle is impounded... are you here to deal with either of those issues?"

"Yeah, probably... but I want to talk to him first... uh... please." The final word emerged as a whisper.

"You plan to leave him in custody?"

"Uh... no... I just want to talk to him before I pay up, you know?"

"No, I don't know. Usually, when a person resists arrest, he has to appear in court, plead, have his day in court, and then pay the penalty before he can enjoy the benefits of freedom... like conversation outside of visiting hours."

Slash seethed, listening to the cop's scornful recital. Spyder had said Slash had to pay up to get The Pest out. Otherwise, he'd just as soon leave him inside to rot for a stretch! But he had no choice if he wanted a quick answer about Willow. "Alright, I'll pay the... uh... fine, and get the ticket for the bike lock-up."

"Right. Wait here, and I'll get the finance clerk to talk to you." Slash drummed his fingers on the counter, more and more antsy as each minute ticked by.

A half hour and five hundred dollars later, Slash, now clothed in his colours once again, led a chastened Diablo to a local bar for a chat.

"Uh... Slash, I swear, I just was takin' Willow for a ride on my bike. She said she liked the thrill, y' know? I didn't touch her, Slash, y' know? I know she's yer ol' lady."

"Well, she ain't, but that don't mean ya get to touch her. She's a stripper, see? They're all off limits, and ya know that!" Diablo squirmed in his seat. "So where is she, bigshot? Why didn't she get picked up by the cops, too?"

"Uh... well... we... went out to the... airport... just for a look-see, y'know? And... uh... the Kraut was there monkeyin' with his rig..."

"Yeah? So? Who cares? He was hired for tomorrow... wasn't he?"

"Yeah... uh... but he talked Willow into sittin' in his copter, and before I knew what happened, he took off with her! I swear, Slash, I never seen it comin'!"

Slash exploded. "WHAT?? YOU FUCKIN' IDIOT!" Every patron in the bar stopped what they were doing to watch the action between the two bikers. Suddenly aware of his voice volume, Slash yanked Diablo by the arm up and out of his chair and hustled him past the bar to the back, where he found the door out into the alleyway behind.

"What do you mean 'before you knew what happened'? Where were you while she was climbin' into the cabin? Jerkin' off somewhere?"

"Jeez, Slash, ya don't gotta insult me like that... Uh... I went to the airport office to get somethin' for the Kraut..."

"Like what?"

"Huh?"

Diablo's dumb act was wearing thin on Slash. "Like what did the Kraut ask you to get? Come on, Pest! Quit yer stallin'! The Kraut is the last person we want diddlin' with our strippers."

"He... asked me to get... uh... his flight log..."

"His flight log? What for? He only needs that if he's flyin' somewhere... Oh my God! You fuckin' SNOT! Were you getting' him to fly you and Willow someplace? And he swiped her out from under ya?"

"I swear, Slash, I didn't hurt her... We... I... uh... y'know..."

"You fucked her!"

"No! ... Uh... yeah..."

Slash could hold back no longer. He swung with an upper cut that dislocated Diablo's jaw and knocked the Pest unconscious. Slash stood for a minute or two nursing his inflamed knuckles, then trudged back into the bar to pay the bill and arrange for Tiny and the chase van to pick up Diablo and bring him back to the Restawhile and see he got patched up. He would have to be kept confined until Slash could figure out what to do about his disobedience. Figuring Diablo should at least have to repay the club the money it had forked out to cover the speeding coupon, Slash first urge was to send him back to Spyder to discipline, but he knew he needed to cool down to think that impulse through. He didn't need Diablo working on Spyder against him.

None of this hassle helped deal with the problem of what had happened to Willow. The more he thought about her, the more infuriated he became until his rage became a white heat that drove him to let the pressure off. His rage lit on Chloe.

Before dealing with Diablo, he had almost decided not to bother with any more snooping in Chloe's room, but something prickled at him. Why would a chick like that listen to a limp-wrist idiot like Liberace? It made no sense! If he couldn't do anything about Willow, at least he could get to the bottom of that phony broad.

Slash made his way back to the Lake Else Hotel and, after checking that Chloe was still in the Cosmobile working with Roxie, he got into her room once again, put the earphones on, and pressed play.

～

VEE WAS HANGING OUT AT THE RESTAWHILE WATCHING "THE YOUNG and the Restless" when she overheard BB having a heated exchange on the phone in the next room. She wasn't able to catch the entire conversation but heard 'Cosmobile' and 'cop snitch' (or is it 'cop bitch'?) and 'tape player' before the door in the adjacent room slammed, and there was silence.

Vee sat stunned, her eyes glued to the television screen, not taking in any of the soap story. Was Chloe's identity blown? It sounded possible, judging from the little she had heard. What else could those overheard words mean? She looked around for Axel, their minder, and saw him with his back to her in the doorway, busy talking in hushed tones to someone in the hall, likely BB.

The phone sat on the table between the twin beds in the room. She knew she didn't have permission to use it, but her fear for Chloe emboldened her. She remembered the Lake Else registration desk phone number and called it, using her body to muffle the whirr of the rotary dial as she selected one number after another. Each ring as she waited for a response seemed to last eons. At last, the receptionist answered. Vee whispered, "Three... one... five, please..."

Again, the phone rang on with no answer until the receptionist interrupted. "The guest must be out, Miss. Do you want to leave a message?"

Vee heard movement behind her as Axel re-entered the room and shut the door. To camouflage her phone call, Vee made as if she were reaching across the side table to grab a copy of Vogue magazine from Fantasia's bed. Holding it up in front of her head, she whispered into the receiver, "Tell her Lucky knows, maybe Wolf, too."

At the other end, there was dead silence, as if the listener were unsure of what Vee had said. "Can you repeat that, please?"

"Lucky knows, maybe Wolf..."

Axel yanked the phone from her hand and swung to swat her. She covered her head with the magazine in her upraised arms, Axel's voice thundering up close to her ear. "What the fuck are you doin' on the phone? You know the rules, you stupid bitch!"

His three-hundred-plus pounds shaking in rage, and his tattooed face purple with righteous spleen, Axel lifted her by one arm and a leg off the bed and tossed her against the wall, where she crumpled in stunned confusion. Her ears were ringing, and she saw dots before her eyes.

"I was thinking of ordering some pizza..."

"You don't need no pizza. You're too fat already."

She wondered if Chloe would get the message.

CHAPTER 53 - INTO THE FRAY: MONDAY, OCTOBER 17

As Chloe was working on Roxie's outfit, she remembered she had left some new *Vogue* and *Elle* magazines in her hotel room. She was running by the reception desk in the Lake Else Hotel lobby when the woman behind the desk waved her over. She had a message for her. Chloe listened in horror to the alert from Vee.

Her heart pounded, the strange metallic taste of fear in her mouth. She shook herself, knowing she must get a handle on her emotions before Slash showed up. What could she do to maximize her chances of making the bust? Or even surviving?

She decided she had to notify Hazel to send back-up. *Damn Luke!* Also, she would try to get a look at that small book she had felt in Slash's inside pocket, betting it was a goldmine of drug dealing contacts across Highway 16. In her hotel room, she checked her pendant camera to make sure the battery was still good, put on her high-button wedge-heel boots with the concealed blade, and grabbed a long, warm, black, hooded coat.

The voice message Chloe left for Hazel was succinct: Wolf will take me soon. Notify Osprey.

She ran back to Roxie to continue the make-over, all the time watching for Slash, who now knew who and what she was. She was in the middle of a facial when Slash roared into the parking lot with Gypsy behind him driving the chase vehicle.

The biker yanked open the door of the Cosmobile and glowered at Chloe.

"Howdy, Steve! Ah'm not quite done here…"

"Yeah, bitch, you are done here! You can cut the fake shit with the Southern belle routine, 'cuz I've been listening to Liberace!" He grabbed her arm and twisted it high behind her back, while he grated insults and threats into her ear, "Bull bitch. Fuckin' fuzz. Piece of shit… I shouldda offed you first thing… now you'll pay…"

Realizing that Roxie, with her face covered in a blue astringent masque, was all ears, Slash stopped and nodded out the door to Gypsy. "Listen, take Roxie here back to the hotel on my sled. Tell BB I'll be along with this piece of garbage soon."

Slash listened for them to go and then, checking the parking lot to make sure they were not being observed, manhandled Chloe out of the Cosmobile and into the chase van, where he handcuffed her inside to the door. All this time, Chloe, knowing her cover was blown, said nothing.

***

Slash took Nora to his hotel room in the Restawhile, searched her and discovered only the layers of padding but no weapon. Stripping her down to nakedness, he hyperventilated, while his anger at the deception bloated into a white-hot fury. This wrath translated into a vicious beating that left Nora lying on the floor, unable to move.

When he knelt down to check if she was conscious, he noticed the pendant on the chain and twisted it almost enough to garrote Chloe before he released the tension. He had come close to crushing her larynx. "That should fix your yapping! I better not hear even a squeak outta you." He retrieved his Beretta from his saddle bag, making sure she saw it before he stuffed it in the back of his pants hidden beneath his denim vest. He left, the hotel door locking behind him. She heard him speaking to someone outside, a biker to stand guard, no doubt.

For a few moments she lay overwhelmed by the pain of the

assault. Her left eye was swelling fast, likely a shiner in the making. The rest of the inventory of her injuries included a very sore jaw, a burning sensation around her throat where the chain had bitten into the skin, and severely bruised ribs.

When she saw his leather jacket left lying on the bed, Nora powered through her pain to hoist herself onto the bed and sit up. Her injuries, while painful, were just superficial, she decided, and she knew she had only this time to check to see whether Slash's little book contained a drug customer list. Listening for the sound of Slash's return, she used her pendant camera to take photos of the twenty-odd pages of the book. She was dismayed to discover it written in Cyrillic, the common script of Serbia. She was sure translation would be available, but knowing how word of any bust would spread, she also knew she had to get this intel into her control's hands without delay. When she heard Slash speaking to the guard outside the door, she stopped photographing and, just in time, shoved the book back into his inside jacket pocket. Slash entered to see her sitting on the side of the bed, her head hung between her legs.

Raising her head, she said nothing and kept her expression neutral. She regarded him through her one good eye. His eyes surveyed the scene, taking in her proximity to his jacket.

"So... not beaten so bad, ya can't get up, bitch-cop? Ya better not have bin nosin' around..." He examined her slim naked figure, noting her clear bronze skin and well-toned muscles. He undid his belt and fly zipper, growling, "You're quite the package underneath all that paddin' shit, ya poser skag... think I'll spend a little time checkin' to see how much more of a phony ya are..."

With that, he pinned her on her stomach on the bed and impaled her from behind, grinding and biting her neck and shoulders. The sexual assault was brutal and quick. Now, she was also bleeding across her back from the bites.

When he rose to leave, he threw her clothes at her. "Get dressed. We're gone in fifteen." At the door, he directed Axel, the guard, to get the four bush gig dancers ready to fly.

For a few moments, she lay as if paralyzed, calming her scrambled thoughts. She felt violated, hollow with humiliation, her sense of self almost shattered. A mental image of Vee's vulnerability galvanized her into action. She would have to act to save Vee, and Vee might help save her, or at least the intel in her pendant. Then, her mind made up, Nora dressed, her aching body protesting with each movement. She couldn't let these brutal animals win. She couldn't allow any more missing and murdered women in this country.

She ensured her blade remained undiscovered in the wedge heel of her boot. It might be all she had between life and death. Aware of the limited time available to relay her intel, she had to hope the door was unlocked and to gamble on not being seen on exiting the room. Edging up to the door, she twisted the knob and breathed a sigh when she felt it turn. In his haste to get away, Slash had neglected to lock the hotel door. After checking the hallway and finding it empty, she sidled to the next room. She knocked softly, praying to find Vee inside. The young blonde asset was her only hope.

Nora thanked her lucky stars when Vee opened the door. Fantasia was packing a bag and paid little attention. Axel must be with Roxie and Bambi. She didn't know where BB was. She just knew she had little time.

"Vee..."

"Chloe, what happened? Oh, God... look at your eye!"

"Never mind my eye. I'm okay. Listen, give this to my cousin Hazel, yeah?" She tucked the pendant on its chain into Vee's hand, patting the girl's fingers closed. "She'll know it's a family keepsake. Don't let anyone see you have it. Right?"

"Yeah, I... I guess..." She stretched out her hand to touch Chloe's eye, but Chloe shook her head. Vee grimaced, her mouth working to find words to answer Chloe. "Hazel? Oh, right." Chloe saw comprehension in Vee's eyes. She would try to get the message through.

***

The replacement helicopter BB had arranged was ready on the pad when they arrived with their bags of dance gear in the chase van. Slash pushed Nora into the rear seat and sat beside her while the pilot stowed the bags in the back and the four dancers, with BB and

Axel, climbed into the middle ones. The pilot was a young, scruffy-looking, bearded guy who said nothing beyond the chatter back and forth to the tower to clear their take-off. Over the racket of the chopper's engine and whirling blades, Slash yelled to BB, "I'll be taking this piece of crap with me after I drop you, Axel and the strippers at NorthCo. Make sure nothing screws up! You and Axel work together until we figure out what to do with Diablo."

BB yelled back, "What's happening with Diablo?"

Slash made a backward flip of his wrist, a dismissive gesture with his hand. "Gypsy is keeping an eye on him until we get back. We'll pick you up in the morning and figure it out then."

The helicopter swung up into the cloud-covered sky. Climbing up out of the town site, there was a spectacular vista of snow-topped mountains and velvety valleys that lay partly shrouded in wisps of cloud. Slash paid no attention to the view.

***

After the drop at NorthCo, Slash told the chopper to head past Kitwanga and towards Meziadin. He was sitting behind the pilot next to Nora, her hands tied with a bungy cord. The hooks poking into the skin of her wrists bit like feral teeth.

The tension in Slash's face suggested his preoccupation with savage options. His merciless glare whenever he looked at her told Nora she was in great danger, her only possible salvation being the helicopter pilot, who was an unknown commodity. Could Slash be paying this guy to shut up about a body dumped in the bush? Or was this young pilot more decent than he appeared? Whatever his role, Nora realized she needed to figure it out soon. Her only real bargaining chip was that she knew the coordinates for Bernhardt's cabin.

"So I guess your regular chopper pilot is busy today?" Nora ventured, the first words she had spoken since Slash took her captive in the Cosmobile. She had trouble making herself heard over the noise inside the helicopter cabin. Her voice was a disembodied croak, her throat still on fire from the throttling earlier. She had pulled her collar up to hide her neckline in case Slash noticed that the pendant was missing.

Slash snarled back, "So that's how you sound? Stupid Southern drawl gone, bitch? Shut the fuck up if you know what's good for you." Slash's scowl was menacing.

Nora, speaking as loud as she could, hazarded another few words, "I know where his cabin is..."

Slash whirled around to face her. "I said, shut up!" He raised his arm as if to strike. "What do you mean, you know where his cabin is? How could you know?" Then he stopped, his expression becoming crafty. "Oh right... you're a cop... you know stuff..."

"I'll tell the pilot the coordinates, but you have to take me there, too."

Slash glowered at her, the hatred in his scrutiny palpable. "Yeah? What for, snitch bitch? He on your hit list, too?"

Nora stared back, waiting to hear if she had a bargaining chip.

"I asked 'what for?' Bitch!"

"He has a girl with him, a dancer..."

"I know that. What's it to you?"

"She's not just any dancer. She's the daughter of an RCMP District Commissioner..."

Slash's eyes widened, and he regarded her with new appreciation. "So, you know how to get there?"

Nora nodded.

"Do it, then. Tell the pilot."

"Wait a sec. Only if I get to go, too."

"Yeah, but no bullshit. Tell the pilot. Then shut up. I'm tired of hearin' your yap. Come to think of it, the phony Southern bit was better..."

Nora restrained by the four-way seatbelt, had to tell Slash the coordinates to relay to the pilot. Slash added, "I wanna get there pronto. There's a girl in trouble..."

Nora was interested to hear the heat in Slash's declaration. The biker cared for Stephanie. Nora hoped they wouldn't be too late.

CHAPTER 54 - WILLOW WHISPERS: MONDAY OCTOBER 16

In Bernhardt's cabin, Willow lay on the bed, gauging the looseness of her bonds, trying to fathom the pilot's thinking. He had made no sexual advance, not even a casual feel of her butt or boobs. She had been expecting rape, and even after Diablo's assault earlier in the day, she would have taken it without complaint because the alternative was to resist, and somehow, she thought that would be fatal.

Why was there a smell of smoke when the stove wasn't yet lit?

He was outside at the moment, chopping. She could hear the whack of an axe, sounding like he was splitting wood and making animal-like grunts as he chopped. Was he hurting? Was he weak? Why was he chopping wood?

This guy was so weird, a cold fish... a robotic nerd... the ultimate loser... a terrifying creep with nothing to lose. He seemed the type who could endure endless pain... and dish it out... That thought made her stomach clench even more. She didn't think he was interested in sex with her, not in the usual way, but the acid in her gut told her she was terrified. She needed to use her wits to get away from him.

Maybe he was open to an appeal to reason... likely he didn't know she was the daughter of a cop. Maybe knowing that might make him hesitate... give her some time to get her hands free... get to that CB radio on the counter...

With as little motion as possible, she twisted her wrists inside the rope ties. The coarse hemp chafed her skin. Within minutes, her persistent effort produced a slickness she knew was blood. Her hands slid more easily now. The rope didn't bite so much, but it was burning rings around her wrists. She kept working until the pain prevailed, forcing her to stop.

She listened. Bernhardt had stopped chopping, but wasn't coming inside. Willow craned her neck, straining to hold her head erect enough to catch the sound of his feet swishing through the poplar leaves piled up on the lake shore.

What was he doing? Raking? Why was he collecting dry leaves? Was he planning to burn them? Why would anyone provide tinder when the bush was already ablaze?

Her throat was scratchy and her eyes watering. The air was becoming smoky. Her mind raced with possibilities, each more horrific than the last. She heard thumps and imagined flames of falling brush licking at the roof, burning through the cedar shake shingles. Out the window, she could see a strange yellow-bronze glow in the overcast sky. She imagined the wall of flame advancing, consuming the cabin. She thrashed more convulsively, stretching her neck and jaw to loosen the gag wrapped across her lower face. The cloth he had stuffed in her mouth was causing her to heave. She suppressed the urge to vomit. Back to the wrist restraints... the rope was slimy with blood now, loose, but not quite enough to slip off.

Outside, the swish of leaves had stopped. Instead, she heard the distant drone of a helicopter. She hoped that meant Slash was coming... When Bernhardt thrust the door of the cabin open, the incoming air was acrid with wood smoke. She was aware of a dull roar beneath the beat of the chopper... there was fire close by.

Bernhardt went to the stove and removed the kettle, pouring hot water into a cup with instant coffee. He leant against the counter and regarded her fetal-curled shape on the bed, sipping at the cup, blowing to cool it down. He nodded towards the sky at the noise of the helicopter and spoke as if to the fiery heavens, "You couldn't hold off coming to check the fire... I cleared some of the tinder close to the cabin... just needed another hour..."

Willow opened her eyes wide at his words.

He's looney! What does he need another hour for?

She groaned, trying to speak through the cloth gag. He put the cup down, walked over to the bed and examined her wrists, tsk-tsking at the blood and abrasions. "Naughty girl... I told you to lie still... you cannot escape... there is no place to run..." He stopped to listen. Hearing the helicopter fading, he leant in to examine her up close, his coffee breath fusty to her nose.

Willow thrashed more frantically, moaning in pain and fear. Bernhardt reacted in fury, walloping her head back and forth until she was subdued. She could barely see, her eyes swelling shut from the assault, but she could discern at eye-level as he stood next to her, that she had aroused him. There was a sizable bulge beneath his fly.

"I'm going to remove your gag. You must not scream... I want you to lie here with me... for now... we don't have much time, you and me..." He was removing his jeans, a large, pink rubber dildo shoved into his shorts falling away as he climbed toward her. He reached behind her head for the gag and untied it, slipping it down to lie encircling her neck.

Her eyes remained glued to the dildo lying beside her on the bed. She raised her gaze to meet his, mocking derision written large in her eyes. Her voice was barely audible, a whispery taunt. "You got no dink? Is that your problem?" She was past caring if he retaliated.

∼

THE ACCURACY OF HER WORDS ACTED LIKE A TRIGGER, SETTING OFF HIS fury again. He fell upon her, spreading her legs and holding them down, his knees on her thighs. He was breathing in great gulps, muttering, "Slut, bitch, slut, bitch..."

Clutching the cloth around her neck, he wound the slack around his hand and twisted. The muscles of his jaw worked in spasms, tics jumping with each kink of the garotte. Willow's face turned a deep mottled red, then purple, as she struggled for air until she was still. The skin colour drained, with barely a tinge of life left, a strange contrast to the shock of bleached hair sprouting from her head.

Bernhardt assessed the girl's state. She looked done for. The stronger smell of smoke roused him to action. He needed to get out of there fast. There was just enough light left. He would fly south of the lake. The fire couldn't jump past the water. He left Willow's limp body on the bed, gambling the fire would reduce both the cabin and the body to ashes. He regretted losing the cabin, but he had no choice. Just then, his attention was caught by the rattle of a helicopter coming from the south across the lake.

∼

LUKE, WITH HIS TWO SUPPORT PERSONNEL, RICK PURVIS AND PETE Wosniak, had used a fire-watch helicopter to fly north of Franz Bernhardt's cabin. They had waited as long as they could to identify where Slash had taken Nora, but they had heard nothing.

They were all dressed in cold-weather, waterproof civvies, gloved and armed with RCMP issue Smith and Wesson 38s and two-way radios. The team would stay in contact with their fire-watch pilot, who was patched in, but muted to another nearby chopper. The RCMP officers had been following its progress on their chopper's radar screen. They were less than a mile apart, but the smoke reduced visibility to a few yards.

"Osprey here. Nearing target. Descending now."

A crackling response: "Roger."

The three fast-roped down the braided cord, landing a hundred yards from the cabin.

CHAPTER 55 - NORA GOES FOR A SWIM: 2300 HOURS MONDAY OCTOBER 16

Out a hundred yards from the lakeshore, the hired helicopter with Slash and Nora on board swooped low to surveil Bernhardt's cabin. Slash had heard a garbled communication come through on the radio–something that sounded like 'osprey'. He yelled to the pilot, "What's that about?"

The pilot shrugged. "There's a fire-watch chopper north of us. Just letting me know..."

"No more talking... I don't want nobody knowing we're here..."

Nora had heard the muffled word 'osprey' as well. Her heart leapt to grasp that Luke was nearby, but even more to realize that the helicopter pilot was someone on her side. Otherwise, why would he have downplayed the use of Luke's codename?

From the air, Nora could see the fire advancing towards the lake's edge with Bernhardt's cabin in its path. Slash craned his neck to catch of glimpse of activity around the cabin. There was the merest hint of smoke coming from the chimney, but the one front window was unlit, with no sign of activity inside. Behind, she could make out the silhouette of a helicopter parked on its landing pad. This had to be the place.

Chloe saw Slash nod when he had finished checking the place

out. She sensed Slash would try to rescue Willow from both Bernhardt and the fire, despite the apparent peril of the situation.

Slash shouted above the rattle of the motor, "Wait! You! Pilot! Turn right down the shoreline and fly back out a couple of hundred yards."

The pilot, confused by the directions, hesitated. Slash unclipped his seatbelt and climbed partway over the seat beside the pilot and poked him in the arm. The helicopter shimmied in the air. The pilot reacted, shouting, "Watch it! You don't mess with me when I'm flying! You wanna crash?"

"Then do as I say. Don't give me no lip! Turn right and fly down the shoreline, and out over the water a little way."

As the chopper swung around, Slash turned to Chloe, unbuckled her seat harness and reached across to unlock the door.

On the dash, an alarm beeped. "What the hell… close that door!" The pilot exploded, seeing the risk of an open door and an unsecured passenger. But Slash was shoving Chloe towards the parallelogram of gusting air. She resisted, clutching the straps of the seatbelt and screaming. Slash kept pushing her through and out into the lake below. She shrieked as she plummeted fifty feet into the water.

Slash couldn't ignore the pilot's agitation as he appeared to change course to hover over the woman thrashing in the water. With his Beretta, Slash shot off a couple of rounds aimed at Chloe and then held the muzzle to the pilot's head. "Don't get cute, fly-boy. Never mind that bitch. Take this thing towards the cabin and hang over the dock so I can drop down there."

"Listen, bud. I hear ya, but ya don't have the right gear. Ya need a rope to do it safe."

"Just do what I fuckin' say. I don't need no sissy rope," Slash scoffed. "After I get down, take off and come back later for me… about an hour."

"Right." The pilot swung low and hovered. Slash exited stumbling, overshooting the dock, so he landed in the waist-high water at the pier's end. The helicopter swung high and withdrew just as a shower of gunshots from the cabin door alerted Slash to Bernhardt's presence. Slash ducked below the edge of the dock to escape this first furious barrage from Bernhardt's Walther, and returned fire, hitting Bernhardt in his shooting arm. Slash had crawled belly-down on the dock to take aim, and during the next assault, he took a bullet in the chest, the force of the shot catapulting him backwards from the dock into the water. From there, he staggered back to hide below the deck, continuing with his remaining strength to take keep track of Bernhardt's movements.

There was a lull in the action, Slash assumed, as Bernhardt refilled his gun's magazine.

Now Bernhardt taunted Slash, "Hey Loverboy, I got Willow, you know. She put up a good fight, but she was a delicious piece of ass. But you know that, right? She just didn't have the staying power... too bad." He stepped onto the dock, searching for Slash to finish him. "It got me off, okay, you know? I always look for that special someone to help me get off."

Bernhardt's taunts hit their mark. Gasping in pain, Slash summoned all his strength to shoot back his hatred for the murderer, exposing his own position by crawling close enough to lunge upward toward Bernhardt, who was crouched on the pier holding his wounded right arm. The biker launched a last volley, then sank.

∾

BACK IN THE BUSH ABOUT A HUNDRED YARDS, LUKE AND HIS TEAM heard the shots and scuttled towards the sound. Behind them, the fire was advancing. They were in radio contact with the fire-watch helicopter, whose pilot was keeping them up to date. They had about a half hour before sunset when the helicopter must leave.

∾

IN THE LAKE, NORA CAUGHT THE SOUND OF DISTANT GUNFIRE. ONE bullet had hit her upper left arm just above the elbow. She could feel the cold water numbing her limbs. The water was glacial; within a minute, her teeth were chattering and her head aching. She discovered that her padded underwear inserts did not act as flotation devices. Quite the opposite, they were bloating with water and acting like lead weights to pull her down. She scrambled to stay afloat, but, dressed with coat and boots, she knew she must divest herself of some of the bulk if she hoped to swim ashore. She had to keep the boots for the knife and the coat for its warmth. The padding had to go. Chloe no longer existed.

Brrr! The water was frigid, just above freezing. With her right hand, Nora yanked her outer layers aside, trying to keep the bulky coat out of the way so she could wrench the boob and butt padding out from the bra and panties. Several times, she went under and emerged gurgling and coughing. Her long blonde wig, which somehow had survived the plunge into the water, came off and floated away.

The pad stitching was stubborn, so she had to yank again and again to separate the foam molds from the underwear. She uttered grunts and groans as she struggled to strip out the sodden forms. "Whose dumb idea was this, anyway? Padded boobs... wadded bum..."

Soon she found herself exhausted, losing blood, swallowing too much water, vomiting and choking. To conserve energy, she was treading water. Looking towards the shore, she saw a fiery glow in the dusk that had intensified during the time since she had noticed it in the helicopter. How close would it come to the lakeshore? Could she crawl ashore without risk? The cold seeping into her core told her she had to make the effort. Close to complete exhaustion, she laboured to swim, dog-paddling to minimize the pain in her left arm, each stroke an agony of cramping muscle.

CHAPTER 56 - KARMA TIME ASSAULT TEAM IN ACTION: 2330 HOURS, SUNDAY, OCTOBER 17

When Luke and his crew neared the cabin, they crouched to use Bernhardt's helicopter to screen their approach. In the cockpit, Luke saw the ignition keys tossed on the seat where Bernhardt had left them.

"Handy bit of luck, eh?" Pulling the door ajar, Luke smiled at Purvis and Wozniak and leant in to pocket the keyring. He hand-signaled Wozniak to guard the back door while he and Purvis checked out the action in the front where the gunfire was continuing. They shadowed the side wall up to where they stopped at a curtained window.

"I wonder if Stephanie is inside..." Luke muttered to Purvis, who shrugged and raised his eyebrows in speculation.

When they reached the spot where the porch attached to the cabin, they saw Slash sprawled chest down, across the planks halfway down the side of the pier, leveling intermittent shots at Bernhardt and then falling back down behind the pier for cover. A crimson flood spurted with each movement. Luke and Wozniak could see that Slash had suffered serious injuries. Bernhardt had his back to the cabin, so Slash was the first to realize that they had company. Slash's shot at Luke alerted Bernhardt to the danger behind him. Luke and Purvis edged back along the cabin wall to avoid the gunfire and gave Bernhardt, who seemed confused about who the newcomers were, time to race back to the porch to dive into the cabin.

∼

Bernhardt came across Wozniak at the back of the cabin where he was standing watch and moved up from behind to knock Wozniak unconscious before he raced towards the helicopter. There he discovered the keys gone. Realizing the attackers, whoever they were, had trapped him unless he left on foot, Bernhardt ran farther into the bush and then doubled back to follow the shoreline east.

∼

At the front of the cabin, Luke and Purvis continued to engage in a firefight with Slash, who was losing blood and body heat from standing in the lake.

"Give up, Dracul! You can't win here!" Moving further out along the base of the pier, Slash ignored Luke's warning and shot off another volley. There was a long pause while he reloaded. "Slavko! We know you're wounded… come out and we'll get a medic to look at you." When he realized he was in a hopeless situation, Slash surrendered, climbing with great difficulty onto the dock and collapsing there. A watery pool of blood spread beneath his unconscious body.

Luke knelt to check for vital signs. Slash's pulse was barely registering because of the loss of blood. He needed medical attention fast.

∼

In the meantime, Purvis ran back to check on Wozniak and discovered him coming to after being knocked out. "Pete! Pete Purvis!" Purvis helped his partner get to his feet and stabilized. He checked his head to discover a fair-sized bump developing. Farther behind the cabin, they saw the helicopter still there, the bush fire crackling in the near distance. "You okay to walk, Pete?"

"Yeah, my head's sore where that beggar got me, but I can see–no double vision. Let's go..."

Together, they entered the cabin and found Stephanie's body stretched out on the rope bed. For a moment they were struck dumb at the sight of the slender girl, her shorn hair dyed bleach-blonde, her pallor, black eyes and neck injuries mute testimony to her mistreatment. Purvis bent over to check her vitals and discovered a weak pulse and shallow breathing.

Purvis turned to Wosniak, "Tell Gallagher Stephanie Benson's still alive! She's very weak, but there's a pulse. We need medevac STAT!"

∼

As Purvis stayed with Stephanie, Wosniak moved out to the front deck where Luke had dragged Slavko up off the pier and was trying to staunch the flow of blood from his chest wound with his scarf. Luke panted, winded from the effort of moving the much bigger man. "His vitals are weak... we gotta get a medevac in here..."

"Uh... Corporal, the girl's inside. We think it's Stephanie Benson, and she's alive, barely. Her hair's cut short and dyed, but she fits the description otherwise. No sign of Bernhardt... but the bush fire is advancing."

Luke moved for his two-way radio. "I'll get the undercover RCMP helicopter pilot to request a medevac for both her and Slavko here. Too bad one of us doesn't have a helicopter licence. We could use Bernhardt's rig to get out of here. Maybe I'll suggest they send another pilot if one's available. That chopper is valuable as seized property. I'll contact our guy to see what he suggests."

Once on the blower to the undercover RCMP pilot who had ferried Slash and Chloe to the cabin, Luke received the bad news. "Slavko pushed a female into the lake, Corporal. She went in several hundred yards to the east of Bernhardt's cabin."

"What the...? What did she look like?"

"Blonde, buxom, heavy make-up… Slavko said she was a cop…"

"Nora! When did she get here? She was supposed to stay in town…."

"I don't know, Corporal. She was part of the party that I picked up in Terrace…"

"And now she's in the lake?"

"Last I saw, she was. He took a couple of shots at her, but I don't know if he hit her…"

Luke spoke to Purvis and Wosniak. "You stay here and wait for the medevac for these two. I need to see what's up with Constable Macpherson." He started trudging along the northern lakeshore toward Fort Saint Jacob.

CHAPTER 57 - CANDY, OSPREY, ANGEL AND THE HAWK: 100 HOURS MONDAY OCTOBER 17

Nora reached the shoreline of the lake, exhausted and sopping wet. She knew the only way to maintain what body heat she had left was to keep moving, so she began a painful, erratic trek westward along the lake shore, having to wade back into the lake to bypass huge outcroppings of spruce-studded granite bluffs.

On one of these forays into the lake, she glanced ahead to the west to see a figure about two hundred yards off, heading in her direction. She ducked down in the water to avoid detection, watching the person making its way with a halting gate, the right arm held stiff against the torso. Whoever it was, he (for the silhouette was masculine) was walking injured. The dull roar of the fire continued to fill the northern sky with a dull, russet glow as smoke added to the murk. The overcast day had threatened rain that never came, but now, as the sun set, the progress of the bush fire became clear. She snorted, thinking how the fire had answered her wish for warmth in spades.

But her immediate need was to identify the wounded walker. It was either Slash or Bernhardt, she decided. Either way, with only a knife, she needed to remain hidden and watch for an opening to get within range to attack, and monitor the progress of the fire in case she had to save herself by once again hanging out in the lake.

She looked for cover in the near distance and recognized a beach head of upturned tree roots caught in a rocky shoreline outcropping. She would get muddy and scratched by thrusting herself into that tangle, but at least she could remain hidden.

The figure continued to advance along the pebbled curve of the lake shoreline. Nora knew she would have to be formidable to survive an encounter with either Slash or Bernhardt. She had a decision to make. She could hide and hope to escape detection until backup arrived, or attack whoever was coming towards her, regardless of who it was.

The question was, was she strong enough to attack and win? Maybe... maybe not. She had lost a lot of blood, and her arm was throbbing from the bullet wound. But her head was clear and the adrenalin rush of the combat made the exposure to cold seem less acute. She felt ready to tackle whoever it was... from behind.

Concerning the walking wounded opponent approaching her, she knew her best chance to survive lay in surprise. She needed some camouflage. The tangle of tree roots was all there was. How could she hide without being entangled? She would risk scratches, maybe even deep gouging, but what alternative was there? The lake was a possible refuge, of course, but it's cold still lay heavy in her bones. She didn't want to go back in the water, unless the wild fire set the root tangle ablaze, something not likely as it was water-logged.

Also, she considered the mindset of her opponent. Whoever it was, that person was expecting Chloe, not Nora, if anyone at all. She imagined his reaction upon discovering that she was an agile and fit woman. That decided advantage helped boost her confidence, so she felt energized, ready to camouflage herself in the fibrous root ball.

∽

LUKE HAD LEFT WOSNIAK AND PURVIS IN THE CABIN TO WAIT FOR THE medevac for Slash and Steph. As he walked along the lakeshore,

Luke weighed the merits of calling in the helicopter to find Nora. It had a search beam, so even though the sun had set, they could use it. However, two facts weighed against using it. Casting back to his memory of the topo map of the area, Luke couldn't remember any place along the shoreline for it to land to pick her up. Then there was the advance of the wildfire. The smoke was making visibility a problem. They would be lucky to get the medevac in to evacuate themselves and the two injured.

No, Luke would have to keep to the lakeshore eastward on foot to find Nora, who he hoped had found her way to shore by now.

Luke now knew that Bernhardt, the predatory killer who has been stalking the highway for over a decade, was heading east toward where he hoped Nora had already emerged from the lake. She would be cold and wet, and without a gun. Slash's injuries were proof Bernhardt carried a gun. Luke knew an overnight hike would get Bernhardt to Fort Saint Jacob, where he could get himself a vehicle. There was no time to waste if Luke wanted Nora unharmed and Bernhardt either dead or captured to face changes. He tried not to think of Nora being harmed.

Night has descended as Luke began his trek along the lakeshore. He was trying to focus on his quarry and not think of Nora being harmed. The light cast by the wild fire danced over him, illuminating the shoreline in an almost kaleidoscopic fashion. The smoke was pervasive, a harsh enough attack on his airways that he had to conserve his energy. He wanted to run, but he had to negotiate an obstacle course of deadfall and small outcroppings, and every so often wade around promontories. He was making lousy time.

∼

TWO HUNDRED YARDS TO THE EAST, NORA HAD WEDGED HERSELF INTO A hollow she had fashioned in the root ball by tearing off some of the fragile web of fibrous roots. She thanked her instincts that she had brought a long coat with a hood which, despite being still wet, somewhat protected her head and arms from the gouging of the larger roots. The spot she had chosen allowed her to watch the advance of the wounded male along the shoreline. The closer he came, the more she was sure it was not Slash. His body shape was wrong. This man was taller and slenderer, without the bulky chest of the biker. So, it was the killer, Bernhardt, she would confront. For a second or so, she debated the virtues of waiting for backup. How long before Bernhardt would be beyond range? Why not let him go, and hope Luke had a helicopter organized to pick him up in Fort Saint Jacob?

Not bloody likely. The last thing I want is Luke making the collar!

As he neared, Nora saw Bernhardt was carrying a firearm, a pistol. This confirmed that her best hope for besting him was to attack from behind, to wait until he had passed, and hope he didn't sense her coming at him with full force. She saw he was wearing only a shirt on top. Nothing would interfere with a quick thrust in and up to the heart, as long as she was lucky enough to miss the ribs. She couldn't risk taking him down with karate unless she could disarm him as a part of the assault. He was holding the weapon in his left hand, a position she bet was unnatural for him. She tried to remember the profile she had studied months before. Was he left-handed? Probably not, she decided.

He was almost abreast of her position, looking haggard and winded, staggering with fatigue, his balance off. It would not be hard to take him down with a blow focused just above the kidneys, but now she was unsure about using her knife. Better to use the knife to disarm him and use his own gun to keep him secure. She knew a knife attack in the back, even on an alleged serial killer, would not stand up to any investigation by IIOBC, the Independent Investigation Office of BC. They would see such an attack as unwarranted, given that the person was running away from her. She psyched herself for the onslaught, remembering she had the advantage of surprise, knowing she could pack a wallop that would take him down and make him give up the pistol.

Untangling herself from the root ball took some time, as she had to take care her movements did not tip him off. Then, she had to creep, keeping crouched down until he was past the point of spotting her. She couldn't risk him looking sideways and catching a glimpse. When she was at last free to make the run at him, she had a soundless sprint of at least fifty yards to complete.

Though she had trained for fitness at Burnaby, she knew her exhaustion, and her wedge-heeled boots, heavy even without the knife inserted, were liabilities. She concentrated on the position of his vital organs in the torso, and aimed herself like a bolt for the right kidney, thinking his injury on that side would predispose him to be more vulnerable there.

She felt ash and smoke in her lungs as she raced forward. The fire was coming closer to the lakeshore. God! She didn't want to subject herself to another dunking!

No! keep your focus!

Bernhardt was the killer. She knew he was. Aiming at breakneck speed for his right kidney, she would punch there first with her fist and then go for his pistol. She would use the knife only to control him if she couldn't dislodge the pistol at the outset.

Nora hit him, a solid mass aimed at his lower back. She caught him by surprise and the pistol flew out of his hand to the left, but remained within his reach. She crawled up his back and held the knife to his jugular. "Easy, Bernhardt, easy. You're injured and tired. Enough now…" Feeling his movement beneath her, she pressed her blade harder against his throat until he stopped struggling, then eased her other arm out to grab the pistol. It lay just outside her reach to the left. Nora could see it glinting in the mottled light from the bushfire.

Her sudden thrust to grab it galvanized Bernhardt into payback. With his left hand, he grabbed at her hair to flip her over his shoulders. But he couldn't get a grip on her short hair. She twisted her torso and landed on her back next to the pistol and, spinning over, scooped it before Bernhardt could get up with his injured shoulder. Bernhardt was open-mouthed. Now, standing over him out of range of his arms, she had the advantage.

"You don't want to get hurt anymore, Bernhardt. I'll shoot if you made a break for it or fight me."

His voice sounded strangled. "Who are you?"

"Constable Nora Macpherson, Mr. Bernhardt. You're under arrest for assault on Vigdis Dahlberg in Brandenhoff on May 29th this year."

He scoffed. "I don't know what you're talking about. I don't know any Vigdis..." He stopped as if to ponder the identity. He cleared his throat and swallowed. "I don't know anyone with that name."

"Does Velvet Dawn ring any bells? Exotic dancer... tall... blonde... likes helicopter rides?"

"Fuck off, bitch, you can't lay this rap on me! I work long hours, and I got contacts, you know?"

"Watch your mouth. I've got better contacts!"

By this point, Nora had gestured him up several times, and he had strained and groaned to raise himself first to sitting, then onto his knees with his one good arm supporting his torso, until he was up and standing. With the pistol, she pointed him the way he had been coming, and they started walking, or in Bernhardt's case, stumbling and coughing, towards his cabin. All the while, the backdrop of bush fire somewhat illuminated the scene in the opaque murk of smoke and ash. Their throats were raw, so twice, Nora gestured the prisoner over to the lake shoreline, where she kicked up water onto his face and shoulders.

When they had been walking for several minutes, Nora could see ahead through the smoke another figure coming towards them. Was it Slash, out to get Bernhardt? The figure was still too far away to be sure. She almost cried out loud when she saw it was Luke. "You're here? Corporal Gallagher..."

"Yeah, I'm after this guy... thanks for stopping him." His warm baritone felt like a tonic. "Nice black eye!" His hazel eyes twinkled.

"Thanks. No problem. I've already told him he's under arrest."

"Oh, have you! Okay, then. We'll just have to make sure he gets to detachment in one piece, eh?" His voice was mocking, but there was a smile on his face. He punched her with a gentle tap on the shoulder. She winced, and he then noticed the hole in her coat and the watery blood stain seeping down the left side of her earth-stained shirt. "You're not in one piece, though, eh? Where'd you get hit?"

"It's nothing... only a flesh wound in my arm. I've been using it to deal with this guy..." nodding in Bernhardt's direction, "so it's bleeding a bit."

"Atta girl... uh... what's that on your cheek? Looks like half a spider..."

"What do you mean?" She swiped at her cheek and discovered a false eyelash clinging by a thread to the edge of her eyelid. "That's all that's left of Chloe, I guess..."

"Uh, by the way, Steph is in the cabin back there, barely alive... uh and Slash..."

"Why didn't you say so? I want to talk to her! Here, you hold on to this guy!" She started sprinting towards the cabin.

∼

PURVIS WAS STANDING OUTSIDE, KEEPING AN EYE ON SLASH WHEN SHE ran up. "Is Steph...?"

"She's conscious in there, but I don't give her much time... I think he damaged her trachea... uh... her windpipe and maybe her spine. She's breathing funny and says she can't feel anything. But she's aware..."

"Oh my god!" Nora felt hollow. She entered the cabin and saw Wosniak was sitting opposite in a chair, keeping watch. She knelt by Steph as she lay on the rope bed. "Hey, Steph, it's Nora..." The girl's pale face, punctuated by her great dark eyes, seemed to shine in the dim space. "Hang in there, Steph. We've got help coming..."

The barest whisper floated up when the girl's lips moved, "You... found... me..."

"Don't talk, Steph, save your energy..." Nora turned to where the front door remained open and caught Purvis's eye. "How far is the medevac?"

Purvis, his ear to his two-way radio, signaled 'five' with his fingers.

Nora turned again to Steph, "Only five minutes until a medic's here, Steph. Don't give up!"

Outside, she could hear Luke arrive with Bernhardt in tow. She heard Luke say, "Sit down, and don't move. Purvis, keep him under guard." Then, he entered the cabin and bent down to speak to Nora, "How is she?"

Nora shook her head, tears pooling in her eyes.

As they both watched, Steph's eyes seemed to dim. Her mouth dropped open. She breathed one last shuddering gasp and was gone. Outside, they could hear the drone of a helicopter circling.

CHAPTER 58 - DEBRIEF, INQUIRY AND AFTERMATH: TUESDAY-FRIDAY, OCTOBER 18-21

Back in Burnaby on an overnight flight, Nora had spent all the Tuesday after the ordeal writing up reports and completing invoices to cover expenses. The haste in doing the reports was routine. There was a danger that the principal players could forget important details if they waited too long to do the debrief. Her exhaustion was palpable as she submitted her expenses. After the Special Ops Finance Department ponied up their portion, she knew she would still be out some money. She would plan to sell the wardrobe pieces and the Cosmobile to recoup some cash.

Around noon on the Tuesday after the operation, the detachment received confirmation for mass arrest when the undercover pilot flew Vee back with BB, Axel and the other dancers. The undercover pilot had arranged for the Terrace detachment to be out in force to arrest the bikers on landing. Vee had handed over the camera pendant to Constable Purvis. The evidence detailing the Devil's Brigade drug operation was all there: the recruitment details, the names of the mules, the enforcement process. Purvis had secured the actual address book from Slavko Dracul's inner jacket pocket, but the thing was so wet from Slash's dunking in the lake that the pages were unreadable. Nora's photos were the only solid evidence to underpin the case against the club. It was a coup.

Slavko Dracul himself was under guard in the Prince George hospital, in serious condition. The shot to his chest had punctured his left lung, just missing the heart. His chances of a full recovery were unclear. If he recovered, he would face trial and jail time.

With Vee's witness statement detailing the role played by the other Devils' Brigade club members, the RCMP issued warrants for Milko Zorman of Edmonton, Dimitrios Zorman, Bogdan Lakovic, and Axel Horvat who would all have human trafficking and drug trafficking charges to start. The mining of Slavko Dracul's telephone list would net more charges, likely the gang-related "being a member of a criminal organization", human trafficking, trafficking of controlled substances, and extortion, at least for the rest of the gang. The Vancouver Police were checking on Tommy Cobb's role in providing dancers to the northern circuit. He could face charges of aiding and abetting the human trafficking counts.

Local prosecutors from the Attorney General's office were tallying up charges against the helicopter pilot Friedrich Bernhardt: abduction, assault, murder. They were interested in linking him to other disappearances along Highway 16. So far, he was not cooperating. Neither he nor any of the Brigade would be eligible for bail.

Nora attended the official debrief on the Thursday. Dave Yang, Luke Gallagher, Bonita Burrows, Rick Purvis, Pete Wosniak, William Benson and Gus MacGillivray, the Program Manager, were in attendance. To begin a wide-ranging meeting which covered every aspect of the operation, Yang as chair, made an announcement, "First, District Commissioner Benson, on behalf of Special Operations Chilliwack, I wish to convey our deepest sympathy for the death of your daughter, Stephanie. And given the circumstances, we especially appreciate your being willing to participate in this debrief." All members of the panel nodded towards Benson, whose grief was etched on his gaunt face. His eyes were puffy with dark bags underneath, mute testimony to several days without rest.

Yang continued, "Constable Macpherson, regarding operation

Karma Time, there is cause for grave concern. With the agreement of senior personnel, I have authorized this debrief as a formal inquiry into your undercover operation. We are doing so because of the quickness with which you revealed your identity to our targets and because we want to allow DC Benson quick access to bereavement leave. Do you have any preliminary comment to make, Constable Macpherson?"

Nora, somewhat in shock, shook her head. She had more or less expected an inquiry, but thought it would take place later, in a few weeks.

What followed was a day-by-day, and sometimes, hour-by-hour summary of Operation Karma Time from October 1st to October 17th. At each point along the way, Yang asked the relevant personnel to verify their roles in the undertaking. The summary was thorough and factual.

Afterwards, Yang began the follow-up, "Nora, we need to question your judgment in a few important circumstances. First, we feel your undercover persona was far too flamboyant to work to infiltrate the Devil's Brigade command structure. We tried to warn you against presenting yourself in such an extravagant fashion, and we believed you had taken our advice. At a meeting on July 26, 1983, we suggested that your undercover identity needed fine-tuning. At that meeting, you seemed to avoid the issue by wanting to discuss funding for your op. Admittedly afterwards, you justified your approach with a successful business plan, but your enthusiasm for that achievement seemed to overshadow the more practical concern for your personal safety and the safety of others involved. Lastly, on October 1st, as you were beginning your op, we let you know we still had reservations about the Chloe LaJoie ID. We wonder about your attitude. Why were you so headstrong? Even a bit of a prima donna? As a member of the Force, you must accept compliance to the dictates of your seniors. Do you have anything we should know that would improve our assessment of your approach?"

Nora sat speechless, unable to deny that they had warned her, that she had gone ahead with her original plan, that she had been headstrong. The operation had been successful up to a point, but she had to admit, the undercover ID had not been foolproof. "No Inspector, I have nothing to add."

"Second, we feel there was not enough attention to detail in a couple of instances. First, for example, Constable Macpherson, how was Stephanie Benson able to escape you at Pine Ridge Resort?"

"I should have used something like a carabiner to secure the truck keys. They never should have fallen out of my pocket."

Luke asked to speak. "I believe Constable Macpherson did all she could to make amends for that one slip." Nora heard Luke's words and smiled her thanks. She wanted to accept the exoneration, but somehow couldn't.

Yang nodded. "Yes, we have on record the various notes made in the Missing Persons file to identify potential avenues of inquiry."

Yang next addressed Luke. "Corporal Gallagher, can you explain why you stopped Constable Macpherson's Cosmobile van when it came through Glacier Lake?"

"Uh..." Luke blushed and opened his mouth like a fish gasping for water. "I... uh... I guess I felt I could justify stopping a vehicle that looked so out-of-place up there."

"And you're sure there was no personal agenda leading you to desire interaction with Constable Macpherson?" Dave Yang stared at Luke.

"Uh... no Inspector. We're... uh... just old friends."

DC Benson interjected, "And were you aware that Slavko Dracul observed your interaction with Constable Macpherson at the time?"

"Uh... no, Inspector. I was not." Luke blushed an even deeper shade of red.

"That was one nugget we got from him before he underwent emergency surgery in Prince George Tuesday morning. He said he suspected Chloe from that point onward." Benson continued, "So it would seem that contact compromised the op, Corporal. I think this will require a note on your file."

"I understand, District Commissioner."

"Another problem detail, Nora," Yang continued, "was the use of the Liberace tape as a cover for your communications from Chilliwack. Did you consider the targets would see this artist as an unlikely musical choice for the woman you were supposed to be?"

"Inspector, in my defence, I did not choose the tape cover sent to me. The communications operatives made that choice in Chilliwack."

"But you made those kinds of arrangements yourself, no?"

"You are correct, Inspector. I did not consider whether the Liberace cover would be a problem. Now, I realized I should have pre-planned those drops with Dolly Parton or Willie Nelson covers, for instance, and made sure the agents used them."

"Finally, we have questioned the use of Vigdis Dahlberg as your asset. Why did you not pursue the possibility of using a trained RCMP operative like Corporal Burrows? She has experience as an exotic dancer and could have been in place soon enough to be useful."

This question blindsided Nora. "Uh... I feel that Vee performed well as an asset and... uh... I also know the Brigade did not discover Vee's involvement. She was valuable because she had seen Franz Bernhardt, so she could ID him for us. No, Inspector, although Bunnie... uh... Corporal Burrows would have worked well as a replacement, I don't feel using Vee... uh... Vigdis was a lapse in judgment on my part."

Yang looked around the table at the assembled members of the inquiry. "Does anyone have anything to add?"

DC Benson spoke up, "I think we should commend Constable Macpherson for having the foresight to photograph the pages of the black address book that Slavko Dracul carried in his jacket breast pocket. The original book was water-soaked by Dracul's dunking in the lake, so that the contents became illegible. Without Nora's photo record, we would not have the intel we need to break up the Brigade's drug-running operation along Highway 16. And we would not have that photo record without the quick thinking of Vigdis Dahlberg, who hid it on her person and passed it along to Corporal Burrows via Constable Purvis when she arrived in Terrace. I don't know what the chances are that Corporal Burrows could have been in place for that drop. Replacing Vee with Bunnie may not have been as successful."

"Is there anyone else who wishes to make a comment? I think we may finish this up fairly soon if there are no further remarks." Yang surveyed the table. When no one said anything, he continued, "Could I ask Chief Inspector MacGillvary and District Commissioner Benson to stay behind while we excuse all others? We should be able to convene again in one hour."

~

THE THREE SENIOR OFFICERS, THEIR FACES IMPASSIVE, RE-ENTERED THE room where the remaining Karma Time personnel had assembled. This time, MacGillvary made the announcement. "There needs to be a report to identify the shortcomings of the op so we can learn from our mistakes. We ask that, as soon as possible, you all complete your portion of the report, let's say, within a week." He stopped to hand out folders labelled with their names to each member of the team. There was a moment's pause while each opened and perused the contents.

"Are there any questions about the contents of these folders?"

There were none. MacGillvary continued, "I realize this inquiry has been hurried. As I explained, this haste is important to document personnel impressions while they are still fresh in memory. We must do all we can to prevent similar errors in the future. To finish on a positive note, there is a bright spot. Since there has been excellent intel acquired, this report, as it stands, will not be damning enough to sideline Constable Macpherson from further undercover work. That being said, this inquiry is adjourned."

~

AFTERWARDS, SHE FLEW BACK TO TERRACE AND SPENT FRIDAY HELPING to fill out the paperwork for the arrests of the Franz Bernhardt and the Devil's Brigade and to complete her portion of the report.

By Saturday, Nora was lounging at Sayrita's Hotel in Prince

George, trying to relax. She had the next two weeks off and had checked in to indulge in luxury for her next four days. Her face and arm were healing and her bruised body recovering with hot tub soaks and massage in the spa. The gunshot wound had proven to be superficial. She would have a small scar on her upper arm.

The effects of Slash's rape were harder to fathom. Mostly, she still felt numb. In fact, she didn't want to think about it or talk about it with anyone. She had been taking the pill for years so wasn't worried about pregnancy, and she would watch for any STD after-effects. However, she couldn't decide whether she should keep the option of counselling open.

On the one hand, she was still kicking herself for getting into that mess in the first place and didn't feel like advertising her stupidity. On the other hand, the debrief had raised some thorny issues. Was she rash and headstrong? A prima donna? Did she have compliance issues? She felt chastised for her mistakes. She determined that, given another chance, she would prove herself worthy of the command's trust. Maybe counselling would help her achieve the insight needed to do so.

Nora felt heartache when she thought about Steph Benson. She couldn't help feeling she should have stopped the young woman's escape from Pine Ridge, and should have found her in time before Bernhardt got to her. She would carry that burden of guilt always and knew she still had to face Bill Benson in person and offer condolences and apologies. Steph had been headstrong and rebellious, but she hadn't deserved to die. Maybe once she dealt with Steph's father, she would feel able to unwind, would feel entitled to relax.

She thought back to her last conversation with Luke. It had been painful. They had been waiting for the results from the Inquiry in Chilliwack, having a coffee in the lunchroom. Nora had told Luke she was going to get some R and R at Sayrita's in Prince George.

"Why don't I join you at Sayrita's? I've got some time coming, and we could decompress together… for old time's sake, eh?"

"Aw, Luke, let me do this on my own time, okay? Maybe we could go out for dinner on your time off, one of the weekend days?"

She still felt ambivalent about Luke. His sweet nature was so appealing.

"That was an awesome job you did with the Karma Time Op, Nora. I have to admit I didn't think you could pull it off, not with that many bad actors in the mix…"

"That's nice of you to say, Luke. I thought you would swoop in and take my collar…"

"Well, I took down Slavko… anyway, now that it's done, you can come back to regular service in Brandenhoff, or even Glacier Lake, where there's an opening for a corporal. You're due for a promotion and that can be it. We can be together…"

"Let me think about it, Luke." She knew she had to let him down easy. Nora felt she had come too far to survive a regular small-town beat. Not that she was disinterested in Luke. In fact her connection to him felt stronger since he had joined her in shepherding Bernhardt to justice. He had been there for her when she needed him, as a partner should be. She still felt so comfortable with him that it scared her, but she wanted to take more risks than he could accept. Nora believed she had a right to make those choices, something she could do only if she remained single. She didn't know how long she would have to scratch this "itch" to become satisfied. In fairness to Luke, she couldn't ask him to wait.

As she was deciding to have dinner with Luke on the weekend to say goodbye–again, her hotel room phone rang.

Who could this be? Is Luke reading my mind? He's the only person I told that I would be here.

When she picked up the phone, it surprised her to hear Bunnie Burrows on the end of the line.

"Nora?"

"Yeah?"

"Sorry to interrupt your R and R, but I thought you'd like to hear that Dave has asked for you to work with me on a new undercover op in the Downtown East Side."

"Really? Seriously? Oh, my god!" After the Debrief-Inquiry, Yang had told her there was room for her skills in Vancouver, where the vice squads were going flat out to keep up with hard drug trade and human trafficking connections in the Down East Side community. He had added that they could use her to work undercover to deal specifically with the prostitution rings. Maybe Chloe was 'dead', but Constable Nora Macpherson could create a new incarnation.

"Don't be so surprised, cupcake." Bunnie's voice interrupted her reflection. "You might have screwed up, but what you accomplished was phenomenal! Right? Don't you forget it! Okay, see you in a couple of weeks!"

"Yeah... uh... how'd you know where to find me?"

"Luke Gallagher... he said you'd be at Sayrita's, and I think he's waiting for an invitation..."

"Did you tell him why you wanted to contact me?"

"Of course not! But he's a bright guy. He might have guessed."

Of course he'd wonder... I guess this will make 'goodbye' a bit easier...

Turn the page to see exciting news about Book Four in this series!

Here is the first chapter of Book Four in The Lost Women Series:
East Side Easy

Chapter 1 - Monday April 29, 1985

The screech of the seagulls was drowned out by the blast of the ferry's horn as it left the Schwartz Bay dock on Vancouver Island. Breezy salt air whipped Jenny's long blonde ponytail into a frenzied twist as she stood on the front deck gazing in deep concentration at the horizon dotted by the smoky green mounds of Gulf Islands. She was looking eastward, imagining what she would do when she reached Vancouver. First, she realized, she would have to figure out how to get from Tsawwassen, the Lower Mainland Ferry Terminal, to the city. There was a Greyhound Bus Line kiosk on the main passenger deck. She would have to use some of her scant cash to buy a ticket.

On her way to the kiosk, she stopped into the ladies' washroom. Catching a glimpse of herself in the wall wide mirror behind the sinks, Jenny stopped to straighten her hair. Standing there, she assessed her image. At fifteen, she had become aware of her stunning beauty: long, natural, blonde hair, sky blue eyes and a fresh, clean complexion. She was lithe and athletic with a background in ballet and gymnastics. She was also angry, scared and two and a half months pregnant.

Jenny had had a huge blow-up with her mom the night before about having sex with her boyfriend, Jeff, in the downstairs family room. Mom had broken down the door and caught them in the act. She recalled the heated interchange, her ears still ringing with the anger in her mother's voice.

"Jenny! What are you two doing in here?" There was no need to answer. Their state of undress on the couch said it all. "Jeff, I think you better leave. I need to have a word with my daughter."

Her mom was shocked that Jenny would take such chances and let her frustration tumble out with every word that followed. "You stupid, stupid girl! Not even a condom? What were you thinking? You're only fifteen! What if you get pregnant? I want you to break it off with Jeff. He clearly has no common sense, either! Oh, Jenny! I don't have the time or energy for this! Can't you see? I'm trying my best, and you just defy me!"

Jenny was humiliated and defiant, at first refusing to engage with her mom, Maggie Sheffield, who stood her ground, demanding some reaction. "Well, what do you have to say for yourself?"

Then the dam burst, and Jenny had screamed at Maggie, "Mind your own business! I'm not one of your social work clients! Besides, you're such a hypocrite! If you can have sleepover boyfriends, why can't I?"

"Well, the obvious answer is that I can't get pregnant!" Jenny, who knew her own condition, said nothing in response, but her anger built into desperation. She decided then to take action, flounced up to her bedroom, packed her backpack, and, when she knew he'd be home, she phoned Jeff to pick her up at school in the morning.

Now she was on the 11:00 am ferry to Vancouver with only one item on the agenda. She had to find someone to help her get rid of the pregnancy. Jeff had given her $200, all the money he had from his job at Burger King, and she had $100 from her Christmas money. That would have to be enough.

The ferry was half empty that Monday morning, with mostly weekend commuter passengers filling up the cafeteria and the lounges. When she arrived at the bus kiosk, Jenny was dismayed to see how high the cost was for a one way ticket from Tsawwassen to downtown Vancouver. The kiosk was closed until 12:00 noon so she decided to sit down to wait. She had to get there somehow to get an abortion. It was such a distasteful word. She felt hollow and sick to even think it. But there it was. She has to find a way to get one, and then she would decide about coming home again.

Jenny wandered to the bow of the ship to sit in the lounge with the widest spread of window. Maybe she would be lucky enough to see some orcas on the crossing. Most of the passengers seated there

CHAPTER 1 - EAST SIDE EASY

were absorbed in reading the newspaper or magazines. One couple appeared interested in what was going on around them.

He was a tall, good-looking, black man with an athlete's build and a goatee, smartly dressed in the latest 'retro' fashion, oatmeal-coloured pleated trousers with a knee-length matching coat. His button-down, collared, smoke-blue shirt was clean and crisp. The young woman with him, in her early twenties, was a statuesque, curly-haired brunette with wide set, teal-coloured eyes and a heavily made-up, plump lips. Her complexion was an unblemished coffee and cream. She wore a stunning low-cut, turquoise dress that clung to her shapely form in all the right places. She was smiling at Jenny, inviting her to sit with them.

"Hi Honey, you look lost... I'm Mary-Jo and this is Felix. We're on our way to downtown Vancouver. How about you? What's your name, sister?"

"Uh... sister?"

"Oh I just use that with any girl until I know her name. We're all family under the skin, no?"

"Uh... sure... uh... I'm Jenny."

"And what are you up to this fine April day?"

"Just on my way to Vancouver, too. Are you in a car?"

"Why yes, we have our car downstairs on the ferry."

"Wow... uh... could I ask a favour?"

"Why sure, Jenny. How can we help?"

Jenny looked over at Felix to see if he was paying attention. "Is it all right with you, sir, if I catch a ride into the city?"

"Oh my!" Felix chuckled. "Don't call me 'sir'... makes me feel old...you don't think I'm old, do you?"

"Oh, heavens, no sir... uh... I mean, Felix?" She looked at Mary-Jo to see if she had the name right. Mary-Jo nodded and smiled.

Felix continued, "So Jenny, what's a beautiful girl like you doing on her own going to Vancouver? If you were mine, I wouldn't be letting you wander around alone like this. Where are your folks?"

"Oh, I'm on my own. I left home this morning for a little while... I have something to do in Vancouver."

CHAPTER 1 - EAST SIDE EASY

"Oh, if you don't mind me asking, what would that be?" Felix bright black eyes were in the meantime assessing her build and apparel. He examined her jeans, sneakers and blue hoody, a hint of distaste in the set of his mouth.

"Uh..." Jenny hesitated. She was too embarrassed to tell these strangers her real purpose for travelling. "I'm going for a tryout at a gymnastics club. They have an 'in' with Cirque du Soleil, and I hope I can get on their list of possible trainees." It wasn't a complete lie. Jenny and her mom had talked about such a try-out, but Maggie had insisted Jenny had to wait until she finished school at eighteen.

Mary-Jo patted her arm. "Why, aren't you the bravest creature! I never could have done that at your age... how old are you, hon?"

"I'll be sixteen in a month or so."

"And you're so gorgeously tall! Oh my, is that a good fit for gymnastics?" Mary-Jo clapped her hand over her mouth as if she knew she has said something inappropriate.

"Uh... I'm not sure. I know that the smaller girls are the ones who do the high-wire stuff, but they have others who are acrobats and tumblers. I just love the sport, so I want to see what's out there."

"Well, Jenny, that's just wonderful." Felix was beaming his approval. "We can give you a ride into town. Where are you going to stay?"

"Oh, I dunno... uh... I don't have a lot of money, so I'll go to the 'Y', probably."

"Oh, Honey! You don't want to go there! It's not clean, love." Mary-Jo was wrinkling her pert little nose in disgust. "I'm sure we can find a bed for you at our place. We have a kind of cooperative arrangement, you know? There are several of us sharing a space. We can always fit in one more." Her voice was rich and warm, her amber eyes glowing with friendliness.

"Uh... gee... I'm not sure... that's very nice of you to offer... I just don't know..." Jenny felt torn. This could save her money for the operation.

"That's okay. You think about it. Why don't we get a coffee or some

CHAPTER 1 - EAST SIDE EASY

lunch? Are you hungry?" Felix was standing up and gathering up his newspaper. Mary-Jo stood and put her shoulder bag on.

Jenny stayed seated. She wasn't hungry; in fact she'd been feeling a bit nauseous. "I'll just stay here, thanks. I'm not really hungry." She noticed Mary-Jo catching Felix's eye, and raising an eyebrow. She hastened to add, "It's nothing. Just a stomach upset. Probably that burrito I ate for breakfast." She forced a chuckle.

Mary-Jo leant down and put her arm around Jenny's shoulders. "Oh, well, come along anyway. If we're going to give you a ride, we don't want to lose sight of each other, now. We'll get you an herbal tea for your tummy, okay?"

Jenny hesitated only for a minute before rising. "Maybe some peppermint tea... my mom gives me that sometimes..."

"Atta girl!" Felix led the way, his coat flapping, his newspaper under his arm.

Turn the page for news from Dianne.

Dear Readers,

I hope you are intrigued by Chapter 1 of *East Side Easy* - coming as soon as I can get it done!

In this story, Nora Macpherson is working undercover in the gritty Downtown Eastside of Vancouver targeting drug pushers and human traffickers. This novel is still in progress, but I hope to have it published in 2023.

If you haven't read the first two books in the series, featuring Nora's work in two different communities along the notorious Highway of Tears, Route 16 in northern British Columbia, they are available here:

Wildwoods Child - Book 1
www.amazon.com/dp/B01ELTGXU6

Road to Ruin - Book 2
www.amazon.com/dp/B082CBQQZY

If you would leave a review about these books on Amazon or any of the indicated social media websites, I would be very grateful.

Getting reviews is crucial for authors. Not only does it provide valuable feedback to us as writers, but it also signals to the publishers that our work is garnering attention, and therefore income and revenue for the promoters. Many thanks!

My website:
www.DianneGillespie.com

Thanks for your support.
Dianne Gillespie

You can follow me on:

- goodreads.com/diannegillespie
- facebook.com/dianne.gillespie.16
- linkedin.com/in/dianne-gillespie-she-her-82220313
- twitter.com/didotflo
- instagram.com/ddgillespieauthor

ALSO BY DIANNE GILLESPIE

The Lost Women Series

Wildwoods Child - Book 1
Road to Ruin - Book 2
Deadly Dark Dance - Book 3
East Side Easy - Book 4 (releasing in 2023)

∼

Living Apart Together: A New Possibility for Loving Couples

Is it possible to be independent... together?
This provocative work follows partners who have struggled to find alternatives to the traditional idea that they must live together to be considered a couple.

∼

For a complete list of Dianne's books, visit DianneGillespie.com

NEXT SERIES AFTER THE LOST WOMEN

Coastal Pacific Pioneers Series

From the exploitation of workers in the logging and mining empires to the shameful mistreatment and dislocation of the Indigenous population, Dianne's next series will bring to light the struggles and triumphs of the diverse populations who explored and built life on Vancouver Island from 1860 to 1900—an era that saw tremendous development and tragedy.

ABOUT THE AUTHOR

Dianne Gillespie is a retired high school teacher who lives on the West Coast on Vancouver Island where she spends her time enjoying the spectacular scenery and natural bounty of the area with her hubby, a retired architect, town planner and writer. After over thirty years teaching in British Columbia, Dianne spent four years teaching English in Dalian, Liaoning, in northeastern China. Dianne's passions are writing, reading, cooking, gardening and armchair politics. She also tutors on-line, teaching high school English and social studies.

DianneGillespie.com

- goodreads.com/diannegillespie
- facebook.com/dianne.gillespie.16
- linkedin.com/in/dianne-gillespie-she-her-82220313
- twitter.com/didotflo
- instagram.com/ddgillespieauthor

Manufactured by Amazon.ca
Bolton, ON

32039664R00199